Edina

Edina

A Novel

Mrs. Henry Wood

MINT EDITIONS

Edina: A Novel was first published in 1876.

This edition published by Mint Editions 2021.

ISBN 9781513281148 | E-ISBN 9781513286167

Published by Mint Editions®

 MINT
EDITIONS

minteditionbooks.com

Publishing Director: Jennifer Newens
Design & Production: Rachel Lopez Metzger
Project Manager: Micaela Clark
Typesetting: Westchester Publishing Services

Contents

PART THE FIRST

I

HEARD AT MIDNIGHT

The village, in which the first scenes of this history are laid, was called Trennach; and the land about it was bleak and bare and dreary enough, though situated in the grand old county of Cornwall. For mines lay around, with all the signs and features of miners' work about them; yawning pit mouths, leading down to rich beds of minerals—some of the mines in all the bustle of full operation, some worked out and abandoned. Again, in the neighbourhood of these, might be seen miners' huts and other dwelling-places, and the counting-houses attached to the shafts. The little village of Trennach skirted this tract of labour; for, while the mining district extended for some miles on one side the hamlet; on the other side, half-an-hour's quiet walking brought you to a different country altogether—to spreading trees and rich pasture land and luxuriant vegetation.

The village street chiefly consisted of shops. Very humble shops, most of them; but the miners and the other inhabitants, out of reach of better, found them sufficiently good for their purposes. Most of the shops dealt in mixed articles, and might be called general shops. The linendraper added brushes and brooms to his cottons and stuffs; the grocer sold saucepans and gridirons; the baker did a thriving trade in home-made pickles. On a dark night, the most cheerful-looking shop was the druggist's: the coloured globes displayed in its windows sending forth their reflections into the thoroughfare. This shop had also added another branch to its legitimate trade—that of general literature: for the one solitary doctor of the place dispensed his own medicines, and the sale of drugs was not great. The shop boasted a small circulating library; the miners and the miners' wives, like their betters, being fond of sensational fiction. The books consisted entirely of cheap volumes, issued at a shilling or two shillings each; some indeed at sixpence. The proprietor of this mart, Edmund Float, chemist and druggist, was almost a confirmed invalid, and would often be laid up for a week at a time. The doctor told him that if he would devote less of his time to that noted hostelry, the Golden Shaft, he might escape these attacks of illness. At these times the business of the shop, both as to drugs and books, was transacted by a young native of Falmouth; one Blase Pellet, who had served his apprenticeship in it and remained on as assistant.

The doctor's name was Raynor. He wrote himself Hugh Raynor, M.D., Member of the Royal College of Physicians. That he, a man of fair ability in his profession and a gentleman as well, should be contented to live in this obscure place, in all the drudgery of a general practitioner and apothecary, may seem a matter of surprise—but his history shall be given further on. His house stood in the middle of the village, somewhat back from the street: a low, square, detached building, a bow window on each side its entrance, and three windows above. On the door, which always stood open in the daytime, was a brass plate, bearing the name, "Dr. Raynor." The bow window to the left was screened by a brown wire blind, displaying the word "Surgery" in large white letters. Above the blind Dr. Raynor's white head, or the younger head of his handsome nephew, might occasionally be seen by the passers-by, or by Mr. Blase Pellet over the way. For the doctor's house and the druggist's shop faced each other; and Mr. Pellet, being of an inquisitive disposition, seemed never tired of peeping and peering into his neighbours' doings generally, and especially into any that might take place at Dr. Raynor's. At either end of this rather straggling street were seated respectively the parish church and the Wesleyan meeting-house. The latter was the better attended; for most of the miners followed their fathers' faith—that of the Wesleyan Methodists.

It was Monday morning, and a cold clear day in March. The wind came sweeping down the wide street; the dust whirled in the air; overhead, the sun was shining brightly. Dr. Raynor stood near the fire in his surgery, looking over his day-book, in which a summary of the cases under treatment was entered. He was dressed in black. A tall, grand-looking, elderly man, very quiet in manner, with a pale, placid face, and carefully-trimmed thin white whiskers. It was eight o'clock, and he had just entered the surgery: his nephew had already been in it half-an-hour. Never a more active man in his work than Dr. Raynor, but latterly his energy had strangely failed him.

"Has any message come in this morning from Pollock's wife, Frank?" he asked.

"No, sir."

"Then I suppose she's better," remarked the doctor, closing the book as he spoke, and moving towards the window.

A square table stood at the end of the room, facing the window.

Behind it was Frank Raynor, making up mixtures, the ingredients for which he took from some of the various bottles ranged upon the shelves behind him. He was a slender, gentlemanly young fellow of four-and-twenty, rather above the middle height, and wore this morning a suit of grey clothes. The thought that passed through a stranger's minds on first seeing Frank Raynor was, How good-looking he is! It was not, however, so much in physical beauty that the good looks consisted, as in the bright expression of his well-featured face, and the sunny, laughing blue eyes. The face wanted one thing—firmness. In the delicate mouth, very sweet and pleasant in form though it was, might be traced his want of stability. He could not say No to a petition, let it be what it might: he was swayed as easily as the wind. Most lovable was Frank Raynor; but he would be almost sure to be his own enemy as he went through life. You could not help liking him; every one did that—with the exception of Mr. Blase Pellet across the road. Frank's hair was golden brown, curling slightly, and worn rather long. His face, like his uncle's, was close-shaved, excepting that he too wore whiskers, which were of the same colour as the hair.

"What a number of men are standing about!" exclaimed Dr. Raynor, looking over the blind. "More even than usual on a Monday morning. One might think they were not at work."

"They are not at work," replied Frank. "As I hear."

"No! what's that for?"

Frank's lips parted with a smile. An amused look sat in his blue eyes as he answered.

"Through some superstition, I fancy, Uncle Hugh. They say the Seven Whistlers were heard in the night."

Dr. Raynor turned quickly towards his nephew. "The Seven Whistlers;" he repeated. "Why, who says that?"

"Ross told me. He came in for some laudanum for his neuralgia. As there is to be no work done to-day, the overseer thought he might as well lie up and doctor himself. A rare temper he is in."

"Can't he get the men to work?"

"Not one of them. Threats and promises alike fail. There's safe to be an accident if they go down to-day, say the men; and they won't risk it. Bell had better not come in Ross's way whilst his present temper lasts," added Frank, as he began to screw a cork into a bottle. "I think Ross would knock him down."

"Why Bell in particular?"

"Because it is Bell who professes to have heard the Whistlers."

"And none of the others?" cried the doctor.

"I fancy not. Uncle Hugh, what *is* the superstition?" added Frank. "What does it mean? I don't understand: and Ross, when I asked him, he turned away instead of answering me. Is it something especially ridiculous?"

Dr. Raynor briefly replied. This superstition of the Seven Whistlers arose from certain sounds in the air. They were supposed by the miners, when heard—which was very rarely, indeed, in this neighbourhood—to foretell ill luck. Accident, death, all sorts of calamities, in fact, might be expected, according to the popular superstition, by those who had the misfortune to hear the sounds.

Frank Raynor listened to the doctor's short explanation, a glow of amusement on his face. It sounded to him like a bit of absurd fun.

"You don't believe in such nonsense, surely, Uncle Hugh!"

Dr. Raynor had returned to the fire, and was gazing into it; some speculation, or perhaps recollection, or it might be doubt, in his grey eyes.

"All my experience in regard to the Seven Whistlers is this, Frank—and you may make the most of it. Many years ago, when I was staying amongst the collieries in North Warwickshire, there arose a commotion one morning. The men did not want to go down the pits that day, giving as a reason that the Seven Whistlers had passed over the place during the night, and had been heard by many of them. I naturally inquired what the Seven Whistlers meant, never having heard of them, and received in reply the explanation I have now given you. But workmen were not so independent in those days, Frank, as they are in these; and the men were forced to go down the pits as usual."

"And what came of it?" asked Frank.

"Of the going down? This. An accident took place in the pit that same morning—through fire-damp, I think; and many of them never came up again alive."

"How dreadful! But that could not have been the fault of the Seven Whistlers?" debated Frank.

"My second and only other experience was at Trennach," continued Dr. Raynor, passing over Frank's comment. "About six years ago, some of the miners professed to have heard these sounds. That same day, as they were descending one of the shafts after dinner, an accident occurred to the machinery—"

"And did damage," interrupted Frank, with increasing interest.

"Yes. Three of the men fell to the bottom of the mine, and were killed; and several others were injured more or less badly. I attended them. You ask me if I place faith in the superstition, Frank. No: I do not. I am sufficiently enlightened not to do so. But the experiences that I have told you of are facts. I look upon them as mere coincidences."

A pause. Frank was going on with his work.

"Are the sounds all fancy, Uncle Hugh?"

"Oh no. The sounds are real enough."

"What do they proceed from? What causes them?"

"It is said that they proceed from certain night-birds," replied Dr. Raynor. "Flocks of birds, in their nocturnal passage across the country, making plaintive sounds; and when these sounds are heard, they are superstitiously supposed to predict evil to those who hear them. Ignorant men are always credulous. That is all I know about it, Frank."

"Did you ever hear the sounds yourself, Uncle Hugh?"

"Never. This is only the third occasion that I have been in any place at the time they have been heard—or said to have been heard—and I have not myself been one of the hearers. There's Bell!" added Dr. Raynor, seeing a man leave the chemist's and cross the street in the direction of his house. "He seems to be coming here."

"And Float the miner's following him," observed Frank.

Two men entered through the doctor's open front-door, and thence to the surgery. The one was a little, middle-aged man, who carried a stout stick and walked somewhat lame. His countenance, not very pleasing at the best of times, just now wore a grey tinge that was rather remarkable. This was Josiah Bell. The one who followed him in was a tall, burly man, with a pleasant face, as fresh as a farm-labourer's; his voice was soft, and his manner meek and retiring. The little man's voice, on the contrary, was loud and self-asserting. Bell was given to quarrel with every one who would quarrel with him; scarcely a day passed but he, to use his own words, "had it out" with some one. Andrew Float had never quarrelled in his life; not even with his quarrelsome friend Bell; but was one of the most peaceable and easy-natured of men. Though only a common miner, he was brother to the chemist, and also brother to John Float, landlord of the Golden Shaft. The three brothers were usually distinguished in the place as Float the druggist, Float the miner, and Float the publican.

"I've brought Float over to ask you just to look at this arm of his, doctor, if you'll be so good," began Bell. "It strikes me his brother is not doing what's right by it."

There was a refinement in the man's accent, a readiness of speech, an independence of tone, not at all in keeping with what might be expected from one of a gang of miners. The fact was, Josiah Bell had originally held a far better position in life. He had begun that life as a clerk in the office of some large colliery works in Staffordshire; but, partly owing to unsteady habits, partly to an accident which had for many months laid him low and lamed him for life, he had sunk down in the world to what he now was—a workman in a Cornish mine.

"Won't the burn heal?" observed Dr. Raynor. "Let me see it, Float."

"If you'd please to be so kind, sir," replied the big man, with deprecation, as he took off his coat and prepared to display his arm. It had been badly burned some time ago; and it seemed to get worse instead of better, in spite of the doctoring of his brother the chemist, and of Mr. Blase Pellet.

"I have asked you more than once to let me look to your arm, you know, Float," remarked Mr. Frank Raynor.

"But I didn't like to trouble you, Master Raynor. I thought Ned and his salves could do for it, sir."

"And so you men are not at work to-day, Bell!" began the doctor, as he examined the arm. "What's this absurd story I hear about the Seven Whistlers?"

Bell's aspect changed at the question. The pallor on his face seemed to become greyer. It was a greyness that attracted Dr. Raynor's attention: he had never seen it in the man's face before.

"They passed over Trennach at midnight," said Bell, in low tones, from which all independence had gone out. "I heard them myself."

"And who else heard them?"

"I don't know. Nobody—that I can as yet find out. The men were all indoors, they say, long before midnight. The Golden Shaft shuts at ten on a Sunday night."

"You stayed out later?"

"I came on to Float the druggist's when the public-house closed, and smoked a pipe with him and Pellet, and sat there, talking. It was in going home that I heard the Whistlers."

"You may have been mistaken, in thinking you heard them."

"No," dissented Bell. "It was in the middle of the Bare Plain. I was stepping along quietly—"

"And soberly?" interposed Frank, with a twinkling eye, and a tone that might be taken either for jest or earnest.

"And soberly," asserted Bell, resentfully. "As sober as you are now, Mr. Frank Raynor. I was stepping along quietly, I say, when the church clock began to strike. I stood to count it, not believing it could be twelve—not thinking I had stayed all that time at the druggist's. It was twelve, however, and I was still standing after the last stroke had died away, wondering how the time could have passed, when those other sounds broke out high in the air above me. Seven of them: I counted them as I had counted the clock. The saddest sound of a wail I've ever heard—save once before. It seemed to freeze me up."

"Did you hear more?" asked Dr. Raynor.

"No. And the last two sounds of the seven were so faint, I should not have heard them if I had not been listening. The cries had broken out right above where I was standing: they seemed to die away gradually in the distance."

"I say that you may have been mistaken, Bell," persisted Dr. Raynor. "The sounds you heard may not have been the Seven Whistlers at all."

Bell shook his head, His manner and voice this morning were more subdued than usual. "I can't be mistaken in *them*. No man can be who has once heard them, Dr. Raynor."

"Is it this that has turned your face so grey?" questioned Frank, alluding to the pallor noticed by his uncle; but which the elder and experienced man had refrained from remarking upon.

"I didn't know it was grey," rejoined Bell, his resentful tones cropping up again.

"It's as grey as this powder," persisted Frank, holding forth a delectable compound he was preparing for some unfortunate patient.

"And so, on the strength of this night adventure of yours, Bell, all you men are making holiday to-day!" resumed the doctor.

But Bell, who did not seem to approve of Frank's remarks on his complexion, possibly taking them as ridicule—though he might have known Frank Raynor better—stood in dudgeon, and vouchsafed no reply. Andrew Float took up the retort in his humble, hesitating fashion.

"There ain't one of us, Dr. Raynor, that would venture down to-day after this. When Bell come up to the pit this morning, where us men was collecting to go down, and said the Seven Whistlers had passed over last night at midnight, it took us all aback. Not one of us would hazard it after that. Ross, he stormed and raged, but he couldn't force us down, sir."

"And the Golden Shaft will have the benefit of you instead!" said the doctor.

"Our lives are dear to us all, sir," was the deprecating reply of Float, not attempting to answer the remark. "And I thank ye kindly, sir, for it feels more comfortable like already. They burns be nasty things."

"They are apt to be so when not properly attended to. Your brother should not have allowed it to get into this state."

"Well, you see, Dr. Raynor, some days he's been bad abed, and I didn't trouble him with it then; and young Pellet don't seem to know much about they bad places."

"You should have come to me. Bell, how is your wife to-day?"

"Pretty much as usual," said surly Bell. "If she's worse, it's through the Seven Whistlers. She don't like to hear tell of them."

"Why did you tell her?"

Josiah Bell lifted his cold light eyes in wonder. "Could I keep such a thing as that to myself, Dr. Raynor? It comes as a warning, and must be guarded against. That is, as far as we can guard against it."

"Has the sickness returned?"

"For the matter of that, she always feels sick. I should just give her some good strong doses of mustard-and-water to make her so in earnest, were I you, doctor, and then perhaps the feeling would go off."

"Ah," remarked the doctor, a faint smile parting his lips, "we are all apt to think we know other people's business best, Bell. Float," added he, as the two men were about to leave, "don't you go in for a bout of drinking to-day; it would do your arm no good."

"Thank ye, sir; I'll take care to be mod'rate," replied Float, backing out.

"The Golden Shaft will have a good deal of his company to-day, in spite of your warning, sir; and of Bell's too," observed Frank, as the surgery-door closed on the men. "How grey and queer Bell's face looks! Did you notice it, Uncle Hugh?"

"Yes."

"He looks just like a man who has had a shock. The Seven Whistlers gave it him, I suppose. I could not have believed Bell was so silly."

"I hope it is only the shock that has done it," said the doctor.

"Done what, Uncle Hugh?"

"Turned his face that peculiar colour." And Frank looked up to his uncle as if scarcely understanding him. But Dr. Raynor said no more.

At that moment the door again opened, and a young lady glanced in. Seeing no stranger present, she came forward.

"Papa! do you know how late it is getting? Breakfast has been waiting ever so long."

The voice was very sweet and gentle; a patient voice, that somehow gave one the idea that its owner had known sorrow. She was the doctor's only child: and to call her a *young* lady may be regarded as a figure of speech, for she was past thirty. A calm, sensible, gentle girl she had ever been, of great practical sense. Her pale face was rather plain than handsome: but it was a face pleasant to look upon, with its expression of sincere earnestness, and its steadfast, truthful dark eyes. Her dark brown hair, smooth and bright, was simply braided in front and plaited behind on the well-shaped head. She was of middle height, light and graceful; and she wore this morning a violet merino dress, with embroidered cuffs and collar of her own work. Such was Edina Raynor.

"You may pour out the coffee, my dear," said her father. "We are coming now."

Edina disappeared, and the doctor followed her. Frank stayed a minute or two longer to make an end of his physic. He then adjusted his coat-cuffs, which had been turned up, pulled his wristbands down, and also passed out of the surgery. The sun was shining into the passage through the open entrance-door; and Frank, as if he would sun himself for an instant, or else wishing for a wider view of the street, and of the miners loitering about it, stepped outside. The men had collected chiefly in groups, and were talking idly, in slouching attitudes, hands in pockets; some were smoking. A little to the left, as Frank stood, on the other side of the way, was that much-frequented hostelry, the Golden Shaft: it was evidently the point of attraction to-day.

Mr. Blase Pellet chanced to be standing at his shop-door, rubbing his hands on his white apron. He was an awkward-looking, under-sized, unfortunately-plain man, with very red-brown eyes, and rough reddish hair that stood up in bristles. When he caught sight of Frank, he backed into the shop, went behind the counter, and peeped out at him between two of the glass globes.

"I wonder what he's come out to look at now?" debated Mr. Blase with himself. "*She* can't be in the street! What a proud wretch he looks this morning!—with his fine curls, and that ring upon his finger!"

"Twenty of them, at least, ready to go in!" mentally spoke Frank, his eyes fixed on the miners standing about the Golden Shaft. "And some of them will never come out all day."

Frank went in to breakfast. The meal was laid in a small parlour, behind the best sitting-room, which was on the side of the passage opposite to the surgery, and faced the street. This back-room looked down on a square yard, and the bare open country beyond: to the mines and to the miners' dwelling-places. They lay to the right, as you looked out. To the left stretched a barren tract of land, called the Bare Plain—perhaps from its dreary aspect—which we shall come to by-and-by.

Edina sat at the breakfast-table, her back to the window; Dr. Raynor sat opposite to her. Frank took his usual place between them, facing the cheerful fire.

"If your coffee's cold, Frank, it is your own fault," said Edina, handing his cup to him. "I poured it out as soon as papa came in."

"All right, Edina: it is sure to be warm enough for me," was the answer, as he took it and thanked her. He was the least selfish, the least self-indulgent mortal in the world; the most easily satisfied.

"What a pity it is about the men:" exclaimed Edina to Frank: for this report of the Seven Whistlers had become generally known, and the doctor's maid-servant had imparted the news to Miss Raynor. "They will make it an excuse for two or three days' drinking."

"As a matter of course," replied Frank.

"It seems altogether so ridiculous. I have been saying to papa that I thought Josiah Bell had better sense. He may have taken more than was good for him last night; and fancied he heard the sounds."

"Oh, I think he heard them," said the doctor. "Bell rarely drinks enough to cloud his faculties, And he is certainly not fanciful."

"But how, Uncle Hugh," put in Frank, "you cannot seriously think that there's anything in it!"

"Anything in what?"

"In this superstition. Of course one can readily understand that a flock of birds may fly over a place by night, as well as by day; and that they may give out sounds and cries on the way. But that these cries should forebode evil to those who may hear them, is not to be credited for a moment."

Dr. Raynor nodded. He was languidly eating an egg. For some time past, appetite had failed him.

"I say, Uncle Hugh, that you cannot believe in such nonsense. You admitted that the incidents you gave just now were mere coincidences."

"Frank," returned the doctor, in his quiet tone, that latterly had seemed to tell of pain, "I have already said so. But when you shall have lived to my age, experience will have taught you that there are some things in this world that cannot be fathomed or explained. We must be content to leave them. I told you that I did not myself place faith in this popular belief of the miners: but I related to you at the same time my own experiences in regard to it. I don't judge: but I cannot explain."

Frank turned a laughing look on his cousin.

"Suppose we go out on the Bare Plain to-night and listen for the Seven Whistlers ourselves; you and I, Edina?"

"A watched pot never boils," said Edina, quaintly, quoting a homely proverb. "The Whistlers would be sure not to come, Frank, if we listened for them."

II

Rosaline Bell

Frank Raynor had been a qualified medical man for some few years; he was skilful, kind, attentive, and possessed in an eminent degree that cheering manner which is so valuable in a general practitioner. Consequently he was much liked by the doctor's patients, especially by those of the better class, living at a distance; so that Dr. Raynor had no scruple in frequently making Frank his substitute in the daily visits. Frank alone suspected—and it was only a half-suspicion as yet—that his uncle was beginning to feel himself unequal to the exertion of paying them.

It was getting towards midday, and Frank had seen all the sick near home at present on their hands, when he started on his walk to see one or two living further away. But he called in at home first of all, to give Dr. Raynor a report of his visits, and to change his grey coat for a black one. Every inch a gentleman looked Frank, as he left the house again, turned to the right, and went down the street with long strides. He was followed by the envious eyes of Mr. Blase Pellet: who, in the very midst of weighing out some pounded ginger for a customer, darted round the counter to watch him.

"He is off *there*, for a guinea!" growled Mr. Pellet, as he lost sight of Frank and turned back to his ginger. "What possesses Mother Bell, I wonder, to go and fancy herself ill and in want of a doctor!"

The houses and the church, which stood at that end of Trennach, were soon left behind; and Frank Raynor was on the wide tract of land which was called the Bare Plain. The first break he came to in its bleak monotony was a worked-out mine on the left. This old pit was encompassed about by mounds of earth of different heights, where children would play at hide-and-seek during the daylight; but not one of them ever approached the mouth of the shaft. Not only was it dangerous, from being unprotected; and children, as a rule are given to running into danger instead of avoiding it; but the place had an evil reputation. Some short time ago, a miner had committed suicide there: one Daniel Sandon: had deliberately jumped in and destroyed himself. Since then, the miners and their families, who were for the most part very superstitious and ignorant, held a belief that the man's ghost haunted the pit; that, on a still night, any one listening down the shaft, might hear his sighs and groans. This caused it to be shunned: scarcely a miner would venture close to it alone after dark. There was nothing to take them near it, for it lay some little distance away from the broad path that led through the centre of the Plain. The depth of the pit had given rise to its appellation, "The Bottomless Shaft:" and poor Daniel Sandon must have died before he reached the end. For any one falling into it there could be no hope: escape from death was impossible.

Frank Raynor passed it without so much as a thought. Keeping on his way, he came by-and-by to a cluster of miners' dwellings, called Bleak Row, lying on the Plain, away to the right. Not many of them: the miners for the most part lived on the other side the village, near the mines. Out of one of the best of these small houses, there chanced to come a girl, just as he was approaching it; and they met face to face. It was Rosaline Bell.

Never a more beautiful girl in the world than she. Two-and-twenty years of age now, rather tall, with a light and graceful form, as easy in her movements, as refined in her actions as though she had been born a gentlewoman, with a sweet, low voice and a face of delicate loveliness. Her features were of almost a perfect Grecian type; her complexion was fresh as a summer rose, and her deep violet eyes sparkled beneath their long dark lashes. Eyes that, in spite of their brightness, had an expression of settled sadness in them: and that sad expression of the eye is said, you know, only to exist where its owner is destined to sorrow. Poor Rosaline! Sorrow was on its way to her quickly, even now. Her dress was of some dark stuff, neatly made and worn; her bonnet was of white straw; and the pink bow at her throat rivalled in colour the rose of her cheek.

Far deeper in hue did those cheeks become as she recognized Frank Raynor. With a hasty movement, as if all too conscious of her blushes and what they might imply, she raised her hand to cover them, making pretence gently to put back her dark and beautiful hair. Nature had indeed been prodigal in her gifts to Rosaline Bell. Rosaline had been brought up well; had received a fairly good education, and profited by it.

"How do you do, Rose!" cried Frank, in his gay voice, stopping before her. "Where are you going?"

She let her hand fall. The rich bloom on her face, the shy, answering glance of her lustrous eyes, were charming to behold. Frank Raynor admired beauty wherever he saw it, and he especially admired that of Rosaline.

"I am going in to find my father; to induce him to come back with me," she said. "My mother is anxious about him; and anxiety is not good for her, you know, Mr. Frank."

"Anxiety is very bad for her," returned Frank. "Is she worse to-day?"

"Not worse, sir; only worried. Father heard the Seven Whistlers last night; and I think that is rather disturbing her."

Frank Raynor broke into a laugh. "It amuses me beyond everything, Rose—those Whistlers. I never heard of them in all my life until this morning."

Rosaline smiled in answer—a sad smile. "My father firmly believes in them," she said; "and mother is anxious because he is. I must go on now, sir, or I shall not get back by dinnertime."

Taking one of her hands, he waved it towards the village, as if he would speed her onwards, said his gay good-bye, and lifted the latch of the door. It opened to the kitchen: a clean and, it might almost be said, rather tasty apartment, with the red-tiled floor on which the fire threw its glow, and a strip of carpet by way of hearthrug. A mahogany dresser was fixed to the wall on one side, plates and dishes of the old willow pattern were ranged on its shelves; an eight-day clock in its mahogany case ticked beside the fireplace, which faced the door. The window was gay with flowers. Hyacinths in their blue glasses stood on the frame half-way up: beneath were red pots containing other plants. It was easy to be seen that this was not the abode of a common miner.

Seated in an arm-chair near the round table, which was covered with a red cloth, her back to the window, was Mrs. Bell, who had latterly become an invalid. She was rubbing some dried mint into powder. By this, and the savoury smell, Frank Raynor guessed they were to have pea-soup for dinner. But all signs of dinner to be seen were three plates warming on the fender, and an iron pot steaming by the side of the fire.

"And now, mother, how are you to-day?" asked Frank, in his warm-hearted and genuine tones of sympathy, that so won his patients' regard.

He drew a chair towards her and sat down. The word "mother" came from him naturally. Two years ago, just after Frank came to Trennach, he was taken ill with a fever; and Mrs. Bell helped Edina to nurse him through it. He took a great liking to the quaint, well-meaning, and rather superior woman, who was so deft with her fingers, and so ready with her tongue. He would often then, partly in jest, call her "mother;" he called her so still.

Mrs. Bell was seven-and-forty now, and very stout; her short grey curls lay flat under her mob-cap; her still bright complexion must once have been as delicately beautiful as her daughter's. She put the basin of mint on the table, and smoothed down her clean white apron.

"I'm no great things to-day, Master Frank. Sometimes now, sir, I get to think that I never shall be again."

"Just as I thought in that fever of mine," said Frank, purposely making light of her words. "Why, my good woman, by this day twelvemonth you'll be as strong and well as I am. Only take heart and have patience. Yours is a case, you know, that cannot be dealt with in a day: it requires time."

Into the further conversation we need not enter. It related to her ailments. Not a word was said by either about that disturbing element, the Seven Whistlers: and Frank went out again, wishing her a good appetite for her dinner.

Putting his best foot foremost, he sped along, fleet as the wind. The Bare Plain gave place to pasture land, trees, and flowers. A quarter-of-an-hour brought him to The Mount—a moderately-sized mansion, standing in its own grounds, the residence of the St. Clares. By the sudden death of the late owner, who had not reached the meridian of life, it had fallen unexpectedly to a distant cousin; a young lieutenant serving with his regiment in India. In his absence, his mother had given up her house at Bath, and taken possession of it; she and her two daughters. They had come quite strangers to the place about two months ago. Mrs. St. Clare—it should be mentioned that they chose to give their name its full pronunciation, Saint Clare—had four children. The eldest, Charlotte, was with her husband, Captain Townley, in India; Lydia was second; the lieutenant and present owner of The Mount came next; and lastly Margaret, who was several years younger than the rest, and indulged accordingly. Mrs. St. Clare was extremely fond of society; and considered that at The Mount she was simply buried alive.

The great entrance-gates were on the opposite side; Frank Raynor never went round to them, unless he was on horseback: when on foot, he entered, as now, by the small postern-gate that was almost hidden by clustering shrubs. A short walk through the narrow pathway between these shrubs, and he was met by Margaret St. Clare: or, as they generally called her at home, Daisy. It frequently happened that she did meet him: and, in truth, the meetings were becoming rather precious to both, most especially so to her. During these two months' residence of the St. Clares at The Mount, Mr. Raynor and Margaret had seen a good deal of each other. Lydia was an invalid—or fancied herself one—and the Raynors had been in attendance from the first, paying visits to The Mount almost every other day. The doctor himself now and then, but it was generally Frank who went.

And Mrs. St. Clare was quite contented that it should be Frank. In this dead-alive spot, Frank Raynor, with his good looks, his sunny presence, his attractive manners, seemed like a godsend to her. She chanced to know that he was a gentleman by birth, having met members of his family before: Major Raynor; and, once, old Mrs. Atkinson, of Eagles' Nest. She did not know much about them, and in her proud heart secretly looked down upon Frank: as she would have looked upon any other general practitioner. But she liked Frank himself, and she very much liked his society, and often asked him to dinner, en famille. The few visiting people who lived within reach did not form a large party; but Mrs. St. Clare brought them together occasionally, and made the best of them.

Margaret St. Clare would be nineteen to-morrow. A slight-made, fair, pretty girl, putting one somehow in mind of a fairy. Her small feet scarcely seemed to touch the ground as she walked, her small arms and hands, her delicate throat and neck, were all perfectly formed. The face was fair and piquante, quiet and rather grave when in repose. Her eyes were of that remarkable shade that some people call light hazel and others amber; and in truth they occasionally looked as clear and bright as amber.

She was fond of dress. Mrs. St. Clare's daughters were all fond of it. Margaret's gown this morning, of fine, light blue texture, fell in soft folds around her, some narrow white lace at the throat. A thin gold chain holding a locket was round her neck. Her hat, its blue ribbons streaming, hung on her arm; her auburn hair was somewhat ruffled by the breeze. As she came forward to meet Frank, her face was lighted up with smiles of pleasure; its blushes were almost as deep as those that had lighted up Rosaline Bell's not half-an-hour ago. Frank took both her hands in silence. His heart was beating at the sight of her: and silence in these brief moments is the finest eloquence. Rapidly indeed was he arriving at that blissful state, described by Lord Byron in a word or two: "For him there was but one beloved face on earth." Ay, and arriving also at its consciousness. Even now it was "shining on him."

She was the first to break the silence. "You are late, Mr. Raynor. Lydia has been all impatience."

"I am a little late, Miss Margaret. There is always a good deal to do on a Monday morning."

Lydia St. Clare might be impatient, but neither of them seemed anxious to hurry in to her. The windows of the house could not be seen from here; evergreens grew high and thick between them, a very wilderness. In fact, the grounds generally were little better than a wilderness; the late owner was an absentee, and the place had been neglected. But it seemed beautiful as Eden to these two, strolling along side by side, and lingering on this bright day. The blue sky was almost cloudless; the sun gilded the budding trees; the birds sang as they built their nests: early flowers were coming up; all things spoke of the sweet spring-time. The sweet spring-time that is renewed year by year in nature when bleak winter dies; but which comes to the heart but once. It was reigning in the hearts of those two happy strollers; and it was in its very earliest dawn, when it is freshest and sweetest.

"See," said Margaret, stooping; "a beautiful double-daisy, pink-fringed! It has only come out to-day. Is it not very early for them?"

He took the flower from her unresisting hand as she held it out to him. "Will you give it me, Daisy?" he asked, in low, tender tones, his eyes meeting hers with a meaning she could not misunderstand.

Her eyes fell beneath his, her fingers trembled as she resigned the blossom. He had never called her by that pet name before; only once or twice had he said Margaret without the formal prefix.

"It is not worth your having," she stammered. "It is only a daisy."

"Only a daisy! The daisy shall be my favourite flower of all flowers from henceforth."

"Indeed, I think you must go in to Lydia."

"I am going in. How the wind blows! You will catch cold without your hat."

"I never catch cold, Mr. Raynor. I never have anything the matter with me."

He put the daisy into his button-hole, its pink and white head just peeping out. Margaret protested hotly.

"Oh, don't; please don't! Mamma will laugh at you, Mr. Raynor. Such a stupid little flower!"

"Not stupid to me," he answered. "As to laughing, Mrs. St. Clare may laugh at it as much as she pleases; and at me too."

The house was gained at last. Crossing the flagged entrance-hall, they entered a very pretty morning-room, its curtains and furniture of pale green, bordered with gold. Mrs. St. Clare, a large, fair woman with a Roman nose, lay back in an easy-chair, a beautifully-worked screen attached to the white marble mantelpiece shading her face from the fire. Her gown was black and white: grey and black ribbons composed her head-dress. She looked half-dead with ennui. Those large women are often incorrigibly idle and listless: she never took up a needle, never cared to turn the pages of a book. She was indolent by nature, and had grown more so during her life in India before the death of her husband, Colonel St. Clare.

But her face lighted up to something like animation when Mr. Raynor entered and went forward. Margaret fell into the background. After shaking hands with Mrs. St. Clare, he turned to the opposite side of the fireplace; where, in another easy-chair, enveloped in a pink morning-wrapper, sat the invalid, Lydia.

She was a tall, fair, Roman-nosed young woman too, promising to be in time as large as her mother. As idle she was already. Dr. Raynor said all she wanted was to exert herself: to walk and take an interest in the bustling concerns of daily life as other girls did; she would talk no more of nervousness and chest-ache then.

Frank felt her pulse, looked at her tongue, and inquired how she had slept; with all the rest of the usual medical routine. Lydia answered fretfully, and began complaining of the dulness of her life. It was this wretched Cornish mining country that was making her worse: she felt sure of it.

"And that silly child, Daisy, declared this morning that it was the sweetest place she was ever in!" added Miss St. Clare, in withering contempt meant for Daisy. "She said she should like existence, as it is just at present, to last for ever!"

Frank Raynor caught a glimpse of a painfully-blushing face in the distance, and something like a smile crossed his own. He took a small phial, containing a tonic, from his pocket, which he had brought with him, and handed it to the invalid.

"You will drive out to-day as usual, of course?" said he.

"Oh, I suppose so," was Miss St. Clare's careless answer. "I don't know how we should live through the hours between luncheon and dinner without driving. Not that I care for it."

"Talking of dinner," interposed Mrs. St. Clare, "I want you to dine with us to-day, Mr. Raynor. Is that a *daisy* in your coat? What an absurd ornament!"

"Yes, it is a daisy," replied Frank, looking down on it. "Thank you very much for your invitation. I will come, if I possibly can."

"I cannot allow you any 'If' in the matter."

Frank smiled, and gave a flick to the lavender glove in his hand. He liked to be a bit of a dandy when he called at The Mount. As to dining there—in truth, he desired nothing better. But he was never quite sure what he could do until the hour came.

"A doctor's time is not his own, you know, Mrs. St. Clare."

"You must really give us yours this evening. Our dinners are insufferably dull when we sit down alone."

So Frank Raynor gave the promise—and he meant to keep it if possible. Ah, that he had not kept it! that he had remained at home! But for that unfortunate evening's visit to The Mount, and its consequences, a great deal of this history would not have been written.

THE DAY WENT ON. NOTHING occurred to prevent Frank's fulfilling his engagement. The dinner hour at The Mount was seven o'clock. It was growing dusk when Frank, a light coat thrown over his evening dress, started for his walk to it, but not yet dark enough to conceal objects. Frank meant to get over the ground in twenty minutes: and, really, his long legs and active frame were capable of any feat in the matter of speed. That would give him ten minutes before dinner for a chat with Daisy: Mrs. and Miss St. Clare rarely entered the drawing-room until the last moment.

"Going off to dine again with that proud lot at The Mount!" enviously remarked Mr. Pellet, as he noted Frank's attire from his usual post of observation, the threshold of the chemist's door. "It's fine to be him!"

"Blase," called his master from within, "where have you put that new lot of camomiles?"

Mr. Blase was turning leisurely to respond, when his quick red-brown eyes caught sight of something exceedingly disagreeable to them: a meeting between Frank and Rosaline Bell. She had come into the village apparently from home: and she and Frank were now talking together. Mr. Blase felt terribly uncomfortable, almost splitting with wrath and envy.

He would have given his ears to hear what they were saying. Frank was laughing and chattering in that usually gay manner of his that most people found so attractive; she was listening, her pretty lips parted with a smile. Even at this distance, and in spite of the fading light, Mr. Blase, aided by imagination, could see her shy, half-conscious look, and the rose-blush on her cheeks.

And Frank stayed talking and laughing with her as though time and The Mount were nothing to him. He thought no harm, he meant no wrong. Frank Raynor never *meant* harm to living mortal. If he had only been as cautious as he was well-intentioned!

"Blase!" reiterated old Edmund Float, "I want to find they new camomiles, just come in. Don't you hear me? What have you done with them?"

Mr. Blase was quite impervious to the words. They had parted now: Frank was swinging on again; Rosaline was coming this way. Blase went strolling across the street to meet her: but she, as if purposely to avoid him, suddenly turned down an opening between the houses, and was lost to sight and to Blase Pellet.

"I wonder if she cut down there to avoid me?" thought he, standing still in mortification. And there was a very angry look on his face as he crossed back again from his fruitless errand.

Daisy was not alone in the drawing-room this evening when Frank arrived. Whether his gossip with Rosaline had been too prolonged, or whether he had not walked as quickly as usual, it was a minute past seven when Frank reached The Mount. All the ladies were assembled: Lydia and Daisy in blue silk; Mrs. St. Clare in black satin. Their kinsman had been dead six months, and the young ladies had just gone out of mourning for him; but Mrs. St. Clare wore hers still.

Daisy looked radiant; at any rate, in Frank's eyes: a very fairy. The white lace on her low body and sleeves was scarcely whiter than her fair neck and arms: one white rose nestled in her hair.

"Dinner is served, madam."

Frank offered his arm to Mrs. St. Clare: the two young ladies followed. It was a large and very handsome dining-room: the table, with its white cloth, and its glass and silver glittering under the wax-lights, looked almost lost in it. Lydia faced her mother; Frank and Daisy were opposite each other. He looked well in evening dress: worthy of being a prince, thought Daisy.

The conversation turned chiefly on the festivities of the following evening. Mrs. St. Clare was to give a dance in honour of her youngest daughter's birthday. It would not be a large party; the neighbourhood did not afford that; but some guests from a distance were to sleep in the house, and remain for a day or two.

"Will you give me the first dance, Daisy?" Frank seized an opportunity of whispering to her, as they were all returning to the drawing-room together.

Daisy shook her head, and blushed again. Blushed at the familiar word, which he had not presumed to use until that day. But it had never sounded so sweet to her from other lips.

"I may not," she answered. "Mamma has decided that my first dance must be with some old guy of a Cornish baronet—Sir Paul Trellasis. *Going*, do you say! Why? It is not yet nine o'clock.

"I am obliged to leave," he answered. "I promised Dr. Raynor. I have to see a country patient for him to-night."

Making his apologies to Mrs. St. Clare for his early departure, and stating the reason, Frank left the house. It was a cold and very light night: the skies clear, the moon intensely bright. Frank went on with his best step. When about half-way across the Bare Plain he met Rosaline Bell. The church clock was striking nine.

"Why, Rose! Have you been all this time at Granny Sandon's?"

"Yes; the whole time," she answered. "I stayed to help her into bed. Poor granny's rheumatism is very bad: she can scarcely do anything for herself."

"Is her rheumatism bad again? I must call and see her. A cold night, is it not?"

"I am nearly perished," she said. "I forgot to take a shawl with me."

But Rosaline did not look perished. The meeting had called up warmth and colouring to her face, so inexpressibly beautiful in the full, bright moonlight. A beauty that might have stirred a heart less susceptible than was Frank Raynor's.

"Perished!" he cried. "Let us have a dance together, Rose." And, seizing her hands, he waltzed round with her on the path, in very lightness of spirit.

"Oh, Mr. Raynor, pray don't! I must be going home, indeed, sir. Mother will think I am lost."

"There! Are you warm now? I must go, also."

And before she could resist—if, indeed, she would have resisted—Frank Raynor snatched a kiss from the lovely face, released her hands, and went swiftly away over the Bare Plain.

There was not very much harm in this: and most assuredly Frank intended none. That has been already said. He would often act without thought; do mad things upon impulse. He admired Rosaline's beauty, and he liked to talk and laugh with her. He might not have chosen to steal a kiss from her in the face and eyes of Trennach: but what harm could there be in doing it when they were alone in the moonlight?

And if the moon had been the only spectator, no harm would have come of it. Unfortunately a pair of human eyes had been looking on as well: and the very worst eyes, taken in that sense, that could have gazed—Mr. Blase Pellet's. After shutting up the shop that night, ill luck had put it into Mr. Pellet's head to take a walk over to Mrs. Bell's. He went in the hope of seeing Rosaline: in which he was disappointed: and was now on his way home again.

Rosaline stood gazing after Frank Raynor. No one but herself knew how dear he was to her; no one ever would know. The momentary kiss seemed still to tremble on her lips; her heart beat wildly. Wrapt in this ecstatic confusion, it was not to be wondered at that she neither saw nor heard the advance of Mr. Pellet; or that Frank, absorbed in her and the dance, had previously been equally unobservant.

With a sigh, Rosaline at length turned, and found herself face to face with the intruder. He had halted close to her, and was standing quite still.

"Blase!" she exclaimed, with a faint cry. "How you startled me!"

"Where have you been?" asked Blase, in sullen tones. "Your mother says you've been out for I don't know how many hours."

"I've been to Granny Sandon's. Good-night to you, Blase: it is late."

"A little too late for honest girls," returned Blase, putting himself in her way. "Have you been stopping out with *him?*" pointing to the fast-disappearing figure of Frank Raynor.

"I met Mr. Raynor here, where we are standing; and was talking with him for about a minute."

"It seems to me you are always meeting him," growled Blase, suppressing any mention of the dance he had seen, and the kiss that succeeded it.

"Do you want to quarrel with me, Blase? It seems so by your tone."

"You met him at dusk this evening as you were going to old Sandon's— if you *were* going there; and you meet him now in returning," continued Blase. "It's done on purpose."

"If I did meet him each time, it was by accident. Do you suppose I put myself in the way of meeting Mr. Raynor?"

"Yes, I do. There!"

"You shall not say these things to me, Blase. Just because you chance to be a fifteenth cousin of my mother's, you think that gives you a right to lecture me."

"You are always out and about somewhere," contended Blase. "What on earth d'you want at old Sandon's for ever?"

"She is sad and lonely, Blase," was the pleading answer, given in a tone of sweet pity. "Think of her sorrow! Poor Granny Sandon!"

"Why do you call her 'Granny'?" demanded Blase, who was in a fault-finding mood. "She's no granny of yours, Rosaline."

Rosaline laughed slightly. "Indeed, I don't know why we call her 'Granny,' Blase. Every one does. Let me pass."

"Every one doesn't. No: you are not going to pass yet. I intend to have it out with you about the way you favour that fool, Raynor. Meeting him at all hours of the day and night."

Rosaline's anger was aroused. In her heart she disliked Blase Pellet. He had given her trouble for some time past in trying to force his attentions upon her. It seemed to her that half the work of her life consisted in devising means to repress and avoid him.

"How dare you speak to me in this manner, Blase Pellet? You have not the right to do it, and you never will have."

"You'd rather listen to the false palaver of that stuck-up gentleman, Raynor, than you would to the words of an honest man like me."

"Blase Pellet, hear me once for all," vehemently retorted the girl. "Whatever Mr. Raynor may say to me, it is nothing to you; it never will be anything to you. If you speak in this way of him again, I shall tell him of it."

She eluded the outstretched arm, ran swiftly by, and gained her home. Blase Pellet, standing to watch, saw the light within as she opened the door and entered.

"*Is* it nothing to me!" he repeated, in a crestfallen tone. "You'll find that out before we are a day older, Miss Rosaline. I'll stop your fun with that proud fellow, Raynor."

III

On the Bare Plain

"In vain I look from height and tower,
No wished-for form I see;
In vain I seek the woodbine bower—
He comes no more to me."

So sang Rosaline Bell in the beams of the morning sun. They came glinting between the hyacinths in the window, and fell on the cups and saucers. Rosaline stood at the kitchen-table, washing up the breakfast-things. She wore a light print gown, with a white linen collar fastened by a small silver brooch.

An expression of intense happiness sat on her beautiful face. This old song, that she was singing to herself in a sweet undertone, was one that her mother used to sing to her when she was a child. The words came from the girl half unconsciously; for, while she sang, she was living over again in thought last night's meeting with Frank Raynor on the Bare Plain.

"Rosie!"

The fond name, called in her mother's voice, interrupted her. Putting down the saucer she was drying, she advanced to the staircase-door, which opened from the kitchen, and stood there.

"Yes, mother! Did you want me?"

"Has your father gone out, Rose?"

"Yes. He said he should not be long."

"Oh no, I dare say not!" crossly responded Mrs. Bell; her tone plainly implying that she put no faith whatever in any promise of the sort. "They'll make a day of it again, as they did yesterday. Bring me a little warm water in half-an-hour, Rose, and I'll get up."

"Very well, mother."

Rose returned to her tea-cups, and resumed her song; resumed it in very gladness of heart. Ah, could she only have known what this day was designed to bring forth for her before it should finally close, she had sunk down in the blankness of despair! But there was no foreshadowing on her spirit.

> "'Twas at the dawn of a summer morn,
> My false love hied away;
> O'er his shoulder hung the hunter's horn,
> And his looks were blithe and gay.

> "'Ere the evening dew-drops fall, my love,'
> He thus to me, did say,
> 'I'll be at the garden-gate, my love'—
> And gaily he rode away."

Another interruption. Some one tried the door—of which Rosaline had a habit of slipping the bolt—and then knocked sharply. Rosaline opened it. A rough-looking woman, miserably attired, stood there: an inhabitant of one of the poorest dwellings in this quarter.

"I wants to know," cried this woman, in a voice as uncouth as her speech, and with a dialect that needs translation for the uninitiated reader, "whether they vools o' men be at work to-day."

"I think not," replied Rosaline.

"There's that man o' mine gone off again to the Golden Shaaft, and he'll come hoam as he did yesternight! What tha plague does they father go and fill all they vools up weth lies about they Whistlers for? That's what I'd like to know. If Bell had heered they Whistlers, others 'ud hev heered they."

"I can't tell you anything at all about it, Mrs. Janes," returned Rosaline, civilly but very distantly; for she knew these people to be immeasurably her inferiors, and held them at arm's-length. "You can ask my father about it yourself; he'll be here by-and-by. I can't let you in now; mother's just as poorly as ever to-day, and she cannot bear a noise."

Closing the door as she spoke, and slipping the bolt, lest rude Mrs. Janes should choose to enter by force, Rosaline took up her song again.

> "I watched from the topmost, topmost height,
> Till the sun's bright beams were o'er,
> And the pale moon shed her vestal light—
> But my lover returned no more."

Whether the men were still incited by a dread of the Seven Whistlers, and were really afraid to descend into the mines, or whether they used the pretext as an excuse for a second day's holiday, certain it was that not a single man had gone to work. Ross, the overseer, reiterated his threats of punishment again and again; and reiterated in vain.

As a general rule, there exists not a more sober race of men than that of the Cornish miners; and the miners in question had once been no exception to the rule. But some few years before this, on the occasion of a prolonged dispute between masters and men, many fresh workmen had been imported from distant parts of England, and they had brought their drinking habits with them. The Cornish men caught them up in a degree: but it was only on occasions like the present that they indulged them to any extent, and therefore, when they did so, it was the more noticeable.

Mr. John Float at the Golden Shaft was doing a great stroke of business these idle days. As many men as could find seats in his hospitable house took possession of it. Amongst them was Josiah Bell. Few had ever seen Bell absolutely intoxicated; but he now and then took enough to render him more sullen than usual; and at such times he was sure to be quarrelsome.

Turning out of the Golden Shaft on this second day between twelve and one o'clock, Bell went down the street towards his home, with some more men who lived in that direction. Dr. Raynor chanced to be standing outside his house, and accosted Bell. The other men walked on.

"Not at work yet, Bell!"

"Not at work yet," echoed Bell, as doggedly as he dared, and standing to face the doctor.

"How long do you mean to let this fancy about the Seven Whistlers hinder you? When is it to end?"

Bell's eyes went out straight before him, as if trying to foresee what and where the end would be, and his tones lost their fierceness. This fancy in regard to the Seven Whistlers—as the doctor styled it—had evidently taken a serious, nay, a solemn hold upon him. Whether or not the other men anticipated ill-fortune from it, most indisputably Bell did so.

"I don't know, sir," he said, quite humbly. "I should like to see the end."

"Are you feeling well, Bell?" continued Dr. Raynor, in a tone of sympathy—for the strange grey pallor was on the man's face still.

"I'm well enough, doctor. What should ail me?"

"You don't look well."

Bell shifted his stick from one hand to the other. "The Whistlers gave me a turn, I suppose," he said.

"Nonsense, man! You should not be so superstitious."

"See here, Dr. Raynor," was the reply—and the tone was lowered in what sounded very like fear. "You know of the hurt I got in the pit in Staffordshire—which lamed me for good? Well, the night before it I heard the Seven Whistlers. They warned me of ill-luck then; and now they've warned me again, and I know it will come. I won't go down the mine till three days have passed. The other men may do as they like."

He walked on with the last words. Mr. Blase Pellet, who had been looking on at the interview from over the way, gazed idly after Bell until he had turned the corner and was out of sight. All in a moment, as though some recollection came suddenly to him, Blase tore off his white apron, darted in for his hat, and ran after Bell; coming up with him just beyond the parsonage.

What Mr. Blase Pellet communicated to him, to put Bell's temper up as it did, and what particular language he used, was best known to himself. If the young man had any conscience, one would think that remorse, for what that communication led to, must lie on it to his dying day. Its substance was connected with Rosaline and Frank Raynor. He was telling tales of them, giving his own colouring to what he said, and representing the latter gentleman and matters in general in a very unfavourable light indeed.

"If he dares to molest her again, I'll knock his head off," threatened Bell to himself and the Bare Plain, as he parted with Pellet, and made his way across it, muttering and brandishing his stick. The other men had disappeared, each within his home. Bell was about to enter his, when Mrs. Janes came out of her one room, her hair hanging, her gown in tatters, her voice shrill. She placed herself before Bell.

"I've been asking about my man. They tells me he es in a-drinking at the Golden Shaaft. I'll twist hes ears for he when he comes out on't And now I'm a-going to have it out with you about they Whistlers! Ef the—"

Mrs. Janes's eloquence was summarily arrested. With an unceremonious push, Josiah Bell put her out of his way, strode on to his own door, and closed it against her.

Rosaline was alone, laying the cloth for dinner. Bell, excited by drink, abused his daughter roundly, accusing her of "lightness" and all sorts of unorthodox things. Rosaline stared at him in simple astonishment.

"Why, father, what can you be thinking of?" she exclaimed. "Who has been putting this into your head?"

"Blase Pellet," answered Bell, scorning to equivocate. "And I'd a mind to knock him down for his pains—whether it's true or whether it's not."

"True!—that I could be guilty of light conduct!" returned Rosaline. "Father, I thought you knew me better. As to Mr. Raynor, I don't believe he is capable of an unworthy thought. He would rather do good in the world than evil."

And her tone was so truthful, her demeanour so consciously dignified, that Bell felt his gloomy thoughts melt away as if by magic; and he wished he *had* knocked Mr. Pellet down.

THE DAY WENT ON TO evening, and tea was being taken at Dr. Raynor's. Five o'clock was the usual hour for the meal, and it was now nearly seven: but the doctor had been some miles into the country to see a wealthy patient, and Edina waited for him. They sat round the table in the best parlour; the one of which the bow-window looked on to the street; the other room was chiefly used for breakfast and dinner.

Its warm curtains were drawn before the window now, behind the small table that held the stand of beautiful white coral, brought home years ago by Major Raynor; the fire burned brightly; two candles stood near the tea-tray. Behind the doctor, who sat facing the window, was a handsome cabinet, a few choice books on its shelves. Frank, reading a newspaper and sipping his tea, sat between his uncle and Edina.

This was the night of the ball at The Mount. Edina was going to it. A most unusual dissipation for her; one she was quite unaccustomed to. Trennach afforded no opportunity for this sort of visiting, and it would have been all the same to Miss Raynor if it had. As she truly said, she had not been to a dance for years and years. Frank was making merry over it, asking her whether she could remember her "steps."

"I am sorry you accepted for me, papa," she suddenly said. "I have regretted it ever since."

"Why, Edina?"

"It is not in my way, you know, papa. And I have had the trouble of altering a dress.

"Mrs. St. Clare was good enough to press your going, Edina—she candidly told me she wanted more ladies—and I did not like to refuse. She wanted *me* to go," added Dr. Raynor, with a broad smile.

"I'm sure, papa, you would be as much of an ornament at a ball as

I shall be—and would be far more welcome to Mrs. St. Clare," said Edina.

"Ornament? Oh, I leave that to Frank."

"I dare say you could dance, even now, as well as I can, papa."

Something like a flash of pain crossed his face. *He* dance now! Edina little thought how near—if matters with regard to himself were as he suspected—how very near he was to the end of all things.

"You looked tired, papa," she said.

"I am tired, child. That horse of mine does not seem to carry me as easily as he did. Or perhaps it is I who feel his action more. What do you say, Frank?"

"About the horse, uncle? I think he is just as easy to ride as he always was."

Dr. Raynor suppressed a sigh, and quitted the room. Frank rose, put his elbow on the mantelpiece, and glanced at his good-looking face in the glass.

"What time do you mean to start, Edina?"

"At half-past eight. *I* don't wish to go in later than the card says—nine o'clock. It is a shame to invite people for so late an hour!"

"It is late for Trennach," acknowledged Frank; "but would be early for some places. Mrs. St. Clare has brought her fashionable hours with her."

At that moment, the entrance-door was pushed violently open, and an applicant was heard to clatter in, in a desperate hurry. Frank went out to see.

Mrs. Molly Janes was lying at home, half killed, in immediate need of the services of either Dr. or Mr. Raynor. Mr. Janes had just staggered home from his day's enjoyment at the Golden Shaft: his wife was unwise enough to attack him in that state; he had retaliated and nearly "done" for her. Such was the substance of the report brought by the messenger—a lad with wild eyes and panting breath.

"You will have to go, Frank," said the doctor. "I am sorry for it, but I am really not able to walk there to-night. My ride shook me fearfully."

"Of course I will go, sir," replied Frank, in his ready way. "I shall be back long before Edina wants me. What are Mrs. Janes's chief injuries?" he asked, turning to the boy.

"He heve faaled on her like a fiend, master," answered the alarmed lad. "He've broke aal her bones to lerrups, he heve."

A bad account. Frank prepared to start without delay. He had left his hat in the parlour; and whilst getting it he said a hasty word to Edina—

he had to go off to the cottages on the Bare Plain. Edina caught up the idea that it was Mrs. Bell who needed him: she knew of no other patient in that quarter.

"Come back as quickly as you can, Frank," she said. "You have to dress, you know. Don't stay chattering with Rosaline."

"With Rosaline!" he exclaimed, in surprise. "Oh, I see. It is not Mrs. Bell who wants me; it is Molly Janes. She and her husband have been at issue again."

With a gay laugh at Edina's advice touching Rosaline, and the rather serious and meaning tone she gave it in, Frank hastened away. The fact was, some odds and ends of joking had been heard in the village lately, coupling Frank's name with the girl's, and they had reached the ears of Edina. She intended to talk to Frank warningly about it on the first opportunity.

When about half-way across the Bare Plain, Frank saw some man before him, in the moonlight, who was not very steady on his legs. The lad had gone rushing forward, thinking to come in at the end of the fight; should it, haply, still be going on.

"What, is it you, Bell!" exclaimed Frank, recognizing the staggerer as he overtook and passed him. "You've had nearly as much as you can carry, have you not?" he added, in light good-nature.

It was Bell. Stumbling homewards from the Golden Shaft. A very early hour indeed, considering the state he was in, for him to quit the seductions of that hostelry. He had been unwise enough to go back to it after his dinner, and there he had sat until now. Had he chosen to keep sober, the matter whispered by Blase Pellet would not have returned to rankle in his mind: as he did not, it had soon begun to do so ominously. With every cup he took, the matter grew in his imagination, until it assumed an ugly look, and became a very black picture. And he had now come blundering forth with the intention of "looking out for himself," as ingeniously suggested by Blase Pellet that day when they were parting. In short, to track the steps and movements of the two suspected people; to watch whether they met, and all about it.

"Perhaps other folks will have as much as they can carry soon," was his insolent retort to Frank, lifting the heavy stick in his hand menacingly. At which Frank only laughed, and sped onwards.

A terribly savage mood rushed over Josiah Bell. Seeing Frank strike off towards Bleak Row, he concluded that it was to his dwelling-house he was bent, and to see Rosaline. And he gnashed his teeth in fury, and gave vent to a fierce oath because he could not overtake the steps of the younger man.

Bursting in at his own door when he at length reached it, he sent his eyes round the room in search of the offenders. But all the living inmates that met his view consisted of his wife in her mob-cap and white apron, knitting, as usual, in her own chair, and the cat sleeping upon the hearth.

"Where's Rosaline?"

Mrs. Bell put down her knitting—a grey worsted stocking for Bell himself—and sighed deeply as she gazed at him. He had not been very sober at dinnertime: he was worse now. Nevertheless she felt thankful that he had come home so soon.

"She's gone out!" he continued, before Mrs. Bell had spoken: and it was evident that the fact of Rosaline's being out was putting him into a furious passion. "Who is she with?"

"Rose went over after tea to sit a bit with Granny Sandon. Granny's worse to-day, poor thing. I'm expecting her back every minute."

Bell staggered to the fireplace and stood there grasping his stick. His wife went on with her knitting in silence. To reproach him now would do harm instead of good. It must be owned that his exceeding to this extent was quite an exceptional case: not many times had his wife known him do it.

"Where's Raynor?" he broke out.

"Raynor!" she echoed, in surprise. "Do you mean Mr. Frank Raynor? I don't know where he is."

"He came in here a few minutes ago."

"Bless you, no, not he," returned the wife, in an easy tone, thinking it the best tone to assume just then.

"I tell ye I saw him come here."

"The moonlight must have misled you, Josiah. Mr. Raynor has not been here to-day. Put down your stick and take off your hat: and sit down and be comfortable."

To this persuasive invitation, Bell made no reply. Yet a minute or two he stood in silence, gazing at the fire; then, grasping his stick more firmly, and ramming his hat upon his head, he staggered out again, banging the door after him. Mrs. Bell sighed audibly; she supposed he was returning to the Golden Shaft.

Meanwhile Frank Raynor was with Mrs. Molly Janes. Her damages were not so bad as had been represented, and he proceeded to treat them: which took some little time. Leaving her a model of artistically-applied sticking-plaster, Frank started homewards again. The night was most beautiful; the sky clear, except for a few fleecy clouds that now and then passed across it, the silvery moon riding grandly above them. Just as Frank came opposite the Bottomless Shaft, he met Rosaline, on her way home from Granny Sandon's.

They stopped to speak—as a matter of course. Frank told her of the affray that had taken place, and the punishment of Molly Janes. While Rosaline listened, she kept her face turned in the direction she had come from, as though she were watching for some one: and her quick eyes discerned a figure approaching in the moonlight.

"Good-night—you pass on, Mr. Frank," she suddenly and hurriedly exclaimed. "I am going to hide here for a minute."

Darting towards the Bottomless Shaft, she took refuge amongst the surrounding mounds: mounds which looked like great earth batteries, thrown up in time of war. Instead of passing on his way, Frank followed her, in sheer astonishment: and found her behind the furthest mound at the back of the Shaft.

"Are you hiding from *me?*" he demanded. "What is it, Rosaline? I don't understand."

"Not from you," she whispered. "Why didn't you go on? Hush! Some one is going to pass that I don't want to see.

"Who is it? Your father? I think he has gone home."

"It is Blase Pellet," she answered. "I saw him at the shop-door as I came by, and I think he is following me. He talks nonsense, and I would rather walk home alone. Listen! Can we hear his footsteps, do you think, sir? He must be going by now."

Frank humoured her: he did not particularly like Blase Pellet himself, but he had no motive in remaining still, except that it was her wish. On the contrary, he would have preferred to be going homewards, for he had not much time to lose. Whistling softly, leaning against the nearest mound, he watched the white clouds coursing in the sky.

"He must have passed now, Rosaline."

She stole cautiously away, to reconnoitre; and came back with a beaming face.

"Yes," she said, "and he has gone quickly, for he is out of sight. He must have run, thinking to catch me up."

"I wonder you were not afraid to go through the mounds alone and pass close to the Bottomless Shaft!" cried Frank, in a tone of raillery, no longer deeming it necessary to lower his voice. "Old Sandon's ghost might have come up, you know, and carried you off.

"I am not afraid of old Sandon's ghost," said Rosaline.

"I dare say not!" laughed Frank.

In a spirit of bravado, or perhaps in very lightness of heart, Rosaline suddenly ran through the zigzag turnings, until she stood close to the mouth of the Shaft. Frank followed her, quickly also, for in truth he was impatient to be gone.

"I am listening for the ghost," said she, her head bent over the yawning pit. It was a dangerous position: the least slip, one incautious step nearer, might have been irredeemable: and Frank put his arm round her waist to protect her.

Another half-moment passed, when— They hardly knew what occurred. A howl of rage, a heavy stick brandished over them in the air, and Rosaline started back, to see her father. Old Bell must have been hiding amongst the mounds on his own score, looking out for what might be seen.

Down came the stick heavily on Frank's shoulders. An instant's tussle ensued: a shout from a despairing, falling man; a momentary glimpse of an upturned face; a cry of horror from a woman's voice; an agonized word from her companion; and all was over. Francis Raynor and the unhappy Rosaline stood alone under the pitiless moonlight.

IV

Waiting for Bell

The fire threw its glow on Mrs. Bell's kitchen—kitchen and sitting-room combined—lighting up the strip of bright carpet before the fender and the red-tiled floor; playing on the plates and dishes on the dresser, and on the blue hyacinth glasses in the window, now closed in by the outer shutters. Stout Mrs. Bell sat by the round table in her white apron and mob-cap, plying her knitting-needles. On the other side the hearth sat a neighbour, one Nancy Tomson, a tall, thin Cornish woman in a check apron, with projecting teeth and a high nose, who had come in for a chat. On the table waited the supper of bread-and-cheese; and a candle stood ready for lighting.

The clock struck nine. Mrs. Bell looked up as though the sound half startled her.

"Who'd heve thought it!" cried the visitor, whose chatter had been going incessantly for the last hour, causing the time to pass quickly. "Be they clock too fast, Dame Bell?"

"No," said the dame. "It's right by the church."

"Well, I'd never heve said it were nine. Your folks es late. I wonder where they be that they don't come hoam."

"No need to wonder," returned Mrs. Bell, in sharp tones, meant for the absentees. "Rosaline's staying with poor Granny Sandon, who seems to have nobody else to stay with her. As to Bell, he is off again to the Golden Shaft."

"You said he had comed in."

"He did come in: and I thought he had come in for good. But he didn't stay a minute; he must needs tramp out again. And he was further gone, Nancy Tomson, than I've seen him these three years."

Dame Bell plied her needles vigorously, as if her temper had got down into her fingers. The visitor plunged into renewed conversation, chiefly turning upon that interesting episode, the encounter between Janes and his wife. At half-past nine, Mrs. Bell put down her knitting and rose from her seat. She was growing uneasy.

"What can keep Rosaline? She never stays out so late as this, let Granny Sandon want her ever so. I'll take a look out and see if I can see her."

Unbolting and opening the door she admitted a flood of pale moonlight: pale, compared with the ruddier glow of the interior. Mrs. Bell peered out across the Bare Plain in the direction of Trennach; and Nancy Tomson, who was always ready for any divertisement, advanced and stretched her long neck over Dame Bell's shoulder.

"It's a rare light night," she said. "But I don't see nobody coming, Mrs. Bell. They keeps to the Golden Shaaft."

Feeling the air cold after the hot fire, Nancy Tomson withdrew indoors again. She was in no hurry to be gone. Her husband made one of the company at the Golden Shaft to-night, and this warm domicile was pleasanter than her own. Dame Bell was about to shut the door, when a faint sound caused her to look quickly out again, and advance somewhat farther than she did before. Leaning against the wall on the other side the window was a dark object: and, to Mrs. Bell's intense surprise, she discovered it to be Rosaline.

Rosaline, in what appeared to be the very utmost abandonment of grief or of terror. Her hands were clasped, her face was bent down. Every laboured breath she took seemed to come forth with suppressed anguish.

"Why, child, what on earth's the matter?" exclaimed the mother. "What are you staying there for?"

The words quickly brought out Nancy Tomson. Her exclamations, when she saw Rosaline, might almost have been heard at Trennach.

Rosaline's moans subsided into silence. She slowly moved from the wall, and they helped her indoors. Her face was white as that of the dead, and appeared to have a nameless horror in it. She sat down on the first chair she came to, put her arms on the table, and her head upon them, so that her countenance was hidden. The two women, closing the front-door, stood gazing at her with the most intense curiosity.

"She heve been frighted," whispered Nancy Tomson. And it did indeed look like it. Mrs. Bell, however, negatived the suggestion.

"Frighted! What is there to frighten her? What's the matter, Rosaline?" she continued, somewhat sharply. "Be you struck mooney, child?"

Nancy Tomson was one who liked her own opinion, and held to the fright. She advanced a step or two nearer Rosaline, dropping her voice to a low key.

"Heve you seen anything o' Dan Sandon? Maybe hes ghost shawed itself to you as you come by the Bottomless Shaaft?"

The words seemed to affect Rosaline so strongly that the table, not a very substantial one, vibrated beneath her weight.

"Then just you tell us whaat else it es," pursued Nancy Tomson, eager for enlightenment—for Rosaline had made a movement in the negative as to Dan Sandon's ghost. "Sure," added the woman to Mrs. Bell, "sure Janes and her be not a-fighting again! Sure he heven't been and killed her! Is it *that* whaat heve frighted you, Rosaline?"

"No, no," murmured Rosaline.

"Well, it must be something or t'other," urged the woman, beside herself with curiosity. "One caan't be frighted to death for nothing. Heve ye faaled down and hurted yerself?"

An idea, like an inspiration, seized upon Mrs. Bell. And it seemed to her so certain to be the true one that she only wondered she had not thought of it before. She laid her hand upon her daughter's shoulder.

"Rosaline! You have heard the Seven Whistlers!"

A slight pause. Rosaline neither stirred nor spoke. To Nancy Tomson the suggestion cleared up the mystery.

"*Thaat's it*," she cried emphatically. "Where was aal my wits, I wonder, thaat I never remembered they? Now doan't you go for to deny it, Rosaline Bell: you have heared they Seven Whistlers, and gashly things they be."

Another pause. A shiver. And then Rosaline slowly lifted her white face.

"Yes," she answered. "The Seven Whistlers." And the avowal struck such consternation on her hearers, although the suggestion had first come from them, that they became dumb.

"Father heard them, you know," went on Rosaline, a look of terror in her eyes, and a dreamy, far-off sound in her voice. "Father heard them. And they mean ill-luck."

"They bode death: as some says," spoke Nancy Tomson, lowering her voice to an appropriate key.

"Yes," repeated Rosaline, in a tone of sad wailing. "Yes: they bode death. Oh, mother! mother!"

But now, Mrs. Bell, although given, like her neighbours, to putting some faith in the Seven Whistlers: for example is contagious: was by no means one to be overcome with the fear of them. Rather was the superstition regarded by her as a prolific theme for gossip, and she altogether disapproved of the men's making it an excuse for idleness.

Had she heard the Whistlers with her own ears, it would not have moved her much. Of course she did not particularly like the Whistlers; she was willing to believe that they were in some mysterious way the harbingers of ill-luck; and the discomfort evinced by her husband on Sunday night, when he returned home after hearing the sounds, had in a degree imparted discomfort to herself. But, that any one should be put into a state of terror by them, such as this now displayed by Rosaline, she looked upon as absurd and unreasonable.

"Don't take on like that, child!" she rebuked. "You must be silly. They don't bode *your* death: never fear. I'll warm you a cup o' pea-soup. There's some left in the crock."

She bustled into the back-kitchen for the soup and a saucepan. Rosaline kept her head down: deep, laboured breathings agitated her. Nancy Tomson stood looking on, her arms folded in her check apron.

"Whereabouts did ye hear they Whistlers, Rosaline?" she asked at length.

But there was no answer.

"On the Bare Plain, I take it," resumed the woman. "Were't a-nigh they mounds by the Shaaft? Sounds echoes in they zigzag paths rarely. I've heard the wind a-whistling like anything there afore now. She be a pewerly lonesome consarn, thaat Shaaft, for waun who has to paas her at night alone."

A moan, telling of the sharpest mental agony, broke from Rosaline. Dame Bell heard it as she was coming in. In the midst of her sympathy, it angered her.

"Rosaline, I won't have this. There's reason in roasting of eggs. We shall have your father here directly, and what will he say? I can tell you, he was bad enough when he went out. Come! just rouse yourself."

"Father heard the Whistlers, and—they—bode—death!" shivered Rosaline.

"They don't bode yours, I say," repeated Dame Bell, losing patience. "Do you suppose death comes to every person who hears the Whistlers?—or ill-luck either?"

"No, no," assented Nancy Tomson, for Rosaline did not speak. "For waun that faals into ill-luck after hearing they Whistlers, ten escapes. I've knowed a whole crowd o' they men hear the sounds, and nought heve come on't to any waun on 'em."

"And that's quite true," said Mrs. Bell.

Rosaline could not be persuaded to try the soup. It was impossible that she could swallow it, she said. Taking a candle; she went up to her room; to bed, as her mother supposed.

"And the best place for her," remarked Dame Bell. "To think of her getting a fright like this!"

But poor Rosaline did not go to bed, and did not undress. Taking her shoes off, that she might not be heard, she began to pace the few yards of her narrow chamber, to and fro, to and fro, from wall to wall, in an anguish the like of which has rarely been felt on earth. She was living over again the night's meeting at the Bottomless Shaft and its frightful ending: she saw the white, upturned, agonized face, and heard the awful cry of despair of him who was falling into its pitiless depths, and was now lying there, dead: and it seemed to her that she, herself, must die of it.

The clock struck ten, and Nancy Tomson tore herself away from the warm and hospitable kitchen, after regaling herself upon the soup rejected by Rosaline. And Dame Bell sat on, knitting, and waiting for her husband.

WHEN ROSALINE, HER HANDS LIFTED in distress, tore away that evening from the Bottomless Shaft, and the tragedy that had been enacted there, and went flying over the Bare Plain towards home, Frank Raynor, recovering from the horror which had well-nigh stunned his faculties, went after her. Two or three times he attempted to say a word to her, but she took no notice of him; only sped the quicker, if that were possible. She never answered; it was as if she did not hear. When they reached the narrow path that branched off to the cottages, there she stopped, and turned towards him.

"We part here. Part for ever.

"Are you going home?" he asked.

"Where else should I go?" she rejoined, in anguish. "Where else can I go?"

"I will see you safe to the door.

"No. No! Good-bye."

And, throwing up her hands, as if to ward him off, she would have sped onwards. But Frank Raynor could not part thus: he had something to say, and detained her, holding her hands tightly. A few hasty words passed between them, and then she was at liberty to go on. He stood watching her until she drew near to her own door, and then turned back on his way across the plain.

In his whole life Francis Raynor had never felt as he was feeling now. An awful weight had settled upon his soul. His friends had been wont to say that no calamity upon earth could bring down Frank's exuberant spirits, or change the lightness of his ways. But something had been found to do it now. Little less agitated was he than Rosaline; the sense of horror upon him was the same as hers.

He was now passing the fatal spot, the Bottomless Shaft; its surrounding hillocks shone out in the moonlight. Frank turned his eyes that way, and stood still to gaze. Of their own accord, and as if some fascination impelled him against his will, his steps moved thitherwards.

With a livid face, and noiseless feet, and a heart that ceased for the moment to beat, he took the first narrow zigzag between two of the mounds. And—but what was it that met his gaze? As he came in view of the Shaft, he saw the figure of a man standing on its brink. The sight was so utterly unexpected, and so unlikely, that Frank stood still, scarcely believing it to be reality. For one blissful moment he lost sight of impossibilities, and did indeed think it must be Josiah Bell.

Only for an instant. The truth returned to his mind in all its wretchedness, together with the recognition of Mr. Blase Pellet. Mr. Blase was gingerly bending forward, but with the utmost caution, and looking down into the pit. As if he were listening for what might be to be heard there: just as the unhappy Rosaline had professed to listen a few minutes before.

Frank had not made any noise; and, even though he had, a strong gust of wind, just then sweeping the mounds, deadened all sound but its own. But, with that subtle instinct that warns us sometimes of a human presence, Blase Pellet turned sharply round, and saw him. Not a word passed. Frank drew silently back—though he knew the man had recognized him—and pursued his way over the Plain.

He guessed how it was. When he and Rosaline had been waiting amidst the mounds for Blase Pellet to pass, Blase had not passed. Blase must have seen them cross over to the spot in the moonlight; and, instead of continuing his route, had stealthily crossed after them and concealed himself in one or other of the narrow zigzags. He must have remained there until now. How much had he seen? How much did he know? If anything had been capable of adding to the weight of perplexity and trouble that had fallen on Frank Raynor, it would be this. He groaned in spirit he pursued his way homeward.

"How late you are, Frank!"

The words, spoken by Edina, met him as he entered. Hearing him come in, she had opened the door of the sitting-room. In the bewildering confusion of his mind, the perplexity as to the future, the sudden shock of the one moment's calamity, which might change the whole current of his future life, Frank Raynor had lost all recollection of the engagement for the evening. The appearance of Edina recalled it to him.

She was in evening dress: though very sober dress. A plain grey silk, its low body and short sleeves trimmed with a little white lace; a gold chain and locket on her neck; and bracelets of not much value. Quite ready, all but her gloves.

"Are—are you going, Edina?"

"*Going!*" replied Edina. "Of course I am going. You are going also, are you not?"

Frank pushed his hair off his brow. The gay scene at The Mount, and the dreadful scene in which he had just been an actor, struck upon him as being frightfully incongruous. Edina was gazing at him: she detected some curious change in his manner, and she saw that he was looking very pale.

"Is anything the matter, Frank? Are you not well?"

"Oh, I am quite well."

"Surely that poor woman is not dead?"

"What woman?" asked Frank, his wits still wool-gathering. Dr. Raynor, leaving his chair by the parlour-fire, had also come to the door, and was looking on.

"Have you been to see more than one woman?" said Edina. "I meant Molly Janes."

"Oh—ay—yes," returned Frank, passing his hand over his perplexed brow. "She'll be all right in a few days. There's no very serious damage done."

"What has made you so long, then?" questioned the doctor.

"I—did not know it was late," was the only excuse poor Frank could think of, as he turned from the steady gaze of Edina: though he might have urged that plastering up Mrs. Molly's wounds had taken time. And in point of fact he did not, even yet, know whether it was late or early.

"Pray make haste, Frank," said Edina. "You can dress quickly when you like. I did not wish, you know, to be so late as this."

He turned to seek his room. There was no help for it: he must go to this revelry. Edina could not go alone: and, indeed, he had no plea for declining to accompany her. Not until he was taking off his coat did he remember the blow on his shoulder. Frank Raynor, in his mind's grievous trouble, had neither felt the pain left by the blow, nor remembered that he had received one.

Yet it was a pretty severe stroke, and the shoulder on which it fell was stiff and aching. Frank, his coat off, was passing his hand gently over the place, perhaps to ascertain the extent of the damage, when the door was tapped at and then opened by Edina.

"I have brought you a flower for your button-hole, Frank."

It was a hot-house flower, white and beautiful as wax. Dr. Raynor had brought it from a patient's house where he had been in the afternoon, and Edina had kept it until the last moment as a small surprise to Frank. He took it mechanically; thanking her, it is true, but very tamely, his thoughts evidently far away. Edina could only note the change: what had become of Frank's light-heartedness?

"Is anything wrong with your shoulder?"

"It has a bit of a bruise, I think," he carelessly answered, putting the flower down on his dressing-table.

She shut the door, and Frank went on dressing, always mechanically. How many nights, and days, and weeks, and years, would it be before his mind would lose the horror of the recent scene!

"I wish to Heaven that she-demon, Molly Janes, had been *there!*" he cried, stamping his foot on the floor in a sudden access of grief and passion. "But for her vagaries, I should not have been called out this evening, and this frightful calamity would not have happened!"

Edina was ready when he went down, cloaked and shawled, a warm hood over her smooth brown hair. The doctor did not keep a close carriage; such a thing as a fly was not to be had at Trennach; and so they had to walk. Mrs. St. Clare had graciously intimated that she would send her carriage for Miss Raynor if the night turned out a bad one. But the night was bright and fine.

"You will be *sure* not to sit up for us, papa," said Edina, while Frank was putting on his overcoat. "It is quite uncertain what time we shall return home."

"No, no, child; I shall not sit up."

When they came to the end of the village, Frank turned on to the roadway, at the back of the parsonage. Edina, who was on his arm, asked him why he did so: the Bare Plain was the nearer way.

"But this is less dreary," was his answer. "We shall be there soon enough."

"Nay, I think the Bare Plain far less dreary than the road: especially on such a night as this," said Edina. "Here we are over-shadowed by trees: on the Plain we have the full moonlight."

He said no more: only kept on his way. It did not matter; it would make only about three minutes' difference. Edina stepped out cheerfully; she never made a fuss over trifles. By-and-by, she began to wonder at his silence. It was very unusual.

"Have you a headache, Frank?"

"No. Yes. Just a little."

Edina said nothing to the contradictory answer. Something unusual and unpleasant had decidedly occurred to him.

"How did you bruise your shoulder?" she presently asked.

"Oh—gave it a knock," he said, after the slightest possible pause. "My shoulder's all right, Edina: don't talk about it. Much better than that confounded Molly Janes's bruises are."

And with the sharp words, sounding so strangely from Frank's good-natured lips, Edina gathered the notion that the grievance was in some way connected with Molly Janes; perhaps the damaged shoulder also. Possibly she had turned obstreperous under the young doctor's hands and had shown fight to him as well as to her husband.

The Mount burst upon them in a blaze of light. Plants, festoons, music, brilliancy! As they were entering the chief reception-room, out-door wrappings removed, Edina missed the beautiful white flower: Frank's coat was unadorned.

"Frank! what have you done with your flower?"

His eyes wandered to the flowers decorating the rooms, and then to his button-hole, all in an absent sort of way that surprised Miss Raynor.

"I fear I must have forgotten it, Edina. I wish you had worn it yourself: it would have been more appropriate. How well it would have looked in your hair!"

"Fancy me with flowers in my hair!" laughed Edina. "But, Frank, I think Molly Janes must have scared some of your wits away."

Their greeting to Mrs. St. Clare over, Frank found a seat for Edina, and stood back himself in a corner, behind a remote door. How terribly this scene of worldly excitement contrasted with the one enacted so short a time ago! He was living it, perforce, over again; going through its short-lived action, that had all been over in one or two fatal moments: this, before him, seemed as a dream. The gaily-robed women sweeping past him with light laughter; the gleam of jewels; the pomp and pageantry: all seemed but the shifting scenes of a panorama. Frank could have groaned aloud at the bitter mockery: here life, gay, heedless, joyous: there DEATH; death violent and sudden. Never before, throughout his days, had the solemn responsibilities of this world and of the next so painfully pressed themselves upon him in all their dread reality.

"Oh, Mr. Raynor! I thought you were not coming! Have you been here long?"

The emotional words came from a fair girl in a cloud of white—Daisy St. Clare. Frank's hand went forward to meet the one held out to him: but never a smile crossed his face.

"How long have you been here, Mr. Raynor?"

"How long? I am not sure. Half-an-hour, I think."

"Have you been dancing?"

"Oh no. I have been standing here."

"To hide yourself? I really should not have seen you but that I am looking everywhere for Lydia's card, which she has lost."

He did not answer: his head was throbbing, his heart beating. Daisy thought him very silent.

"I have had my dance with Sir Paul Trellasis," said Daisy, toying with her own card, a blush on her face, and her eyes cast down.

At any other moment Frank would have read the signs, and taken the hint: she was ready to dance with *him*. But he never asked her: he did not take the gilded leaves and pencil into his own hands and write down his name as many times as he pleased. He simply stood still, gazing out with vacant eyes and a sad look on his face. Daisy at length glanced up at him.

"Are you ill?" she inquired.

"No; only tired."

"Too tired to dance?" she ventured to ask, after a pause, her pulses quickening a little as she put the suggestive question.

"Yes. I cannot dance to-night, Miss Margaret."

"Oh, but why?"

His breath was coming a little quickly with emotion. Not caused by Daisy, and her hope of dancing; but by that terrible *recollection*. Subduing his tones as far as possible, he spoke.

"Pray forgive me, Miss Margaret: I really cannot dance to-night."

And the cold demeanour, the discouraging words, threw a chill upon her heart. What had she done to him, that he should change like this?

With a bearing that sought to be proud, but a quivering lip, Margaret turned away.

He caught her eye as she was doing so; caught the expression of her face, and read its bitter disappointment. The next moment he was bending over her, pressing her hand within his.

"Forgive me, Daisy," he whispered, in pleading tones. "Indeed it is not caprice: I—I cannot dance to-night. Go and dance to your heart's content, and let me hide myself here until Miss Raynor is ready to leave you. The kindest thing you can do is to take no further notice of me."

He released her hand as he spoke, and stood back again in his dark corner. Margaret turned away with a sigh. Her pleasure in the evening had flown.

"And he never wished me any good wishes! It might just as well not have been my birthday."

V

MISSING

There was commotion next morning at Trennach, especially about the region of the Bare Plain and the cottages in Bleak Row. Josiah Bell had disappeared. Mrs. Bell had sat up half the night waiting for him; then, concluding he had taken too much liquor to be able to find his way home, and had either stayed at the Golden Shaft or found refuge with Andrew Float, she went to bed. Upon making inquiries this morning, this proved not to be the case. Nothing seemed to be known of Josiah Bell. His comrades professed ignorance as to his movements: the Golden Shaft had not taken him in; neither had Andrew Float.

Mrs. Bell rose early. People in a state of exasperation, lose sight of physical weakness: and this exactly expresses Dame Bell's state of mind. It was of course necessary that she should be up, in order to give Bell a proper lecture when he should make his appearance. Whilst dressing, she saw Nancy Tomson's husband outside, apparently starting for Trennach. Throwing a warm shawl over her shoulders, she opened the window.

"Tomson!" she called out. "Tomson!"

The man heard and looked up, his face leaden and his eyes red and inflamed. Last night's potations were not yet slept off.

"What was the reason my husband did not come home?"

Tomson took a few moments to digest the question. Apparently his recollection on the point did not quickly serve him.

"I doan't know," said he. "Didn't Bell come hoam?"

"No, he didn't."

"Baan't he come hoam?"

"No, he has not come. And I think it was a very unfriendly thing of the rest of you not to bring him. You had to come yourselves. Did you leave him at the Golden Shaft?"

"Bell warn't at tha Golden Shaaft," said Tomson.

"Now don't you tell me any of your untruths, Ben Tomson," returned the dame. "Not at the Golden Shaft! Where else was he?"

"I'll take my davy Bell were not weth us at tha Golden Shaaft last evening!" said the man. "He cleared out at dusk."

"But he went back to it later."

"He never did—not as I saw," persisted Tomson; who was always obstinate in maintaining his own opinion.

"Was Andrew Float there?" asked Mrs. Bell.

"Andrew Float? Yes, Float was there."

"Then I know Bell was there too. And don't you talk any more nonsense about it, Ben Tomson. Bell was too bad to get home by himself, and none of you chose to help him home; perhaps you were too bad yourselves to do it. And there he has stayed till now; either at the Golden Shaft, or with Float the miner: and you'd very much oblige me, Tomson, if you'd hunt him up."

She shut the casement, watched Tomson start on his way to Trennach, and, presently, went down to breakfast. Rosaline was getting it ready as usual, looking more dead than alive.

"We'll wait a bit, Rose, to see whether your father comes. Don't put the tea in yet."

Rose was kneeling before the fire at the moment. She turned at the words, a wild look in her eyes, and seemed about to say something; but checked herself.

Half-an-hour passed: Dame Bell growing more angry each minute, and rehearsing a sharper reception for Bell in her mind. At last they sat down to breakfast. Rose could not eat; she seemed ill: but her mother, taken up with the ill-doings of the truant, did not observe her as much as she would otherwise have done. Breakfast was at an end, although Mrs. Bell had lingered over it, when Tomson returned; and with him appeared the tall ungainly form of Float the miner.

"Well?" cried the dame, rising briskly from her chair in expectation, as Tomson raised the latch of the door.

"Well, 'tis as I said," said Tomson. "Bell didn't come back to the Golden Shaaft last night after he cleared out just afore dark. He ain't nowheres about as we can see."

Mrs. Bell looked from one to the other: at Tomson's rather sullen countenance, at Float's good-natured one. She might have thought the men were deceiving her, but she could see no motive for their doing so. Unless, indeed, Bell was lying somewhere in Trennach, so ill after his bout that they did not like to tell her.

"Where is he, then, I should like to know?" she retorted, in reply to Tomson.

"Caan't tell," said Tomson. "None o' they men heve seen him."

"Now this won't do," cried Dame Bell. "You must know where he

MRS. HENRY WOOD

is. Do you suppose he's lost? Don't stand simpering there on one leg, Andrew Float, but just tell me where he is hiding."

"I'd tell ye if I knew, ma'am," said Andrew, in his meek way. "I'd like to know where he is myself."

"But he was at the Golden Shaft last night: he must have been there," insisted the dame, unable to divest herself of this opinion. "What became of him when the place shut up? What state was he in?"

"No, ma'am, he was not there," said Andrew, mildly, for he never liked contradicting.

"Stuff!" said Mrs. Bell. "There was nowhere else for him to go to. What did you do with him, Andrew Float?"

"I heve done naught with him," rejoined Andrew. "He kep' I and they t'other soes awaiting all the evening for him at the Golden Shaft; but he didn't come back to't."

"I know he was at the Golden Shaft pretty nigh all yesterday," retorted Mrs. Bell, angrily.

"He were," acknowledged Andrew. "He come back after his dinner, and stayed there along o' the rest of us: but he was pewerly silent and glum; we couldna get a word from him. Just as they were a-lighting up, Bell he gets off the settle, and puts on his hat; and when we asked where he was going, he said to do his work. Upon that, one o' they sees—old Perkins, I think it were—wanted to know what work; but Bell wouldn't answer him. He'd be back by-and-by, he said; and went out."

"And he did not go back again?" reiterated Dame Bell.

"No, ma'am, he didn't. Though we aal stayed a bit later than usual on the strength of expecting him."

"It's very strange," said she. "He came home here about seven o'clock, or between that and half-past—I can't be sure as to the exact time. I thought he had come for good; he was three-parts tipsy then, and I advised him to sit down and make himself comfortable. Not a bit would he heed. After standing a minute or so, twirling his stick about, and asking where Rosaline was, and this and the other, he suddenly pushes his hat down over his eyes, and out he goes in a passion—as I could tell by his banging the door. Of course he was going back to the Golden Shaft. There can't be a doubt of it."

"He never came to the Golden Shaft, ma'am," said Float.

"I say," cried Tomson at this juncture, "what's amiss with Rosaline?"

During the above conversation, Rosaline had stood at the dresser, wiping the plates one by one, and keeping her back to the company, so that they did not see her face. But it chanced that Tomson went to the fire to light his pipe, just as Rosaline's work came to an end. As she crossed the kitchen to the staircase, Tomson met her and had full view of her. The man stared after her in surprise: even when she had disappeared up the stairs and shut the door behind her, he still stood staring; for he had never seen in all his life a face to equal it for terror. It was then that he put his question to Mrs. Bell.

"Didn't your wife tell you what it was that frightened her, Ben Tomson?" was the dame's query.

"My wife have said ne'er a word to me since yesterday dinnertime, save to call me a vool," confessed Tomson. "Her temper be up. Rosaline do look bad, though!"

"She heard the Seven Whistlers last night," explained Mrs. Bell. "It did fright her a'most to death."

"What!—they Whistlers here again laast night?" cried Tomson, his eyes opening with consternation.

Dame Bell nodded. "Your wife and me were sitting here, Ben Tomson, waiting for Rosaline to come in, and wondering why Granny Sandon kept her so late. I opened the door to see if I could see her coming across the Plain—or Bell, either, for the matter o' that—and there she was, leaning again' the wall outside with terror. We got her indoors, me and Nancy Tomson, and for some time could make nothing of her; she was too frighted to speak. At last she told us she had heard the Seven Whistlers as she was coming over the Plain."

But now this statement of Mrs. Bell's unconsciously deviated from the strict line of truth. Rosaline had not "told" them that she heard the Seven Whistlers on the Plain. When her mother suddenly accused her of having heard the Whistlers, and was backed in the suggestion by Nancy Tomson, poor Rosaline nodded an affirmative, but she gave it in sheer despair. She could not avow what had really frightened her; and the Seven Whistlers—which she had certainly *not* heard—served excellently for an excuse. The two women of course adopted the explanation religiously, and they had no objection to talk about it.

"They Whistlers again!" resumed Tomson, in dismay. "Ross, he's raging just like a bear this morning, threatening us weth law and what not; but he *caan't* expect us to go down and risk our lives while they boding Whistlers be glinting about."

"There, never mind they Whistlers," broke in Mrs. Bell, who

MRS. HENRY WOOD

sometimes fell into the native dialect. "Where's Bell got to? that's what I want to know."

Of course Tomson could not say. Neither could Float. The latter made the most sensible suggestion the circumstances admitted of—namely, that they should go and search for him. Mrs. Bell urged them to do so at once and to make haste about it. Bell would be found in Trennach fast enough, she said. As he had not taken refuge in Float's the miner's house, he had taken it in somebody else's, and was staying there till he grew sober.

On this day, Wednesday, Trennach was again taking holiday, and laying the blame on the Seven Whistlers. But this state of things could not last. The men knew that; and they now promised the overseer, Ross, whose rage had reached a culminating point, that the morrow should see them at work. One wise old miner avowed an opinion that three days would be enough to "break the spell o' they Whistlers and avert evil."

So the village street was filled with idlers, who really, apart from smoking and drinking, had nothing to do with themselves. It was a little early yet for the Golden Shaft: and when Andrew Float and Tomson arrived amongst them with the account that Josiah Bell had not been seen since the previous evening or been home all night, and that his wife (or as Tomson phrased it in the local vernacular, his woman) couldn't think where he had got to and had put a rod in pickle for him: the men listened. With one accord, they agreed to go and look for Bell: and they set about it heartily, for it gave them something to do.

But Josiah Bell could not be found. The miners' dwellings were searched, perhaps without a single exception, but he had not taken refuge in any one of them. Since quitting the Golden Shaft the previous evening at dusk, as testified to by the men who were there, only two persons, apart from his wife, could remember to have seen him: Blase Pellet, and the Rector of Trennach, the Reverend Thomas Pine. Mr. Pellet, standing at his shop-door for recreation at the twilight hour, had seen Bell pass down the street on his way from the inn, and noticed that he was tolerably far gone in liquor. The clergyman had seen and spoken to Bell a very few minutes later.

Chancing to meet the men on their search this morning, Mr. Pine learnt that Josiah Bell was missing. The clergyman always made himself at home with the men, whether they belonged to his flock or were Wesleyans. He never attempted to interfere in the slightest degree with their form of worship, but he constantly strove by friendly persuasion to lead them away from evil. The Wesleyan minister was obliged to him for it: he himself was lame, and could not be so active as he would have liked. Mr. Pine did much good, no doubt: but this last affair of the Whistlers, and the consequent idleness, had been too strong for him. Latterly Mr. Pine had also been in very indifferent health; the result of many years' hard work, and no holiday. Dr. Raynor had now told him that an entire rest of some months had become essential to him; without it he would inevitably break down. He was a tall, thin, middle-aged man with a worn face. Particularly worn, it looked, as he stood talking to the group of miners this morning.

"I saw Bell last evening myself," observed Mr. Pine. "And I was very sorry to see him as I did, for he could hardly walk straight. I was coming off the Plain and met him there. He had halted, and was gazing about, as if looking for some one: or, perhaps, in doubt—as it struck me—whether he should go on home, or, return whence he had come; which I supposed was from that favourite resort of yours, my men, the Golden Shaft. 'Better go straight home, Bell,' I said to him. 'I'm going that way, sir,' he answered. And he did go that way: for I watched him well on to the Plain."

"Well, we caan't find him nohow, sir," observed Andrew Float. "What time might that have been, sir, please?"

"Time? Something past seven. I should think it likely that Bell lay down somewhere to sleep the liquor off," added the clergyman, preparing to continue his way. "It is not often Bell exceeds as he did yesterday, and therefore it would take more effect upon him." The Bells, it may as well be remarked, were church people.

"Most likely he have faaled down, as tha paarson says; but he's a vool for lying there still," observed the men amongst themselves, as they turned off to pursue the search. Frank Raynor was out on his round this morning, as usual, and paid a visit to Molly Janes, whom he found going on satisfactorily. In passing Mrs. Bell's window, he saw Rosaline: hesitated, and then lifted the latch and went in. He stayed a minute or two talking with her alone, the mother being upstairs: and left her with the one word emphatically repeated: "Remember."

When Tomson went home to his midday meal, he opened Mrs. Bell's door to inform her that there were no tidings of her husband. Dame Bell received the information with incredulity. Much they had searched! she observed to her daughter, as Tomson disappeared: they had just sat themselves down again at the Golden Shaft; that was what they had done. Which accusation was this time a libel. She resolved to go and look after him herself when she had eaten her dinner. As to Rosaline, she did not know what to make of her. The girl looked frightfully ill, did not speak, and every now and then was seized with a fit of trembling.

"Such nonsense, child, to let the Whistlers frighten you into this state!" cried Mrs. Bell, tartly.

Retiring to her room after dinner, she came down by-and-by with her things on. Rosaline looked surprised.

"Where are you going, mother?"

"Into Trennach," said Dame Bell. "There's an old saying, 'If you want a thing done, do it yourself.' I shall find your father, I'll be bound, if he is to be found anywhere."

"You will be so tired, mother."

"Tired! Nonsense. Mind you have tea ready, Rosaline. I shall be sure to bring him back with me; I'm not going to stand any nonsense: and you might make a nice bit of buttered toast; he's fond of it, you know."

Stepping briskly across the Plain, Mrs. Bell went onwards. Nothing induces activity like a little access of temper, and she was boiling over with indignation at her husband. The illness from which she was suffering did not deprive her of exertion: and in truth it was not a serious illness as yet, though it might become so. Symptoms of a slow, inward complaint were manifesting themselves, and Dr. Raynor was doing his best to subdue them. Privately he feared the result; but Dame Bell did not suspect that yet.

Dr. Raynor and his nephew stood in the surgery after their midday dinner, the doctor with his back to the fire, Frank handing some prepared medicines, for delivery, to the boy who waited for them. As the latter went out with his basket, Blase Pellet ran across the road and came in, apron on, but minus his hat.

"Could you oblige us with a small quantity of one or two drugs, sir?" he asked of Dr. Raynor: mentioning those required. "We are out of them, and our traveller won't call before next week. Mr. Float's respects, sir, and he'll be much obliged if you can do it."

"I dare say we can," replied Dr. Raynor. "Just see, Frank, will you?"

As Frank was looking out the drugs, Mr. Pine came in. He was rather fond of running in for a chat with the doctor and Frank at leisure moments. Frank was an especial favourite of his, with his unaffected goodness of heart and his genial nature.

"A fine state of things, is it not!" cried the clergyman, alluding to the idlers in the streets. "Three days of it, we have had now."

"They will be at work to-morrow, I hear," said the doctor.

"Has Bell turned up yet?"

"No. The men have just told me they don't know where to look for him. They have searched everywhere. It seems strange where he can have got to."

Blase Pellet, standing before the table, waiting for the drugs, caught Frank's eye as the last words were spoken. A meaning look shot out from Pellet, and Frank Raynor's gaze fell as he met it. It plainly said, "*You* know where he is:" or it seemed so to Frank's guilty conscience.

"The fellow must have seen all!" thought Frank. "What on earth will come of it?"

Some one pushed back the half-open door, and stepped in with a quick gait and rather a sharp tongue: sharp, at least, this afternoon. Dame Bell: in her Sunday Paisley shawl, and green strings to her bonnet.

"If you please, Dr. Raynor—I beg pardon, gentlefolk"—catching sight of the clergyman—"if you please, doctor, could you give me some little thing to quiet Rosaline's nerves. She heard the Seven Whistlers last night, and they have frightened her out of her senses."

"Heard the Seven Whistlers!" repeated the clergyman, a hearty smile crossing his face.

"She did, sir. And pretty nearly died of it. I'm sure last night I thought she would have died. I'd never have supposed Rosaline could be so foolish. But there; it is so; and to-day she's just like one dazed. Not an atom of colour in her face; cowed down so as hardly to be able to put one foot before the other; and every other minute has a fit of the shivers."

To hear this astounding account of the hitherto gay, light-hearted, and self-contained Rosaline Bell, surprised the surgery not a little. Dr. Raynor naturally asked for further particulars; and Dame Bell plunged into the history of the previous night, and went through with it.

"Yes, gentlefolk, those were her very words—almost all we could get out of her: 'Father heard them and they boded death.' I—"

"But you should have tried to reason her out of such nonsense," interrupted Dr. Raynor.

"*Me* tried!" retorted Dame Bell, resenting the words. "Why, sir, it is what I did do. Me and Nancy Tomson both tried our best; but all she answered was just what I now tell you: 'Father heard the Whistlers, and they boded death.'"

Mr. Blase Pellet, standing with the small packet of drugs in his hand, ready to depart, but apparently unable to tear himself away, glanced up at Frank with the last words, and again momentarily met his eye. A slight shivering passed through Frank—caught perhaps from hearing of Rosaline's shiverings—and he bent his face over a deep drawer, where it could not be seen; as if searching for something missing.

"Well, it is a pity Rosaline should suffer herself to be alarmed by anything of the sort," observed Dr. Raynor; "but I will send her a composing draught. Are you going home now, Mrs. Bell?"

"As soon as I can find my husband, sir. I've come in to look for him. Tomson wanted to persuade me that he and Andrew Float and a lot more of them had been hunting for him all the morning; but I know better. Bell is inside one of their houses, sleeping off the effects of drink."

"The men have just told me they can't find him," said the clergyman. "I know they have been searching."

"There's an old saying, sir, 'If you want a thing well done, do it yourself.' I repeated it to Rose before I came out. Fine searching, I've no doubt it has been!—the best part of it inside the Golden Shaft. I'm going to look him up myself—and if you please, Dr. Raynor, I'll make bold to call in, as I go back, for the physic for Rosaline."

Unbelieving Mrs. Bell departed. Blase Pellet followed her. Dr. Raynor told Frank what to make up for Rosaline, and then he himself went out with Mr. Pine.

A few minutes afterwards, Edina softly opened the surgery-door, and glanced in. She generally came cautiously, not knowing whether patients might be in it or not. But there was only Frank. And Frank had his arms on the desk, and his head resting on them. The attitude certainly told of despondency, and Edina stood in astonishment: it was so unlike the gay-hearted young man.

"Why, Frank! What is the matter?"

He started up, and stared, bewildered, at Edina: as if his thoughts had been far away, and he could not in a moment bring them back again. Edina saw the trouble in his unguarded face, but he smoothed it away instantly.

"You have not seemed yourself since last night, Frank," said she in low tones, as she advanced further into the room. "Something or other has happened, I am sure. Is it anything that I can set right?—or help you in?"

"Now, Edina, don't run away with fancies," rejoined he, as gaily as though he had not a care in the world. "There's nothing at all the matter with me. I suppose I had dropped asleep over the physic. One does not stay out raking till three o'clock in the morning every day, you know."

"You cannot deceive me, Frank," rejoined Edina, her true, thoughtful eyes fixed earnestly upon him. "I—I cannot help fancying that it is in some way connected with Rosaline Bell," she added, lowering her voice. "I hope you are not getting into any entanglement: falling in love with her; or anything of that sort?"

"Not a bit of it," readily answered Frank.

"Well, Frank, if I can do anything to aid you in any way, you have only to ask me; you know that," concluded Edina, perceiving he was not inclined to speak out. "Always remember this, Frank: that in any trouble or perplexity, the best course is to look it straight in the face, freely and fully. Doing so takes away half its sting."

Meanwhile Dame Bell was pursuing her search. But she found that she could not do more than the miners had done towards discovering her husband. Into this house, out of that one, inquiring here, seeking there, went she, but all to no purpose. She was not uneasy, only exasperated: and she gave Mr. Blase Pellet a sharp reprimand upon his venturing to hint that there might exist cause for uneasiness.

The reprimand occurred as she was returning towards home. After her unsuccessful search, she was walking back down the street of Trennach in a state of much inward wonder as to where Bell could be hiding, and had nearly reached Dr. Raynor's, when she saw Float the druggist standing at his shop-door, and crossed over to enlarge upon the mystery to him. Mr. Blase Pellet came forward, as a matter of course, from his place behind the book-counter to assist at the conference.

"Bell is safe to turn up soon," remarked the druggist, who was a peaceable man, after listening to Mrs. Bell for a few minutes in silence.

"Turn up! of course he will turn up," replied the dame. "What's to hinder it? And he will have such a dressing from me that I don't think he'll be for hiding himself again in a hurry."

Upon that, Blase Pellet, partially sheltered behind the burly form of the druggist, spoke.

"Suppose he never does turn up? Suppose he is dead?—or something of that kind."

The suggestion angered Mrs. Bell.

"Are you a heathen, Blase Pellet, to invent such a thought as that?" she demanded in wrath. "What do you suppose Bell's likely to die from?—and where?"

Leaving Mr. Pellet to repent of his rashness, she marched over to Dr. Raynor's for the composing draught promised for Rosaline. And when Mrs. Bell went home with it she fully expected that by that time the truant would have made his appearance there.

But he had not done so. Rosaline had prepared the tea and toast, according to orders, but no Bell was there to partake of it. Nancy Tomson shared it instead. All the rest of the evening Dame Bell was looking out for him; and exchanging suggestions with her neighbours, who kept dropping in. Rosaline scarcely spoke: not at all unless she was spoken to. The same cold, white hue sat on her face, the same involuntary shiver at times momentarily shook her frame. The gossips gazed at her curiously—as a specimen of the fright those dreaded Whistlers had power to inflict.

They sat up again half the night, waiting for Bell, but waiting in vain; and then they went to rest. Mrs. Bell did not sleep as well as usual: she was disturbed with doubts as to where he could be, and by repeated fancyings that she heard his step outside. Once she got up, opened the casement, and looked out; but there was nothing to be seen; nothing except the great Bare Plain lying bleak and silent in the silver moonlight.

VI

Dining at the Mount

When another day dawned upon Trennach, and still Josiah Bell had not returned, his wife's exasperation gave place to real anxiety. She could not even guess what had become of him, or where he could be. Suspicion was unable to turn upon any particular quarter; not a shadow of foundation appeared for it anywhere. Had the man taken refuge in one of the miners' houses, as she had supposed, there he would still be; but there he was not. Had he stretched himself on the Bare Plain to sleep off the stupidity arising from drinking, as suggested by Mr. Pine, there he would have been found. No: the miners' dwellings and the Plain were alike guiltless of harbouring him; and Mrs. Bell was puzzled nearly out of her wits.

It cannot be said that as yet fear of any fatal accident or issue assailed her. The mystery as to where her husband could be was a great mystery, at present utterly unaccountable; but she never supposed that it would not be solved by his reappearance sooner or later. And she would have been quite ready to put down any hint of the kind, as she had put down Mr. Pellet's hint the previous day. Mrs. Bell fully believed that this day would not pass without bringing him home: and she was up with the lark, and down before Rosaline, in anticipation of it.

The miners had returned to their work this morning, and to their usual habits of sobriety: all things were quiet out of doors. The world was going on in its old groove; just as though, but for the absence of Bell, no ill-omened flock of Whistlers had come to raise a commotion in it.

This had been another night of sleeplessness for Rosaline, another prolonged interval of remorse and terror. She had undressed the previous night, and got into bed; and there she lay until morning, living through her fits of despondency, and striving to plan out the future. To stay at Trennach would, she felt, be simply impossible; if she did, she should die of it; she firmly believed that only to pass the Bottomless Shaft again, and look at it, would kill her. Discovery must come, she supposed, sooner or later; but she dared not stay in the place to face it.

Mrs. Bell was a native of Warwickshire. Her sister had married a Cornish man, who kept a shop in Falmouth. His name was John Pellet, and he was cousin to Blase Pellet's father. So that in point of fact there was no relationship between the Bells and Blase, although Blase enlarged upon their "cousinship," and Rosaline admitted it. They were merely connections. Mrs. Pellet had a small business as a milliner: she had no children, and could well attend to it. She and her husband, what with his trade and her work, were very comfortably off. She was fond of Rosaline, and frequently had her at Falmouth. It was to this refuge that Rosaline's thoughts now turned. She determined to go to it without delay. But so many neighbours came in during breakfast, inquiring after Bell, that she found no opportunity to speak of it then.

"Mother," she said, coming into the kitchen after attending to the upstairs rooms, Mrs. Bell having this morning undertaken to put away the breakfast-things: "Mother, I think I shall go to Falmouth."

"Go where?" cried Dame Bell, in surprise.

"To Aunt Pellet's."

"Why, what on earth has put that into your head, Rose?" demanded Mrs. Bell, after a prolonged pause of amazement.

Rosaline did not answer immediately. She had caught up the brass ladle, that chanced to lie on the table, and a piece of wash-leather from the knife-box, and was rubbing away at the ladle.

"Aunt will be glad to see me, mother. She always is."

"Glad to see you? What of that? Why do you want to go just now? And what are you polishing up that ladle for?" went on Mrs. Bell, uniting the grievances. "The brasses and tins had a regular cleaning last Saturday, for I gave it 'em myself."

Again Rosaline did not speak. As Mrs. Bell glanced at her, waiting for some rejoinder, she was struck with the girl's extreme pallor, her look of utter misery. Rosaline burst into tears.

"Oh, mother, don't hinder me!" she cried imploringly, dropping the ladle, and raising her hands in supplication. "I *can't* stay here. I must go away."

"You are afraid of hearing the Seven Whistlers again!"

"Let me go, mother; let me go!" piteously sobbed Rosaline. And her mother thought she had never seen any one in so deplorable a state of agitation before.

"Well, well, child, we'll see," said the dame, too much concerned to oppose her. "I wish the Whistlers had been somewhere. It is most unreasonable to let them take hold of your nerves in this way. A bit of an absence will put you all right again, and drive the thought out of your head. You shall go for a week, child, as soon as your father comes home."

"I must go to-day," said Rosaline.

"To-day!"

"Don't keep me, mother," besought Rosaline. "You don't know what it is for me here. These past two nights! have never closed my eyes; no, not for a moment. Let me start at once, mother! Oh, let me go! I shall have brain-fever if I remain."

"Well, I never!" cried Mrs. Bell, other words failing her to express her astonishment. "I never did think you could have put yourself into this unseemly fantigue, child; no, not for all the Whistlers in the air. As to starting off to Falmouth to-day, why, you could not have your things ready."

"They can be ready in half-an-hour," returned Rosaline, eagerly, her lips feverish with excitement. "I have already put them together."

"Well, I'm sure!—taking French leave, in that way, before you knew whether you might go or not! There, there; don't begin to cry and shake again. There's an afternoon train. And—and perhaps your father will be in before that."

"It is the best train I could go by," said Rosaline, turning to hang up the ladle on its hook by the dresser.

"It's not the best; it's the worst," contradicted Dame Bell. "Not but what it may be as well if you do go. I'm ashamed of the neighbours seeing you can be so silly and superstitious. The train does not get into Falmouth till night-time."

"Oh yes, it does," said Rosaline, anxiously: "it gets in quite early enough. Why, mother, I shall be at Aunt Pellet's soon after dark." And she crossed the kitchen with a quicker step than had been seen since that past miserable Tuesday night, and opened the staircase-door.

"And suppose your father does *not* come home first?" debated Mrs. Bell, not quite pleased with the tacit leave she had given. "How will you reconcile yourself to going away in the uncertainty, Rose?"

Rose did not answer. She only ran up the stairs, shutting the door behind her. "What in the world does ail the child?" exclaimed Dame Bell, considerably put out. "It's my belief the fright has turned her head. Until now she has always laughed at such things."

But Mrs. Bell made no further opposition to the journey. A discerning woman in most kinds of illness, she recognized the fact that change of some sort might be necessary for Rosaline. Still Bell did not return, and still the day went on.

In the afternoon Rosaline was ready to start, with a bandbox and handbag. Nancy Tomson had volunteered to accompany her to the station.

"I might perhaps have managed the walk to the train; I don't know; it's a goodish step there and back," said Dame Bell, as Rosaline stood before her, to say good-bye. "But you see, child, I want to wait in for your father. I shouldn't like him to find an empty house on his return."

Rosaline burst into a fit of sobbing, and laid hold of her mother as if seeking protection from some visible terror. And once again Mrs. Bell was puzzled, and could not make her out at all.

"Oh, mother dear, take care of yourself! And forgive me for all the ill I have ever done. Forgive, forgive me!"

"Goodness bless me, child, there's nothing to forgive that I know of!" testily cried Dame Bell, not accustomed to this sort of sensational leave-taking. "I shall take care of myself; never fear. Mind you take care of *your*self, Rose: those steam railways are risky things to travel by: and give my love to your aunt and my respects to Pellet."

"And we hed better be going," put in Nancy Tomson, who had put on her Sunday cloak and bonnet for the occasion. "They trains don't wait for nobody."

They were in ample time for this one: perhaps Rosaline had taken care of that: arriving, in fact, twenty minutes too soon. Rosaline entered it when it came up, and was steamed away.

In returning, Nancy Tomson saw Frank Raynor. He was on horseback; riding along very leisurely.

"Good-day," said he, nodding to her in passing. "Been out gallivanting?" he added in his light way.

"I heve been a-seeing Rosaline Bell off by one o' they trains, sir," answered the woman. And Frank checked his horse as he heard it and sat as still as a statue.

"Where has she gone to?"

"Off on a maggot to Falmouth. They Whistlers went and give her a prime fright, sir: she heve hardly done shaking yet, and looks as gashly as you please. She heve gone to her aunt's to forget it."

"Oh, to be sure," carelessly assented Frank: and rode on.

A few minutes afterwards, when near Trennach, he met Mrs. St. Clare's carriage; herself, two ladies, and Lydia seated within it. The coachman pulled up by orders. Of course Frank had to do the same.

"Have you been to The Mount, Mr. Raynor?"

"No, I have been across to Pendon," he answered, keeping his hat off; and the breeze took advantage of that to stir the waves of his bright hair.

"This makes two days that we have seen nothing of you," said Mrs. St. Clare. "You have not been near us since Tuesday night."

A faint flush passed over his face. He murmured something about having been very busy himself—concluded they were occupied: but he spoke rather confusedly, not at all with the usual ready manner of Frank Raynor.

"Well, we shall see you this evening, Mr. Raynor. You are coming to dine with us."

Very hastily he declined the invitation. "I cannot come, thank you," he said. "I shall have patients to see, and must stay at home."

"But you must come; you are to come," rejoined Mrs. St. Clare. "I have seen Dr. Raynor, and he has promised that you shall. Finally, Mr. Raynor, you will very much oblige me by doing so."

What further objection could Frank make? None. He gave the required assent, together with a sweeping bow, as the carriage drove on.

"What a bright-looking, handsome man!" exclaimed one of the ladies to Mrs. St. Clare. "I really do not remember, though, to have seen him the night of the ball, as you say I did."

"Oh, he stuck himself in a corner all the night," put in Lydia. "I don't believe he came out of it once, or danced at all."

"He is too good-looking for a doctor. I should tremble for my daughters' hearts."

"*Being* a doctor, there is, I hope, no cause for me to tremble for the hearts of mine," haughtily rejoined Mrs. St. Clare. "Not but that he is of fairly good family and expectations: the eldest son of Major Raynor and the heir to Eagles' Nest."

Mrs. St. Clare, unconsciously to herself, was not altogether correct in this statement. But it may pass for the present.

Frank rode home. Dr. Raynor was out; and he went into the parlour to Edina. She sat in the bow window, prosily darning stockings.

"Why did Uncle Hugh promise Mrs. St. Clare that I should dine at The Mount to-night? Do you know, Edina?"

"Because she invited you, I suppose. I saw the carriage at the door and papa standing at it as he talked to them. Don't you care to go?"

"Not this evening—particularly."

"Papa just looked in here afterwards and said would I tell you that you were to dine at The Mount. I thought you were fond of dining there, Frank."

"So I am sometimes. Where is Uncle Hugh?"

"He has been sent for to the parsonage. Mr. Pine is not well."

AGAIN FRANK RAYNOR—AND THIS time sorely against his will—sat at Mrs. St. Clare's brilliant dinner-table. He could see why she had made so great a point of his coming: only one gentleman was present besides himself. In fact, there was only Frank in all Trennach to fall back upon. Dr. Raynor never dined out: the Rector pleaded ill-health. Most of the guests who had been staying in the house had left it this morning after their two nights' sojourn: those remaining—General Sir Arthur Beauchamp, Lady and Miss Beauchamp, and a young married woman, Mrs. Fox—were to leave on the morrow. It fell to Frank's lot to take in Lady Beauchamp: she it was who had expressed doubts as to the stability of young ladies' hearts, if exposed to the attractions of Mr. Raynor. Margaret, as it chanced, sat on Frank's left hand; and Margaret, for the time being, was supremely happy.

"Are you better than you were on Tuesday night, Mr. Raynor?" she took occasion to ask him in a whisper, when a buzz of conversation was going on.

"Better? I was not—" not ill, Frank was about to respond in surprise, and then recollected himself. "Oh, thank you, yes, Margaret. I was rather out of sorts that night."

"Mr. Raynor, what is this story about some man being lost?" asked Mrs. St. Clare, from the head of the table. "One of the miners, we hear, has mysteriously disappeared and cannot be found."

Frank's face flushed hotly, and he would have given the world to avoid the subject. But he could not: and he related the particulars.

"But where is it supposed that he can be, this Josiah Bell?" asked the general. "Where should *you* think he is, Mr. Raynor?"

Perhaps no one at the table, with the exception of Margaret, noticed that the young surgeon was somewhat agitated by the topic: that his breath seemed a little laboured as he answered the repeated questions, and that his complexion changed from red to pale. Margaret silently wondered why the disappearance of a miner should so affect him.

"Are there any old pits, used out and abandoned, that the man could have fallen into?" asked the sensible general.

A strangely-vivid flush now on Frank Raynor's face. A marked hesitation in his voice, as he replied.

"Not—not any—that are easy of access, I fancy, Sir Arthur."

"Well, the man must be somewhere, dead or alive. You say it is not at all thought that he would run away."

"Oh no; his friends say he would not be likely to do that."

"He has a very beautiful daughter, has he not?" spoke Lydia to Frank, from the opposite side of the table.

"Yes, she is nice-looking."

"Nice-looking is not the word for it, Mr. Raynor—as we are told," persisted Lydia. "We hear she is strictly, faultlessly beautiful. Fancy that, for the daughter of a common miner!"

Miss St. Clare's tone seemed to savour of mockery—as her tones often did. Frank, straightforward and true-hearted to the core, answered rather warmly.

"The man has come down in life; he was not always a common miner: and Rosaline is superior in all ways to her station. She *is* very beautiful."

"You seem to know her well."

"Oh, very well," carelessly replied Frank.

"We should not have been likely to hear of the affair at all: of the man's disappearance, or that he had a daughter who was celebrated for her looks; but for mamma's maid," said Lydia, more slightingly; for in truth she considered it a condescension even to speak of such people. "Tabitha has relatives in Trennach: she paid them a visit this morning, heard the news about the missing man, and entertained us with it on her return."

"I should like to see this Rosaline," spoke Lady Beauchamp. "I am a passionate admirer of beauty. You do, by some rare chance, now and again, find it wonderfully developed in a girl of the lower orders."

"Well, it is to be hoped the poor man will be found all right," concluded Sir Arthur.

And, with that, the conversation turned to some other topic—to Frank's intense relief. But Margaret St. Clare still marvelled at the interest he had betrayed: and she was fated to remember it, to her cost, in the time to come.

VII

EDINA'S ROMANCE

In the days gone by there were three of the brothers Raynor: Francis, Henry, and Hugh. Francis entered the army; Henry the church; and Hugh the medical profession. With the two former we have at present nothing to do. Hugh Raynor passed his examinations satisfactorily, and took all his degrees—thus becoming Dr. Raynor. Chance and fortune favoured him. He was at once taken by the hand by an old doctor who had an excellent practice in Mayfair, and became his assistant and frequent companion. The old doctor had one only child, a daughter, who was just as much taken with Hugh (and he with her) as was her father. They were married; and on the death of the old doctor shortly afterwards, Dr. Raynor succeeded to a good deal of the practice. He was quite a young man still, thoroughly well intentioned, but not so prudent as he might have been. He and his wife lived rather extravagantly, and the doctor sometimes found himself short of ready-money. They resided in the house that had been the old doctor's; and they heedlessly, and perhaps unconsciously, made the mistake of beginning where he had left off: that is, they continued their housekeeping on the same scale as his: maintained the same expenses, horses, carriages and entertainments. The result was, that Dr. Raynor in the course of four or five years found himself considerably involved. In an evil moment, thinking to make money by which to retrieve his fortunes, he embarked his name (and as much money as he could scrape together) in one of the bubble schemes of the day. A scheme which—according to its prospectus, its promoters' assertions, and the credulous doctor's own belief—was certain to realize an immense fortune in no time.

Instead of that, it realized poverty and ruin. The scheme failed— the usual result—and Dr. Raynor found himself responsible for more money than he would ever make in this world. Misfortunes, it has been too often said, do not come singly: Dr. Raynor proved an example of it. Just before the bubble burst, he lost his wife; and the only one element of comfort that came to him in the midst of his bitter grief for her, was to know that she died before the other blow fell.

A frightful blow it was, almost prostrating Dr. Raynor. The creditors of the ruthless company took all from him: even to the gold watch upon his person. They sold up his furniture, his books, his carriages and horses, everything; and they told him he might thank their leniency that they did not imprison him until he could pay up the scores of thousands they made out he was responsible for. The fact was, the promoters of the company, and those of its directors who possessed funds, had gone over to the Continent; and there remained only the poor doctor, innocent and honourable, to come upon.

Turned out of house and home, his name in the papers, his prospects gone, Dr. Raynor felt he should be glad to die. He did not even attempt to retain his practice, which was a great mistake; his only care was to escape from the scene of his prosperity and hide his humiliated head for ever. His little child, Edina, the only one he had, was five years old; and for her sake he must try and keep a roof over his head and find bread to eat. So he looked out for employment after a time, as far away from London and in as obscure a corner of the land as might be, and obtained it amidst the collieries in North Warwickshire, as assistant to a general practitioner. After remaining there for some years, he heard of an opening at a place in Cornwall. The surgeon of the place, Trennach, an old man, who wanted to retire, chanced to know Dr. Raynor, and wrote to offer him the succession upon very easy terms. It was accepted, and the doctor removed to Trennach. The returns from the practice were very small at first, he found, scarcely enabling him to make way, for it lay almost entirely amongst the poor; but subsequently Dr. Raynor dropped into a better class of practice as well through the death of another surgeon some two or three miles from Trennach. And here, in Trennach, he remained; a sad and silent man ever since the misfortune of his early days; and lived as retired a life as might be. His only care, his constant companion, had been his beloved child, Edina. He had trained her to be all that a woman should be: true, earnest, thoughtful, good. Mrs. Pine, who had no children of her own, had helped him, and been to Edina almost as a second mother. Not many women in this world were like Edina Raynor.

The only sister of the three brothers Raynor had married a London banker, Timothy Atkinson, the junior partner in the house of Atkinson and Atkinson. When Edina was two-and-twenty years of age, she went on a visit to her aunt in London. Mr. and Mrs. Timothy Atkinson, who had married rather late in life, were childless; and in these later years Mrs. Atkinson had become an invalid. She was also eccentric and capricious; and, for the first few days after her arrival, Edina thought she should not enjoy her visit at all. Timothy Atkinson was a sociable little man, but he spent all his time in the business downstairs—for they lived at the banking-house. His cousin, the head and chief, disabled by illness, rarely came to business now; it all lay on Timothy's shoulders. No one seemed to have any time to give to Edina.

But soon a change came. George Atkinson, the son of the elder partner, found out Edina; and perhaps pitying her loneliness, or out of courtesy, constituted himself her cavalier. He was nine or ten years older than Edina: a good-looking, rather silent young man of middle height and grave courtesy, with a pleasant voice and thoughtful face. He was not strong, and there had been some talk of his having been ordered to travel for his health; but the death of his mother had intervened and prevented it. But, though a silent man to the world in general, he was eloquent to Edina. At least, she found him so. As though they had been the actual cousins that Mrs. Atkinson sometimes called them, he was allowed to take her everywhere. To the theatres, the opera, the gardens, all the shows and sights of London, Edina was entrusted to the care of George Atkinson. Sometimes Mrs. Atkinson was with them; more often she was not.

And better care he could not have taken of her, or shown himself more solicitous for her comfort, had she been his sister or cousin. Honourable, instinctively kind, upright and noble, there was in George Atkinson a chivalrous devotion to women, that could only betray itself in manner and tell upon those on whom it was exercised. It told upon Edina. Highly educated, and possessing a fund of general information, he was a most agreeable companion. Before one-half of their few weeks' intercourse together had passed, she had learned to love George Atkinson with a lasting affection.

Many a half-hour did he spend talking to her in low gentle accents of his recently dead mother. His love, his reverence, his still lively grief for her loss, was expressed in the truest and most tender terms. This alone would have taken Edina's heart by storm. She believed there lived not another man in the world who was so true a gentleman, so estimable and admirable in all respects as George Atkinson. Indeed he was very much so, as young men go; and neither Edina nor any other girl need feel anything but pride at being chosen by him.

Poor Edina! It was the one great mistake of her life. Whilst George Atkinson had no ulterior thought of her, hope was whispering to her heart the possibility that they might pass their future lives together. And oh, what an Eden it would have been for Edina! She loved him with all the intensity of a pure young heart; a heart in its virgin freshness. Whilst he, though no doubt liking her very much indeed; nay, perhaps even loving her a little just in one corner of his heart; had no thought, no intentions beyond the present hour. He knew he was not strong; and he meant to see what travelling far and wide would do to make him so. Consequently the idea of marriage had not entered his head.

It was only on the last day of her stay, the one previous to her departure for home, that the revelation came to Edina, and her eyes were opened all too abruptly. They were together in the drawing-room in the half-hour before dinner. Mr. Timothy Atkinson had not come up from the counting-house, his wife was in her chamber, dressing. It was a lovely day in late spring. Edina stood by one of the open windows, which had been made into a sort of small fernery. The western sunlight was playing upon the leaves, and touching her own smooth hair and her fair young face.

"It is very beautiful—but I think very delicate," observed Edina, speaking of a new specimen of fern just planted, which they were both looking at. "Do you think it will live?"

George Atkinson passed his fingers under the small leaf, and somehow they met Edina's. He did not appear to notice the momentary contact; *her* pulses thrilled at it.

"Oh yes, it will live and flourish," he answered. "In six months' time you will see what it will be."

"*You* may see," she said, smiling. "It will be a great many more months than six, I suppose, before I am here again. Perhaps it may be years."

"Indeed, Edina, you are more likely to be here in six months' time than I am. But for my mother's death and my father's failing health, I should have left before this."

"But you will return?" said Edina.

"Some time I may do so. I cannot answer for it.

"What do you mean, George?"

"Not very much," he answered, with a grave and kindly smile in his dark grey eyes. "An idea crosses my mind now and then, that when once I am in those genial lands, where the skies are blue and the winds temperate, I shall be in no hurry to quit them again. Of course I don't say that I shall remain there for life; but—it might happen so."

MRS. HENRY WOOD

A pang, sharp as a two-edged sword, struck Edina. "What, and abandon your country for ever, and—and home ties?"

"As to home ties, Edina, I shall have none then. There is only my father now. Of course my future movements will be regulated with reference to him as long as he is with us. But—I fear—that may not be very much longer. As you know."

She made a slight movement of assent; and bent her head over the ferns.

"And I shall not be likely to make home ties for myself," went on George Atkinson, unconscious of the anguish he was inflicting. "I shall never marry."

"Why?" breathed Edina.

"I scarcely know why," he replied, after a pause, as if searching for a reason. "I have never admitted the thought. I fancy I shall like a life of change and travel best. And so—when once we part, Edina—and that must be to-morrow, you say, though I think you might have remained longer—it is hard to say when we shall meet again. If ever."

"Halloa, who's here? Oh, it is you, George; and Edina! Where's your aunt? Dinner must be nearly ready."

The interruption came from brisk little Timothy Atkinson, who bounded into the room with quick steps and his shining bald head.

As Edina turned at his entrance, George Atkinson caught the expression of her face; the strange sadness of its eyes, its extreme pallor. She looked like one who has received a shock. All at once a revelation broke upon him, as if from subtle instinct. For an instant he stood motionless, one hand pushing back his brown hair; hair that was very much the same shade as Edina's.

"It may be better so," he said in a whisper, meeting her yearning eyes with his earnest gaze. "At any rate, I have thought so. Better for myself, better for all."

The tall, portly frame of Mrs. Timothy Atkinson, clothed with rich crimson satin, rolled into the room, and the conversation was at an end. And with it, as Edina knew, her life's romance.

"God bless you, Edina," George Atkinson said to her the next day, as he attended her to the station with Mr. Timothy, and clasped her hand at parting. "When I return to England in years to come—if ever I do return—I shall find you a blooming matron, with a husband and a flock of children about you. Farewell."

And as Edina sat back in the swiftly-speeding railway-carriage, not striving, in these early moments of anguished awakening to do battle with her breaking heart, she knew that the blow would last her for all time. Dr. Raynor thought her changed when she arrived home: he continued to think her so as the days went on. She was more quiet, more subdued: sad, even, at times. He little knew the struggle that was going on within her, or the incessant strivings to subdue the recollection of the past: and from henceforth she endeavoured to make duty her guide.

Never a word was exchanged between father and daughter upon the subject; but probably Dr. Raynor suspected something of the truth. About a year after Edina's return from London, a gentleman who lived a few miles from Trennach made her an offer of marriage. It would have been an excellent match in all respects; but she refused him. Dr. Raynor, perhaps feeling a little vexed for Edina's sake, asked her the reason of her rejection. "I shall never marry, papa," she answered, her cheek flushing and paling with emotion. "Please do not let us ever talk of such a thing; please let me stay at home with you always."

Nothing more was said, then or later. No one else came forward for her, and the matter dwindled down into a recollection of the past. Edina got over the cruel blow in time, but it exercised an influence upon her still.

And that had been Edina Raynor's romance in life, and its ending.

MRS. HENRY WOOD

VIII

Rose-coloured Dreams

The sweet spring sunshine lay upon Trennach, and upon Dr. Raynor's surgery. Francis Raynor stood in it, softly whistling. Two sovereigns lay on the square table, amongst the small scales and the drugs and the bottles, and he was looking down upon them somewhat doubtfully. He wanted to convey this money anonymously to a certain destination, and hardly knew how to accomplish it. Sovereigns were not at all plentiful with Frank; but he would, in his open-heartedness, have given away the last he possessed, and never cast regret after it.

"I know!" he suddenly cried, taking up a sheet of white paper. "I'll pack them up in an envelope, direct it to her, stick a stamp on it, and get Gale the postman to deliver it on his round. Dame Bell is as unsuspicious as the day, and will think the money is sent by Rosaline—as the last was. As to Gale—he is ready to do anything for me and Uncle Hugh: he gets his children doctored for nothing. It's a shame he is so badly paid, poor fellow!"

Several weeks had gone on since the disappearance of Josiah Bell, and it was now close upon May. Bell had never returned: nothing could be heard of him. Mrs. Bell knew not what to make of it: she was a calm-natured, unemotional woman, and she took the loss more easily than some wives might have taken it. Bell was missing: she could make neither more nor less of it than that: he might come back some time, and she believed he *would* do so: meanwhile she tried to do the best she could without him. In losing him, she had lost the good wages he earned, and they had been the home's chief support. She possessed a very small income of her own, which she received quarterly—and this had enabled them to live in a better way than most of the other miners—but this alone was not sufficient to keep her. A managing, practical woman, Mrs. Bell had at once looked out for some way of helping herself in the dilemma, and found it. She took in two of the unmarried miners as lodgers—one of them being Andrew Float, and she began to knit worsted stockings for sale. "I shall get along somehow till Bell returns," was her cheerful remark to the community.

Rosaline was still at Falmouth—and meant to remain there. She wrote that she was helping her aunt with her millinery business, was already clever at it, and received wages, which she intended to transmit to her mother. The first instalment—it was not much—had already come. Frank Raynor had just called Dame Bell unsuspicious as the day. She was so. But, one curious fact, in spite of the freedom from suspicion, was beginning to strike her: in all the letters written by Rosaline she had never once mentioned her father's name, or inquired whether he was found.

Frank Raynor, elastic Frank, had recovered his spirits. It was perhaps impossible that one of his light and sanguine temperament should long retain the impression left by the dreadful calamity of that fatal March night. Whatever the precise details of the occurrence had been, he had managed outwardly to shake off the weight they had thrown upon him, and in manner was himself again.

Perhaps one thing, that helped him to do this, was his altered opinion as to the amount of knowledge possessed by Blase Pellet. At first he had feared the man; feared what he knew, and what evil he might bring. But, as the days and the weeks had gone on, and Blase Pellet did not speak, or give any hint to Trennach that he had anything in his power to betray, Frank grew to think that he really knew nothing; that though the man might vaguely suspect that something wrong had occurred that night, he was not actually cognizant of it. Therefore Frank Raynor had become in a measure his own light and genial self again. None could more bitterly regret the night's doings than he did: but his elastic temperament could throw off all sign of remorse; ay, and often its recollection.

The thing that troubled him a little was Mrs. Bell's position. It was through him she had been deprived of the chief means which had kept her home; therefore it was only just, as he looked upon it, that he should help her now. Even with the proceeds from the lodgers and the stockings, and with what Rosaline would be enabled to send her, her weekly income would be very much smaller than it had been. Frank wished with his whole heart that he could settle something upon her, or make her a weekly allowance; but he was not rich enough to do that. He would, however, help her a little now and again in secret—as much as he was able—and this was the destination of the two sovereigns. In secret. It would not do to let her or any one else know the money came from him, lest the question might be asked, What claim has she upon you that you should send it to her? To answer that truthfully would be singularly inconvenient.

Trennach in general could of course make no more of the disappearance of Bell than his wife made. It was simply not to be understood. Many and many an hour's discussion took place over it in the pits; or at the Golden Shaft, to the accompaniment of pipes and beer; many a theory was started. The man might be here, or he might be there; he might have strolled this way, or wandered that way—but it all ended as it began: in uncertainty. Bell was missing, and none of them could divine the cause. And the Seven Whistlers, that he heard on the Sunday night or thought he heard, had certainly left no damage behind them for the miners. The men might just as well have been at work those three days for all the accident that had occurred in the mines. Perhaps better.

Seated at the window of what was called the pink drawing-room at The Mount, from the colour of its walls, were Mrs. St. Clare and her daughter Lydia. The large window, shaded by its lace curtains, stood open to the warm bright day. Upon the lawn was Margaret in her white dress, flitting from flower to flower, gay as the early butterflies that sported in the sunshine. Lydia, a peculiar expression on her discontented face, watched her sister's movements.

Frank Raynor had just gone out from his morning visit, carrying with him an invitation to dine with them in the evening. Lydia was really better; she no more wanted the attendance of a doctor than her sister wanted it: but she was devoured by ennui still, and the daily, or almost daily, coming of Frank Raynor was the most welcome episode in her present life. She had learned to look for him: perhaps had learned in a very slight degree to *like* him: at any rate, his presence was ever welcome. Not that Lydia would have suffered herself to entertain serious thoughts of the young surgeon—because he was a surgeon, and therefore far beneath her notice in that way—but she did recognize the fascination of his companionship, and enjoyed it. Latterly, however, an idea had dawned upon her that some one else enjoyed it also—her sister—and the suspicion was extremely unwelcome. Lydia was of an intensely jealous disposition. She would not for the world have condescended to look upon Frank Raynor as a lover, but her jealousy was rising, now that she suspected Daisy might be doing so, somewhat after the fashion of the dog-in-the-manger. That little chit, Daisy, too, whom she looked upon as a child!—there was some difference, she hoped, between nineteen and her own more experienced age of five-and-twenty! She was fond of Daisy, but had not the least intention of being rivalled by her; and perhaps for the child's own sake, it might be as well to speak.

As Frank went out, he crossed Daisy's path on the lawn. They turned away side by side, walking slowly, talking apparently of the flowers; lingering over them, bending to inhale their perfume. Mrs. St. Clare, a new magazine and a paper-knife in her hand—for she did make a pretence of reading now and then, though it was as much a penance as a pleasure—glanced up indifferently at them once, and then glanced down again at her book. But Lydia, watching more observantly, saw signs and wonders: the earnest gaze of Frank's blue eyes as they looked into Daisy's; the shy droop in hers; and the lingering pressure of the hands in farewell. He went on his way; and Daisy, detecting in that moment her sister's sharp glance from the window, made herself at once very busy with the beds and the flowers, as if they were her only thought in life.

"Mamma!"

The tone was so sharp that Mrs. St. Clare lifted her head in surprise. Lydia's voice was usually as supinely listless as her own.

"What is it, Lydia?"

"Don't you think that Daisy wants a little looking after?"

"In what way?"

"Of course I may be mistaken in my suspicions. But I think I am not. I will assume that I am not."

"Well, Lydia?"

"She and Mr. Raynor are flirting desperately."

Mrs. St. Clare made no reply whatever. Her eyes fixed inquiringly on Lydia's, kept their gaze for a moment or so, and then fell on the magazine pages again. Lydia felt a little astonished: was this indignation or indifference?

"Did you understand me, mamma?"

"Perfectly, my dear."

"Then—I really do not comprehend you. Don't you consider that Daisy ought to be restrained?"

"If I see Daisy doing anything that I very much disapprove, I shall be sure to restrain her."

"Have you not noticed, yourself, that they are flirting?"

"I suppose they are. Something of the sort."

"But *surely*, mamma, you cannot approve of Mr. Raynor! Suppose a serious attachment came of it, you could not suffer her to marry him!"

Mrs. St. Clare turned her book upside down upon her knee, and spoke in the equable manner that characterized her, folding her arms idly in the light morning scarf she wore.

"It never occurred to me, Lydia, until one day, a week or two ago, that any possibility could arise of what you are mentioning. Mr. Raynor's visits here are merely professional. Even when he comes by invitation to dinner, I consider them as partaking of that nature: to look upon them in any other light never entered my mind. On this day, however, I saw something that, figuratively speaking, opened my eyes."

"What was it?" asked Lydia.

"It occurred on the day that the Faulkners were to have come to us, and did not. Mr. Raynor dined here in the evening. After dinner I dropped into a doze; there, on the sofa"—pointing to the other end of the room. "When I awoke it was quite dusk; not dark; and Mr. Raynor and Daisy were standing together at this open window; standing very close indeed to each other. Daisy was leaning against him, in fact; and he, I think, had one of her hands in his. You were not in the room."

"It was the evening I had so bad a headache, through vexation at those stupid people not coming!" cried Lydia, angrily. "I had gone upstairs, I suppose, to take my drops. But what did you do, mamma? Order Mr. Raynor from the house?"

"No. Had I acted on my first impulse, I might have done that, Lydia. But instinct warned me to take time for consideration. I did so. I sat quite still, my head down on the cushion as before, they of course supposing me to be still asleep, and I ran the matter rapidly over in my mind. The decision I came to was, not to speak hastily; not *then*; to take, at any rate, the night for further reflection: so I coughed to let them know I was awake, and said nothing."

"Well?" cried Lydia, impatiently.

"I went over the affair again at night with myself, looking at it from all points of view, weighing its merits and demerits, and trying to balance one against the other," pursued Mrs. St. Clare. "The result I came to was this, Lydia: to let the matter take its course."

Lydia opened her eyes very widely. "What, to let—to let her marry him?"

"Perhaps. But you jump to conclusions too rapidly, Lydia."

"Why, he is only a common medical practitioner!"

"There of course lies the objection. But he is not a 'common' practitioner, Lydia. If he were so, do you suppose I should invite him here as I do, and make much of him? He is a gentleman, and the son of a gentleman. In point of fact," added Mrs. St. Clare, in a lower tone, as if the acknowledgment might only be given in a whisper, "our branch of the St. Clare family is little, if any, better than the Raynors—"

"Mamma, how can you say so?" burst forth Lydia. "It is not true. And the Raynors have always been as poor as church mice."

"And—I was going to say," went on Mrs. St. Clare with equanimity— "he is the heir to Eagles' Nest."

Lydia sat back in her chair, a scowl on her brow. She could not contradict that.

"In most cases of this kind there are advantages and disadvantages," quietly spoke Mrs. St. Clare, "and I tried, as I tell you, to put the one side against the other, and see which was the weightier. On the one hand there is his profession, and his want of connections; on the other, there is Eagles' Nest, and his own personal attractions. You are looking very cross, Lydia. You think, I see, that Daisy might do better."

"Of course she might."

"She might or she might not," spoke Mrs. St. Clare, impressively. "Marriage used to be called a lottery: but it is a lottery that seems to be getting as scarce now as the lotteries that the old governments put down. For one girl who marries, half-a-dozen girls do not marry. Is it, or is it not so, Lydia?"

No response. Mrs. St. Clare resumed.

"And it appears to me, Lydia, that the more eligible girls, those who are most worthy to be chosen and who would make the best wives, are generally those who are left. Have you been chosen yet?—forgive me for speaking plainly. No. Yet you have been *waiting* to be chosen—just as other girls wait—for these six or seven years. Daisy may wait in the same manner; wait for ever. We must sacrifice some prejudices in these non-marrying days, Lydia, if we are to get our daughters off at all. If an offer comes, though it may be one that in the old times would have been summarily rejected, it is well to *consider* it in these. And so, you see, my dear, why I am letting matters take their course with regard to Daisy and Mr. Raynor."

"He may mean nothing," debated Lydia.

"Neither of them may mean anything, if it comes to that," said Mrs. St. Clare, relapsing into her idly indifferent manner. "It may be only a little flirtation—your own word just now—on both sides; pour faire passer le temps."

"And if Daisy loses her heart to him, and nothing comes of it? You have called him attractive yourself."

"Highly attractive," composedly assented Mrs. St. Clare. "As to the rest, it would be no very great calamity that I know of. When once a girl has had a little love affair in early life, and has got over it, she is always the more tractable in regard to eligible offers, should they drop in. No, Lydia, all things considered—and I have well considered them—it is the better policy not to interfere. The matter shall be left to take its course."

"Well, I must say, Daisy ought not to be allowed to drift into love with a rubbishing assistant-surgeon."

"She has already drifted into it, unless I am mistaken," said Mrs. St. Clare, significantly; "has been deep in it for some little time past. My eyes were not opened quickly enough; but since they did open, they have been tolerably observant, Lydia. Why—do you suppose I should wink at their being so much together, unless I intended the matter to go on? Don't they stroll out alone by moonlight and twilight, in goodness knows what shady walks of the garden, talking sentiment, looking at the stars, and bending over the same flowers? Twice that has happened, Lydia, since I have been on the watch: how many times it happened before, I can't pretend to say."

Lydia remained silent. It was all true. Where had her own eyes been? Daisy would walk out through the open French window— she remembered it now—and he would stroll out after her: while Mrs. St. Clare would be in her after-dinner doze, and she, Lydia, lying back in her chair with the chest-ache, or upstairs taking her drops. Yes, it was all true. And what an idiot she had been not to see it—not to suspect it!

"We cannot have everything; we must, as I say, make sacrifices," resumed Mrs. St. Clare. "I could have wished that Mr. Raynor was not in the medical profession, especially in its lower branch. Of course at present he can only be regarded as altogether unsuitable for Daisy: but that will be altered when the major comes into Eagles' Nest. Frank will then no doubt quit the profession, and—"

"The singular thing to me is, that he should ever have entered it," interrupted Lydia. "Fancy the heir to Eagles' Nest making himself a working apothecary! It is perfectly incongruous."

"It seems so," said Mrs. St. Clare. "I conclude there must have been some motive for it. Perhaps the major thought it well to give him a profession; and when he had acquired it sent him to this remote place to keep him out of mischief. It will be all right, Lydia, when they come into Eagles' Nest. The major will of course make Frank a suitable allowance as his heir. The major is already getting in years: Frank will soon come into it."

"As to that old Mrs. Atkinson, she must intend to live to a hundred," remarked Lydia, tartly. "How many centuries is it since we saw her in London?—and she was old then. She ought to give up Eagles' Nest to the major and live elsewhere. If it be the beautiful place that people say it is, she might be generous enough to let some one else have a little benefit out of it."

Mrs. St. Clare laughed. "Old people are selfish, Lydia; they prefer their own ease to other people's. I dare say we shall be the same if we live long enough."

From this conversation, it will be gathered that the check thrown upon Frank Raynor's pleasant intercourse with Margaret St. Clare by the unknown calamity (unknown to the world) that had so mysteriously and suddenly happened, had been only transitory. For a week or two afterwards, Frank had paid none but strictly professional visits to The Mount; had been simply courteous to its inmates, Daisy included, as a professional man, and nothing more. He had not danced with Daisy on her birthday; he had not given her any more tender glances, or exchanged a confidential word with her. But, as the first horror of the occurrence began to lose its hold upon his mind, and his temperament recovered its elasticity, his love returned to him. He was more with Daisy than ever; he *sought* opportunities to be with her now: formerly they had only met in the natural course of things. And so they, he and she, were living in an enchanted dream, whose rose-coloured hues seemed as if they could only have come direct from Eden.

And Frank Raynor, never famous for foresight or forethought at the best of times, fell into the belief that Mrs. St. Clare approved of him as a future aspirant for her daughter's hand and tacitly encouraged their love. That she must see they were intimate with an especial intimacy, and very much together, he knew, and in his sanguine way he drew deductions accordingly. In this he was partly right, as the reader has learnt; but it never entered into his incautious head to suppose that

Mrs. St. Clare was counting upon his coming in for future wealth and greatness.

They stood once more together on this same evening, he and Daisy, gazing at the remains of the gorgeous sunset. Dinner over, Daisy had strolled out as usual into the garden; he following her in a minute or two, without excuse or apology. In his assumption of Mrs. St. Clare's tacit encouragement, he believed excuse to be no longer necessary. Clouds of purple and crimson, flecked with gold, crowded the west; lighting up Daisy's face, as they stood side by side leaning on the low iron gate, with a hue as rosy as the dream they were living in.

"I should like to see the sunsets of Italy," observed Margaret. "It is said they are very beautiful."

"So should I," promptly replied Frank. "Perhaps some time we may see them together."

Her face took a brighter tint, though there was nothing in the sky to induce it. He passed his hand along the gate, until it rested on hers.

"Mamma talks of going abroad this summer," whispered Daisy. "I do not know whether it will be to Italy."

"I hope she will not take you with her!"

"It is Lydia's fault. She says this place tires her. And possibly," added Daisy, with a sigh, "when once we get abroad, we shall stay there."

"But, my darling, you know that must not be. I could not spare you. Why, Daisy, how could we live apart?"

Her hand, clasped tenderly, lay in his. Her whole frame thrilled as the hand rested there.

"Shall you always stay on at Trennach?" she questioned in low tones.

"Stay on at Trennach!" he repeated, in surprise. "I! Why, Daisy, I hope to be very, very soon away from it. I came to my uncle two years ago, of my own accord, to gain experience. Nothing teaches experience like the drudgery of a general practice: and I was not one of those self-sufficient young students who set up after hospital work with M.D. on their door-plate, and believe themselves qualified to cure the world. It is kill or cure, haphazard, with some of them."

"And—when you leave Trennach?" she asked, her clear eyes, clear this evening as amber, gazing out, as if she would fain see into the future.

"Oh, it will be all right when I leave Trennach; I shall get along well," returned Frank, in his light, sanguine fashion. "I—I don't care to praise myself, Daisy, but I am clever in my profession; and a clever man must make his way in it. Perhaps I should purchase a share in a West-end practice in town; or perhaps set up on my own account in that desirable quarter."

The bright hope of anticipation lighted Daisy's beautiful eyes. Frank changed his tone to one of the sweetest melody. At least, it sounded so to her ear.

"And with one gentle spirit at my hearth to cheer and guide me, the world will be to me as a long day in Paradise. My best and dearest you know what spirit it is that I covet. Will she say me nay?"

She did not say anything just now; but the trembling fingers, lying in his hand, entwined themselves confidingly within his.

"I know you will get on," she murmured. "You will be great sometime."

"Of course I shall, Daisy. And keep carriages and horses for my darling wife; and the queen will knight me when I have gained name and fame; and—and we shall be happier than the live-long day."

The bright colours in the sky faded by degrees, leaving the grey twilight in their stead. Before them lay the sloping landscape, not a living soul to be seen on it; immediately behind them was the grove of laurels, shutting them out from view. In this favourable isolation, Frank passed his arm around Daisy's waist, and drew her face to his breast.

"Nothing shall ever separate us, Daisy. Nothing in this world."

"Nothing," she murmured, speaking between his passionate kisses. "I will be yours always and for ever."

"And there will be no trouble," remarked he, in sanguine impulse, as they turned reluctantly from the gate to regain the house. "I mean no opposition. I am my own master, Daisy, accountable to none; and your mother has seen our love and sanctions it."

"Oh, do you think she does sanction it?" exclaimed Daisy, drawing a deep breath.

"Why, of course she does," replied Frank, speaking in accordance with his belief. "Would Mrs. St. Clare let us linger out together, evening after evening, if she did not see and sanction it? No, there will be neither trouble nor impediment. Life lies before us, Daisy, fair as a happy valley."

Tea waited on the table when they got in. Mrs. St. Clare was sleeping still; Lydia looked very cross. Frank glanced at his watch, as if doubting whether he could stay longer.

Daisy's pretty hands, the lace meant to shade them falling back, began to busy themselves with the tea-cups. It awoke Mrs. St. Clare.

She drew her chair at once to the tea-table. Frank pushed Lydia's light couch towards it.

"We were speaking to-day of Eagles' Nest," observed Mrs. St. Clare—and she really did not introduce the subject with any ulterior view; simply as something to talk about. "It's a very nice place, is it not?"

"Very—by all accounts," replied Frank. "I have not seen it."

"Indeed! Is not that strange?"

"My aunt Atkinson has never invited me there. None of us have been invited, except the major. And he has not been there for several years."

"How is that? Major Raynor is the next heir."

"Well, I scarcely know how it is. He and Mrs. Atkinson are not very good friends. There was some quarrel, I fancy."

"Mrs. Atkinson must be very old."

"About seventy-four, I believe."

"Not more than that! I thought she was ninety at least."

"I was saying to-day," put in Lydia, "that those old people ought to give up their estates to the heir. It is unreasonable to keep Major Raynor so long out of his own."

Frank smiled. "He would be very glad if she did give it up, I dare say; but I don't know about the justice of it. Elderly people, as a rule, cling to their homes. I once knew an old lady who was unexpectedly called upon to give up the home in which she had lived for very many years, and it killed her. Before the day for turning out came, she was dead."

"At any rate, Mr. Raynor, *you* will not be kept out of it so long when it comes to your turn," remarked Mrs. St. Clare: "for I suppose the major is very nearly as old as Mrs. Atkinson."

Frank's honest blue eyes went straight into those of the speaker with a questioning glance.

"I beg your pardon: kept out of what?"

"Of Eagles' Nest."

His whole face lighted up with amusement at the mistake she was making.

"I shall never come into Eagles' Nest, Mrs. St. Clare."

"Never come into Eagles' Nest! But the major comes into it."

"The major does. But—"

"And you are his eldest son."

Frank laughed outright. Freely and candidly he answered—with never a thought of reserve.

"My dear lady, I am not Major Raynor's son at all. His eldest son is my cousin Charley. It is he who will succeed to Eagles' Nest."

Mrs. St. Clare stared at Frank. "Good Heavens!" she murmured under her breath. "You are not the son of Major Raynor?"

"No, I am his nephew. My father was the clergyman."

"I—I have heard Major Raynor call you his son!" she debated, hardly believing her own ears. "He has called you so to my face."

"He often does call me so," laughed Frank. "I fear—he is—proud of me—dear, fond old uncle!"

"Well, I never was so deceived in all my life!" exclaimed Mrs. St. Clare.

IX

PLANNING OUT THE FUTURE

It has been already said that there were originally three of the brothers Raynor: Francis, who was an officer in her Majesty's service; Henry the clergyman; and Hugh the doctor. The youngest of these, Hugh, was the first to marry by several years; the next to marry was Henry. Henry might have married earlier, but could not afford it: he waited until a living was given to him. In the pretty country rectory attached to his church, he and his wife lived for one brief year of their married life: and then she died, leaving him a little boy-baby, who was named Francis after the clergyman's eldest brother. Some ten years later the Reverend Henry Raynor himself died; and the little boy was an orphan, possessed of just sufficient means to educate him and give him a start in life in some not too costly profession. When the time came, he chose that of medicine, as his Uncle Hugh had done before him.

The eldest of the three brothers was the last to marry: Captain Raynor. He and his young wife led rather a scrambling sort of life for some years afterwards, always puzzled how to make both ends of their straitened income meet; and then a slice of good fortune (as the captain regarded it) befell him. Some distant relative left him an annuity of five hundred a-year. Five hundred a-year in addition to his pay seemed riches to the captain: whilst his unsophisticated and not too-well-managing wife thought they were now clear of shoals for life.

Very closely upon this, the captain obtained his majority. This was succeeded by a long and severe attack of illness; and the major, too hastily deciding that he should never be again fit for active service, sold out. He and his wife settled down in a pretty cottage-villa, called Spring Lawn, in the neighbourhood of Bath, living there and bringing up their children in much the same scrambling fashion that they had previously lived. No order, no method; all good-hearted carelessness, good-natured improvidence. Just as it had been in their earlier days, so it was now: they never knew where to look for a shilling of ready-money. That it would be so all through life with Major Raynor, whatever might be the amount of his income, was pretty certain: he was sanguine, off-hand, naturally improvident. The proceeds from the sale of his commission had all vanished, chiefly in paying back-debts; the five hundred a-year was all they had to live upon, and that five hundred would die with the major: and, in short, they seemed to be worse off now than before the annuity came to them. Considering that they spent considerably more than the five hundred yearly, and yet had no comfort to show for it, and that debts had gathered again over the major's head, it was not to be wondered at that they were not well off. The major never gave a thought to consequences; debt sat as lightly upon him as though it had been a wreath of laurel. If he did feel slightly worried at times, what mattered it: he should, sooner or later, come into Eagles' Nest, when all things would be smooth as glass. A more prudent man than the major might have seen cause to doubt the absolute certainty of the estate coming to him. *He* did not; he looked upon the inheritance of it as an accomplished fact.

The reader has probably not forgotten Mr. and Mrs. Timothy Atkinson—at whose house Edina had stayed so many years ago. Changes had taken place since then. Both the partners in the bank, Timothy and his cousin (they were only second cousins), were dead: and the firm had long been Atkinson and Street. For, upon the death of the two old men, Mr. George Atkinson, their sole successor, took his managing clerk, Edwin Street, into partnership. The bank was not one of magnitude—I think this has already been said—only a small, safe, private one. The acting head of it was, to all intents and purposes, Edwin Street: for Mr. George Atkinson passed the greater portion of his time abroad, coming home only every two or three years. George Atkinson was well off, and did not choose to worry himself with the cares of business: had the bank been given up to-morrow, he would have had plenty of money without it. During his later life, Mr. Timothy Atkinson had invested the chief portion of his savings in the purchase of an estate in Kent, called Eagles' Nest. He was not a rich man, as bankers go, never having been an equal partner in the firm; drawing from it in fact only a small share. His death was somewhat sudden, and occurred during one of his sojourns at Eagles' Nest. Mrs. Atkinson, his widow; not less portly than of yore, and still very much of an invalid; summoned her two brothers to attend the funeral: Major Raynor from Bath, Dr. Raynor from Trennach. The major went up at once: Dr. Raynor sent a refusal; his excuse, no idle one, being that he could not leave his patients. The season was one of unusual sickness, and he had no one to take his place. This refusal Mrs. Atkinson, never a very genial woman, or at all cordial with her brothers, resented.

When Mr. Timothy Atkinson's will was opened, it was found that he had left everything he possessed to his wife unconditionally. Consequently the estate was now at her own disposal. Though a pretty, compact property, it was not a large one: worth some two thousand a-year, but capable of great improvement.

On the day following the funeral, Mrs. Atkinson went up to her house in London, the major accompanying her. There she found George Atkinson, who had just arrived in England; which was an agreeable surprise to her. He had always been a favourite of hers, and he would be useful to her just now.

"I shall leave it to you, George," she suddenly observed one morning, a few days after this, as they sat together looking over letters and papers.

"Leave what to me, aunt?" For he had called her "aunt" in the old days, and often did so still.

"Eagles' Nest."

George Atkinson laid down the bundle of letters he was untying, and looked questioningly at the old lady, almost as though he doubted her words.

"I am sure you cannot mean that."

"Why not, pray?"

"Because it is a thing that you must not think of doing. You have near relatives in your brothers. It is they who should benefit by your will."

"My brothers can't both inherit the place," retorted the old lady.

"The elder of them can—Major Raynor."

"I like you better, George, than I like him."

"I am very glad you like me—but not that your liking should render you unjust to your family," he returned, firmly but gently. "Indeed, dear Mrs. Atkinson, to prefer me to them would be an act of the greatest injustice."

"My will ought to be made at once," said the old lady.

"Certainly. And I hope you will not as much as mention my name in it," he added with a smile. "I have so very much of my own, you know, that a bequest from you would be altogether superfluous."

The conversation decided Mrs. Atkinson. She sent for her lawyer, Mr. John Street, and had her will drawn up in favour of Major Raynor. Legacies to a smaller or larger amount were bequeathed to a few people, but to Major Raynor was left Eagles' Nest. Her brother Hugh, poor Dr. Raynor of Trennach, was not mentioned in it: neither was Edina.

The will was made in duplicate; Mrs. Atkinson desired her solicitor to retain possession of one copy; the other she handed to Major Raynor. She affixed her own seal to the envelope in which the will was enclosed, but allowed him first to read it over.

"I don't know how to thank you, Ann, for this," said the major, tears of genuine emotion resting on his eyelashes. "It will be good news for Mary and the young ones."

"Well, I'm told it's the right thing to do, Frank," answered the old lady: who was older than any of her brothers, and had domineered over them in early life. "I suppose it is."

So Major Raynor went back to Spring Lawn with the will in his pocket; and he considered that from that hour all his embarrassments were over. And Mrs. Atkinson gave up her house in London, and stationed herself for life at Eagles' Nest. While George Atkinson, after a month's sojourn, went abroad again.

But now, as ill-fortune had it, Major Raynor had chanced, since that lucky day, to offend his sister. The year following the making of the will, being in London on some matter of business, he took the opportunity to go down to Eagles' Nest—and went without asking permission, or sending word. Whether that fact displeased Mrs. Atkinson, or whether she really did not care to see him at all, certain it was that she was very cross and crabbed with him, her temper almost unbearable. The major had a hot temper himself on occasion, and they came to an issue. A sharp quarrel ensued; and the major, impulsive in all he did, quitted Eagles' Nest that same hour. When he reached Spring Lawn, after staying another week in London to complete his business, he found a letter awaiting him from his sister, telling him that she had altered her will and left Eagles' Nest to George Atkinson.

"Stupid old thing!" exclaimed the major, laughing at what he looked upon as an idle threat. "As if she would do such a thing as that!" For the major had never the remotest idea that she had once intended to make George Atkinson her heir.

And from that hour to this, the major had not once seriously thought of the letter again. He had never since seen Mrs. Atkinson; had never but once heard from her; but he looked upon Eagles' Nest as being as certainly his as though it were already in his possession. Once every year at Christmas-time he wrote his sister a letter of good wishes; to which she did not respond. "Ann never went in for civilities," would observe the major.

The one exception was this. When his eldest son, Charles, had attained his sixteenth year, the major mentioned the fact in the annual letter to his sister. A few days afterwards, down came the answer from her of some half-dozen lines: in which she briefly offered Charles an opening (as she called it) in life: meaning, a clerkship in the bank of Atkinson and Street, which her interest would procure for him. Master Charles, who had far higher notions than these, as befitted the heir to Eagles' Nest, threw up his head in disdain: and the major wrote a letter of refusal, as brief as the old lady's offer. With that exception, they had never heard from her.

The major and his wife were both incredibly improvident; he in spending money; she in not knowing how to save it. Yielding and gentle, Mrs. Raynor fell in with anything and everything done by her husband, thinking that because he did it, it must be right. She never suggested that they might save cost here, and cut it off there; that this outlay would be extravagant, or that unnecessary. There are some women really not capable of forethought, and Mrs. Raynor was one of them. As to doing anything to advance their own interest, by cultivating Mrs. Atkinson's favour, both were too single-minded for such an act; it may be said too strictly honourable.

It was with them, his uncle and aunt, that Frank Raynor had spent his holidays when a boy, and all his after-intervals of leisure. They were just as fond of Frank as they were of their own children: he was ever welcome. The major sometimes called him "my son Frank," when speaking of him to strangers; very often indeed "my eldest boy." As to taking people in by so doing, the major had no thought of the sort; but there is no doubt that it did cause many a one, not acquainted with the actual relationship, to understand and believe that Frank was in truth the major's son. Possibly their names being the same—Francis—contributed to the impression. Amongst those who had caught up the belief, was Mrs. St. Clare. She had occasionally met the Major and Mrs. Raynor in Bath, though the acquaintanceship was of the slightest. When her son, young St. Clare, came into possession of The Mount, and it was known that she was going to remove there, the major, meeting her one day near the Old Pump-room, said to her, in the openness of his heart, "I'll write to Trennach to my boy Frank, and tell him to make himself useful to you." "Oh," returned Mrs. St. Clare, "have you a boy at Trennach?" "Yes, the eldest of them: he is with his uncle the doctor," concluded the major, unsuspiciously. Had he thought it would create mischief, or even a false impression, he would have swallowed the Pump-room before he had spoken it. That the major was the presumptive heir to Eagles' Nest was well known: and Mrs. St. Clare may be excused for having, under the circumstances, carried with her to her new abode the belief that Frank would succeed him in the estate.

On the night that the enlightenment took place—when Frank so candidly and carelessly disabused Mrs. St. Clare's mind of the impression—he perceived not the chill that the avowal evidently threw upon her. That it should affect her cordiality to him he could never have feared. A more worldly man, or one of a selfish nature, would have seen in a moment that his not being heir to Eagles' Nest rendered him a less eligible parti for Margaret; but Frank Raynor, in worldliness, as in selfishness, was singularly deficient. And he left The Mount when tea was over, quite unconscious that anything had occurred to diminish the favour in which he was held by its mistress.

Not with that was his mind occupied as he walked home; but rather with thoughts of the future. Daisy was to be his; she had promised it; and Frank would have taken her to himself to-morrow, could he have provided her with bread-and-cheese. How to do this was puzzling his brain now.

He took the road home over the Bare Plain. Never, since the night of that fatal tragedy, had Frank Raynor taken it by choice: he always chose the highway. But to-night he had a patient lying ill in the cottages on the Plain; and Dr. Raynor had said to him, "Call in and see Weston, Frank, as you return." The visit paid, he continued his way homewards. It was a light night: there were neither stars nor moon: but a white haze seemed to veil the sky, and lighted up surrounding objects. Frank looked towards the Bottomless Shaft as he passed it; his fascinated eyes turning to it of their own accord. Bringing them back with an effort and a shudder, he quickened his pace, and went onwards with his burthensome secret.

"Will it lie hidden there for ever?" he said, half aloud. "Pray Heaven that it may!"

Dr. Raynor was sitting in the small room behind his surgery; a room chiefly used for private consultations with patients; in his hand was a medical journal, which he was reading by lamplight. He put it down when Frank entered.

"I want to ask you something, Uncle Hugh," began Frank, impulsively, as though what he was about to say was good news. "Should I have any difficulty, do you think, in dropping into a practice when I leave you?"

"You do mean to leave me, then, Frank?" returned Dr. Raynor, without immediately replying to the question.

"Why, of course I do, Uncle Hugh," said Frank, in slight surprise. "It was always intended so. I came here, you know, for two years, and I have stayed longer than that."

"And you would not like to remain altogether, and be my partner and successor?"

"No," replied Frank, very promptly. "It would be a poor living for two people; my share of it very small, for I could not expect you to give me half the profits. And there are other reasons against it. No, Uncle Hugh; what I want to do is, to jump into some snug little practice in a place where I shall get on. Say in London."

A smile crossed the more experienced doctor's lips. Young men are sanguine.

"It is not easy to 'jump into a snug little practice,' Frank."

"I know that, sir: but there are two ways in which it may be done. One way is, to purchase a share in an established practice; another, to set up well in some likely situation, with a good house and a plate on the door, and all that, and wait for patients to drop in."

"But each of those ways requires money, Frank."

"Oh, of course," acquiesced Frank, lightly, as though money were the most ordinary commodity on earth.

"Well, Frank, where would you find the money? You have not saved much, I take it, out of the salary you have from me."

"I have not saved anything: I am never a pound to the good," answered Frank, candidly. "Clothes cost a good deal, for one thing."

"When gentlemen dress as you do, and buy their kid gloves by the dozen," said the doctor, archly. "Well, whence would you find the means to set yourself up in practice?"

"That's what I want to ask you about, Uncle Hugh. I dare say you remember, when there was so much talk about that will of my aunt Ann's, that it was said I had a share in it."

"Indeed, Frank, I don't. I remember I was told that she had not left anything to me; and I really remember no more."

"Then you cannot tell me what the amount was?" exclaimed Frank, in accents of disappointment. "I thought perhaps Uncle Francis might have told you."

Dr. Raynor shook his head. "I have no idea, Frank, whether it was one pound or one thousand. Or many thousands."

"You see, sir, if I knew the exact sum, I could think about my plans with more certainty."

"Just so, Frank. As it is, your plans must be somewhat like castles in the air."

"I recollect quite well Uncle Francis telling me that I came in for a good slice. That was the exact phrase: 'in for a good slice.' He had read the will, you know. I wonder he did not mention it to you."

"All I recollect, or know, about it is, that Francis wrote me word that nothing was left to me. He said he had remonstrated with Ann—your aunt—at leaving my name out of the will, and that she ordered him, in return, to mind his own business. I do not care for it myself; I do not, I am sure, covet any of the money Ann may leave; though I could have wished she had not quite passed over Edina."

"She must have a good deal of money, Uncle Hugh, apart from Eagles' Nest."

"I dare say she has."

"And, if Uncle Francis comes in for that money, I should think he would make over half of it to you. I should, were I in his place."

"Ah, Frank," smiled the doctor, "people are not so chivalrously generous in this world; even brothers."

"I should call it justice, not generosity, sir."

"If you come to talk of justice, you would also be entitled to your share, as Henry's son. He was equally her brother."

"But I don't expect anything of the kind," said Frank. "Provided I have enough to set me up in practice, that's all I care for."

"You would not have that until your aunt dies."

"To be sure not. I am not expecting it before. But what has struck me is this, Uncle Hugh—I have been turning the thing over in my mind as I walked home—that I might, without any dishonour, reckon upon the money now."

"In what way? How do you mean?"

"Suppose I go to some old-established man in London who, from some cause or other—advancing years, say—requires some one to relieve him of a portion of his daily work. I say to him, 'Will you take me at present as your assistant, at a fair salary, and when I come into my money'—naming the sum—'I will hand that over to you and become your partner?' Don't you think that seems feasible, sir?"

"I dare say it does, Frank."

"But then, you see, to do this, I ought to know the exact sum that is coming to me. Unless I were able to state that, I should not be listened to. That's why, sir, I was in hopes that you could tell me what it was."

"And so I would tell you if I knew it, Frank. I do not think Francis mentioned to me that you would come in for anything. I feel sure, if he had done so, I should remember it."

"That's awkward," mused Frank, thoughtfully balancing the paper-knife he had caught up from the table. "I wonder he did not tell you, Uncle Hugh."

"To say the truth, so do I," replied Dr. Raynor. "It would have been good news: and he knows that I am equally interested with himself in the welfare of Henry's orphan son. Are you sure, Frank, that you are making no mistake in this?"

"I don't think I am. I was staying at Spring Lawn when the major came home from Aunt Atkinson's after her husband's death, and he brought her will with him. He was telling us all about it—that Eagles' Nest was to be his, and that there were several legacies to different people, and he turned to me and said, 'You come in for a good slice, Frank.' I recollect it all, sir, as though it had taken place yesterday."

"Did he mention how much the 'slice' was?"

"No, he did not. And I did not like to ask him."

There was a pause. Dr. Raynor began putting the papers straight on the table, his usual custom before retiring for the night. Frank had apparently fallen into a reverie.

"Uncle Hugh," he cried, briskly, lifting his head, his face glowing with some idea, his frank blue eyes bright with it, "if you can spare me for a couple of days, I will go to Spring Lawn and ask Uncle Francis. I should like to be at some certainty in the matter."

"I could spare you, Frank: there's nothing particular on hand that I cannot attend to myself for that short time. But—"

"Thank you, Uncle Hugh," interrupted Frank, impetuously. "Then suppose I start to-morrow morning?"

"But—I was about to inquire—what is it that has put all this into your head so suddenly?"

Frank's eager eyes, raised to the doctor's face, fell at the question. A half-conscious smile parted his lips.

"There's no harm, sir, in trying to plan out one's future."

"None in the world, Frank. I only ask the reason for your setting about it in this—as it seems to me—sudden manner."

"Well—you know, Uncle Hugh—I—I may be marrying some time."

"And you have been fixing on the lady, I see, Frank!"

A broad smile now shone upon Frank's face. He was sending the paper-knife round in circles on the table, with rather an unnecessary noise. Dr. Raynor's thoughts were going hither and thither; he could not recall any individual in the neighbourhood of Trennach likely to be honoured by Frank's choice. In an instant an idea flashed over him—an idea that he did not like.

"Frank! can it be that you are thinking of one of the Miss St. Clares?"

"And if I were, sir?"

"Then—I fear—that there may be trouble in store for you," said the doctor, gravely. "Mrs. St. Clare would never sanction it."

"But she has sanctioned it, Uncle Hugh. She sanctions it every day of her life."

"Has she told you so?"

"Not in words. But she sees how much I and Daisy are together, and she allows it. *That* will be all right, Uncle Hugh."

"Daisy? Let me see? Oh, that is the young one: she is a nice little girl. I cannot say I like the elder. But—"

"But what, sir?"

"You are by nature over-sanguine, Frank; and I cannot help thinking that you are so in this. Rely upon it, there is some mistake here. Mrs. St. Clare is a proud, haughty woman, remarkably alive, unless I am in error, to self-interest. She would not be likely to give a daughter to one whose prospects are so uncertain as yours."

"But I am wishing to make my prospects more certain, you see, uncle. And I can assure you she approves of me for Daisy."

"Well, well; if so, I am glad to hear it. Nevertheless it surprises me. I should have supposed she would look higher for suitors for her daughters. The little girl is a nice girl, I say, Frank, and you have my best wishes."

"Thank you, Uncle Hugh," warmly repeated Frank, rising, his face flushing with pleasure as he met the doctor's hand. "Of course you understand that it must not yet be talked of: I must first of all speak to Mrs. St. Clare."

"I shall not be likely to talk of it," replied Dr. Raynor.

X

Major and Mrs. Raynor

The windows of Spring Lawn stood open to the afternoon sun. It was a small, pretty white house, half cottage, half villa, situated about three miles from Bath. A latticed portico, over which crept the white clematis, led into a miniature hall: Major Raynor could just turn round in it. On either side was a small sitting-room, the dining-room on the left, the drawing-room on the right.

The scrambling midday dinner was over. Somehow all the meals seemed to be scrambling at the major's, from the utter want of order, and of proper attendance. Only two servants were kept, a cook and a nurse: and *they* could not always get their wages paid. When Edina was there, she strove to bring a little comfort out of the chaos: but that was only a chance event; a brief and rare occasion, occurring at long intervals in life. Some wine stood on the old table-cover, with a plate of biscuits. On one side of the table sat the major; a tall and very portly man, with a bald head and a white moustache, looking every day of his nine and-sixty years. He had been getting on for fifty when he married his young wife; who was not quite eight-and-thirty yet: a delicate, fragile-looking woman, with a small fair face and gentle voice, mild blue eyes, a pink colour, and thin light brown hair quietly braided back from it. Mrs. Raynor looked what she was: a gentle, yielding, amiable, helpless woman; one who could never be strong-minded in any emergency whatever, but somehow one to be loved at first sight.

She sat half turned from the table—as indeed did the major opposite, their faces towards the window—her feet on a footstool, and her hands busy with work, apparently a new frock she was making for one of her younger children. She wore a faded muslin gown, green its predominant colour; a score of pins, belonging to the work in process, in her waistband.

They were talking of the weather. The major was generally in a state of heat. That morning he had walked into Bath and back again, and got in late for dinner, puffing and steaming, for it was an up-hill walk. He liked to have a fly one way at least; but he had not always the money in his pocket to pay for it.

"Yes, it was like an oven in the sun, Mary," continued he, enlarging upon the weather. "I don't remember any one single year that the heat has come upon us so early."

"That's why I have a good deal of sewing to do just now," observed Mrs. Raynor. "We have had to take to our summer things before they were ready. Look at poor dear little Robert! The child must be melted in that stuff frock."

"What's the nurse about?—can't she make him one?" asked the major.

"Oh, Francis, she has so much to do. With all these children! She does some sewing; but she has not time for very much."

The major, sipping his wine just then, looked at the children, sitting on the grass-plot. Four of them, in whose ages there was evidently more than the usual difference between brothers and sisters. One looked an almost grown-up young lady. That was Alice. She wore a washed-out cotton dress and a frayed black silk apron. Alfred was the next, aged ten, in an old brown-holland blouse and tumbled hair. Kate, in another washed-out cotton and a pinafore, was eight: and Robert was just three, a chubby, fat child in a thick woollen plaid frock. They were stemming cowslips to make into balls, and were as happy as the day was long.

"I saw Mrs. Manners in Bath this morning," resumed the major. "She says she is coming to spend a long day here."

"I hope she won't come until Bobby's new frock is finished," said Mrs. Raynor, her fingers plying the needle more swiftly at the thought. "He looks so shabby in that old thing."

"As if it mattered! Who cares what children have on?"

"Oh, I forgot to tell you, Francis—the butcher asked to see me this morning: he came over for orders himself. He says he must have some money."

"Oh, does he?" returned the major, with careless unconcern. "I don't know when I shall have any for him, I'm sure. Did you tell him so?"

"I did not go to him: I sent Charley. I do hope he will not stop the supply of meat!"

"As if he would do that!" cried the major, throwing up his head with a beaming smile. "He knows I shall come into plenty of money sooner or later."

At this moment the children came rushing with one accord to the window, and stood—those who were tall enough—with their arms on the sill, Alice with the cowslips gathered up in her apron. Little

Robert—often called Baby—who toddled up last, could only stretch his hands up to the edge of the sill.

"Mamma—papa," said Alice, a graceful girl, with the clearly-cut Raynor features and her mother's mild blue eyes, "we want to have a little party and a feast of strawberries and cream. It would be so delightful out here on the grass, with tables and chairs, and—"

"Strawberries are not in yet," interrupted the major. "Except those in the dearer shops."

"When they are in, we mean, papa. Shall we?"

"To be sure," said papa, as pleased with the idea as were the children. "Perhaps we could borrow a cow and make some syllabubs!"

Back ran the children to the grass again, to plan out the anticipated feast. Alice was seventeen; but in mind and manners she was still very much of a child. As they quitted the window, the room-door opened, and a tall, slender, well-dressed stripling entered. It was the eldest of them all, Charles Raynor. He also had the well-formed features of the Raynors, dark eyes and chestnut hair; altogether a very nice-looking young man.

"Why, Charley, I thought you were out!" cried his father.

"I have been lying down under the tree at the back, finishing my book," said Charley. "And now I am going into Bath to change it."

It was the greatest pity—at least most sensible people would have thought it so—to see a fine, capable young fellow wasting the best days of his existence. This, the dawning period of his manhood, was the time when he ought to have been at work, preparing himself to run his career in this working world. Instead of that, he was passing it in absolute idleness. Well for him that he had no vice in his nature: or the old proverb, about idle hands and Satan, might have been exemplified in him. All the reproach that could at present be cast on him was, that he was utterly useless, thoroughly idle: and perhaps he was not to blame for it, as nothing had been given him to do.

Charles Raynor was not brought up to any profession or business. Various callings had been talked of now and again in a desultory manner; but Major and Mrs. Raynor, in their easy-going negligence, had brought nothing to pass. As the heir to Eagles' Nest, they considered that he would not require to use his talents for his livelihood: Charles himself decidedly thought so. Gratuitous commissions in the army did not seem to be coming Major Raynor's way; he had not the means to purchase one: and, truth to tell, Charles's inclinations did not tend towards fighting. The same drawback, want of money, applied to other possibilities: and so Charles had been allowed to remain unprofitably at home, doing nothing; very much to his own satisfaction. If obliged to choose some profession for himself, he would have fixed on the Bar: but, first of all, he wanted to go to one of the universities. Everything was to be done, in every way, when Eagles' Nest dropped in: *that* would be the panacea for all present ills. Meanwhile, Major Raynor was content to let the time slip easily away, until that desirable consummation should arrive, and to allow his son to let it slip away easily too.

"Charley, I wish you'd bring me back a Madeira cake, if you are going into Bath."

"All right, mamma."

"And, Charley," added the major, "just call in at Steer's and get those seeds for the garden."

"Very well," said Charley. "Will they let me have the things without the money?"

"Oh yes. They'll put them down."

Charley gave a brush to his coat in the little hall, put on his hat, and started, book in hand. As he was passing the children, they plied him with questions: where he was going, and what to do.

"Oh, I'll go too!" cried Alfred, jumping to his feet. "Let me go with you, Charley!"

"I don't mind," said Charley. "You'll carry the book. How precious hot it is! Take care you don't get a sunstroke, Alice."

Alice hastily pulled her old straw hat over her forehead, and went on with her cowslips. "Charley, do you think you could bring me back a new crochet-needle?" she asked. "I'll give you the old one for a pattern."

"Hand it over," said Charley. "I shall have to bring back all Bath if I get many more orders. I say, youngster, you don't think, I hope, that you are going with me in that trim!"

Alfred looked down at his blouse, and at the rent in the hem of his trousers.

"What shall I put on, Charley? My Sunday clothes? I won't be a minute."

The boy ran into the house, and Charles strolled leisurely towards the little gate. He reached it just in time to meet some one who was entering. One moment's pause to gaze at each other, and then their hands were clasped.

"Frank!"

"Charley!"

"How surprised I am! Come in. You are about the last fellow I should have expected to see."

Frank laughed gaily. He enjoyed taking them by surprise in this way; enjoyed the gladness shining from their eyes at sight of him, the hearty welcome.

"I dare say I am. How are you all, Charley? There are the young ones, I see! Is that Alice? She *has* grown!"

Alice came bounding towards him, dropping the yellow blossoms from her apron. They had not seen him since the previous Christmas twelvemonth, when he had spent a week at Spring Lawn. Little Robert did not know him, and stood back, shyly staring.

"And is this my dear little Bob?" cried Frank, catching him up and kissing him. "Does he remember brother Frank? And—why, there's mamma!—and papa! Come along."

The child still in his arms, he went on to meet Major and Mrs. Raynor, who were hastening with outstretched hands of greeting.

"This sight is better than gold!" cried the major. "How are you, my dear boy?"

"We thought we were never to see you again," put in Mrs. Raynor. "How good of you to come!"

"I have come to take just a peep at you all. It seems ages since I was here."

"Are you come for a month?"

"A month!" laughed Frank. "For two days."

"Oh! Nonsense!"

And so the bustle and the greetings continued. Major Raynor poured out a glass of wine, though Frank protested it was too hot for wine, especially after his walk from Bath. Mrs. Raynor went to see her cook about sending in something substantial with tea. Charles deferred his walk, and the young ones seduced Frank to the grass-plot to help with the cowslips.

And Frank never gave the slightest intimation that he had come from Trennach for any purpose, except that of seeing them. But at night, when bedtime came and Mrs. Raynor went upstairs, leaving the major, as usual, to finish his glass and pipe, Frank drew up his chair for a conference, Charley being present.

He then disclosed the real purport of his visit—namely, to ascertain from Major Raynor the amount of money coming to him under

Mrs. Atkinson's will. Explaining at the same time why he wished to ascertain this: his intention to get into practice in London, and the ideas that had occurred to him as to the best means of accomplishing it. Just as he had explained the matter to Dr. Raynor at Trennach, the previous night.

"You see, Uncle Francis, it is time I was getting a start in life," he urged. "I am half-way between twenty and thirty. I don't care to remain an assistant-surgeon any longer."

"Of course you don't," said the major, gently puffing away. "Help yourself, Frank."

"Not any more, thank you, uncle. And so, as the first preliminary step, I want you to tell me, if you have no objection, what sum Aunt Ann has put me down for."

"Can't recollect at all, Frank."

"But—don't you think this idea of mine a good one?—getting some well-established man to take me in on the strength of this money?" asked Frank, eagerly. "I cannot see any other chance of setting up."

"It's a capital idea," said the major, taking a draught of whisky-and-water.

"Well, then, Uncle Francis, I hope you will not object to tell me what the amount is."

"My boy, I'd tell you at once, if I knew it. I don't recollect it the least in the world."

"Not recollect it!" exclaimed Frank.

"Not in the least."

It was a check for Frank. His good-natured face looked rather blank. Charley, who seemed interested, sat nursing his knee and listening.

"Could you not recollect if you tried, uncle?"

"I am trying," said the major. "My thoughts are back in the matter now. Let me see—what were the terms of the will? I know I had Eagles' Nest; and—yes—I think I am right—I was also named residuary legatee. Yes, I was. That much I do remember."

Frank's face broke into a smile. "It would be strange if you forgot *that*, uncle. Try and remember some more."

"Let me see," repeated the major, passing his unoccupied hand over his bald head. "There were several legacies, I know; and I think—yes, I do think, Frank—your name stood first on the list. But, dash me if I can recollect for how much."

"Was it for pounds, hundreds, or thousands?" questioned Frank.

"That's what I can't tell. Hang it all my memory's not worth a rush now. When folks grow old, Frank, their memory fails them."

"I remember your words to me at the time, Uncle Francis: they were that I came in for a good slice."

"Did I? When?"

"When you came back from London, and were telling my aunt about the will. I was present: it was in this very room. 'You come in for a good slice, Frank,' you said, turning to me."

"Didn't I say how much?"

"No. And I did not like to ask you. Of course you knew how much it was?"

"Of course I did. I read the will."

"I wish you could remember."

"I wish I could, Frank. I ought to. I'll sleep upon it, and perhaps it will come to me in the morning."

"Where is the will?" asked Charles, speaking for the first time. "Don't you hold it, papa?"

Major Raynor took his long pipe from his mouth, and turned the stem towards an old-fashioned walnut bureau that stood by the side of the fireplace. The upper part of it was his own, and was always kept locked; the lower part consisted of three drawers, which were used indiscriminately by Mrs. Raynor and the children.

"It's there," said the major. "I put it there when I brought it home, and I've never looked at it since."

As if the thought suddenly came to him to look at it then, he put his pipe in the fender, took a bunch of keys from his pocket, and unlocked the bureau. It disclosed some pigeon-holes above, some small, shallow drawers beneath them, three on each side, and one deeper drawer in the middle. Selecting another key, he unlocked this last, pulled the drawer right out, and put it on the table. Two sealed parchments lay within it.

"Ay, this is it," said the major, selecting one of them. "See, here's the superscription: 'Will of Mistress Ann Atkinson.' And that is my own will," he added, nodding to the other. "See, Charley: you'll know where to find it in case of need. Not that any of you would be much the better for it, my lad, as things are at present. They will be different with us when Eagles' Nest falls in."

Frank had taken the packet from the major's hand, and was looking at the seal: a large red seal, with an imposing impression.

"I suppose you would not like to open this will, uncle? Would it be wrong to do so?"

The major shook his head, slowly but decisively. "I can't open it, Frank. Although I know its contents—at least, I knew them once—to open it would seem like a breach of confidence. Your aunt Ann sealed the will herself in my presence, after I had read it. 'Don't let it be opened until my death,' she said, as she handed it to me. And so, you see, I should not like to do it."

"Of course not," readily spoke Frank. "I could not wish you to do so. Perhaps, uncle, you will, as you say, recollect more when you have slept upon it."

"Ay, perhaps so. I have an idea, mind you, Frank, that it was a very good slice; a substantial sum."

"What should you call substantial?" asked Frank.

"Two or three thousand pounds."

"I do hope it was!" returned Frank, his face beaming. "I could move the world with that."

But the major did not return the smile. Sundry experiences of his own were obtruding themselves on his memory.

"We are all apt to think so, my boy. But no one knows, until they try it, how quickly a sum of ready-money melts. Whilst you are saying I'll do this with it, or I'll do that—hey, presto! it is gone. And you sit looking blankly at your empty hands, and wonder what you've spent it in."

Taking the drawer, with the two wills in it, he put it back in its place, locking it and the bureau safely as before. And then he went up to bed to "sleep upon it," and try and get back his recollection as to an item that one of those wills contained.

Morning came. One of the same hot and glorious days that the last few had been: and the window was thrown open to the sun. It shone on the breakfast-table. The children, in their somewhat dilapidated attire, but with fresh, fair, healthy faces and happy tempers, sat round it, eating piles of bread-and-butter, and eggs ad libitum. Mrs. Raynor, in the faded muslin gown that she had worn the day before, presided over a dish of broiled ham, whilst Alice poured out the coffee. It seemed natural to Mrs. Raynor that she should take the part, no matter at what, that gave her the least trouble: kind, loving, gentle, she always was, but very incapable.

The major was not present. The major liked to lie in bed rather late in a morning; which was not good for him. But for his indolent habits, he need not have been quite so stout as he was. Frank Raynor glanced at the bureau, opposite to him as he sat, and wondered whether his uncle had recollected more about the one desired item of the will within it during his sleep.

"Has Uncle Francis had a good night, aunt?" asked Frank, who was inwardly just as impatient as he could be for news, and perhaps thought he might gather some idea by the question.

"My dear, he always sleeps well," said Mrs. Raynor. "*Too* well, I think. It is not good for a man of his age."

"How can a man sleep too well, mamma?" cried one of the children.

"Well, my darling, I judge by the snoring. Poor papa snores dreadfully in his sleep."

"Will he be long before he's down, do you suppose, Aunt Mary?"

"I hear him getting up, Frank. He is early this morning because you are here."

And, indeed, in a minute or two the major entered: his flowery silk dressing-gown—all the worse for wear, like the children's clothes—flowing around him, his hearty voice sending forth its greeting. For some little time the children kept up an incessant fire of questions; Frank could not get one in. But his turn came.

"Have you remembered that, Uncle Francis, now that you have slept upon it?"

The major looked across the table. Just for the moment he did not speak. Frank went on eagerly.

"Sometimes things that have dropped out of our memory come back to us in a dream. I have heard of instances. Did it chance so to you last night, uncle?"

"My dear boy, I dreamt that a great big shark with open jaws was running after me, and I could not get out of the water."

"Then—have you not recollected anything?"

"I fear not, Frank. I shall see as the day goes on."

But the day went on, and no recollection upon the point came back to Major Raynor. He "slept upon it" a second night, and still with the same result.

"I am very sorry, my boy," he said, grasping Frank's hand at parting, as they stood alone together on the grass-plot for a moment. "Goodness knows, I'd tell you if I could. Should the remembrance come to me later—and I dare say it will: I don't see why it should not—I'll write off at once to you at Trennach. Meanwhile, you may safely count on one thing—that the sum's a good one."

"You think so?" said Frank.

"I more than think so; I'm next door to sure of it. It's in the thousands. Yes, I feel certain of that."

"And so will I, then, uncle, in my own mind." It would have been strange had Frank, with his sanguine nature, not felt so, thus encouraged. "I can be laying out my plans accordingly."

"That you may safely do. And look here, Frank, my boy: even should it turn out that I'm mistaken—though I know I am not," continued the open-hearted major, "I can make it up to you. As residuary legatee—and I remember that much correctly now—I should be sure to come into many thousands of ready-money; and some of it shall be yours, if you want it."

"How good you are, uncle!" cried Frank, his deep-blue eyes shining forth their gratitude.

"And I'll tell you something more, my boy. Though I hardly like to speak of it," added the major, dropping his voice, "and I've never mentioned it at home: for it would seem as though I were looking out for poor Ann's death, which I wouldn't do for the world. Neither would you, Frank."

"Certainly not, Uncle Francis. What is it?"

"Well, I had a letter the other day on some business of my own from Street the lawyer. He chanced to mention in it that he had been down to Eagles' Nest: and he added in a postscript that he was shocked to see the change in your aunt Ann. In fact, he intimated that a very short time must bring the end. So you perceive, Frank, my boy—though, as I say, it sounds wrong and mean to speak of it—you may go back quite at your ease; for all the money you require will speedily be yours."

And Frank Raynor went back accordingly, feeling as certain of the good fortune coming to him, as though it had been told down before his eyes in golden guineas.

XI

Scheming

The light of the hot and garish day had almost faded from the world, leaving on it the cool air, the grateful hues of twilight. Inexpressibly grateful was that twilight to Frank Raynor and the pretty girl by his side, as they paced unrestrainedly, arm-in-arm, the paths of that wilderness, the garden at The Mount. The period of half-breathed vows and tender hints had passed: each knew the other's love, and they spoke together confidentially of the future.

After the unpleasant truth—that Frank was not heir to Eagles' Nest—had so unexpectedly dawned on Mrs. St. Clare, she informed her daughter Margaret that the absurd intimacy with Mr. Raynor must be put aside. Margaret, feeling stunned for a minute or two, plucked up courage to ask why. Because, answered Mrs. St. Clare, it had turned out that he was not the heir to Eagles' Nest. And Margaret, whose courage increased with exercise, gently said that that was no good reason: she liked Mr. Raynor for himself, not for any prospects he might or might not possess, and that she could not give him up. A stormy interview ensued. At least it was stormy on the mother's part: Margaret was only quiet, and inwardly firm. And the upshot was, that Mrs. St. Clare, who hated contention, as most indolent women do, finally flew into a passion, and told Margaret that if she chose to marry Mr. Raynor she must do so; but that she, her mother, and The Mount, and the St. Clare family generally, would wash their hands of her for ever after.

When once Mrs. Clare said a thing, she held to it. Margaret knew that; and she knew that from henceforth there was no probability, one might almost write possibility, of inducing her mother to consent to her marriage with Frank Raynor. Margaret was mistress of her own actions in one sense of the word: when Colonel St. Clare died he left no restrictions on his daughters. All his money; it was not much; was bequeathed to his wife, and was at her own absolute disposal; but not a word was said in his will touching the free actions of his children. Mrs. St. Clare knew this; Daisy knew it; and that, in the argument, gave the one an advantage over the other.

But Mrs. St. Clare, in the dispute, committed a fatal error. When people are angry, they often say injudicious things. Had she said to Margaret, I forbid you to marry Mr. Raynor, Margaret would never have thought of disobeying the injunction: but when Mrs. St. Clare said, "If you choose to marry him, do so, but I shall wash my hands of you," it put the idea into Margaret's head. Mrs. St. Clare had used the words because they came uppermost in her anger, never supposing that any advantage could be taken of them. To her daughter they wore a different aspect. Right or wrong—though of course it was wrong, not right—she looked upon it as a half-tacit permission: and from that moment the idea of marrying Frank with no one's approval but her own, took possession of her. To lose him seemed terrible in Margaret's eyes; she would almost as soon have lost life itself: and instinct whispered a warning that in a short time Mrs. St. Clare would contrive to separate them, and they might never meet again.

It was of this terrible prospect of separation, or rather of avoiding the prospect, that Mr. Raynor and Margaret were conversing in the twilight of the summer's evening. For once they had met and could linger together without restraint. Mrs. St. Clare and Lydia had gone to a dinner-party ten miles away: Margaret had not been invited; the card said Mrs. and Miss St. Clare; and so they could not take her. Mrs. St. Clare, divining perhaps that her absence might be thus made use of, had proposed to Lydia that Margaret should be the one to go; but Lydia, selfish as usual, preferred to go herself. Mr. Raynor was no longer a visitor at The Mount. Mrs. St. Clare, after the rupture with Margaret, wrote a request to Dr. Raynor that for the future he would attend himself; but she gave no reason. So that the lovers had not had many meetings lately.

All the more enjoyable was the one this evening. Frank had gone over on speculation. Happening to hear Dr. Raynor say that Miss St. Clare was going out to dinner with her mother, he walked over on the chance of seeing Margaret. And there they were, absorbed in each other amidst the sighing trees and the scented flowers.

Frank, open-natured, single-minded, had told her every particular of his visit to Spring Lawn: what he had gone for, what the result had been, and that his uncle the major had assured him of the large sum he might confidently reckon upon inheriting under Mrs. Atkinson's will. To this hour Frank knew not the full truth of Mrs. St. Clare's altered manner; for Margaret, in her delicacy, did not give him a hint as to

Eagles' Nest. "Mamma thinks that you—that you are not rich enough to marry," poor Margaret had said, stammering somewhat in the brief explanation. But, as he was now pointing out to Margaret with all his eloquence, the time could not be very far off when he should be quite rich enough.

"Shall you not consider it so, Daisy? When I have joined some noted man in London, to be paid well for my present services, with the certainty of being his partner at no distant date? We should have a charming house; I would take care of that; and every comfort within it. Not a carriage; not luxuries; I could not attempt that at first; but we could afford, in our happiness, to wait for them."

"Oh yes," murmured Daisy, thinking that it would be Paradise.

"If I fully explain all this to your mother—"

"It would be of no use; she would not listen," interrupted Daisy. "I—I have not told you all she said, Frank; I have not liked to tell you. One thing we may rest assured of—she will never, never give her consent."

"But she must give it, Daisy. Does she suppose we could give each other up? You and I are not children, to be played with; to be separated without rhyme or reason."

"In a short time—I do not know how short—mamma intends to shut up The Mount and take me and Lydia to Switzerland and Italy. It may be *years* before we come back again, Frank; years and years. I dare say I should never see you again."

"I'm sure you speak very calmly about it, Daisy! Almost as if you liked it!"

Looking down at her he met her reproachful eyes and the sudden tears the words had called up in them.

"My darling, what is to be done? You cannot go abroad with them: you must remain in England."

"As if that would be possible!" breathed Daisy. "I have no one to stay with; no relatives, or anything. And if I had, mamma would not leave me."

"I wish I could marry you off-hand!" cried thoughtless Frank, speaking more in the impulse of the moment than with any real meaning in what he said.

Daisy sighed: and put her cheek against his arm. And what with one word and another, they both began to think it might be. Love is blind, and love's arguments, though specious, are sadly delusive. In a few minutes they had grown to think that an immediate marriage, as private as might be, was the only way to save them from perdition. That is, to preserve them one to another: and that it would be the very best mode of proceeding under their untoward lot.

"The sooner it is done, the better, Daisy," cried Frank, going in for it now with all his characteristic eagerness. "I'd say to-morrow, if I had the license, but I must get that first. I hope and trust your mother will not be very angry!"

Daisy had not lifted her face. His arm was pressed all the closer. Frank filled up an interlude by taking a kiss from the sweet lips.

"Mamma said that if I did marry you, she should wash her hands of me," whispered Daisy.

"Said that! Did she! Why, then, Daisy, she must have seen herself that it was our best and only resource. I look upon it almost in the light of a permission."

"Do you think so?"

"Of course I do. And so do you, don't you? How good of her to say it!"

With the blushes that the subject called up lighting her face, they renewed their promenade amidst the trees, under the grey evening sky, talking earnestly. The matter itself settled, ways and means had to be discussed. Frank's arm was round her; her hand was again clasped in his.

"Our own church at Trennach will be safest, Daisy; safest, and best: and the one most readily got to. You can come down at an early hour: eight o'clock, say. No one will be much astir here at home, and I don't think you will meet any one en route. The road is lonely enough, you know, whether you take the highway or the Bare Plain."

Daisy did not answer. Her clear eyes had a far-off look in them, gazing at the grey sky.

"Fortune itself seems to aid us," went on Frank, briskly. "At almost any time but this we might not have been able to accomplish it so easily. Had I gone to Mr. Pine and said, I want you to marry me and say nothing about it, he might have demurred; thought it necessary to consult Dr. Raynor first, or invented some such scruple; but with Pine away and this new man here the matter is very simple. And so, Daisy, my best love, if you will be early at the church the day after to-morrow, I shall be there waiting for you."

"What do you call early?"

"Eight o'clock, I said. Better not make it later. We'll get married, and not a soul will be any the wiser."

"Of course I don't mean it to be a real wedding," said Daisy, blushing violently, "with a tour, and a breakfast, and all that, Frank. We can just go into the church, and go through the ceremony, and come out again at different doors; and I shall walk home here, and you will go back to Dr. Raynor's. Don't you see?"

"All right," said Frank.

"And if it were not," added Daisy, bursting into a sudden flood of tears, "that it seems to be the only way to prevent our separation, and that mamma must have had some idea we should take it when she said she would wash her hands of me, I wouldn't do such a dreadful thing for the world."

Frank Raynor set himself to soothe her, kissing the tears away. A few more minutes given to the details of the plan, an urgent charge on Daisy to keep her courage up, and to be at the church in time, and then they separated.

Daisy stood at the gate and watched him down the slight incline from The Mount, until he disappeared. She remained where she was, dwelling upon the momentous step she had decided to take; now shrinking from it instinctively, now telling herself that it was her sole chance of happiness in this world, and now blushing and trembling at the thought of being his wife, though only in name, ere the setting of the day-after-to-morrow's sun. When she at length turned with slow steps indoors, the lady's-maid, Tabitha, was in the drawing-room.

"Is it not rather late for you to be out, Miss Margaret? The damp is rising. I've been in here twice before to see if you wouldn't like a cup of tea."

"It is as dry as it can be—a warm, lovely evening," returned Margaret. "Tea? Oh, I don't mind whether I take any or not. Bring it, if you like, Tabitha."

With this semi-permission, the woman withdrew for the tea. Margaret looked after her and knitted her brow.

"She has been watching me and Frank—I *think*. I am sure old Tabitha's sly—and fond of interfering in other people's business. I hope she won't go and tell mamma he was here—or Lydia."

This woman, Tabitha Float, had only lived with them since they had come to The Mount: their former maid, at the last moment, declining to quit Bath. Mrs. St. Clare had made inquiries for one when she reached The Mount, and Tabitha Float presented herself. She had recently left a family in the neighbourhood, and was staying at Trennach with her relatives, making her home at the druggist's. Mrs. St. Clare engaged her, and here she was. She proved to be a very respectable and superior servant, but somewhat fond of gossip; and in the latter propensity was encouraged by Lydia. Amidst the ennui which pervaded the days of Miss St. Clare, and of which she unceasingly complained, even the tattle of an elderly serving-maid seemed an agreeable interlude.

Not a word said Frank Raynor of the project in hand. Serious, nay solemn, though the step he contemplated was, he was entering upon it in the lightest and most careless manner—relatively speaking—and with no more thought than he might have given to the contemplation of a journey.

He had remarked to Margaret—who, in point of prudence, was not, in this case, one whit better than himself—that fortune itself seemed to be aiding them. In so far as that circumstances were just now, through the absence of the Rector of Trennach, more favourable to the accomplishment of the ceremony than they could have been at another time, that was true. The Reverend Mr. Pine had at length found himself obliged to follow the advice of Dr. Raynor, and had gone away with his wife for three months' rest. A young clergyman named Backup was taking the duty for the time; he had only just arrived, and was a stranger to the place. With him, Frank could of course deal more readily in the affair than he would have been able to do with Mr. Pine.

Morning came. Not the morning of the wedding, but the one following the decisive interview between Frank and Margaret. In the afternoon, Frank made some plea at home for visiting a certain town, which we will here call Tello, in search of the ring and the marriage license. It happened that the Raynors had acquaintances there; and Edina unsuspiciously bade Frank call and see them. Frank went by rail, and was back again before dusk.

Taking his tea at home, and reporting to Edina that their friends at Tello were well and flourishing, Frank went out later to call at the Rectory. It was a gloomy sort of dwelling, the windows looking out upon the graves in the churchyard. Mr. Backup was seated at his early and frugal supper when Frank entered. He was a very shy and nervous young man; and he blushed at being caught eating, as he started up to receive Frank.

"Pray don't let me disturb you," said Frank, shaking hands, and then sitting down in his cordial way. "No, I won't take anything, thank you"— as the clergyman hospitably asked him to join him. "I haven't long had tea. I have come to ask you to do me a little service," continued Frank, plunging headlong into the communication he had to make.

MRS. HENRY WOOD

"I'm sure I shall be very happy to—to—do anything," murmured Mr. Backup.

"There's a wedding to be celebrated at the church tomorrow morning. The parties wish it to be got over early—at eight o'clock. It won't be inconvenient to you, will it, to be ready for them at that hour?"

"No—I—not at all," stammered the young divine, relapsing into a state of inward tumult and misgiving. Not as to any doubt of the orthodoxy of the wedding itself, but as to whether he should be able to get over his part of it satisfactorily. He had never married but one couple in his life: and then he had made the happy pair kneel down at the wrong places, and contrived to let the bridegroom put the ring on the bride's right-hand finger.

"Not at all too early," repeated he, striving to appear at his ease, lest this ready-mannered, dashing young man should suspect his nervousness on the score of his sense of deficiency. "Is it two of the miners' people?"

"You will see to-morrow morning," replied Frank, laughing, and passing over the question with the most natural ease in the world. "At eight o'clock, then, please to be in the church. You will be sure not to keep them waiting?"

"I will be there before eight," said Mr. Backup, rising as Frank rose.

"Thank you. I suppose it is nothing new to you," lightly added Frank, as a passing remark. "You have married many a couple, I dare say."

"Well—not so many. In my late curacy, the Rector liked to take the marriages himself. I chiefly did the christenings: he was awkward at holding the babies."

"By the way, I have another request to make," said Frank, pausing at the front-door, which the clergyman had come to open for him. "It is that you would kindly not mention this beforehand."

"Not mention? I don't quite understand," replied the bewildered young divine. "Not mention what?"

"That there's going to be a wedding to-morrow. The parties would not like the church to be filled with gaping miners; they wish it to be got over quite privately."

"I will certainly not mention it," readily assented Mr. Backup. "For that matter, I don't suppose I shall see any one between now and then. About the clerk—"

"Oh, I will see him: I'll make that all right," responded Frank. "Good-evening."

He went skimming over the grave-mounds to the opposite side of the churchyard, with little reverence, it must be owned, for the dead who lay beneath: but when a man's thoughts are filled with weddings, he cannot be expected to be thinking about graves. Crossing a stile, he was then close to the clerk's dwelling: a low, one-storied cottage with a slanting roof, enjoying the same agreeable view as the Rectory. The clerk's wife, a round, rosy little woman, was milking her goat in the shed, her gown pinned up round her.

"Halloa, Mrs. Trim! you are doing that rather late, are you not?" cried Frank.

"Late! I should think it is late, Master Frank," answered Mrs. Trim, in wrath. She was familiar enough with him, from the fact of going to the doctor's house occasionally to help the servant. "I goes over to Pendon this afternoon to have a dish o' dea with a friend there, never thinking but what Trim would attend to poor Nanny. But no, not a bit of it. Draat all they men!—a set o' helpless vools. I don't know whaat work Trim's good for, save to dig tha graves."

"Where is Trim?"

"Indoors, sir, smoking of his pipe."

Frank stepped in without ceremony. Trim, who was sexton as well as clerk, sat at the kitchen-window, which looked towards the field at the back. He was a man of some fifty years: short and thin, with scanty locks of iron-grey hair, just as silent as his wife was loquacious, and respectful in his manner. Rising when Frank entered, he put his pipe down in the hearth, and touched his hair.

"Trim, I want to send you on an errand," said Frank, lowering his voice against any possible eavesdroppers, and speaking hurriedly; for he had patients still to see to-night, "Can you take a little journey for me to-morrow morning?"

"Sure I can, sir," replied Trim. "Anywhere you please."

"All right. I went to Tello this afternoon, and omitted to call at the post-office for some letters that may be waiting there. You must go off betimes, by the half-past seven o'clock train; get the letters—if there are any—and bring them to me at once. You'll be back again long before the sun has reached the meridian, if you make haste. There's a sovereign to pay your expenses. Keep the change."

"And in what name are the letters lying there, sir?" asked the clerk, a thoughtful man at all times, and saluting again as he took up the gold piece.

"Name? Oh, mine: Francis Raynor. You will be sure not to fail me?"

The clerk shook his head emphatically. He never failed any one.

"That's right. Be away from here at seven, and you'll be in ample time for the train, walking gently. Don't speak of this to your wife, Trim: or to any one else."

"As good set the church-bell clapping as tell her, sir," replied the clerk, confidentially. "You need not be afraid of me, Mr. Frank. I know what women's tongues are: they don't often get any encouragement from me."

And away went Frank Raynor, over the stile and the mounds again, calling back a good-evening to Mrs. Trim; who was just then putting up her goat for the night.

Scheming begets scheming. As Frank found. Open and straightforward though he was by nature and conduct, he had to scheme now. He wanted the marriage kept absolutely secret at present from every one: excepting of course from the clergyman who must of necessity take part in it. For this reason he was sending Clerk Trim out of the way, to inquire after some imaginary letters.

Another little circumstance happened in his favour. Eight o'clock was the breakfast-hour at Dr. Raynor's. It was clear that if Frank presented himself to time at the breakfast-table, he could then not be standing before the altar rails in the church. Of course he must absent himself from breakfast, and invent some excuse for doing so. But this was done for him. Upon quitting the clerk's and hastening to his patients, he found one of them so much worse that it would be essential to see him at the earliest possible hour in the morning. And this he said later to the doctor. When his place was found vacant at breakfast, it would be concluded by his uncle and Edina that he was detained by the exigencies of the sick man.

But, if Fortune was showing herself thus kind to him in some respects, Fate was preparing to be less so. Upon how apparently accidental and even absurd a trifle great events often turn. Or, rather, to what great events, affecting life and happiness, one insignificant incident will lead! The world needs not to be told this.

XII

THE WEDDING

"Papa, will you come to breakfast? Oh dear! what is the matter?"

Edina might well ask. She had opened the door of the small consulting-room as the clock was chiming eight—the knell of Frank Raynor's bachelorhood—to tell her father that the meal was waiting, when she saw not only the hearth and the hearthrug, but the doctor himself enveloped in a cloud of soot, and looking as black as Erebus.

"I said yesterday the chimney wanted sweeping, Edina."

"Yes, papa, and it was going to be done next week. Have you been burning more paper in the chimney?"

"Only just a letter: but the wind carried it up. Well, this is a pretty pickle!"

"The room shall be done to-day, papa. It will be all right and ready for you again by night."

Dr. Raynor took off his coat and shook it, and then went up to his room to get the soot out of his whiskers. The fact was, seeing the letter go roaring up the chimney, he stooped hastily to try to get it back again, remembering what a recent blazing piece of paper had done; when at that moment down came a shower of soot, and enveloped him.

As he was descending the stairs again, the front-door was opened with a burst and a bang (no other words are so fitting to express the mad way in which excited messengers did enter), and told the doctor that he was wanted there and then by some one who was taken ill and appeared to be dying. Drinking a cup of coffee standing, the doctor followed the messenger. It had all passed so rapidly that Edina had not yet commenced her own breakfast.

"Hester," she said, calling to the maid-servant, "papa has had to go out, and Mr. Frank is not yet in. You shall keep the coffee warm, and I will run at once to Mrs. Trim and see if she can come to-day. We must breakfast later this morning."

Hastily putting on her bonnet and mantle, Edina went down the street towards the churchyard. The entrance to the church was at the other end, facing the open country, the parsonage was there also: on this side, near to her, stood the clerk's house. She could go to it without entering the graveyard; and did so. Trying the door, she found it fastened, which was unusual at that hour of the morning. It was nothing for the door to be fastened later, when the clerk and his wife were both abroad; the one on matters connected with his post, the other doing errands in the village, or perhaps at some house helping to clean. Edina gave a sharp knock with the handle of her umbrella, which she had brought with her; for dark clouds, threatening rain, were coursing through the sky. But the knock brought forth no response.

"Now I do hope she is not out at work to-day!" exclaimed Edina, referring to Mrs. Trim. "The sweep *must* come to the room; and Hester cannot well clean up after him with all her other work. There's the ironing about. If she has to do the cleaning to-day, I must do that."

Another knock brought forth the same result—nothing. Edina turned to face the churchyard, and stood thinking. The goat was browsing on the green patch close by.

"If I could find Trim, he would tell me at once whether she's away at work or not. She may have only run out on an errand. It is curious he should be out: this is their breakfast-time."

Suddenly, as she stood there in indecision, an idea struck Edina: Mrs. Trim was no doubt dusting the church. She generally did it on Saturday, and this was Thursday: but, as Edina knew, if the woman was likely to be occupied on the Saturday, she took an earlier day for the duty.

Lightly crossing the stile, Edina went through the churchyard and round the church to the entrance-porch. Her quick eyes saw that, though apparently shut, the door was not latched; and she pushed it open.

"Yes, of course: Mary Trim expects to be busy to-morrow and Saturday, and is doing the dusting to-day," soliloquized Edina, deeming the appearances conclusive. "Well, she will have to make haste here, and come to us as soon as she can."

But it was no Mrs. Trim with her gown turned up, and a huge black bonnet perched forward on her head, that Edina saw as she went gently through the inner green-baize door. A very different sight met her eyes; a soft murmur of reading broke upon her ears. The church was not large, as compared with some churches, though of fairly good size for a country parish: and she seemed to come direct upon the solemn scene that was being enacted. At the other end, before the altar, stood, side by side, Frank Raynor and Margaret St. Clare: facing them was the new clergyman, Mr. Backup, book in hand.

Edina was extremely practical; but at first she really could not believe her eyesight. She stood perfectly motionless, gazing at them as one in a trance. They did not see her; could not have seen her without turning round; and Mr. Backup's eyes were fixed on his book—which, by the way, seemed to tremble a little in his hands, as though he were being married himself. Coming to a momentary pause, he went on again in a raised voice; and the words fell thrillingly on the ear of Edina.

"I require and charge you both, as ye will answer at the dreadful day of judgment, when the secrets of all hearts shall be disclosed, that if either of you know any impediment, why ye may not be lawfully joined together in Matrimony, ye do now confess it. For be ye well assured, that so many as are coupled together otherwise than God's word doth allow are not joined together by God; neither is their Matrimony lawful."

The words, one by one, fell not only on Edina's ear; they touched her soul. Oh, was there no impediment? Ought these two silly people, wedding one another in this stolen fashion, and in defiance of parental authority—ought they to stand silent under this solemn exhortation, letting it appear that there was none? Surely this deceit ought, of itself, to constitute grave impediment! Just for the moment it crossed Edina's mind to come forward, and beg them to reflect; to reflect well, ere this ceremony went on to the end. But she remembered how unfitting it would be: she knew that she possessed no right to interfere with either the one or the other.

Drawing softly back within the door, she let it close again without noise, and made her way out of the churchyard. It appeared evident that neither the clerk nor his wife was in the church: and, if they had been, Edina could not have attempted then to speak to them.

As one in a dream, went she, up the street again towards home. The clouds had grown darker, and seemed to chase each other more swiftly and wildly. But Edina no longer heeded the wind or the weather. They might, in conjunction with burning paper, send the soot down every chimney in the house, for all the moment it was to her just now. She was deeply plunged in a most unpleasant reverie. A reverie which was showing her many future complications for Frank Raynor.

"Good-morning, Miss Edina! You be abroad early, ma'am."

The voice was Mrs. Trim's: the black bonnet, going down with the rest of herself in a curtsy, was hers also. She carried a small brown jug in her hand, and had met Edina close to the doctor's house. Edina came out of her dream.

"I have been to see after you, Mrs. Trim, and could not get in. The door was locked."

"Dear now, and I be sorry, Miss Edina! I just went to carry a drop o' coffee and a morsel of hot toast to poor Granny Sandon: who heve got nobody much to look after her since Rosaline Bell left. So I just locked the door, and brought tha key away weth me, as much to keep the Nanny-goat out as for safety. She heve a way of loosing herself, Miss Edina, clever as I thinks I ties her, and of coming into the house: and they goats butts and bites at things, and does no end o' mischief."

"Your husband is out, then?"

"He heve gone off somewhere by rail, Miss Edina. I could na get out of him where 'twas, though, nor whaat it were for. They men be closer nor waax when they want to keep things from ye; and Trim, he be always close. It strikes me, though, he be went somewhere for Mr. Raynor."

"Why do you think that?" cried Edina, quickly.

"Well, I be sure o' one thing, Miss Edina—Trim had no thought o' going off anywhere when I come hoam last evening from Pendon; for after we had had a word or two about his not seeing to tha goat, he says to I he was going to do our garden up to-day: which would na be afore it wants it. Mr. Frank, he come in then, and was talking to Trim in tha kitchen, they two together; and, a-going to bed, Trim asks for a clean check shirt, and said he was a-staarting out in the morning on business. And, sure enough, he heve went, Miss Edina, and I found out as he heve went by one o' they trains."

Edina said no more. She marshalled the chattering woman indoors to look at the state of the doctor's room, and to tell her it must be cleaned that day. Mrs. Trim took off her shawl there and then, and began to prepare for the work.

The doctor had returned, and Hester was carrying the breakfast in. Edina took her place at the table, and poured out her father's coffee.

"Is Frank not in yet?" he asked, as she handed it to him.

"Not yet, papa."

"Why, where can he be? He had only Williamson to see."

Edina did not answer. She appeared to be intent on her plate. Fresh and fair and good she looked this morning, but she seemed to be lost in thought. The doctor observed it.

"You are troubling yourself about that mess in my study, child!"

"Oh no, indeed I am not, papa. Mary Trim is already here."

"Are you sure Frank's not in the surgery, Edina?" said Dr. Raynor again presently.

Knowing where Frank was, and the momentous ceremony he was taking part in—though by that time it had probably come to an end—Edina might safely assure the doctor that he was not in the surgery. Dr. Raynor let the subject drop: Frank had called in to see some other patient, he supposed, on his way home from Williamson's; and Edina, perhaps dreading further questions, speedily ended her breakfast, and went to look after Mrs. Trim and household matters.

When the Reverend Titus Backup awoke from his slumbers that morning, the unpleasant thought flashed on his mind that he had a marriage ceremony to perform. Looking at his watch, he found it to be half-past seven, and up he started in a flurry. Having lain awake half the night, he had overslept himself.

"Has the clerk been here for the key of the church, Betsy?" he called to the old servant, just before he went out.

"No, sir."

It wanted only about eight minutes to eight then. Mr. Backup, feeling somewhat surprised, for he had found Clerk Trim particularly attentive to his duties, walked along the passage to the kitchen, and took the church-key from the nail where it was kept. Opening the church himself, he then went round to the clerk's house, and found it locked up.

Quite a hot tremor seized him. *Without* the clerk and his experience, it would be next door to impossible to get through the service. Alone, he might break down. He should not know what to say, or where to place the couple; or when to tell them to kneel down, when to stand up; or where the ring came in, or anything.

Where *was* the clerk? Could he have made some mistake as to the hour? However, it wanted yet some minutes to eight. Crossing the churchyard, he entered the church, put on his surplice, carried the Prayer-book into the vestry, and began studying the marriage service as therein written.

Frank Raynor came up to the church a minute after the clergyman entered it, and waited in the porch, looking out for his intended bride. Eight o'clock struck; and she had promised to be there before eight. Why did she not come? Was her courage failing her? Did the black clouds, gathering overhead, appal her? Had Mrs. St. Clare discovered all, and was preventing her? Frank thought it must be one or other of these calamities.

MRS. HENRY WOOD

There he stood, within the shelter of the porch, glancing to the right and left. He could not go to meet her because he did not know which way she would come: whether by the sheltered roadway, or across the Bare Plain. That was one of the minor matters they had forgotten to settle between themselves.

As Frank was gazing about, and getting into as much of a flurry as was possible for one of his easy temperament, light, hasty steps were heard approaching; and Margaret, nervous, panting, agitated, fell into his arms.

"My darling I thought you must be lost."

"I could not get away before, Frank. Of all mornings, Lydia must needs choose this one to send Tabitha to my room for some books from the shelves. Now, these did not do; then, others did not do: the woman did nothing but run in and out. And the servants were about the passages: and oh, I thought I should never get away!"

A moment given to soothing her, to stilling her beating heart, and they entered the church together. Margaret threw off the thin cloak she had worn over her pretty morning dress of white-and-peach sprigged muslin, almost as delicate as white. She went up the church, flushing and paling, on Frank's arm: Mr. Backup came out of the vestry to meet them. In a few flowing and plausible words, Frank explained that it was he himself who required the parson's services, handed him the license, and begged him to get the service over as soon as possible.

"The clerk is not here," answered the bewildered man, doubly bewildered now.

"Oh, never mind him," said Frank. "We don't want the clerk."

An older and less timid clergyman might have said, I cannot marry you under these circumstances: all Mr. Backup thought of was, getting through his own part in it. It certainly did strike him as being altogether very strange: the question even crossed him whether he was doing rightly and legally: but the license was in due form, and in his inexperience and nervousness he did not make inquiries or raise objections. When he came to the question, Who giveth this Woman to be married to this Man, and there was no response, no one indeed to respond, he visibly hesitated; but he did not dare to refuse to go on with the service. An assumption of authority, such as that, was utterly beyond the Reverend Titus Backup. He supposed that the clerk was to have acted in the capacity: but the clerk, from some inexplicable cause, was not present. Perhaps he had mistaken the hour. So the service proceeded to its close, and Francis Raynor and Margaret St. Clare were made man and wife.

They proceeded to the vestry; the clergyman leading the way, Frank conducting his bride, her arm within his, the ring that bound her to him encircling her finger. After a hunt for the register, for none of them knew where it was kept, Mr. Backup found it, and entered the marriage. Frank affixed his signature, Margaret hers; and then the young clergyman seemed at a standstill, looking about him helplessly.

"I—ah—there are no witnesses to the marriage," said he. "It is customary—"

"We must do without them in this case," interrupted Frank, as he laid down a fee of five guineas. "It does not require witnesses to make it legal."

"Well—no—I—I conclude not," hesitated the clergyman, blushing as he glanced at the gold and silver, and thinking how greatly too much it was, and how rich this Mr. Raynor must be.

"And will you do me and my wife a good turn, Mr. Backup," spoke Frank, ingenuously, as he clasped the clergyman's hand, and an irresistible smile of entreaty shone on his attractive face. "*Keep it secret.* I may tell you, now it is over and done, that no one knows of this marriage. It is, in fact, a stolen one; and just at present we do not wish it to be disclosed. We have our reasons for this. In a very short time, it will be openly avowed; but until then, we should be glad for it not to be spoken about. I know we may depend upon your kindness."

Leaving the utterly bewildered parson to digest the information, to put off his surplice and to lock up the register, Frank escorted his bride down the aisle. When she stopped to take up her cloak and parasol, he, knowing there were no spectators, except the ancient and empty pews, folded her in his arms and kissed her fervently.

"Oh, Frank! Please!—please don't! We are in church, remember." And there, what with agitation and nervous fear, the bride burst into a fit of hysterical tears.

"Daisy! For goodness' sake!—not here. Compose yourself, my love. Oh, pray do not sob like that!"

A moment or two, and she was tolerably calm again. No wonder she had given way. She had literally shaken from head to foot throughout the service. A dread of its being interrupted, a nervous terror at what she was doing, held possession of her. Now that it was over, she saw she

MRS. HENRY WOOD

had done wrong, and wished it undone. Just like all the rest of us! We do wrong first, and bewail it afterwards.

"You remain in here, please, Frank; let me go out alone," she said, catching her breath. "It would not do, you know, for us to go out together, lest we might be seen. Good-bye," she added, timidly holding up her hand.

They were between the green-baize door now and the outer one. Frank knew as well as she did that it would be imprudent to leave the church together. He took her hand and herself once more to him, and kissed her fifty times.

"God bless and keep you, my darling! I wish I could see you safely home."

Daisy's suggestion, a night or two ago, of their leaving the church by different doors, had to turn out merely a pleasant fiction, since the church possessed but one door. She lightly glided through it when Frank released her, and went towards home the way she had come, that of the shady road, her veil drawn over her face, her steps fleet. He remained where he was, not showing himself until she should be at a safe distance.

"If I can only get in without being seen!" thought poor Daisy, her heart beating as she sped along. "Mamma and Lydia will not be downstairs yet, I know; and all may pass over happily. How high the wind is!"

The wind was high indeed, carrying Daisy very nearly off her feet. It took her cloak and whirled it over her head in the air. As ill-luck had it, terrible ill-luck Daisy thought, who should meet her at that moment but the Trennach dressmaker. She had been to The Mount to try dresses on.

"Mrs. St. Clare is quite in a way about you, Miss Margaret," spoke Mrs. Hunt, who was not pleased at having had her walk partly for nothing. "They have been searching everywhere for you."

"I did not know you were expected this morning," said poor Daisy, after murmuring some explanation of having "come out for a walk."

"Well, Miss Margaret, your mamma was good enough to say I might come whenever it was most convenient to me: and that's early morning, or late evening, so as not to take me out of my work in the daytime. I thought I might just catch you and Miss St. Clare when you were dressing, and could have tried on my bodies without much trouble to you."

"What bodies are they?" asked Margaret. "I did not know that anything was being made."

"They are dresses for travelling, miss. Mrs. St. Clare gave me a pattern of the material she would like, and I have been getting them.

"Oh, for travelling," repeated Margaret, whose mind, what with one thing and another, was in a perfect whirl. "Will you like to go back, and try mine on now."

But the dressmaker declined to turn back. She was nearer Trennach now than she was to The Mount, and her apprentice had no work to go on with until she arrived at home to set it for her. Appointing the following morning, she continued her way.

Daisy continued hers. It was a most unlucky thing that the dressmaker should have gone to The Mount that morning of all others! What a fuss there would be! And what excuse could she make for her absence from home? There was only one, as it seemed to Daisy, that she could make—she had been out for a walk.

But the shifting clouds had now gathered in a dense mass overhead, and the rain came pouring down. Daisy had brought no umbrella: nothing but a fashionable parasol about, large enough for a doll: one cannot be expected on such an occasion to be as provident as the renowned Mrs. McStinger. The wind took Daisy's cloak, as before; the drifting rain-storm half blinded her. Before she reached home, her pretty muslin dress, and her dainty parasol, and herself also, were wet through.

"Now where have you been?" demanded Mrs. St. Clare, pouncing upon Daisy in the hall, and backed by Tabitha; whilst Lydia, who had that morning risen betimes, thanks to the exacting dressmaker, looked on from the door of the breakfast-room.

"I went for a walk," gasped Daisy, fully believing all was about to be discovered. "The rain overtook me."

"What a pickle you are in," commented Lydia.

"*Where* have you been for a walk?" proceeded Mrs. St. Clare, who was evidently angry.

"Down the road," said Daisy, in an almost inaudible voice, the result of fear and emotion. "It—it is pleasant to walk a little before the heat comes on. I—I did not know it was going to rain."

"Pray, how long is it since you found out that it is pleasant to walk a little before the heat comes on?" retorted Mrs. St. Clare, with severe sarcasm. "How many mornings have you tried it?"

"Never before this morning, mamma," replied Daisy, with ready earnestness, for it was the truth.

"And pray with whom have you been walking?" put in Lydia, with astounding emphasis. "Who brought you home?"

"Not any one," choked Daisy, swallowing down her tears. "I walked home alone. You can ask Mrs. Hunt, who met me. Mamma, may I go up and change my things?"

Mrs. St. Clare said neither yes nor no, but gave tacit permission by stretching out her hand towards the staircase. Daisy ran the gauntlet of the three faces as she passed on: her mother's was stern, Lydia's supremely scornful, Tabitha's discreetly prim. The two ladies turned into the breakfast-room, and the maid retired.

"It is easy enough to divine what Daisy has been up to," spoke Lydia, whose speech was not always expressed in the most refined terms. She sat back in an easy-chair, sipping her chocolate, a pink cloak trimmed with swan's-down drawn over her shoulders; for the rain and the early rising had made her feel chilly.

"Oh, I don't know," said Mrs. St. Clare, crossly. She detested these petty annoyances.

"I do, though," returned Lydia. "Daisy has been out to meet Frank Raynor. Were I you, mamma, I should not allow her so much liberty."

"Give me the sugar, Lydia, and let me take my breakfast in peace."

Daisy, locking her door, burst into a fit of hysterical tears. Her nerves were utterly unstrung. It was necessary to change her garments, and she did so, sobbing wofully the while. She wished she had not done what she had done; she wished that Frank could be by her side to encourage and shield her. When she had completed her toilet, she took the wedding-ring from her finger, attached it to a bit of ribbon, and hid it in her bosom.

"Suppose I should never, never be able to wear it openly?" thought Daisy, with a sob and a sigh. "Suppose Frank and I should never see each other again! never be able to be together? If mamma carries me off abroad, and he remains here, one of us might die before I come back again."

XIII

UNDER THE STARS

"Can you spare me a moment, Frank?"

"Fifty moments, if you like, Edina," was the answer in the ever-pleasant tones. "Come in."

The day had gone on to its close, and Edina had found no opportunity of speaking to Frank alone. The secret of which she had unexpectedly gained cognizance that morning was troubling her mind. To be a party to it, and to keep that fact from Frank, was impossible to Edina. Tell him she must: and the sooner the better. After tea, he and the doctor had sat persistently talking together until dusk, when Frank had to go out to visit a fever-patient in Bleak Row. Running upstairs to change his coat, Edina had thought the opportunity had come, and followed him to his chamber.

She went in after his hearty response to her knock. Frank, quick in all his movements, already had his coat off, and was taking the old one from the peg where it hung. Edina sat down by the dressing-table.

"Frank," she said, in low tones—and she disliked very much indeed to have to say it, "I chanced to go into the church this morning soon after eight o'clock. I—I saw you there."

"*Did* you?" cried Frank, coming to a pause with his coat half on. "And—did you see anything else, Edina?"

"I believe I saw all there was to see, Frank. I saw you standing with Margaret St. Clare at the altar-rails, and Mr. Backup marrying you.

"Well, I never!" cried Frank, with all the amazing ease and equanimity he might have maintained had she said she saw him looking on at a christening. "Were you surprised, Edina?"

"Surprised, and a great deal more, Frank. Shocked. Grieved."

"I say, though, what took you to the church at that early hour, Edina?"

"Chance, it may be said. Though I am one of those, you know, who do not believe that such a thing as chance exists. I went after Mrs. Trim, found her house shut up, and the thought she might be in the church, cleaning. Oh, Frank, how could you do anything so desperately imprudent?"

"Well, I hardly know. Don't scold me, Edina."

"I have no right to scold you," she answered. "And scolding would be of no use now the thing is done. Nevertheless, I must tell you what a very wrong step it was to take; lamentably imprudent: and I think you must, yourself, know that it was so. I could never have believed it of Margaret St. Clare."

"Do not blame Daisy, Edina. I persuaded her to take it. Mrs. St. Clare has been talking of marching her off abroad; and we wanted, you see, to secure ourselves against separation."

"And what are you going to do, Frank?"

"Oh, nothing," said easy Frank. "Daisy's gone back to The Mount, and I am here as usual. As soon as I can make a home for her, I shall take her away."

"Make a home where?"

"In some place where there's a likelihood of a good practice. London, I dare say."

"But how are you to live? A good practice does not spring up in a night, like a mushroom."

"That's arranged," replied Frank, as perfectly confident himself that it was arranged as that Edina was sitting in the low chair, and he was finally settling himself into his coat. "My plans are all laid, Edina, and Uncle Hugh knows what they are. It was in pursuance of them that I went over to Spring Lawn. I will tell you all about it to-morrow: there's no time to do so now."

"Papa does not know of what took place this morning?"

"No. No one knows of that. We don't want it known, if we can help it, until the time comes when all the world may know."

"Meaning until you have gained the home, Frank?"

"Meaning until I and Daisy enter upon it," said sanguine Frank.

Edina's hand—her elbow resting on her knee—was raised to support her head: her fingers played absently with her soft brown hair: her dark thoughtful eyes, gazing before her, seemed to see nothing. Whether it arose from the fact that in her early days, when Dr. Raynor's means were narrow, she had become practically acquainted with some dark phases of existence, or whether it was the blight that had been cast on her heart in its sweet spring-time, certain it was, that Edina Raynor was no longer of a sanguine nature. Where Frank saw only sunshine in prospective, she saw shadow. And a great deal of it.

"You should have made sure of the home first."

"Before making sure of Daisy? Not a bit of it, Edina. We shall get along."

"That's just like you, Frank," she exclaimed petulantly, in her vexation. "You would as soon marry ten wives as one, the law allowing it, so far as never giving a thought to what you were to do with them."

"But the law would not allow it," laughed Frank.

"It is your great fault—never to think of consequences."

"Time enough, Edina, when the consequences come."

She did not make any rejoinder. To what use? Frank Raynor would be Frank Raynor to the end of time. It was his nature.

"It is odd, though, is it not, that you, of all Trennach, should just happen to have caught us?" he exclaimed, alluding to the ceremony of the morning. "But you'll not betray us, Edina? I must be off down, or Uncle Hugh will be calling to know what I'm doing."

Edina rose, with a sigh. "No, I will not betray you, Frank: you know there is no danger of that: and if I can help you and Daisy in any way, I will do it. I was obliged to tell you what I had seen. I could not keep from you the fact that it had come to my knowledge."

As Frank leaped downstairs, light-hearted as a boy, Dr. Raynor was crossing from the sitting-room to the surgery. He halted to speak.

"I forgot to tell you, Frank, that you may as well call this evening on Dame Bell: you will be passing her door."

"Is Dame Bell ill again?" asked Frank.

"I fear so. A woman came for some medicine for her to-day."

"I thought she was at Falmouth."

"She is back again, it seems. Call and see her as you go along: you have plenty of time."

"Very well, Uncle Hugh."

The Bare Plain might be said to specially deserve its name this evening as Frank traversed it. In the morning the wind had been high, but nothing to what it was now. It played amidst the openings surrounding the Bottomless Shaft, going in with a whirr, coming out with a rush, and shrieked and moaned fearfully. The popular belief indulged in by the miners was, that this unearthly shrieking and moaning, which generally disturbed the air on these boisterous nights, proceeded not from the wind, but from Dan Sandon's ghost. Frank Raynor of course had no faith in the ghost—Dan Sandon's, or any other—but he shuddered as he hastened on.

The illness, more incipient than declared as yet, from which Mrs. Bell was suffering, had seemed to cease with her trouble. Her husband's mysterious disappearance was followed by much necessary exertion, both of mind and body, on her own part; and her ailments almost left her. Dr. Raynor suspected—perhaps knew—that the improvement was only temporary; but he did not tell her so. Dame Bell moved briskly about her house during this time, providing for the comforts of her lodgers, and waiting for the husband who did not come.

Rosaline did not come, either. And her prolonged absence seemed to her mother most unaccountable, her excuses for it unreasonable. As the days and the weeks had gone on, and Rosaline's return seemed to be no nearer than ever, Dame Bell grew angry. She at length made up her mind to go to Falmouth and bring back the runaway with her own hands.

Easier said than done: as Mrs. Bell found. When after two days' absence, she returned to her home on the Bare Plain, she returned alone: her daughter was not with her. This was only a few days ago. The dame had been ailing ever since, some of the old symptoms having returned again—the result perhaps of the travelling—and she had that day sent a neighbour to Dr. Raynor's for some medicine.

Frank Raynor made the best of his way across the windy plain, and lifted the latch of Dame Bell's door. She stood at the table, ironing by candle-light, her feet resting upon an old thick mat to keep them from any draught. Frank, making himself at home as usual, sat down by the ironing-board, telling her to go on with her occupation, and inquired into her ailments.

"You ought not to have taken the journey," said Frank, promptly, when questions and answers were over. "Travelling is not good for you."

"But I could not help taking it," returned Dame Bell, beginning upon the wristbands of a shirt she was ironing. "When Rosaline never came home, and paid no attention to my ordering her to come home, it was time I went to see after her."

"She has not come back with you?"

"No, she has not," retorted Dame Bell, ironing away with a viciousness that imperilled the wristband. "I couldn't make her come, Mr. Frank. Cords would not have dragged her. Of all the idiots! to let those Whistlers frighten her from a place for good, like that!"

"The Whistlers?" mechanically repeated Frank, his eyes fixed on the progress of the ironing.

"It's the Whistlers, and nothing else," said Mrs. Bell. "I didn't send word to her or her aunt that I was on my way to Falmouth: I thought I'd take 'em by surprise. And I declare to you, Mr. Frank, I hardly believed my eyes when I saw Rosaline. It did give me a turn. I was that shocked—"

"But why?" interrupted Frank.

"She's just as thin as a herring. You wouldn't know her, sir. When I got to the place, there was John Pellet's shop-window flaming away, and lighting up the tins and fire-irons, and all that, which he shows in it. I opened the side-door, and went straight up the stairs to the room overhead, knowing I should most likely find Rosaline there, for it's the room where my sister Pellet does her millinery work. My sister was there, standing with her back to me, a bonnet on each of her outstretched hands, as if she was comparing the blue bows in one with the pink bows in the other; and close to the middle table, putting some flowers in another bonnet, was a young woman in black. I didn't know her at first. The gas was right on her face, but I declare that I didn't know her. She looked straight over at me, and I thought what a white and thin and pretty face it, was, with large violet eyes and dark circles round 'em: but as true as you are there, Mr. Frank, I didn't know her for Rosaline. 'Mother!' says she, starting up: and I a'most fell on the nearest chair. 'What ever has come to you, child?' I says, as she steps round to kiss me! 'you look as though you had one foot in the grave.' At that she turns as red as a rose: and what with the bright colour, and the smile she gave, she looked a little more like herself. But there: if I talked till I tired you, sir, I could make out no more than that: she's looking desperately ill and wretched, and she won't come home again."

Frank made no rejoinder. The ironing went on vigorously: and Mrs. Bell's narrative with it.

"All I could say was of no use: back with me she wouldn't consent to come. All her aunt could say was of no use. For, when she found how lonely I was at home, and how much I wanted Rosaline, my sister, though loth to part with her, said nature was nature, and a girl should not go against her mother. But no persuasion would bring Rosaline to reason. She'd live with me, and glad to, she said, if I'd go and stay at Falmouth, but she could not come back to Trennach. Pellet and his wife both tried to turn her: all in vain."

"Did she give any reason for not coming back?" questioned Frank: and one, more observant than Dame Bell, might have been struck with the low, subdued tones he spoke in.

"She gave no reason of her own accord, Mr. Frank, but I got it out of her. 'What has Trennach done to you, and what has the old house on the Plain done to you, that you should be frightened at it?' I said to her. For it's easy to gather that she is frightened in her mind, Mr. Frank, and Pellet's wife had noticed the same ever since she went there. 'Don't say such things, mother,' says she, 'it is nothing.' 'But I will say it,' says I, 'and I know the cause—just the shock you had that Tuesday night from the Seven Whistlers, and a fear that you might hear them again if you came back; and a fine simpleton you must be for your pains!' And so she is."

"Ah, yes, the Seven Whistlers," repeated Frank, absently.

"She could not contradict me. She only burst into tears and begged of me not to talk of them. Not talk, indeed! I could have shook her, I could!"

"We cannot help our fears," said Frank.

"But for a girl to let they sounds scare her out of house and home and country, is downright folly," pursued Dame Bell, unable to relinquish the theme, and splitting the button of the shirt-collar in two at one stroke of the angry iron. "And she must fright and fret herself into a skeleton besides! But there," she resumed, in easier tones, after folding the shirt, "I suppose she can't help it. Her father was just as much afraid of 'em. He never had an atom o' colour in his face from the Sunday night he heard the Whistlers till the Tuesday night when he disappeared. It had a curious grey look on it all the while."

Frank rose. He remembered the grey look well enough. "If Rosaline likes Falmouth best, she is better there, Mrs. Bell. I should not press her to return."

"If pressing would do any good, she'd have her share of it," rejoined Mrs. Bell, candidly. "But it won't. I did press, for the matter of that. When I'd done pressing on my score, I put it on the score of her father. 'Don't you care to be at home to welcome your poor lost father when he gets back to it—for he's sure to come back, sooner or later,' says I: and I'm sure my eyes ran tears as I spoke. But no: she just turned as white as the grave, Mr. Frank, and shook her head in a certain solemn way of hers, which she must have picked up at Falmouth: and I saw it was of no use, though I talked till doomsday. There she stops, and there she will stop, and I must make the best of it. And I wish those evil Whistlers had been at the bottom of the sea!"

Frank was in a hurry to depart: but she went on again, after taking breath.

"She is earning money, and her aunt is glad to have her, and takes care of her, and she says she never saw any girl so expert with her fingers and display so much taste in bonnets as Rosaline. But that does not mend the matter here, Mr. Frank, and is no excuse for her being such a goose. 'Come and take a room in Falmouth, mother,' were her last words when I was leaving. But I'd like to know what a poor lone body like me could do in that strange place."

"Well, good-evening, Mrs. Bell," said Frank, escaping to the door. But the loquacious tongue had not quite finished.

"When I was coming back in the train, Mr. Frank, the thought kept running in my mind that perhaps Bell would have got home whilst I'd been away: and when I looked round the empty house, and saw he was not here, a queer feeling of disappointment came over me. Do you think he ever will come back, sir?"

Some "queer feeling" seemed to take Frank at the question, and stop his breath. He spoke a few words indistinctly in answer. Mrs. Bell did not catch them.

"And whether it was through that—expecting to see him and the consequent disappointment—I don't know, Mr. Frank; but since then I can't get him out of my mind. Day and night, Bell is in it. I am beginning to dream of him: and that's what I have not done yet. Nancy Tomson says it's a good sign. Should you say it was, sir?"

"I—really don't know," was Frank's unsatisfactory reply. And then he succeeded in making his final exit.

"I wish she wouldn't bring up her husband to me!" he cried, lifting his hat that his brow might get a little of the fresh wind, which blew less fiercely under the cottages. "Somehow she nearly always does it. I hate to cross the threshold."

A week or two went on: a week or two of charming weather and calm blue skies: The day fixed for the departure of Mrs. St. Clare from The Mount came and passed, and she was still at home, and likely to be there for some time to come. "Man proposes, but Heaven disposes." Every day of our lives we have fresh proofs of that great fact.

On the very day of Daisy's impromptu wedding, her sister Lydia showed herself more than usually ailing and grumbling. She felt cold and shivery, and sat in the pink cloak all day. The next morning she seemed really ill, not fancifully so, was hot and cold alternately. Dr. Raynor was sent for. The attack turned out to be one of fever. Not as yet of infectious fever—and Dr. Raynor hoped he should prevent its going on to that. But it was rather severe, and required careful watching and nursing.

Of course their departure for foreign lands was out of the question. They could not leave The Mount. Mrs. St. Clare, who was very anxious, for she dreaded a visitation of infectious fever more than anything else, spent most of her time in Lydia's room. Once in a way, Frank Raynor appeared at The Mount in his uncle's place. Dr. Raynor was fully given to understand that his own attendance was requested, not his nephew's: but he was himself getting to feel worse day by day; he could not always go over, walking or riding; and on those occasions Frank went instead. Mrs. St. Clare permitted what, as it appeared, there was no remedy for, and was coldly civil to the young doctor.

But this illness of Lydia's, and Mrs. St. Clare's close attendance in her room, gave more liberty to Daisy. Scarcely an evening passed but she, unsuspected and unwatched, was pacing the shrubberies and the secluded parts of that wilderness of a garden with Frank. There, arm-in-arm, they walked, and talked together of the hopeful future, and the enchanted hours seemed to fly on golden wings.

> *"Love took up the glass of Time, and turned it in his glowing hands,*
> *Every moment, lightly shaken, ran itself in golden sands.*
> *Love took up the harp of Life, and smote on all the chords with might,*
> *Smote the chord of Self, that, trembling, passed in music out of sight."*

Whatever of reality, of fruition, the future might bring, it could never be to them what this present time was, when they wandered together in the sweet moonlight, with the scent of the night-flowers around them, and the soft sighing wind, and the heart's romance.

Never an evening but Daisy stole out to watch from the sheltered gate for the coming of her lover; scarcely an evening that Frank failed to come. When he did fail, it was through no fault of his. Daisy would linger and linger on, waiting and watching, even when all sensible hope of his coming must have died out; and when compelled to return indoors with a reluctant step, she would think fate cruel to her, and sigh heavily.

"The time may come when we shall live with each other and be together always, in place of just this little evening walk up and down the paths—and oh, how I wish the time was come now!" poor Daisy would say to her own heart.

One evening it was Daisy who failed to be at the trysting-place. Lydia was getting better, was able to sit up a little, morning and evening. The greater danger, feared for her, had been prevented: and under her own good constitution—for she had one, in spite of her grumblings and her imaginary ailments—and Dr. Raynor's successful treatment, she was recovering rapidly. This evening, lying back in an easy-chair, it had pleased her to order Daisy to read to her. Daisy complied willingly: she was ever more ready to help Lydia than Lydia was to accept her help; but when a long spell of reading had been got through, and the room was growing dim, Daisy, coming to the end of a chapter, closed the book.

"What's that for?" asked Lydia, sharply, whose peevishness was coming back to her with her advance towards convalescence. "Read on, please."

"It is growing dusk," said Daisy.

"Dusk—for that large print!—nonsense," retorted Lydia. The book was a popular novel, and she felt interested in it.

"I am tired, Lydia: you don't consider how long I have been reading," cried Daisy, fretting inwardly: for the twilight hour was her lover's signal for approach, and she knew he must be already waiting for her.

"You have only been reading since dinner," debated Lydia: "not much more than an hour, I'm sure. Go on."

So Daisy was obliged to go on. She dared not display too much anxiety to get away, lest it might betray that she had some motive for wishing it. A secret makes us terribly self-conscious. But by-and-by it really became too dark to see even the large print of the fashionable novel of the day, and Lydia exhibited signs of weariness; and Mrs. St. Clare, who had been dozing in another arm-chair, woke up and said Lydia must not listen any longer. Daisy ran down to the yellow room, and sped swiftly through the open glass-doors.

It was nearly as dark as it would be. The stars were shining; a lovely opal colour lingered yet in the west. Frank Raynor, hands in pockets, and whistling softly under his breath, stood in the sheltered walk. A somewhat broad walk, where the trees met overhead. Daisy flung herself into his arms, and burst into tears. Tried almost beyond bearing by her forced detention, it was thus her emotion, combined perhaps with a little temper, expended itself.

"Why, Daisy! What is the matter?"

"I could not get to you, Frank. Lydia kept me in, reading to her, all this time."

"Never mind, my darling, now you have come."

"I thought you would go away; I feared you might think I forgot, or something," sighed Daisy.

"As if I could think that! Dry your eyes, my dear one."

Placing her arm within his, Frank led her forward, and they began, as usual, to pace the walk. It was their favourite promenade; for it was so retired and sheltered that they felt pretty safe from intruders. There, linked arm-in-arm, or with Frank's arm round her waist, as might be, they paced to and fro; the friendly stars shining down upon them through the branches overhead.

Their theme was ever the same—the future. The hopeful future, that to their eyes looked brighter than those twinkling stars. What was it to be for them, and how might they, in their enthusiasm, plan it out? In what manner could Frank best proceed, so as to secure speedily a home-tent, and be able to declare to the world that he and Margaret St. Clare had spent a quarter-of-an-hour in the grey old church at Trennach one windy morning, when he had earned the right to take her away with him and cherish her for life?

To this end the whole of their consultations tended; on this one desired project all their deliberations centred. The sooner Frank could get away from Trennach, the sooner (as they both so hopefully believed) would it be realized. Never a shadow of doubt crossed either of them in regard to it. Frank was too sanguine, Daisy too inexperienced, to see any clouds in their sky. The days to come were to be days of brightness: and both were supremely unconscious that such days never return after the swift passing of life's fair first morning.

"You see, Daisy, the delay is not my fault," spoke Frank. "My uncle has been so very unwell this last week or two, so much worse, that I don't like to urge the change upon him. Only to-day I said to him, 'You know I am wanting to leave you, Uncle Hugh,' and his reply was, 'Do not speak of it just immediately, Frank: let things be as they are a very little longer.' Whilst he is feeling so ill, I scarcely like to worry him."

"Of course not," said Daisy. "And as long as I can walk about here with you every evening, Frank, I don't care how long things go on as they are now. It was different when I feared mamma was going to carry me off to the end of the world. It was only that fear, you know, Frank, that made me consent to do what I did that morning. I'm sure I tremble yet when I think how wrong and hazardous it was. Any one might have come into the church."

"Where's your wedding-ring, Daisy?" he asked: and it may as well be said that he had never told her some one did come in.

"Here," she answered, touching her dress. "It is always there, Frank."

"I have written to-day to a friend of mine in London, Daisy, asking if he knows of any good opening for me—or of any old practitioner in a first-class quarter who may be likely to want some younger man to help him. I dare say I shall receive an answer with some news in it in a day or two."

"I dare say you will. Who is he, Frank?"

"A young fellow named Crisp, who has the best heart in the world. He—"

A sudden grasping of his arm by Daisy, just after they had turned in their walk; a visible shrinking, as if she would hide behind him; and a faint idea that he saw some slight movement of the foliage at the other end of the avenue, stopped Frank's further words.

"Did you see, Frank?" she whispered. "Did you see?"

"I fancied something stirred, down there. What was it?"

"It was Tabitha. I am certain of it. I saw her the moment we turned. She might have been watching us ever so long; all the way up the walk; I dare say she *was* doing so. Oh, Frank, what shall I do? She will go in and tell mamma."

"Let her," said Frank. "The worst she can say is, that we were walking arm-in-arm together. I cannot think why you need be so fearful, Daisy. Your mother must know that we do meet out here, and she must tacitly sanction it. She used to know it, and sanction it too."

Daisy sighed. Yes, she thought, her mother might, at any rate, suspect that they met. It was not so much *that* which Daisy feared. But, the one private act she had been guilty of lay heavily on her conscience; and she was ever haunted with the dread that any fresh movement would lead to its betrayal.

Saying good-night to each other, for it was growing late, Frank departed, and Daisy went in. Her mother was shut up in the drawing-room, and she went on straight to her sister's chamber. There an unpleasant scene awaited her. Lydia, not yet in bed—for she had refused to go, and had abused Tabitha for urging it—lay back still in the easy-chair. Could looks have annihilated, Daisy would certainly have sunk from those cast on her by Lydia, as she entered.

And then the storm began. Lydia reproached her in no measured terms, and with utter scorn of tone and manner, for the "clandestine intimacy," as she was pleased to call it, that she, Daisy, was carrying on with Frank Raynor.

It appeared that after the candles were lighted, and Mrs. St. Clare had gone down, Lydia, declining to go to bed, and wanting to be amused, required Daisy to read to her again. Tabitha was sent in search of Daisy, and came back saying she could not find her anywhere: she was not downstairs, she was not in her chamber. "Go and look in the garden, you stupid thing," retorted Lydia: "you know Miss Daisy's for ever out there." Tabitha—a meek woman in demeanour, who took abuse humbly—went to the garden as directed, searched, and at length came upon Miss Daisy in the avenue, pacing it on the arm of Mr. Raynor. Back she went, and reported it to Lydia. And now Lydia was reproaching her.

"To suffer yourself to meet that man clandestinely after night has fallen!" reiterated Lydia. "And to stay out with him!—and to take his arm! You disgraceful girl! And when, all the while, he does not care one jot for *you!* He loves some one else."

Daisy had received the tirade on herself in silence, but she fired up at this. "You have no right to say *that*, Lydia," she cried. "Whether he loves me, or not, I shall not say; but, at any rate, he does not love any one else."

"Yes, he does," affirmed Lydia.

"He does not," fired Daisy. "If he does, who is it?"

"No one in his own station—more shame to him! It is that girl they call so beautiful—who lost her father. Rose—Rose—what's the name?—Rosaline Bell. Frank Raynor loves her with his whole heart and soul."

"Lydia, how dare you say such a thing?"

"*I* don't say it. I only repeat it. Ask Trennach. It is known all over the place. They used to be always together—walking on the Bare Plain by night. The girl has gone away for a time; and the gentleman, during her absence, amuses himself with you. Makes love to you to keep his hand in."

Daisy's heart turned sick and faint within her. Not at Lydia's supreme sarcasm, but at the horrible conviction that there must be something in the tale. She remembered the past evening at the dinner-table—and the recollection came rushing into her mind like a barbed arrow—when Sir

Arthur Beauchamp and others were questioning Frank about this very girl and her beauty, and she—Daisy—had been struck with the emotion he betrayed; with his evidently shrinking manner, with the changing hue of his face. Did he in truth love this girl, Rosaline Bell?—and was she so very beautiful?

"How did you hear this, Lydia?" asked Daisy, in tones from which all spirit was quenched.

"I heard it from Tabitha. She knows about it. You can ask her yourself."

And Daisy did ask. As it chanced, the maid at that moment entered the room with some beef-tea for Lydia; and Daisy, suppressing her pride and her reticence, condescended to question her. Tabitha answered freely and readily, as if there were nothing in the subject to conceal, and with a palpable belief in its truth that told terribly upon Daisy. In fact, the woman herself implicitly believed it. Mr. Blase Pellet had once favoured her with his version of the story, and Tabitha never supposed that that version existed in Mr. Pellet's own imagination, and in that alone.

"I—don't think it can be *true*, Tabitha," faltered poor Daisy, her heart beating wildly. "She was not a lady."

"It's true enough, Miss Margaret. Blase Pellet wanted her himself, but she'd have nothing to say to him—or to any one else except Mr. Raynor. Pellet is related to the Bells, and knew all about it. What he said to me was this: 'Raynor is after her for ever, day and night, and she worships the ground he treads on!' Those were his very words, Miss Margaret."

Margaret, turning hot and cold, and red and white, made her escape from the room, and took refuge in her own. In that first moment of awakening, she felt as though her heart must break with its bitter pain. Jealousy, baleful jealousy, had taken possession of her: and no other passion in this life can prey upon our bosoms so relentlessly, or touch them with so keen a sting.

XIV

IN THE CHURCHYARD

Trennach churchyard was lonely at all times, but it looked particularly so in the twilight of a dull evening. The trees took fantastic shapes; the headstones stood out like spectres; the grave-mounds reminded you unpleasantly that you yourself must sometime lie beneath them.

Especially grey were the skies this evening; for, though it was summer weather, the day had been gloomy: and Mr. Blase Pellet, sitting in the middle of the churchyard on the stump of an old tree, looked grey and gloomy as the weather and the graves.

Since the departure from Trennach of Rosaline Bell—for whom Mr. Blase Pellet did undoubtedly entertain a fond and sincere affection, whatever might have been his shortcomings generally—he had found his evening hours, when the chemist's shop was closed for the night, hang heavily on his hands. With the absence of Rosaline, the two chief relaxations in which Mr. Blase had employed his leisure were gone: namely, the cunning contrivances to meet her, either at home or abroad; and watching the movements of Frank Raynor. The young man's jealousy of the latter and Rosaline burnt as fiercely as ever, tormenting him to a most unreasonable degree: though, indeed, when was jealousy ever amenable to reason? There was no longer any personal intercourse between Frank Raynor and Rosaline; Blase knew quite well that could not be, for Frank was at Trennach, and she was at Falmouth; but he had felt as sure, ever since she went, that their intercourse was carried on by letter, as that he was now sitting on the stump of the old tree.

Jealousy needs no proof to confirm its fancies: our great master-mind has told us that it makes the food it feeds on. And upon this airy, unsubstantial kind of food had Mr. Pellet been nourishing his suspicions of the supposed correspondence—which existed in his imagination alone. He had watched the postman in a morning, he had waylaid him, and by apparently artless questions had got him to disclose to whom the letter was addressed which he had just left at Dr. Raynor's: and the less proof he could find of the suspected postal intercourse, the brighter his jealousy burned. For it was not often that the postman could say the letter, which he might have chanced to leave at the doctor's house, was for Mr. Frank Raynor. Sometimes it would be for the doctor himself, sometimes for Miss Raynor; but very rarely for Frank. Frank's correspondence did not seem to be an extensive one. This might possibly have satisfied an ordinary young man; it only tended to strengthen Mr. Blase Pellet's raging doubts: and now, on this ill-favoured evening, those doubts had received "confirmation strong as proofs of holy writ."

Since, like Othello, he had found his occupation gone, Mr. Blase Pellet was rather at a loss to know what to do with his evenings. To render him justice, it must be admitted that he did not follow the fashion, and spend them, however soberly, at the Golden Shaft. He was a steady, well-conducted young man, superior to his apparent position, and better in some respects than many of his neighbours. Finding the hours lying on his hands, he took to looking in unceremoniously at the houses of his acquaintants, so to pass a more or less agreeable interlude. This evening he had so favoured Clerk Trim; and it was in crossing the churchyard, after quitting that functionary's dwelling, that he had come to an anchor on the tree-stump. Bitter anger was aroused within him; raging jealousy; a tumultuous thirst for revenge. For, in the clerk's house he had just been furnished, as he believed, with the confirmation yearned for.

When Frank Raynor had so lightly sent Clerk Trim to Tello, to inquire for certain imaginary letters at the post-office there, he little thought what grave consequences would arise from it in the future. Simply for the sake of getting the clerk out of the way during the ceremony of the stolen marriage, he had invented this fruitless errand. When the clerk came back in the course of the day, and reported that no letter was lying for him at the post-office at Tello, the man added, "And I've taken care not to mention to a soul, sir, where I have been, as you desired; neither will I." "Oh, thank you, but I don't in the least mind now whether you mention it or not," rejoined Frank, in the openness of his heart. For, his object attained, it did not matter to him if the whole world knew that he had sent the clerk to Tello.

Clerk Trim, naturally a silent man, had experienced no temptation to mention it, in spite of the release given him: but on this evening, talking with Blase Pellet of Tello, he chanced to say that he had been there not long ago. Mr. Blase expressed some surprise at this, knowing that journeys were rare events with the clerk; and then Trim mentioned what he had gone for: to inquire for a letter at the Tello post-office for Mr. Frank Raynor.

That was enough. And a great deal more than enough. Blase instantly jumped to the conclusion that it was through the Tello post-office that the correspondence with Rosaline was carried on. And perhaps it was not unnatural that he should think so. The scarcity of letters arriving for Frank at Trennach was accounted for now.

Forth he came, boiling and bursting, crossed the stile, and dropped down on the tree-stump, unable to get any farther. The very fact of the correspondence being carried on clandestinely made it more cruel for him. With his bitter indignation mingled a great deal of despair. In that one miserable moment he began to see that he might indeed lose Rosaline. To lose her would have been anguish unspeakable; but to see another gain her was simply torment—and that other the detested gentleman, Frank Raynor. Blase Pellet had not a very clear idea of social distinctions, and he saw no particular incongruity in Frank's making her his wife.

"I've kept quiet as yet about that past night's work," said Mr. Pellet to himself, "but I'll speak now. I kept quiet for her sake, knowing what pain it would bring her; not for his; and because—"

"Well, any way," he resumed, after the long pause which succeeded his sudden break-off, "I must feel my way in it. If I could only drive him away from Cornwall for good, that would be enough; and then I'd draw in again. I heard him tell old Float that he meant to be off to London soon and settle there: let him go, and leave me and Rose and these parts alone. I'll help to start him there; and when he's gone I'll keep silent again. But now—how much will it be safe to say?—and *what* can I say?—and how can I set about it?"

Leaning forward, his hands placed on his knees, pressing them almost to pain, his eyes fixed on the opposite hedge, he went on with his thoughts. Blase Pellet was of an extremely concentrative nature: he could revolve and debate doubts and difficulties in his own mind, until he saw his way to bringing them out straight in the end, just as patiently and successfully as a Cambridge student will work out a problem in mathematics. But the difficulty Blase was trying to solve now was not an easy one.

"I *can't* say I saw it," debated he. "I can't say I heard it. If I did, people would ask five hundred questions as to where I was, and how it came about, and why I did not give the alarm—and I might have to tell all. I don't care to do that. I won't do it, unless I'm forced. Let him go away and leave her alone hereafter, and he shall get off scot-free for me. If I told of him, I should have to tell of her—that she was present—and she wouldn't like it; neither should I, for I'd be sorry to bring pain and exposure on her. She ought to have denounced him at the time—and she was a regular simpleton for not doing it: but still it would not be pleasant for me to be the one to complain that she was there and witnessed it all. No, no: I may not say I know *that*: I dare not say I was a witness myself. I must find some other way."

The other way seemed to be very far off. Mr. Pellet took his eyes from the hedge, and his hands from his knees; but only to fix them on the same places again. The stump of the tree was as uneasy a seat as its once green and flourishing topmost bough must have been, to judge by the restlessness that was upon him as he sat there.

"Could I say I dreamt it?" cried he, suddenly, ceasing his shuffling, and holding his head bolt upright. "*Could* I? I don't see any other way. Let's think it out a bit."

The thinking out took a tolerably long time yet, and Mr. Pellet did not seem altogether to like his idea. It was very nearly dark when he at length rose from the stump, sighing heavily.

"I must be uncommonly cautious," said he. "But it's just one of those ticklish things that admit of no openings but one. If Rosaline got to know that I saw—and told—she'd just fling me over for ever. I think a word or two of suspicion will be enough to drive him away, and that's all I want."

Now, in the main, Blase Pellet was not a hard-hearted or vindictive young man. His resentment against Frank Raynor arose from jealousy. Even that resentment, bitter though it was, he did not intend, or wish, to gratify to anything like its full extent. Believing that certain testimony of his could place Frank's neck in jeopardy, he might surely be given credit for holding his tongue. It is true that his caution arose from mixed motives: the dread of exasperating or in any way compromising Rosaline; the dislike to mixing himself up with the doings of that past night; and the genuine horror of bringing any man to so dire a punishment, even though that man were Frank Raynor.

Pondering upon these various doubts and difficulties, and failing to feel reassured upon them in his own mind—or rather upon the result if he moved in the matter—Mr. Pellet went slowly home through the dark and deserted street; and ascended straight to his chamber, which was an attic in the roof. There, he came to an anchor by the side of his low bed in much the same musing attitude that he had sat on the tree-stump, and "thought it out" again.

"Yes, it must be a dream," he decided at length, beginning to take off his coat preparatory to retiring. "There is no other way. I must not say I was there and saw it—they'd turn round upon me and cry, Why did you not tell at the time?—and what could I answer? Moreover, I can't, and I won't bring in Rosaline's name—which I should have to do if I stated the truth outright. But I can say I dreamt that Bell is lying at the bottom of the shaft; and keep up the commotion for a short while. They can't turn round on me for *that*. Folks do dream, as all the world knows."

With this final resolve, Mr. Blase Pellet retired to bed, to dream real dreams instead of inventing them.

As THE DAYS WENT ON at The Mount, the lovers' meetings became more rare. Far from being able to steal out every evening, Margaret found that she could hardly get out at all. She was virtually a prisoner, as far as her evening's liberty was concerned. Either she had to remain in, reading to Lydia, or playing cards with her, or else Mrs. St. Clare would have her in the drawing-room. Upon only half a movement of Daisy's towards the open glass-doors, Mrs. St. Clare would say: "You cannot go out in the evening air, Daisy: I shall have you ill next."

Evening after evening Frank Raynor betook himself to the grounds about The Mount, and lingered in their wilderness, waiting for Daisy. Evening after evening he had to return as he came, without having seen her. But one evening, when his patience was exhausted, and he had taken the first step for departure, Daisy came flying through the trees and fell into his arms.

"I was determined to come," she said, with a nervous catching of the breath. "I am watched, Frank; I am perpetually hindered. Mamma has just gone to her room with a headache, and I ran out. Oh, Frank, this cannot go on. I have so wanted to see you."

"It has been uncommonly hard, I can tell you, Daisy, to come here, one evening after another, and to have to go back as I came."

"This is the *first* opportunity I have had. It is indeed, Frank. And if that Tabitha should come prying into the drawing-room, as I know she will, and finds me gone out of it, I don't care. No, I don't."

He took her upon his arm and they paced together as formerly. The moon was bright to-night, and flickered through the leaves on to Daisy's head.

"Of course this cannot go on," observed Frank, in assent to what she had just said. "I should make a move at once, but for one thing."

"What sort of move?"

"Leaving Trennach. The reason I have not done so, is this, Daisy. In speaking again the other morning to my uncle, telling him that I must go to London, he made no further opposition to it: only, he begged me to remain with him until Edina returned—"

"Where is she going?" interrupted Daisy.

"To Bath. On a week or ten days' visit to Major and Mrs. Raynor. Daisy, I should not *like* to leave my uncle alone; he is not well enough to be left; and therefore I will stay as he wishes. But as soon as Edina is back again, I will go to London, and see about our future home."

"Yes," said Daisy. "Yes."

She spoke rather absently. Indeed, in spite of the first emotion, she appeared to be less lively than usual; more preoccupied. The fact was, she wanted to ask Frank a question or two, and did not know how to do it.

"Edina goes to-morrow," he resumed. "She intends to be back in a week's time; but I give her a day or two longer, for I know how unwilling they always are at Spring Lawn to let her come away. After that, I wind up with the doctor, and go to London. And it will not be very long then, Daisy, before I return to claim you. I shall soon get settled, once I am on the spot and looking out: the grass will not grow under my feet. It won't take above a week or two."

How sanguine he was! Not a shadow of doubt rested on his mind that the "week or two" would see him well established. Daisy did not answer. Had Frank chanced to turn his head as they walked, he would have seen how white her face was.

It was a simple question that she wished to ask. And yet, she could not ask it. Her dry and quivering lips refused to frame the words. "Were you so very intimate with Rosaline Bell?—and did you really love her?" Easy words they seemed to say; but Daisy could not get them out in her terrible emotion.

And so, they parted, and she had not spoken. For the hour was late already, and she feared to remain out longer. And Frank went home unsuspecting and unconscious.

It was on the following morning that certain rumours were afloat in Trennach. They had arisen the previous day: at least, two or three people professed to have then heard them. The miners congregated in groups to discuss the news; Float the chemist and other tradesmen stood at their shop-doors, exchanging words on the subject with the passers-by. It was said that Josiah Bell was lying in the Bottomless Shaft. Instead of having walked off in some mysterious manner, to return some day as mysteriously—as his wife believed—he was lying dead in that deep pit on the Bare Plain.

But—whence arose these rumours? what was their foundation? No one could tell. Just as other unaccountable rumours that float about us and are whispered from one to another in daily intercourse, it seemed that none could trace their source. "They say so." Yes, but who are "they"?

This same morning was the morning of Edina's departure for the neighbourhood of Bath. Frank was about to drive her to the railway-station. The doctor's gig was already at the door, the small trunk strapped on behind: for she never encumbered herself with much luggage. Frank was in the surgery, busying himself until she appeared, and talking with his uncle, when the door opened, and Ross the overseer came in. He had not been well lately, and came occasionally to the surgery for advice.

"Have you heard this new tale they've got hold of now, doctor?" asked he, whilst Dr. Raynor was questioning him about his symptoms. "It's a queer one."

"I have heard no tale," said the doctor. "What is it?"

"That the missing man is lying at the bottom of the old shaft on the Plain."

"What missing man?"

"Josiah Bell."

A moment's startled pause; a rush of red to his brow; and then Frank spoke up hastily.

"What an utter absurdity! Who says so?"

"It is being said among the men," replied Ross, turning towards him. "They can talk of nothing else this morning."

The colour was receding from Frank's face, leaving it whiter than usual.

"Bell at the bottom of the shaft!" exclaimed Dr. Raynor. "But why are they saying this? Who says it?"

Ross pointed to the groups of men in the street, some of whom were in view of the window. "All of them, doctor. They are talking of nothing else."

"What are their grounds for saying this?"

"I haven't got to them yet. I don't think they know themselves."

Since the first hasty words, Frank had remained silent, apparently paying attention to his physic-bottles. He spoke again now in a sharp, grating tone; which was very unusual in him, and therefore noticeable.

"It is not likely that there are any grounds for it. I wonder, Ross, you can come here and repeat such nonsense!"

"The place is buzzing with it; that's all I know," replied Ross, rather sulkily, as he went out. He could never bear to be found fault with.

Dr. Raynor followed him to the door. After glancing up and down the street at the men collected there, he returned to the surgery.

"It is evident that something or other is exciting them," he observed to Frank. "I wonder what can have given rise to the report?"

"Some folly or other, Uncle Hugh. It will soon die away again."

Dr. Raynor stood near the window, his eyes fixed on the outer scenes, his mind far away. Frank, who had made an end of his physic, stood buttoning his coat.

"I have never believed anything but the worst, since Bell's disappearance," said the doctor. "Others have expected him to return: I never have. Where he may be, I know not: whether accident, or some other ill, may have chanced to him, I know not: but I entertain no hope that the man is still living."

There was a pause. "Have you any reason for saying that, sir?" asked Frank, somewhat hesitatingly.

"No reason in the world," replied Dr. Raynor. "At least, no sufficient reason. I am an old man, Frank, and you are a young one; and what I am about to say you will probably laugh at. I did not like Bell's look when we last saw him."

Frank was at a loss to understand: and said so.

"I did not like that grey look on his face," continued the doctor. "Do you remember it?"

"Yes, I do, Uncle Hugh. It was very peculiar. Sometimes when a person is ill, or going to be ill, the face turns quite grey from loss of colour, and we say to them, You are looking grey this morning. But the shade on Bell's face was quite different from that."

"Just so," assented the doctor. "And it takes a practised eye—or, I would rather say, an eye possessing innate discernment—to distinguish the one shade from the other: but it is unmistakable. The grey hue on Bell's face I have observed three times before during my life, in three different men; and in each case it was the forerunner of death."

Dr. Raynor's voice had become solemn. Frank, far from laughing, seemed to catch it as he spoke.

"Do you mean the forerunner of fatal illness, sir?"

"Only in one of the cases, Frank. The man had been ill for a long time, but his death was quite sudden and unexpected. The other two had no illness whatever: they died without it."

"From accident?"

"Yes, from accident. I should not avow as much to any one but you, Frank, and run the risk of being ridiculed: but I tell you that when I saw Bell come in that morning, with that peculiar grey on his face, it shocked me. I believed then, as firmly as I ever believed anything in my life, that the man's hours were numbered."

Frank neither stirred nor spoke. Just for the moment he might have been taken for a statue.

"Where Bell is, or where he went to, I know not; but from the time I first heard of his disappearance, I feared the man was dead," added Dr. Raynor. "The probability was, I thought, that he had fallen down in some fit, which had been, or would be, fatal. And I confess the marvel to me throughout has been that his body could not be found. If this rumour be true—that he is lying at the bottom of the used-up shaft—the marvel is accounted for."

"But—is it likely to be true, sir?" cried Frank, in remonstrance.

"Very likely, I think," replied the doctor. "Though I cannot imagine what should bring him *there*."

"Are you ready, Frank?" asked Edina, appearing in her grey plaid shawl and plain straw bonnet. "Good-bye, papa. I have been looking for you."

Dr. Raynor stooped to kiss his daughter quietly: he was not a demonstrative man. Hester was at the door: the boy held the horse's head. Frank helped Edina in; and, taking the reins, followed her.

"You will not stay too long, Edina?"

"Only the eight or nine days I am going for, papa."

They drove on. It was a lovely summer's day; and Edina, who enjoyed the sunshine, the balmy atmosphere, the blue sky, the waving trees, sat still and looked about her. Frank was unusually silent. In point of fact, the rumour he had just heard, touching Bell, had almost dumfounded him. Edina might have wondered at his prolonged silence, but that she was deep in thought herself.

"Frank," she began, as they neared the station, "I wish you would answer me a question."

He glanced quickly round at her, dread in his heart. Did the question concern the Bottomless Shaft?

"Do you know whether anything is wrong with papa?"

It was a great relief; and Frank, ever elastic, brightened up at once.

"Wrong with him? In what way, Edina?"

"With his health. In the last few weeks he seems to have changed so very much: sometimes he seems quite like a broken-down old man. Don't you see that he is ill, Frank?"

"Yes, I am sure he is," replied Frank, readily. "But I don't know what can be the matter with him."

"It seems to me that he wants rest."

"He has more rest than he used to have, Edina; I save him all I can. There are some crotchety old patients who *will* have him, you know."

"I hope it is nothing serious! Do you think he will soon be better?"

Frank touched the horse with the whip: which perhaps made his excuse for not answering. "Had Uncle Hugh been in his usual health, I should have left him before this," he observed. "But I want to see him stronger first. He might chance to get some fellow in my place who would not be willing to take most of the work on his own shoulders."

"Left him to set up for yourself, do you mean, Frank?"

"To be sure. I ought to, you know," he added, with a slight laugh.

She understood. It was the first time Frank's stolen marriage had been alluded to by either of them, since the day it took place.

"How are you getting on, Frank?" she asked, in low tones, as he drew up outside the station. "You and Daisy?"

"Not getting on at all. She is there, and I am elsewhere. Now and then I see her for five minutes in their garden; but that's pretty nearly stopped now. Until last night, she has been unable to escape from the house for I don't know how long. Of course it is not a lively condition of things."

"It seems to me to be just the same with you as though you had not been married."

"It is precisely the same, Edina."

XV

LOOKING OUT FOR EDINA

In the bow-window of the shabby dining-room at Spring Lawn stood Major Raynor, his wife and children. They were on the tiptoe of expectation, waiting for Edina. A vehicle of some kind could be discerned at a distance; opinions differed as to whether it was a fly or not. The evening sunbeams fell athwart the green lawn and on the flowers, whose perfume mingled with that of the hay, lying in cocks in the adjoining field.

"I am sure it *is* a fly," cried little Kate, shading her eyes that she might see the better.

"And I tell you it is not," retorted Alfred. "That thing, whatever it is, is coming at a snail's pace, like a waggon. Do you suppose Edina would come in a waggon, little stupid?"

"I don't think it is a waggon," said Major Raynor, who had the aid of an opera-glass. "It has two horses, at any rate. The driver is whipping them up, too: and see—it is coming along now at a smart pace. I should say it is a fly."

Every now and then the vehicle lost itself behind trees and hedges and turnings from the temporary glimpses they caught, it seemed to have something like a cart-load of luggage upon its roof. Which was extremely unlikely to belong to Edina.

On it came: its rumble could now be heard, though it was no longer visible. All ears were bent to it: and when it had reached the narrow avenue that led to the garden it was heard to turn off the road and rattle down.

"It is a fly," spoke Alice, triumphantly. "And it is bringing Edina."

Charles strolled out to the gate. Away tore the children after him, shouting Edina's name in every variety of voice. Major and Mrs. Raynor followed, and were just in time to witness the drawing-up of the vehicle.

It was not a fly. It was a large, lumbering, disreputable conveyance that plied daily between Bath and sundry villages, and was called Tuppin's van. Disreputable as compared with a genteel, exclusive Bath fly that carried gentlefolk. This was used only by the lower classes; people who knew nothing about "society."

Nevertheless, Edina was in it. Old Tuppin, throwing the reins across his horses, had left his box to go round to the door, which opened at the back like an omnibus. A sudden silence had fallen on the children. Edina got out. And Tuppin, touching his hat to Major and Mrs. Raynor, selected her trunk from the luggage on the roof, and placed it inside the gate. Three outside male passengers watched the proceedings.

Edina put a shilling into Tuppin's hand. He thanked her, ascended to his seat, touched his horses, turned them round, and drove up the avenue with a clatter. Edina was smothered with greetings and kisses on the lawn.

"But how could you come in that van, Edina?"

"There were very few carriages at the station, Charley. The only one I could see wanted to charge six shillings. This van—but I call it an omnibus—was waiting for a passenger, and I took advantage of it."

"It is Tuppin's van," persisted Charley. "No one ever travels by it, except servants."

"No one with a full pocket, perhaps," smiled Edina, with her imperturbable good-humour. "I paid a shilling only, and came very comfortably."

"There was an old woman inside as well as you, Edina," cried Alfred.

"Yes. It was she who came by the same train, and got out at the station. She is housekeeper, she told me, in some family near here."

Edina caught up little Bobby as she spoke, and the matter dropped. But an impression remained on the minds of the elder children that Edina was more stingy than ever, or she would never have travelled in Tuppin's van when there was a fly to be had for the hiring. Certainly Edina's were saving ways. Contrasted with their own reckless ones, they appeared "stingy." But the time was to come when they would learn how mistaken was the impression, and how they had misjudged her.

"And how are you getting on, Uncle Francis?" asked Edina.

"Going backwards, my dear. What with no money, so to say, coming in, and everything going out—"

The major stopped for want of adequate words to express the position. Edina resumed.

"But you have some money coming in, Uncle Francis. You have your income."

"But what is it, my dear, as compared with the expenses? Besides, to tell you the truth, it is always forestalled. There always seems to be such a lot to pay."

MRS. HENRY WOOD

"How uneasy it must make you!"

"Not a bit of it," spoke the major, cheerily. "With Eagles' Nest in prospective, it does not matter at all, Talking of Eagles' Nest, Edina, have you heard anything of your aunt Ann lately?"

"We never do hear from her, Uncle Francis. Papa writes to her sometimes, and I write, but we never receive any answer."

"I fear she is on her last legs."

The major spoke solemnly, with quite a rueful expression of countenance. Badly though he wanted the money his sister's death would bring, and estranged from him though she was, he could not and did not think of it in any spirit but a sad one.

"I have heard from London two or three times lately, Edina, from my lawyer: John Street, you know. And in each letter he has given me a very poor account of Mrs. Atkinson. Her death, poor soul, must be very near."

It had been nearer than the major, or even his lawyer, anticipated. She was dead even then. At the very moment the major was talking of her she was lying dead at Eagles' Nest. Had been dead three or four hours.

The news reached them in the morning. A letter was delivered at Spring Lawn, and was carried up, as usual, to the major in bed. No one took any particular notice of the letter; as a rule, the major's letters were only applications from creditors, and could not be supposed to interest the household. Mrs. Raynor was seated at breakfast with her three elder children and Edina, when a sudden bumping on the floor above, and shouting in the major's voice, considerably startled them.

"Good gracious! he must have fallen out of bed!" cried poor Mrs. Raynor.

"And upset his coffee," said Charley, with a laugh.

But it was nothing of the sort. The major had jumped up to dress in hot haste, and was calling out to them between whiles. He had received news of the death of his sister, Mrs. Atkinson; and was going up forthwith to Eagles' Nest.

"Shall I go too, papa?" asked Charley.

"I don't mind, my boy. I suppose we can scrape up enough money for the tickets."

Of course the children were all in commotion. Alfred marched up to the nursery, and drew the blinds down.

"What is that for, Master Alfred?" demanded nurse, who was dressing Kate's doll; Kate herself standing by to watch the process.

"Ah, you don't know," replied Alfred, bursting with impatience to deliver his news, yet withholding it tantalizingly.

"No, I don't," said the nurse, who was often at war with Alfred. "You will have the goodness, sir, to draw the blinds up again, and leave them alone."

"I choose to have them down, nurse."

"You will choose to walk out of my nursery in a minute or two," retorted the nurse. "Wait till I've fixed this frock on. It would be a precious good thing if you were at school, Master Alfred!"

"But I am not going to school," cried Alfred, in irrepressible delight, the good news refusing to be kept down any longer. "I'm going somewhere else. Old Aunt Atkinson's dead, and papa has come into Eagles' Nest and a large fortune, Madam Nurse! And he is going up there so-day; and Charley's going; and we shall go directly. Eagles' Nest! Won't I have a pony to myself!—and a double-barrelled gun!—and a whole shopful of sweet-stuff!"

Vaulting over little Robert, who sat on the floor staring at him, he caught Kate in the exuberance of his anticipations, and whirled her round until she was giddy. Then, attempting a leap across the table, he caught his foot on the edge; and boy, table, and a heavy pincushion that was on it, called a "doctor," all came down together. The noise was something wonderful. It brought up Edina and Alice.

"Whatever is it, nurse?"

"Only one of Master Alfred's freaks, ma'am. He thought he would leap over the table."

Alfred was holding his handkerchief to his nose. He would not acknowledge that it bled.

"We thought the house was falling," said Alice. "It was worse than papa. He gave us the first fright."

"And all because he has come into some money, he says, Miss Raynor," put in the nurse, who was angrily picking up the table, "and the money is to buy him everything under the sun."

"Unseemly boasting, Alfred!" cried Edina. "Had you no thought for your poor aunt?"

"I don't see why I should have, Edina," returned the boy, boldly. "I never saw Aunt Atkinson in my life: why should I pretend to be sorry for her?"

"I never said you were to pretend anything, child. Sorrow is real enough, and perhaps, Alfred, you will find that it comes to you often

MRS. HENRY WOOD

enough in life, without assuming it. But there is a great difference between feigning sorrow, and being especially elated. As to the fortune, it may not make very much difference to you in any way."

"Oh, won't it though, Edina! Charley's not going to get it all."

"About the blinds, ma'am? Are they to be kept down?"

"I don't know, nurse. I will ask Mrs. Raynor."

"What an old croaker she is!" exclaimed Alfred, as Edina left the room.

"A bit of one," assented Alice.

"That she is not, Miss Alice," said the nurse. "If you were all only half as good as Miss Edina Raynor!"

When the sum necessary for the journey came to be ascertained, it was found that the major and all his household could not scrape it together: though it sounds like a ridiculous fact. Edina came forward with help; and so it was managed.

"I trust it will be all right, Uncle Francis," whispered Edina, earnestly, as she crossed the lawn with the major when he was departing.

"Right in what way, my dear?"

"That you will inherit Eagles' Nest."

"Oh, that *is* all right," replied the major. "My letter tells me so. Everything is willed to me. Poor Ann! Good-bye, my dear: be sure you stay until we return. What a hot walk we shall have into Bath!" added the major, taking off his hat and rubbing his brow in anticipation. "But there's no help for it; no conveyance of any kind at hand. I should be glad even of Tuppin's van this morning."

Edina stood at the gate, and watched them up the avenue, Charley carrying the black portmanteau. In her steadfast eyes there lay a certain expression of *rest*. With her habit of looking forward to the dark side of things as well as to the bright, Edina had never felt quite assured upon the point of the major's inheritance: it was welcome, indeed, to hear that this was placed beyond doubt. What would that helpless, improvident family have done without it!

A hand stole itself within Edina's arm. She turned her soft dark eyes, to see Mrs. Raynor; who looked, as usual, very mild about the face, and very limp about the dress. The children had rushed indoors again, and were restlessly running from room to room in the excitement of their new prospects, discussing the wonders that would become theirs, now wealth and greatness had fallen upon them. Their minds were picturing the future residence at Eagles' Nest all gold, and glitter, and gladness: life was to be as one long Lord Mayor's day.

"It is a great strain removed, Edina!"

"What is, Mary?" For Edina had never called this young wife of her uncle's "Aunt." It had been "Mary" from the first. They were not so very many years removed from one another in age.

"All the distress and contriving about money. I have never said much to you, for where was the use; but you don't know what a strain it has been, what shifts we have been put to."

"I do," said Edina. "I can only too readily imagine it. For many years the same strain lay on me and papa: at Trennach, and before we went to Trennach. It is removed in a degree, for the necessity for saving does not exist as it did, but we are careful still. I learnt economy in my pinafores, Mary. Your children could not understand my coming here in Tuppin's van yesterday, when I might have hired a fly: but it saved five shillings. Papa urges economy upon me still, and practises it himself. I think he does so for my sake."

"Ah! what *could* you do, Edina, if anything happened to your father, and you were left without the means to live?"

Edina laughed at the consternation expressed in Mrs. Raynor's voice. To this really helpless woman, the being left without means seemed the very greatest of all earthly calamities.

"I should have no fear for myself, Mary. I could go out as useful companion; or governess; or even as housekeeper. Few places where I could be practically useful would come amiss to me."

"I am sure of that," said Mrs. Raynor.

They were strolling across the grass-plat arm-in-arm, Mrs. Raynor stooping to pluck a flower here and there: a June rose; a pink; a sprig of syringa. Silence had supervened. Mrs. Raynor was puzzling her brains over the children's mourning: what would, and what would not be necessary, and how it would all get made.

"What are you going to do with Charles?" suddenly asked Edina.

"With Charles! I'm sure I don't know. Why, Edina?"

"It is so sad to see a fine young fellow, as he is, with all his wits and capabilities about him, spending his days in idleness. I had meant to talk to Uncle Francis about it to-day. I do think, Mary, it has been a great mistake."

"Well, dear, perhaps it has," replied the equable woman. "But you see, it takes so much money to bring young men on in life: and we had no money to spare."

"Then, where money is wanting, they should be 'brought on' in some way that does not need money," rejoined Edina. "Charles has been absolutely idle; and only for the want of proper direction. Even Frank saw the error. When he returned to us the last time from his short stay here, he said what a pity it was."

"Charles wanted to be a barrister, I fancy. But the major could not take any steps in it without money."

"Then I would place him in a lawyer's office as a temporary clerk, that he might be acquiring some knowledge of law while he waited."

"I declare we never thought of that," cried Mrs. Raynor. "Perhaps Charley would not have liked it, though."

"Perhaps not. I should have done it, for all that, had I been Uncle Francis. Nothing in the world is so bad to a young man as indulging in idle habits. Has Charles been reading law books?"

"No; only novels," said Mrs. Raynor. "Oh, it will all be right, Edina, now that he has Eagles' Nest to look forward to. Of course, he could look forward to it before; but there was always the doubt when we should come into it. Suppose Mrs. Atkinson had lived to be a hundred? Some people do. Where should we all have been then? or even to eighty or ninety?"

"I'm sure I don't know," said Edina, smiling. "Suppose Uncle Francis should live to be a hundred, Mary? Where would Charley be in that case?"

"But, Edina, what would it matter? With a beautiful place like Eagles' Nest and means to keep it up, the children would always be sure of a home and of welcome there. It would be Charley's as much as ours—"

"Oh, mamma! What do you think? Papa has gone without his shaving-tackle, and without his boots!"

The salutation came from the children, who all came wildly rushing forth again. They had been visiting the major's dressing-room, and discovered that these indispensable articles had been left behind.

"They are his light summer boots, too; those with the long name," said Alice. "He cannot walk about much in any others."

"Dear, dear, dear!" lamented Mrs. Raynor. "He must have put on those tight, patched ones by mistake—and they always blister his heels. How will he manage to get to Bath?"

EAGLES' NEST WAS NOT LARGE, but it was one of the prettiest places in all Kent. A long, low, ancient house of grey stone, covered in places with ivy. Some of its old-fashioned mullioned casements had been replaced (many people said spoilt) by modern windows, opening to terraces, undulating lawns, and beds of brilliant flowers. Few old houses have so gay an appearance as this house had: perhaps owing to the new windows and to other alterations. The entrance-door was approached by three or four broad, low steps. Gothic casements of rich and blended colours threw their tints upon the tesselated hall. Rooms opened on either side: bright rooms, that had a very *home* look about them, and in which one felt that it would be a privilege to pass a great portion of one's life. The estate had been well kept up by Mrs. Atkinson. It was worth about two thousand a-year; but was still capable of much improvement.

When Major Raynor and his son arrived in the course of the afternoon, they were received by Mr. Street, the solicitor to the late Mrs. Atkinson. He was brother to Mr. Edwin Street, the acting partner in the Atkinson bank. John Street was the elder of the brothers; a man of sixty now, well known in London as a quiet and most respectable practitioner. He was reserved in manner; not at all what could be called "genial," and rather severe than benevolent; strictly just, but perhaps not generous.

As the fly that brought the major and his son from the nearest station rattled up, Mr. Street appeared at the hall-door: a little man in spectacles, with cold light eyes and very scanty hair.

"I am glad you have come, Major Raynor."

"And I'm sure I'm glad to see that you have," returned the major, cordially holding out his hand. "I might have found myself in a fog without you. I had your letter this morning."

"We received news of Mrs. Atkinson's death yesterday afternoon; her coachman was sent up with the tidings, and I wrote to you at once," observed Mr. Street. "As you are sole inheritor, excepting a few trifling legacies, and also executor, I thought it well, as I stated in my letter, that you should be here."

"Just so," said the major. "When did you arrive yourself?"

"I came down this morning."

"And I and Charley started off in a hurry to catch the ten-o'clock train—and I came away in my wrong boots—and Charley has been laughing at me. You don't know him, Street—my eldest son and heir. Charley, come here, sir, and be introduced to Mr. Street."

Charles Raynor had been looking out from the open window. He had never seen so pretty a place before as this one, lying under the June sunshine. Hay was being made here, just as it had been in Somerset: and the sweet smell came wafted to him on the summer breeze. The lawns were beautifully kept, the flowers were perfect; shrubs clustered around, trees waved above. In the distance was stretched out a beautiful landscape, than which nothing could be more charming. Close by, curled the blue smoke from the little village of Grassmere, hidden by trees from the view of Eagles' Nest. Surely in this spot man could find all that his heart desired Charley sighed as he turned to the call: the lad had a strong love for the beauties of nature.

"Had this been left to others instead of to ourselves, how I should envy them, now that I have seen it!" said Charles to himself. And he was not thinking then of any pecuniary return.

Mr. Street looked keenly at him. He saw a tall, slender, good-looking young man; who, in manner at least, appeared somewhat indifferent, not to say haughty.

"A proud young dandy, who thinks the world was made for him," decided the lawyer in his own mind.

"In any profession, young sir?" asked Mr. Street.

"Not yet," replied Charles. "I shall have, I expect, to go to college before thinking of one. If I think of one at all."

"Better enter one," said Mr. Street, shortly. "The pleasantest life is the one that has its regular occupation; the most miserable a life of idleness."

"That's true," put in the major. "Since I left the service, I have been like a fish out of water. Sometimes, before the day has well begun I wish it was ended, not knowing what to do with myself."

"Not many weeks ago, Mrs. Atkinson was talking to me about that very thing, major. She fancied you would have done better not to sell out."

"Ay; I've often said so myself. Poor Ann! I should like to have seen more of her. But she had her crotchets, you know, Street. Did she suffer much at the last, I wonder?"

"No, she went off quite easily, as one who is worn out. She is lying in the red room: I have been up to see her. A good woman; but, as you observe, major, crotchety on some points."

"Why, would you believe it, Street, she once thought of disinheriting me."

"I know it," replied the lawyer. "It was the year following her husband's death. And perhaps," he added, with as much of a smile as ever came to his lips, "you owe it to me that she did not do so."

"Indeed! How was that?"

"I received a letter from her, calling me here for the purpose, she said, of altering her will. Away I came, bringing the will with me—for I held one copy of it, as you may remember, Major Raynor, and you the other. 'I want to disinherit my brother,' were the first words she said to me; 'I shall leave Eagles' Nest to George Atkinson: I always wished him to have it.' Of course I asked her the why and the wherefore. 'Francis has affronted me, and he shall not inherit it,' was all the explanation I could get from her. Well, major, I talked to her, and brought her into a more reasonable frame of mind: and the result was, that I carried the original will back to town with me, unaltered."

"Poor Ann! poor Ann!" re-echoed the major.

"About the arrangements?" resumed Mr. Street. "If I can be of any use to you, major—"

"Why, you can be of every use," interrupted the major. "I don't know how to manage anything."

Mr. Street had brought the will down with him to-day, and it was thought right to open it at once. Major Raynor found that the recollection he had retained of its general contents was pretty accurate, excepting on one point. Eagles' Nest was left to him as it stood, with all its contents and appurtenances; and he was made residuary legatee: therefore, whatever moneys might have accumulated or been invested in shares or stock, would become his, after all claims and legacies were paid. The one point on which his memory had not served him, regarded the bequest to Frank Raynor. Instead of its being "among the thousands," as he had confidently believed, and led Frank to believe, it was only among the hundreds. And not very advanced in them, either. Five hundred pounds, neither more nor less. The major looked at the amount ruefully.

"I'm sure I can't tell how I came to fancy that it was so much more, Charley," said he. "I am very sorry. It will be a disappointment for Frank."

"But can't you make it up to him, father?" suggested Charles. "There must be a great deal of accumulated money, as Mr. Street says: you might spare Frank a little of it."

"Why, to be sure I can," heartily returned the major, his eyes beaming. "It did not strike me. But I should have thought of it myself, Charley, later on."

"A great deal of accumulated money, regarded from a moderate point of view," spoke the lawyer, in confirmation. "Mr. Timothy Atkinson left a fair sum behind him, the interest upon which must have been accumulating until now. And his widow did not, I am sure, live up to anything like the revenues of this estate."

"What is it all invested in?—where is it lying?" asked the major.

"We must see to that."

"But don't you know?"

"No. Mrs. Atkinson managed her monetary affairs herself, without reference to me. My brother knows all about everything, I dare say; but he is, and always has been, as close as wax."

"Perhaps the money is deposited with him?"

"I think not," said the lawyer. "I know he once, close though he is, said something to me to the effect that it was not. The securities, bonds and vouchers, and so forth, are no doubt lying in his hands."

The funeral took place, Mr. Street again coming down for the ceremony. He was accompanied by his brother, Mr. Edwin Street. Dr. Raynor had declined the invitation sent him: he was not well enough to undertake the long journey; and Frank could not be spared.

Some conversation occurred between the brothers, on the way down, about the above-mentioned securities; but the banker at once said they were not deposited with him. In the after-part of the day, when the funeral was over, Lawyer Street mentioned this to Major Raynor, and said they were no doubt "somewhere in the house."

A thorough search ensued: old Mrs. Atkinson's maid, an elderly and confidential attendant of many years, taking part in it. She showed them every possible place of security, locked and unlocked, in which such deeds could be placed. But no deeds were found.

"I still think they must be in your strong boxes at the bank," observed the lawyer to his brother, when he and Major Raynor returned to the room where they had left Mr. Edwin Street and Charles.

"But I assure you they are not," replied the banker, who bore a striking resemblance to his brother, and had the same cold manner. "When Mrs. Atkinson made her will, she lodged with us certain bonds of India Stock, just about sufficient to pay the legacies she bequeathed in that will when the time should come—as it has come now. She told me that she intended the stock to be applied to that purpose. We hold the bonds still; and the interest, which we have regularly received for her, has been added to her current account with us: but we hold no other securities."

"What an odd thing!" cried the major. "Where can they be?"

"When our second partner, Mr. Timothy Atkinson, died," continued the banker, "he left a certain sum in the bank to his wife's account, upon which she was to receive substantial interest. But about a year afterwards she withdrew this sum, and invested it elsewhere."

"Where? What in?"

"I cannot tell. I never knew. I understood from her that it was invested; but I knew no more. We have never had any money of hers since—excepting of course the current account, paid in from the revenues of this estate. And we hold no securities of hers, besides these Indian bonds that I have spoken of."

"Was the sum she withdrew a large one?" asked the major.

"It was between fourteen and fifteen thousand pounds."

"And she must have added ever so much to that," observed the lawyer. "She has not lodged her superfluous income with you?" he added to his brother.

"No. I have said so. We hold nothing but her current account. That has been replenished by her when necessary; but we have had nothing more. It is certainly strange where the vouchers for her property can be. I suppose," added the banker, more slowly, "she did not invest the money in some bubble scheme, and lose it?"

"The very same thought was crossing my mind," spoke his brother.

"But you don't think that probable, do you, Street?" cried Major Raynor, turning rather hot.

A pause ensued. Lawyer Street was evidently thinking out the probabilities. They waited, and watched him.

"I must confess that circumstances look suspicious," he said at length. "Else why so much secrecy?"

"Secrecy?"

"Yes. If Mrs. Atkinson placed the money in any well-known safe investment, why was she not open about it: get me to act for her, and lodge the securities at the bank? She did neither: she acted for herself—as we must suppose—and kept the transaction to herself. The inference is, that it was some wild-goose venture that she did not care to speak about. Women are so credulous."

"What a gloomy look-out!" put in the major.

"Oh, well, we have only been glancing at possibilities, you know," observed Mr. Street. "I dare say the securities will be found—and the money also."

"Right, John," assented the banker. "Had Mrs. Atkinson found her money was being lost, she would assuredly have set you to work to recover it. I think we may safely assume that, Major Raynor!"

XVI

Commotion

B e sure you stay until we return," had been the charge left to Edina
Raynor by her uncle. But the major found himself detained longer
than he had expected, and she went away from Spring Lawn without
again seeing him or Charles.

During the short period of her absence from Trennach—nine days—
her father had changed so much for the worse that she started when
she saw him. As he came out of his house to welcome her, all Edina's
pulses stood still for a moment, and then coursed on with a bound. In a
gradual, wasting illness, not very apparent to those around, it is only on
such an occasion as this that its progress can be judged of.

"Papa, you have been ill!"

"True, Edina, but I am mending a little now."

"Why did you not send for me?"

"Nay, my dear, there was not any necessity for that."

A substantial tea-table had been spread, and in a very few minutes
Edina was presiding at it; her travelling things off, her soft brown hair
smoothed, her countenance wearing its usual cheerful gravity. Not a
gravity that repelled: one that insensibly attracted, for it spoke of its
owner's truth, and faith, and earnestness, of her goodwill to all about
her. Sitting there, dispensing cups of tea to the doctor and Frank, she
was ready to hear the news of all that had transpired in the village
during her absence.

Almost the first item that greeted her was the stir about Josiah Bell,
of which she had previously heard nothing. It had not subsided in the
least, but rather increased: the man so long missing was now supposed
to be lying at the bottom of the deep shaft. But the supposition could
only be traced back to a very insecure source indeed: nothing more than
a dream of Mr. Blase Pellet's.

"A dream!" exclaimed Edina, in the midst of her wonder.

"So Pellet says," replied Dr. Raynor.

"But, papa, can there be any foundation for it? I mean for the fact,
not the dream."

"The very question we all asked when the rumour arose, Edina. At

MRS. HENRY WOOD

first it could not be traced to any source at all; there was the report, but whence it came seemed a mystery. At last, by dint of close and patient investigation, chiefly on the part of Float the publican, it was traced to Blase Pellet, and he said he had dreamt it."

"Then, after all, it has no real foundation," cried Edina.

"None but that. I questioned Pellet myself, asking him how he came to spread such a report about. He replied that he did not spread the report that Bell was lying there, only that he dreamt he was there."

"I should have thought Blase Pellet a very unlikely man to have dreams, papa, and to relate them."

"So should I," assented the doctor, significantly. "So unlikely, that I cannot help suspecting he did not have this one."

Frank Raynor, who had risen and crossed to the window, as if attracted by something in the street, half turned at this remark, but immediately turned back again. Edina looked inquiringly at her father.

"I could not help fancying, as I listened to him, that Pellet was saying it with a purpose," observed the doctor. "His manner was peculiar. If I may so describe it—shuffling."

"I scarcely understand you, papa. You think he did not have the dream? That he only said he had it; and said it to answer some purpose of his own?"

"Just so, Edina."

"But what could be his purpose?"

"Ah, there I am at fault. We may discover that later. If he did say it with a purpose, I conclude it will not end here."

"Well, it sounds rather strange altogether," observed Edina. "Frank, do you mean to let your tea get quite cold?"

Frank Raynor returned to his place. He drank his tea, but declined to eat, and began to speak of Mrs. Atkinson's will.

"Did you hear any particulars about it, Edina?"

"No," replied Edina. "Excepting the one fact that she did not make a second will. There were doubts upon the point, you know."

"Uncle Francis never entertained any doubt about it, Edina; and he was the best judge, I think, of what his sister would or would not do. I am very glad, though, for his and Charley's sake."

"For all their sakes," added Edina.

"I rather wonder we have not heard from him," resumed Frank. "The funeral took place three or four days ago."

"You were not able to go to it, papa?" said Edina.

"No, child. Neither could Frank be spared. It would have taken three days, you see, to go and return comfortably."

Rising from the tea-table as soon as he could make a decent excuse for it, for he had no business calls on his time this evening, Frank set off on his usual walk to The Mount. On five evenings, since Edina left, had he so gone; but never with any success: not once had Daisy come out to him. She was being watched closer than ever.

"And I suppose I shall have my walk for nothing this evening also!" thought Frank, as he plucked a wild-rose from a fragrant roadside hedge. "This shall not go on long: but I should like to present myself to Mrs. St. Clare with an assured sum to start us in life. I wonder Uncle Francis does not write! He must know I am anxious—if he thinks about it at all. Up to his ears in his new interests, he forgets other people's."

Fortune favoured Frank this evening. As he approached the outer gate of The Mount, he saw Daisy standing at it, very much to his surprise.

"Mamma's lawyer has come over on business, and she is shut up with him," began Daisy, her eyes dancing with delight. "She told me to go up to Lydia, but Lydia is asleep, and I came out here."

"I have wanted to see you so much, Daisy," said Frank, as he gave her his arm, and they passed under the broad elm-trees. "My aunt, Mrs. Atkinson, is dead."

"We saw it in the papers," answered Daisy.

"It is from her that I expect money, you know. Every day, I look for a letter from my uncle Francis, telling me what sum it is that I inherit. And then I shall present myself to your mother. I have so longed to tell you this."

"I have longed to see you," returned Daisy, her pulses beating wildly with various and very mixed feelings, her face flushing and paling. "I—I—I want to ask you something, Frank."

"Ask away, my love," was his reply. But he noticed her emotion.

"Perhaps you will not answer me?"

"Indeed I will, Daisy. Why not?"

"It is about—Rosaline Bell." She could scarcely get the words out for agitation.

Frank was startled. It was quite evident that he was unprepared for any such topic. It seemed to *frighten* him. Else why that sudden change of countenance, that sudden dropping of Daisy's arm? Her heart fell.

MRS. HENRY WOOD

"What of her?" asked Frank, quite sharply. For in truth he believed Daisy was about to question him, not of Rosaline herself, but of that mysterious rumour connected with her father and the Bottomless Shaft; and it grated terribly on all his nerves.

"I see it is true," gasped Daisy. "Oh! why did you marry *me?*"

"What is true?" returned Frank, unpleasantly agitated.

"That you—that you—were fond of Rosaline Bell. You loved her all along. Before you loved me!"

The charge was so very different from what he had been fearing, that Frank felt for the moment bewildered: bewildered in the midst of his inexpressible relief. He stood still, turned so that Daisy faced him, and gazed into her eyes.

"*What* is that you say, my dear? I really do not understand."

Daisy shook and shivered, but did not speak.

"That I love Rosaline Bell? I never loved her. What in the name of wonder put such an idea into your head?"

For answer Daisy burst into tears. "She—she was so beautiful!"

"Beautiful! Of course she is beautiful. And I admired her beauty, Daisy, if it comes to that, as much as other people did. But as to loving Rosaline Bell, that is a mistake. I never felt a spark of love for her. What a goose you must be, Daisy! And why on earth should you have taken up the fancy just now?"

Daisy sobbed too much to answer. She almost believed what he said, for no doubt lay in his earnest tone, and she suffered herself to be soothed. She would have quite believed it but for Frank's signs of discomfiture at the introduction of the girl's name. Frank held her to him as they walked under the trees, and kissed her tear-stained face from time to time.

"You need not doubt my love, Daisy. That at least is yours."

They parted more hopefully than usual, for Frank assured her it could not be above a day or two ere he claimed her openly; and Daisy felt that she might believe him in all respects; and she resolutely flung her jealousy to the winds.

"Fare you well, my darling. A short time now—we may count it by hours—and this tantalizing life will be over."

He went home by way of the Bare Plain. And by so doing—and it was not very often now that he chose that route—fell into an adventure he had not bargained for. Round and about the Bottomless Shaft had collected a crowd of men, who were making very much of a commotion.

It appeared that the rumours, touching Josiah Bell, had this night reached what might be called a climax. Miners had gone off from various quarters to the alleged scene of Mr. Blase's dream, and were plunging into the mystery con amore. As many as could press around the pit's mouth were holding on one to another for safety and bending dangerously over it: as if by that means they could solve the problem of who and what might be lying within its depths. Others stood at a distance, momentarily taking their pipes out of their mouths to make their free comments. Mrs. Bell, hearing of the stir, had tied a yellow silk square (once Josiah's Sunday-going handkerchief) over her cap, and come out to make one of the throng. It was a very light, hot night, daylight scarcely departed, and the western sky bright with a pale amber. The rugged faces of the miners and the red glow from their pipes, coupled with the commotion that stirred them, made up a strange scene.

"Are you here, Mrs. Bell?" cried Frank, as he discerned her on the outskirts of the crowd. "What is the matter?"

"There's nothing the matter," interposed Blase Pellet. And Frank turned on his heel to face the speaker in the moment's impulse, for he had not known that he was there. "What the plague all the town has come out for like this, I can't think. Let them mind their own business."

"But we consider that it is our business, don't you see, Blase," put in Andrew Float, in his civil way. "Our poor vanished soe is either lying there in aal they stones and ashes, or he is not; and we'd like to make sure which it be."

"Well, then, he is *not* there," returned Blase: and he disappeared amidst the throng.

"Has anything fresh arisen?" inquired a quiet voice at this juncture— that of Dr. Raynor—addressing both Frank and Mrs. Bell, who were standing side by side. The doctor, observing from his window a number of people, evidently in excitement, making for the Bare Plain, had come forth himself to learn what the movement meant.

"I can't find out that there's anything fresh, sir," was the dame's answer. "Amid such confusion one don't easily get to the bottom of things. Andrew Float says 'twas just a thought that took a few of 'em as they sat talking of Bell at the Golden Shaft—that they'd come off and have a look down the pit's mouth; and the news spread, and others collected and followed. But I hardly think anything so simple could have brought all these."

"They must have some reason for coming," remarked the doctor, gazing at the ever-increasing crowd.

MRS. HENRY WOOD

"Blase Pellet has just said there is no reason," rejoined Frank. "I should advise you not to stand out here any longer," he added, to Mrs. Bell.

"Blase Pellet's no one to go by: he says one thing to-day, and another to-morrow," rejoined Dame Bell, as she turned on the path that led to her home; they turning with her.

"I think the dreams that he says he has, are certainly not very much to go by," observed Dr. Raynor, quietly.

"Oh, but that dream was a good deal," said Dame Bell. "And I've never had a good night's rest, sir, since I heard it, and that's more than a week ago. I can't sleep at night for thinking of it."

"I am sorry to hear you say so, Mrs. Bell: I thought you possessed better sense. Pellet must have been very foolish to tell you about it."

"It wasn't him that did tell me, Dr. Raynor. Leastways, not off-hand. It was Nancy Tomson. She came into my place one morning, when I was down on my knees whitening the hearth-flag; and I saw how scared her face looked. 'Guess what they be saying now,' says she: 'they've got a tale that your husband is lying in the Bottomless Shaft.' Well, sir, I stared at her, sitting back, as I knelt, with the stone in my hand: for you see I thought she meant he was lying there asleep; I really thought no worse. 'Go along with you, Nancy,' says I; 'as if Bell would lay himself down to sleep near that shaft!' 'Oh, it's not near it, but in it,' says she; 'and he's not sleeping, but dead.' Well, doctor, though I found every soul in the place saying the same thing, for four-and-twenty hours I could not get to learn why they said it. Andrew Float told me at last. He said it was through a dream of Blase Pellet's."

Dr. Raynor, listening attentively, made no comment.

"I had Pellet before me, sir, and he made a clean breast of it. He had not intended to let me know it, he said—and I don't think he had; but I did know it, and so it was no use holding out. It was a dreadful dream, he said. He had seen my poor husband lying at the bottom of that deep shaft, dead: seen him as plain as he had ever seen anything in all his life. When he woke up, his hair was standing on end with horror."

"Ah," said the doctor quietly, his tone one of utter disbelief, though Mrs. Bell did not detect it. "Did he intimate, pray, how long Bell had been lying there?"

"It was just what I asked him, sir, when I could get my breath again. A good three months, he was sure, he said. Which must have brought it back, sir, you see, to the time of his disappearance."

"Yes, I do see," observed the doctor, rather pointedly. "Well, I do not put any faith in dreams, Mrs. Bell, and I would advise you not to put any either. Good-night. Go in as soon as you can."

Dr. Raynor turned homewards, making a circuit to avoid the throng. Frank began whistling softly to himself, as a man sometimes does when absorbed in thought.

"What is your opinion of this, Frank?" asked the doctor, abruptly.

"I can form none, sir. Why they should collect—"

"Not that," interrupted the doctor. "One fool makes many. I spoke of Blase Pellet's alleged dream. I, myself, believe he had nothing of the kind: his manner, when I spoke with him about it, was not satisfactory: but what puzzles me is, his motive for saying that he had the dream. Some men are gifted with a propensity for astounding their fellow-creatures with marvellous tales. To create a sensation they'd say they have been hung, drawn, quartered, and brought to life again. But Pellet is not one of these; he is quiet, reticent and practical."

Frank made no reply. They were very close now to the Bottomless Shaft, and to the crowd surging around it.

"I could almost think that he *knows* Bell is there," resumed the doctor, lowering his voice. "If so, he must have been privy to the accident—if it was an accident—that sent poor Bell down. Perhaps took part in it—"

"Oh no, no!" incautiously spoke Frank. "It is not likely that he would take part in anything of the sort, Uncle Hugh," he added in quieter tones.

"If I don't quite think it, it is because there are one or two stumbling-blocks in the way," went on Dr. Raynor with composure. "Had Pellet been a witness to any accident—any false slip of Bell's, for instance; on the edge of the pit—he would have spoken of it at the time. Had he taken any part in it—inadvertently, of course, Pellet would not do so willingly—and hushed it up, he would not be likely to invent a dream now, and so draw attention again to what had nearly died away. Nevertheless, I am sure there is something or other in this new stir of Mr. Pellet's that does not appear on the surface."

Dr. Raynor quitted the subject, to the intense relief of his nephew; took off his hat in the warm night, and began to talk of the evening star, shining before them in all its brilliancy.

"A little while, Frank, a few more weeks, or months, or years, as may be, given to the fret and tear of this earthly life, and we shall, I suppose, know what these stars are; shall have entered on our heavenly life."

MRS. HENRY WOOD

Major Raynor's anticipated letter reached Frank on the following morning. As he opened it, a bank-note for twenty pounds dropped out: which the generous-hearted major had sent as an earnest of his goodwill.

My Dear Boy,

"I am sorry to have to tell you that the legacy left you by your aunt Ann is only five hundred pounds. I confess that I thought it would have turned out to be at least three thousand. Of course I shall make it up to you. We cannot yet put our hands upon the securities for the accumulated savings; but as soon as we do so, you shall have a cheque from me for three thousand pounds.

"I hope my brother is better, and Edina well. I wish she could be at Spring Lawn to help in the packing up, and all the rest of it. They come up to Eagles' Nest next week: and how they will get away without Edina to start them, I cannot imagine. My best affection to all.

"Ever your attached uncle,

Francis Raynor

"I wonder how it is," mused Frank, as he slowly folded the letter, "that in all our troubles and necessities, we instinctively turn to Edina?"

XVII

Brought to the Surface

The Reverend Titus Backup, in charge just now of the spiritual welfare of Trennach, had read out the banns of marriage on three separate Sundays, between Aaron Pitt, bachelor, and Naomi Perkins, spinster. On the Monday morning following the last announcement, Aaron, who was a young miner, and Naomi, who was nothing at all, and not good for much, either, in the shape of usefulness, presented themselves at the church with their respective friends, for the purpose of being united in matrimony.

This was the second marriage ceremony that Mr. Backup had had to perform since his sojourn at Trennach. He got through it pretty much as he had got through the first: namely, with a good deal of inward doubt and hesitation, but successfully as to the result; inasmuch as he was able, at the conclusion, to pronounce the couple man and wife without having broken down.

Clerk Trim was present, flourishing in all the importance of his office. Mrs. Trim also. Being on intimate terms with the parties in private life, Mrs. Trim had smartened herself up, and stepped into the church to look on, making one with the rest at the altar-rails. After the ceremony, came the business in the vestry. Trim took out the register book, and was opening it to place it before Mr. Backup, when a fresh entry, caught his eye. The clerk knew every page of the register as well as he knew his own Sunday shoes: which were made after the fashion of pumps, adorned with big ties of black ribbon.

"Mercy'pon us!" cried he in his astonishment. "Here's a new marriage wrote down!"

The exclamation caused the party to gather round him. Mr. Backup, remembering the circumstances of the marriage, and that he himself was in the well-kept secret, turned nervous at once.

"Why, it's—it's—it's Mr. Frank Raynor!" went on the clerk, staring at the page, and mastering its revelations slowly in his consternation. "And Miss—Miss— Well, if ever I was so struck in my life! Did you marry them, sir?" holding out the book to the parson. "Is that your reverence's own signature?"

His reverence took the book, muttered something quite foreign to the subject, that no one in the world could hear distinctly, himself included, and proceeded to enter the present marriage. As it was upon the same page, the parties signing it after him had the satisfaction of gratifying their own curiosity; and read, plainly as ink could show it, the names of Francis Raynor and Margaret St. Clare.

Now, had Clerk Trim haply been alone when he made this discovery, he, being a reticent and prudent man, would probably have kept the news to himself. But unfortunately he was not alone. Six or eight people were present, besides the parson; and, half of them being females, the reader may be left to judge what chance there was of its being kept secret.

The first to spread it abroad was Mrs. Trim. The wedding company having dispersed—without any invitation to her to accompany them to the house of the bride's mother and partake of the feasting, of which she had cherished a slight hope—Mrs. Trim betook herself to Float the druggist's. She had no particular work on hand that morning, and thought she could not do better than consecrate it to gossip. Mrs. Float, who was so far an invalid as to be unable to do much for herself, having been crippled years ago by an attack of rheumatic-fever, was in her usual chair by the fireside in the small parlour behind the shop, and Blase Pellet was pouring out some hot milk for her. Let the weather be ever so warm, Mrs. Float would not go without her fire: and perhaps she needed it. She was a stout, easy sort of woman, who took the best and the worst sides of life equally calmly; even her husband's attachment to the Golden Shaft. Of Blase Pellet she was very fond: for he was always ready to render her little services, as he might have been to a mother. Blase Pellet had his good and his bad qualities—as most people have: it was chiefly on the subject of Rosaline Bell that he was crazed.

"I'll do that," said Mrs. Trim, taking the warming-can from him. "You are wanted in the shop, Mr. Pellet. A customer followed me in."

Putting the can within the fender, she gave the cup to Mrs. Float; and at the same time regaled her with an account of the discovery in the register. Mrs. Float, lifting the cup to her mouth with her crippled hands, listened and stared, and for once felt some surprise; whilst Blase Pellet, behind the counter, changing one volume for another, caught a word here and there.

"What's that you have been saying about Mr. Raynor?" he demanded, reappearing before Mrs. Trim, after despatching the customer. "I don't believe a word of it."

"Then you can disbelieve it," was the tart retort; for Mrs. Trim did not like cold water thrown upon her assertions. "Mr. Baackup himself maarried him; there's his reverence's own name writ to the wedding."

"Married him to Miss St. Clare?"

"To Miss Margaret St. Clare. That's the pretty one. Don't you go disputing a body's word again, Blase Pellet. Fact es fact. Did you suppose they'd write down a lie? They registers 'ud be pewerly ticklish consarns to sarve out in thaat form."

A summons at the other counter with some copper money, called Mr. Blase away again. This time he was wanted to make up a complicated prescription for hair-oil; comprising various choice ingredients. Whilst he was doing it, his thoughts ran in so deep a groove that he scented it with oil of turpentine instead of bergamot. And when the purchaser complained, Mr. Blase, after sniffing and looking, and finding out what he had done, being powerless to alter it, protested that it was a new scent just come down from London.

"What a fool I have been!" ran his reflections. "If it is Miss St. Clare that he has been in love with—and married her, too, in secret—it can't have been Rosaline Bell: and when Rosaline said, poor girl, that there was nothing between them, she must have told the truth. And there I've been and gone and stirred up all this blessed commotion about the old man!—and who is to know whether I shall be able to lay it?"

At any rate, Mr. Blase Pellet endeavoured to "lay" it. He went forth at once, and earnestly assured every one who would listen to him, that he found he had been mistaken in fancying he had had the dream.

It chanced that on this same Monday morning, Frank Raynor was about to depart for London. Whatever disorder might have fastened upon Dr. Raynor, one thing was certain—it fluctuated greatly. And though only a few days had elapsed since the return of Edina, he had so visibly improved, both in appearance and strength, that she thought he was getting well: and Frank felt less scruple in leaving him.

Frank, in his sanguine way, believed he had only to go to London to drop into some good thing; that the one and the other would be, as it were, a simultaneous process. On the spot one can do anything, he observed, when discussing the point with Dr. Raynor. Dr. Raynor did not oppose his going. Rather the contrary. If Frank went at all, now was the best time: for he knew that this spurt of health in himself, this renewed capacity of exertion, would not last long. During his stay in

London, Frank was to look out for, and engage, an assistant for his uncle; a qualified medical man, who might become the partner of Dr. Raynor, and might eventually succeed to his practice. In short, it was just the same sort of thing that Frank was hoping to find for himself with some first-rate medical man in London.

On the previous day, when the congregation was pouring out of church, after Mr. Backup's sermon, Frank and Daisy had contrived to exchange a few words, under cover of the crowd. He told her that he was at length starting for town; and should only return to claim her. It might be in a week's time—if he were fortunate and found what he wanted at once; or it might be a fortnight. Longer than that it could not be; for his uncle had given that as the extreme limit of his absence. Daisy returned the brief pressure of his hand, which he managed to give unseen, and glanced at him with her bright eyes, that had a whole sea of hope in their depths. The world looked very fair to them; and they felt that they had need of patience to endure this enforced separation before they might enter on its enjoyment together.

On that same Sunday evening, Dr. Raynor spoke finally to Frank. They were sitting together, talking of this approaching sojourn in town: and of the great things it was to accomplish.

"Frank," said the doctor, rousing himself from a reverie, "has it ever occurred to you that in carrying out the idea of settling in London, you may be throwing away the substance for the shadow?"

Frank Raynor's gay blue eyes took a wondering expression as they went out to the speaker.

"In what way, Uncle Hugh?"

"It seems to me that the very thing you are about to seek there is lying ready to your hand here."

Frank understood now. "You mean that I should remain with you, Uncle Hugh?"

"Yes. As my partner now, Frank. As my successor hereafter."

Frank Raynor slightly shook his head, but made no other answer.

"I say to you, Frank, what I would say to no one else: that the time before some one must succeed to my place and practice is growing limited. It may be only a few weeks; it may be a few months: more than twelve months I do not think it can be. If—"

"Oh, Uncle Hugh!"

"Let me finish. I know I have your sympathy, my boy, and your best wishes, but all the sympathy and the good wishes in the world cannot alter the fiat which I fear has gone forth. Hear me, Frank. This has become a good practice now: it is a thousand pities that you should reject it and let it fall to a stranger."

"But, if I get a better practice than this in London, Uncle Hugh?" he argued. "I mean, a more lucrative one."

"But that is uncertain."

"Not very uncertain," said sanguine Frank.

"At any rate, you will have to pay for it. Pay in proportion to its merits."

"Of course. But I can do that. Uncle Francis is going to make up my legacy to three thousand pounds, you know."

"I know that he says so."

"But—you can't doubt his word!" cried Frank, his eyes lifted again in genuine amazement.

"Not his word, Frank: no, nor his intention: both are honest as the day. I only doubt his power."

"His power! What, with all that accumulated money just dropped into his hands!"

"But it has not yet dropped into them. It seems that a doubt exists as to where the money is, or even whether any exists at all."

"Oh, Uncle Hugh, it is sure to be found. I dare say it has already turned up."

"Well, I hope it has, Frank, and that you will reap all you expect. Let it pass so. Still, you must spend the money to ensure a practice; and the practice may not turn out as lucrative as you may be led to expect. The practice here is certain; you need not spend any money in securing it; and in a short time, a little sooner or a little later, it will be all in your hands."

"Uncle Hugh, you are very generous, very thoughtful for me; but indeed I could not settle at Trennach. There are reasons—"

Frank pulled up hastily. He was going on to say that for certain reasons this one small spot, in the whole length and breadth of the world's surface, was barred to him. Rather would he pass his life in some desert unfrequented by man, than within sight and sound of the Bare Plain.

"I do not like Trennach," he went on. "I could not remain here. For the last two or three months," he added, in his candour, "I have been as restless as possible, wanting to get away from it."

"You want to be amongst a more civilized community," said the doctor, good-naturedly.

"Well—yes, Uncle Hugh. I do—when one is setting up for life."

"Then there's nothing more to be said," concluded Dr. Raynor.

So Frank held to his plan and his journey, and this morning was starting in pursuance of it. Never again, as he hoped, should he be living at Trennach. Just a few days, as it was arranged, he would remain to introduce the new doctor—who would probably come down when he did—to people and places; and then he would bid it farewell for ever, carrying Daisy with him.

Taking leave of his uncle and Edina, he set out to walk to the station, his light overcoat thrown back, and greeting every one he met with a kindly word and a gay smile. The sky overhead was blue and calm, giving promise that the day would be fair to its end; just as Frank's hopeful heart seemed to assume that his life's journey would be fair throughout its course.

"Good-morning, Mr. Raynor."

The salutation came from the young parson. He stood leaning on the stile of the Rectory garden, which overlooked the high-road. Frank, answering cordially, was intending to pass onwards. But Mr. Backup motioned to retard him.

"I am off to London," said Frank, gaily. "Can I do anything for you?"

"I will not detain you a moment; I want to say just a word," spoke the clergyman, feeling already uncommonly shy and nervous at the thought of what that word was. "Mr. Raynor, I—I—I beg you to believe that I have implicitly kept secret that—that matter which you requested me to keep. But—"

"I know you have," cried Frank, extending his hand in token of gratitude, "and I thank you heartily. Not a soul knows of it."

"But—I was about to say that I fear it is a secret no longer. Another wedding took place in the church this morning, and the clerk read the entry of yours in it. Other people read it. They saw it in signing the book."

The information was about as complete a damper for Frank Raynor as could have been administered to him. He stood perfectly still, his lips settling into a grave expression. Not that Frank cared very much that the fact itself should transpire: he had thought lately that if it did so, it might be a stroke of good luck for him, by giving him Daisy, who was now kept from him. But what struck him was, that if this were true, it would stop his journey to London. Instead of going there, he must bend his steps to The Mount; for he could not leave Daisy to bear the brunt of the discovery alone.

"I knew Aaron Pitt was to be married this morning, but I declare that I never gave a thought to the register," spoke he aloud. "They saw it, you say. Did they make any comment?"

"A few comments were made. Clerk Trim was so much surprised that he asked whether it was really my signature, and whether I married you. It crossed my mind to say you did not wish it talked about just at present, and to beg them to keep it secret. But as so many people were there I thought it would be quite useless to do so."

"Quite useless," decided Frank. "Well, this has come upon me unexpectedly, and—and it will change my immediate plans. I must go on to The Mount now, instead of to the station."

"I am very sorry," began the clergyman, as nervously as though it were through some fault of his own. "There are not two registers, you see, Mr. Raynor, and—"

"Oh, don't be sorry," interrupted Frank, recovering his spirits and his lightness of heart and tone. "I'm not sure but it may turn out for the best. Upon my return from London, a few days hence, I was going to declare it myself."

Shaking hands warmly, Frank continued his way, striding over the ground at a great rate. Instead of branching off at the turning that led to the railway, he strode straight on towards The Mount.

"All for the best," he repeated to himself, referring to his parting words to the parson. "It may end in my taking Daisy up with me to-day. It shall end so, if my will is worth anything."

Boldly went he to The Mount, knocking and ringing freely. Far from feeling small for having, so to say, run away with the prettiest daughter of the house, for which act he might expect reproach and obloquy, he seemed to think he had come on some errand that merited reward. One of the men-servants threw open the door.

"Can I see Mrs. St. Clare?"

"Mrs. St. Clare is not at home, sir."

"Indeed!" returned Frank, in surprise. For it was not her habit to go out so early.

"My mistress and the young ladies have left home this morning, sir," explained the man. "They have gone for a week or so."

"Where to?"

"I don't know, sir. It was uncertain. Perhaps as far as Malvern: Miss Lydia likes Malvern: or perhaps only to one of the seaside places on this coast."

"You cannot tell me where a letter would find Mrs. St. Clare?"

"No, sir. My mistress said that all letters might wait here until she came back."

So there was no help for it: he could not make the communication to Mrs. St. Clare. But in all probability she would hear nothing of the news before her return. Daisy would be sure to write to him, and Edina had been requested to forward his letters to town.

"It must have been rather a sudden thought of Mrs. St. Clare's, this going from home: was it not?"

"Quite so, sir. It was Miss Lydia who started it, while the ladies were sitting in the drawing-room yesterday afternoon. Tabitha never heard a word about packing up, sir, till she was at her tea."

Frank looked at his watch. There might still be time to catch his train if he started at once for the station. He set out; and just accomplished it. But that he did so was owing to the fact that the train, as usual, came up considerably behind its time.

It is a great deal easier in this world to raise a storm than to allay one: and so Mr. Blase Pellet found to his cost. He had thoroughly aroused the public mind on the subject of the missing miner; and the public mind refused to be calmed again.

Day by day, since the discovery in the register, did the astounding news of Frank's private marriage make a deeper impression upon Blase Pellet. He saw things now with very different eyes from what he had formerly seen them. He told himself that Rosaline's version of her intimacy with Mr. Raynor—namely, that it bore no particular intimacy, and had nothing hidden beneath its surface—was the truth. The relief to himself was wonderfully great. All his love for her, that he had been angrily trying to repress, increased tenfold: and he began to see that the love might indeed go on to fruition. At least, that if it did not do so, the fault would lie in his own insensate folly. If he could only stop this commotion about Bell, so that the man might rest where he was, undiscovered, he should make his way with Rosaline. But the public seemed anything but inclined to let it stop there: and Blase Pellet gave many a hard word to the said public. Just at present Trennach appeared to have nothing to do but to go about suggesting disagreeable surmises.

One story led to a second; one supposition to another. From the first startling rumour, that Bell might be lying at the bottom of the shaft (as shown to Mr. Pellet in a remarkable dream), Trennach passed on to believing that he was there; and, next, to say that he must be searched for.

In vain Blase Pellet, mortified, agitated, and repentant, sought to prove that Bell was not there; that no foundation could exist for the notion; that he was now fully convinced his dream had not been a dream at all, but the baseless fabric of a fancy. Trennach did not listen to him. Excitement had gone too far for that. It was just possible, of course, that poor Bell might not be in the pit; but they thought he was there; and, at any rate, they meant to see for themselves. As simple-minded, well-meaning Andrew Float expressed it: "Dreams didna come for nought." Blase Pellet could have bitten out his false tongue. How easy the future would now have seemed but for this storm! Frank Raynor removed from his path by marriage, his own success with Rosaline could only be a question of time: but if this stir, which he had invoked, could not be stilled, and it went on to any discovery, Rosaline would probably make it an excuse for throwing him off for ever. That it would in any case grieve and anger her frightfully, and that she would detect the falsity of his "dream," he knew by instinct; and Blase felt tempted to wish he had been born dumb.

When we go out of our way to delude the world from interested motives, and do it, moreover, by a lie, the chances are that the step recoils unpleasantly upon us. In some way or other we are repaid in our own coin. It may not be immediately; it may not be for years to come; but rely upon it, it does come home to us sooner or later. We see the blind folly we were guilty of: not to speak of the sin: and we cry out in our flood-tide of repentance, Oh, that I had not quitted the straightforward path! As Blase Pellet was crying now.

The owner of the land, one of those mine-owners whose wealth is fabulous, became interested in the case. He came forward, and gave orders that the pit should be examined, to ascertain whether or not the missing man was there. The necessary machinery was soon brought into requisition—where wealth commands, difficulties are lightened—and the Bottomless Shaft was searched.

Yes. Josiah Bell was brought up to the surface. His attire was recognized as that which he had worn the day of his disappearance: and there remained no doubt that he had met his death that same night by falling down the pit.

Amidst startling commotion, an inquest was called. Of course the question now was, how he got down there: a question that puzzled his friends and the world in general. For it was a well-known fact that Bell gave way to superstitious fancies, and would not be likely to approach the shaft alone at night.

But no evidence came forward that could throw light on the mystery. Those who had seen him last in life—the pitmen with whom he had been drinking at the Golden Shaft, and his wife at home, who had been the last person, so far as was known, to exchange a word with him—told what they had to tell. Their testimony amounted to nothing. Neither, for that matter, did Mr. Blase Pellet's. Very much to his dismay, Mr. Pellet was summoned as a witness, and was sharply questioned by the coroner about his dream.

And Blase, in sheer helplessness and some terror, took up the dream again; the dream which he had been trying lately to repudiate. No other course than to take it up seemed open to him, now that matters had come to this pass and Bell had been actually found. If he disowned the dream, the next inquiry would be, How then did you come to know anything of the matter: what told you that the man was lying there? So, with clouded face and uneasy voice, Mr. Blase gave the history of his dream: and when asked by a juryman why he had gone about lately protesting that he was sure he had not had any dream, he replied that, seeing the public were growing so excited, he had deemed it better to disavow it, thinking it might calm them down again. The coroner, who seemed to be unfortunately sceptical as to dreams in general, eyed the witness keenly, and made him repeat the dream—at least what he remembered of it—three times over. Blase declared he had never been able to recollect much of it, except the fact that he had seen Bell lying at the foot of the pit, dead. And then he had awakened in a state of inconceivable fright.

"Had you any animosity against the deceased during his life?" questioned the coroner, still regarding the witness intently.

"Oh dear, no, sir," returned Blase. "We were always the best of friends. He was a sort of relation of mine. At least his wife is."

That no animosity had existed between them could be testified to by the community in general, as the coroner found. He was looking at Blase still.

"And you positively state, young man, that you had no grounds whatever, except this dream, for suspecting or knowing that the deceased was down the shaft?"

Blase coughed. "None."

"You do not know how he got down?"

"Good gracious I know! Not I, sir."

Blase had answered readily, and with much appearance of earnestness. The coroner was conscious that dim doubts of Mr. Blase Pellet's strict veracity were floating in his own mind, chiefly arising from his incredulity as to dreams; but the doubts were not sufficient to act upon, neither did he perceive that they could be in any way supported. So he released the witness. And the inquest came to an end, the jury returning an open verdict—

"That Josiah Bell met with his death through falling down the pit; but that what caused his fall there was no evidence to show."

XVIII

A Subtle Enemy

He never went near the pit of his own free will! He was lured to it and thrown into it. Or he was first killed, and then cruelly put there out of the way."

The speaker was Mrs. Bell: who had at last assumed the widow's dress and cap. Her audience consisted of her daughter Rosaline, the Aunt Pellet from Falmouth, Blase Pellet, and two or three neighbours. The aunt and Rosaline had arrived from Falmouth to attend the funeral. Rosaline, at first, had absolutely refused to come; she "felt afraid," she said, with much trembling and many bitter tears; she did not like to look upon the dead, even though it was her poor father: and she also felt too ill to travel. But John Pellet and his wife overruled these objections. They told her it was an "unnatural state of feeling;" one that might not be indulged: and the aunt, who was coming to Trennach herself, brought Rosaline with her, partly by persuasion, partly by force.

Her plea of illness might indeed have been allowed. Thin, white, worn, with a manner that seemed to be for ever starting at shadows, Rosaline looked little like the gay and blooming girl once known to Trennach. Trennach gazed at her with amazed eyes, wondering what Falmouth could have done to her in that short period, or whether the Seven Whistlers, which had so startled her at home, could have followed her to that populous town. Sitting in her mother's kitchen, her back to the light, her cheek resting on her hand, Rosaline listened in silence to the conversation, two of the company especially regarding her—Blase Pellet and Nancy Tomson. Nancy openly avowed that she had never seen any young woman so changed in her life; while Blase Pellet, though mentally acknowledging the change, was taking in draughts of her wondrous beauty.

"No living body of men have queerer fancies than miners, especially these Cornish miners: and poor Josiah, though he was not Cornish at all, as we know, had his," pursued Dame Bell, chiefly addressing her sister, a tall, thin woman, who had arrived fashionably attired in crape and bombazine, with a veil to her bonnet. Not that she wore her bonnet now, for this was the next morning, and the day of the funeral.

"Hardly a man about here would venture close up to that shaft at night: and if you go out and ask them one by one, Sarah, you'll find I am telling you nothing but truth," pursued the widow. "Since Dan Sandon threw himself headlong in, and was killed, the men won't go near it for fear of seeing him. Neither would Bell; and—"

"Perhaps he fell into it accidentally, Ann," interrupted Mrs. Pellet.

"I don't say but he might have done so. If he was at the edge of the pit, looking down, or anything of that sort, he might have overbalanced himself. But I do say that he was not there alone. I ask what took him there at all; and I ask who was with him?"

Pertinent questions. Rosaline, chancing to look up, met the gaze of Blase Pellet. Each started slightly, and dropped their eyes, as though to look at one another were a crime.

"Let us put it down as an accident; for argument's sake," urged the widow. "That he was too close to the pit's mouth, and fell in. It might have been so. But in that ease, I repeat, he was not alone. At least one man must have been with him—perhaps more than one. Why did he, or they, not give the alarm? Why did he not come straight away, and say, 'Poor Bell has fallen into the shaft, and what's to be done?' Can any of you answer me that question?"

"It stands to reason that that's what anybody would do," observed Mrs. Pellet. "But who could have been with him?"

"Not waun o' tha men owns to it," put in Nancy Tomson. "What should heve taaken 'em up to that there ghashly shaaft at night, they aal ask; or Bell either?"

"No, not one owns to it; and, as far as I can see, there was nothing to take them there," assented Mrs. Bell. "Therefore I say it was no accident. Bell was just carried there, living or dead, and put away out o' sight."

"What shall you do about it?" asked Mrs. Pellet, in a scared tone.

"What can I do but wait? Wait until some disclosure turns up."

"If it never does turn up."

"But it will turn up," confidently asserted Dame Bell.

"So say I," spoke Nancy Tomson. "When once a thing o' this kind es led up to by dreams, it won't stop at the beginning. They dreams es strange indexes sometimes, and Mr. Blase Pellet there didna heve his for nothing. Without that dream the poor man might just heve laid on in thaat shaaft as he faalled, and never been found i' this world."

Mr. Blase Pellet, listening to this, shot a glance of intense aggravation at the speaker. Rosaline looked up at him. It was a steady gaze this time, and one that betrayed unqualified contempt.

"Was it a very bad dream?" asked his relative from Falmouth, this being the first opportunity she had had of questioning Blase upon the subject.

"Bad enough," shortly replied Pellet; and, with the words, he made a sudden détour to the front-door, and took up his standing outside in the sunshine.

The movement led to a general dispersion. Nancy Tomson and the other neighbours departed; Mrs. Pellet went upstairs; Dame Bell passed into the back-kitchen to see about their own and her lodgers' dinner: for the ordinary day's work must go on even on the saddest occasions; and Rosaline remained in the room alone.

"I am very sorry I had that dream."

Lifting her eyes, Rosaline saw the speaker beside her—Blase Pellet.

"So am I," she shortly answered, in a significant way, that certainly gave him no encouragement to proceed.

"And still more sorry that I spoke of it abroad, Rosaline: for I see that it is giving you pain."

"Pain!" she exclaimed, a whole world of anguish in her tone: ay, and of resentment also.

"But it shall be the endeavour of my life to atone to you for it, Rosaline. My best care, my truest love, shall be devoted to you. Daily and hourly—"

"Be quiet, Blase," she interrupted, the flash in her eye, the hot flush upon her cheek, rendering her for the moment almost more than beautiful. "We will understand one another at once, and finally. To talk of such a thing as 'love,' or 'care,' to me is worse than useless. My path lies one way, your path lies another: it will not be my fault if they ever cross each other again."

"You do not mean this," he said, after a pause.

"I do mean it. I used to mean it: as you know. I shall mean it always."

"Have you heard that Raynor is married?" asked Blase.

"Yes," she answered in constrained tones, her flushed cheek fading to whiteness.

"Then, perhaps, as he is out of our way, you will think of me, Rosaline. If not now—"

"Neither now nor ever, Blase. Do not deceive yourself."

With a quick movement, she evaded his outstretched hand that would have sought to detain her, and ran up the stairs. Leaving Mr. Blase Pellet excessively discomfited: but not as much so as a less hopeful swain would have been.

"It was a little too soon to speak," reasoned he with himself: "I must wait a while."

OF ALL THE SCENES CONNECTED with Bell's disappearance and his recovery, none caused more excitement than that of the funeral. It was fixed for a late hour—six o'clock in the afternoon. This was to enable the pitmen to be present. The Reverend Titus Backup made no sort of objection to it. Had they settled it for midnight, he had been equally agreeable. The hour for the interment came, and people flocked to it from far and near. Not only did the local miners attend, but also gangs of men from more distant mines. Mr. Backup had never seen such a crowd in his life. Near the grave a small space was left for Mrs. Bell and the other mourners; but in the churchyard and adjacent parts; including a portion of the Bare Plain, the spectators thronged.

Rosaline was not there. Blase was. In right of his relationship to the Pellets of Falmouth, Blase had been invited to the funeral; and made one of the mourners, with a flow of crape to his hat. Whether Rosaline had meant to make one also did not clearly appear, though no one thought of doubting it; but just before the time of starting, she was seized with a fainting-fit: not quite losing consciousness, but lying back powerless in her chair, and looking white as death. Nancy Tomson, who was to be of the procession, was the first to recognize the dilemma it placed them in.

"Whaat es to be done?" she cried. "It willna never do to keep *him*, and the paarson, and they folks waiting; but she caan't walk like thic!"

"Him" applied to poor Bell. At least, to what remained of him. For the convenience of the inquest and other matters, he had been placed in a shelter bordering the Bare Plain, partly room, partly shed, when first brought up from the pit, and had not been removed from it. It was there that the mourners would meet the coffin and attend it to the church.

"True," put in Mrs. Trim; who had deemed it neighbourly to look in upon the widow Bell at this sorrowful hour and see what was to be seen. "They funerals don't waait for nobody: specially when they heve been put off aalmost to sunset."

"No; it will not do to keep it waiting," breathed Rosaline, with weak and trembling lips. "Do you go on; all of you. I will follow if I am able, and catch you up."

Nancy Tomson feebly offered to remain with her, seeing that good feeling demanded as much consideration, but she did not at all mean the offer to be accepted, for she would not have missed the ceremony for the world. It was not every day she had the chance of filling a conspicuous position at a funeral; and such a funeral as this. Rosaline promptly declined her company, saying she felt much better now, and preferred to come after them alone.

So the mourners departed, followed at a respectful distance by many neighbours and others, who had collected to watch and wait for their exit. The chief crowd had gathered about that other building, for which these were making their way. Men, women and children, all went tramping towards it across the Plain: and in a few minutes Bleak Row was as absolutely deserted as though it were a city of the dead.

Rosaline slowly rose from her seat, dragged her chair outside, and sat down in the evening sunshine. Thankful was she to be alone. No eye was on her. The houses were empty; the Bare Plain, stretching out around and beyond, lay silent and still, save for that moving mass of human beings, pressing farther and farther away in the distance. The open air seemed necessary to her if she would continue to breathe. When somewhat more composed, she put up her hands in the attitude of prayer, bent forward till her forehead touched them, and sat with her eyes closed.

A Prayer-book lay on her knee. She had brought it out, intending to follow the service, soon about to begin. But she could not do so. There she sat, never once moving her attitude, scattered passages of the service recurring now and again to her memory, and ascending to heaven from the depths of her anguished heart. Poor Rosaline Bell! There were moist eyes and wrung feelings amidst those mourners standing round the grave, but none of them could know anything of the desperate distress that was *her* portion. None, none.

But now, it was perhaps a somewhat singular coincidence that just as Frank Raynor had come unexpectedly upon that excited throng, collected round the Bottomless Shaft on the Bare Plain, a few nights before his departure for London, so he should in like manner come quite as unexpectedly upon this throng, gathered at Bell's funeral. The one had not surprised him more than the other did. He had been just a fortnight absent in London; this was the day of his return, and he was now walking home from the station. All the excitement consequent upon the finding of Bell had taken place during these two weeks of Frank's absence. There had been commotion (the result of Blase Pellet's "dream") before his departure, with much talking and surmising; but all movement in the matter had taken place since then.

In a letter written to him by Edina, Frank had learnt that Bell was found. But he learnt nothing more. And he certainly had not anticipated coming upon the funeral, and this concourse of people collected at it, as he passed the churchyard on his way from the station to his uncle's, on this, the evening of his return.

Before he knew what it all meant, or could quite make out whether his eyes were not playing him false, he found himself accosted by the clerk's wife. Mrs. Trim, seeing his surprise, told all she knew, intensely gratified by the favourable opportunity, and a good deal that she did not know. Frank listened in silence.

"Yes, sir, he was found there, down deep in the pit shaaft, and they jurymen never brought et in waun way nor t'other, whether he was throwed down wilful, or faaled in accidental, but just left folks to fight out the question for their own selves. It were a dreadful thing for him, anyway, poor man; to heve been lying there aal thic while."

"I never saw so many people at a funeral in my life," observed Frank, making no special comment on her words.

He mechanically moved a step and looked over the hedge that skirted the graveyard. Mrs. Trim continued her information and remarks: detailing the mourners by name, and stating that Rosaline was seized with a faintness when they were starting, and so remained at home alone.

"Alone!" cried Frank.

"Aal alone, entirely," repeated Mrs. Trim. "Every soul from aal parts es here, Mr. Frank; as you may see. She said perhaps she'd follow ef she felt equal to't; but she's not come. She and her aunt talks o' going back to Falmouth to-morrow; but the widow, poor thing, es against it. Thaat's the aunt, sir: that tall thin woman."

Frank Raynor rapidly debated a question with himself. He very much wished to say a few words to Rosaline in private: what if he seized this occasion for doing so? If she were indeed going away on the morrow, he might find no other opportunity. Yes: at any rate he would make the attempt.

Turning somewhat abruptly from the clerk's wife, in the very middle of a sentence, Frank made a détour on the outskirts of the crowd, and strode rapidly away over the Bare Plain. Rosaline was sitting just in the same position, her head bowed, her hands raised. His footsteps aroused her.

Respecting her grief as he had never respected any grief yet, feeling for her (and for many other things connected with the trouble) from the bottom of his heart, uncertain and fearful of what the ultimate end would be, Frank took her hand in silence. She gazed up at him yearningly, almost as though she did not at once recognize him, a pitiful expression on her face. For a short time he did not speak a word. But that which he had come to say must be said, and without delay: for already the ceremony had terminated, and the procession of mourners, with the attendant crowd, might be seen slowly advancing towards them across the Bare Plain.

"It has almost killed me," moaned Rosaline. "I should be thankful that he is found, but for the fear of what may follow: thankful that he has had Christian burial. But there can be no more safety now. There was not very much before."

"Nay," spoke Frank. "I think it is just the contrary. Whilst the affair lay in uncertainty, it might be stirred up at any moment: now it will be at rest."

"Never," she answered. "Never so long as Blase Pellet lives. He has brought this much about; and he may bring more. Oh, if we could only escape from him!"

Frank, still holding her hand, in his deep compassion, spoke to her quietly and kindly for a few moments. She seemed to listen as one who hears not, as one whom words cannot reach or soothe; her eyes were fixed on the ground, her other hand hung listless by her side. But now the first faint hum of the approaching crowd struck upon her half-dulled ear; she raised her eyes and saw for the first time what caused it. First in the line walked her mother and aunt, their black robes and hoods lighted up by the setting sun. And as if the sight of those mourning garments put the finishing touch to her already distracted mind and conveyed to it some sudden terror, Rosaline gave a faint scream and fell into a fit of hysterics, almost of convulsions. Frank could not leave her, even to dash indoors for water. He put his arm round her to support her.

"Whaat on airth es it, sir?" demanded Nancy Tomson, who was the first to speak when the group of hooded women came up.

"It is only an attack of hysterics, brought on by the sight of your approach," said Frank. "It is a sad day for her, you know; and she does not seem very strong. Will you be so good as to get some water."

"I thought it must be your ghost, Mr. Frank," spoke poor Mrs. Bell, in her subdued tones, as she put back her hood. "Believing you were in London—"

"I am back again," he shortly interrupted. "Seeing your daughter sitting here, I turned aside to speak a word of sympathy to her."

The hysterics subsided as quickly as they had come on; and Rosaline, declining the water, rose and passed into the house. The women pressed in after her, leaving Blase Pellet outside. As to the crowd of voluntary attendants, they had already slackened their steps in the distance, and seemed uncertain what next to do: whether to disperse their various roads, or to remain talking with one another, and watching the house.

This virtually left Frank and Blase Pellet alone. Blase took off his tall Sunday hat, and rubbed his brow with his white handkerchief, as though the heavy hat and the burning sun had left an unpleasant sensation of heat there. It was, however, neither the hat nor the sun that had put him into that access of warmth; it was the sight of Frank Raynor. Of Frank Raynor holding Rosaline's hand in his, holding herself, in fact, and bending over her with what looked like an impulse of affection.

A most disagreeable idea had flashed into Mr. Pellet's head. A dim, indistinct idea, it is true, but none the less entertained. Married man though Frank Raynor was, as the world of Trennach knew, he might not have given up his love for Rosaline! He might be intending to keep that sentiment on; keep her to himself, in short, to laugh and chatter with whenever they should meet, to the destruction of other people's hopes, including those of Blase Pellet. And Blase, in the plenitude of his wrath, could have struck him to the earth as he stood.

How mistaken people can be! How wildly absurd does jealousy make them! Nothing could be further from the thoughts of Frank Raynor: he was at honest peace with all the world, most certainly intending no harm to Rosaline, or to any one else. At peace even with that unit in it, Blase Pellet: and in the plenitude of his good-nature he addressed him cordially.

"You have made one of the followers of poor Bell, I see. The affair is altogether a sad one."

"Yes, it is," replied Blase Pellet. "We have been putting him into his grave; and matters, so far, are hushed up. But I don't say they are hushed for good. I could hang some people to-morrow, if I liked."

MRS. HENRY WOOD

The intense bitterness of his tone, the steady gaze of his meaning eyes, proved that this man might yet become a subtle enemy. Frank's courage fell.

"What do you mean?" he asked. But for the very life of him he could not make his voice quite so free and independent as usual.

"It does not matter saying now what I mean, Mr. Raynor. Perhaps I never shall say it. I would rather not: and it won't be my fault if I do. *You keep out of my way*, and out of somebody else's way, and I dare say I shall be still, and forget it. Out of sight, out of mind, you know, sir."

Frank, deigning no reply, turned into the house to see if there was anything he could do for Rosaline. And then he walked away rapidly towards Trennach.

Mrs. St. Clare had not yet returned to the Mount, but she was expected daily. Frank had received three or four letters from Daisy, re-posted to him in London by Edina, but not one of the letters had he been able to answer in return. They were going about from place to place in obedience to Lydia's whims, Daisy said, and it was simply impossible to give any certain address where a letter would find her. Every day for a week past had her mother announced her intention of turning her steps homeward on the morrow: and every morrow, as it dawned, had her steps been turned to some fresh place instead.

But Frank was now in a fever of impatience for their return. The legacy of five hundred pounds was ready to be paid him, and he meant to take Daisy away on the strength of it. He had no settled plans as yet: these had been delayed by the uncertainty attending the larger sum promised him; the three thousand pounds. It is true that Frank had made inquiries in London; had seen two old-established medical men who were thinking of taking a partner. But each of them wanted a good sum paid down as equivalent; and neither of them seemed to be so sanguine on the score of Frank's coming into the three thousand pounds as he himself was. With his usual candour, he had disclosed the full particulars of the doubts, as well as of the expectations. So, with the future still undecided, here he was, at Trennach again: but only to make preparations for finally leaving it.

With regard to the assistant for Dr. Raynor, he had been more fortunate, and had secured the services of one whom he judged to be in every way eligible. It was a Mr. Hatman. This gentleman was coming down on the morrow. He and Frank were to have travelled together, but Mr. Hatman could not complete his arrangements quite as soon as he had expected: and Frank dared not delay even another day, lest Mrs. St. Clare should return to the Mount. He could not leave Daisy to bear alone the brunt of the discovery of their marriage. Mr. Hatman was to have a three-months' trial. At the end of that period, if he were found to suit the doctor, and the doctor and the place suited him, he would remain for good.

It was not often that Dr. Raynor found fault or gave blame. But on the night after Frank's return, when they were shut up alone together, he took Frank severely to task. Common report had carried the news of the marriage to him; and he expressed his opinion upon it very freely.

"It was perhaps a hasty thing to do, sir, and was entered upon without much thought," admitted Frank, after he had listened. "But we did not care to lose one another."

"Well, I will say no more," returned Dr. Raynor. "The thing cannot be undone now. There's an old saying, Frank, which is perhaps more often exemplified than people think for: 'Marry in haste and repent at leisure.' I wish this case of yours may prove an exception, but I can scarcely hope it."

"We shall get along all right, Uncle Hugh."

"I trust you may."

"I told Hatman about it—he is a very nice fellow, and you will be sure to like him, uncle—and he wished me and Daisy good luck. He says his mother's was a runaway match, and it turned out famously."

On the day but one following; that is, the day after Mr. Hatman's arrival at Trennach; Mrs. St. Clare and her daughters returned to the Mount: not reaching it, however, until late at night, for they had missed the earlier train they had meant to travel by.

Frank went up betimes the next morning. His interview with Mrs. St. Clare took place alone. She was surprised and indignant at what he had to disclose—namely, that the marriage ceremony had passed between himself and her daughter Margaret. But, on the whole, she was more reasonable than might have been expected.

"I wash my hands of it altogether, Mr. Frank Raynor, of her and of you, as I said I would—though you may be sure that when I spoke I never contemplated so extreme a step as this. But that I cannot disbelieve what, as you say, is so easily proved, I should have thought it impossible to be true. Daisy has always been docile and dutiful."

"I will make her the best of husbands; she shall never know an hour's care with me," spoke Frank earnestly, his truthful blue eyes and the sincerity of his face expressing more than words could do.

"But what of your means of keeping her?" asked Mrs. St. Clare, coldly.

"By the aid of the three thousand pounds I have mentioned, I shall obtain a first-class practice in London," returned he in his most sanguine manner. "I trust you will not despise that position for her. If I am very successful, I might even some day be made a baronet, and Daisy would be Lady Raynor."

"A charming prospect!" returned Mrs. St. Clare, in mocking tones, that rather took Frank and his earnestness aback. "Well, I wash my hands of you both, Mr. Francis Raynor. As Daisy has made her bed so must she lie on it."

Daisy was summoned to the conference. She came in with timid steps; and stood, tearful and trembling, in her pretty morning dress of pale muslin. It chanced to be the one she was married in. Frank Raynor drew her arm within his, and stood with her.

"You may well shrink from me, unhappy girl!" cried Mrs. St. Clare. "What have you done with your wedding-ring?"

With trembling hands, Daisy produced it, attached to its blue ribbon. Frank took it from her, broke the ribbon, and placed the ring on its proper finger.

"Never again to be taken off, my dear," he said. "Our troubles are over."

She was to be allowed to remain at the Mount until the afternoon— which Mrs. St. Clare called a great concession—and then she and Frank would start on the first stage of their journey. Daisy might take a box of apparel with her; the rest should be forwarded to any address she might choose to give.

Back went Frank again to Dr. Raynor's to prepare for his own departure. Very busy was he that day. Now talking with his uncle, now with Edina, now with Mr. Hatman; and now running about Trennach to shake hands with all the world in his sunny-natured way. A hundred good wishes were breathed by him. Even to Blase Pellet Frank gave a kindly word and nod at parting.

It was late in the afternoon when he, in a close carriage provided for the occasion, went up to the Mount for Daisy. She was ready, and came out, attended to the door by Tabitha: Mrs. St. Clare and Lydia did not appear. Thence she and Frank drove to the station: and found they had five minutes to spare.

Frank had been seeing to the luggage, when Daisy came out of the waiting-room to meet him. It was one of those small stations that contain only one waiting-room for all classes.

"There's the most beautiful girl that I ever saw sitting inside, Frank," she said in an undertone.

"Is there?" he carelessly remarked.

"I could not keep my eyes from her, she is so lovely. But she looks very ill."

They turned into the waiting-room together. And, to Daisy's extreme surprise, she, the next moment, saw Frank go up and speak to this girl; who was sitting there with an elderly companion, both in deep mourning. Daisy, her gaze fixed on the beautiful face, wondered who they could be.

But there was no further time for waiting. The train came puffing in, and all was bustle. Daisy saw Frank again shake hands cordially with this delicate-looking girl, and whisper a few farewell words to her. She was evidently not departing by this train: probably by one going in the opposite direction.

"Who was it, Frank?" questioned Daisy, when they were at length seated in the carriage.

"It is Rosaline Bell. She and her aunt are going back to Falmouth."

"*That* Rosaline Bell!" exclaimed Daisy, her face flushing deeply. "I—I—did not know she was so beautiful."

PART THE SECOND

I

AT EAGLES' NEST

In a luxurious chamber at Eagles' Nest, where the carpet was soft as moss to the tread, and the hangings were of silk, and the toilette ornaments were rich and fragile, sat Edina Raynor. Her elbow rested on the arm of the chair, her thoughtful face was bent on her hand, her eyes were taking in the general aspect of the room and its costly appurtenances.

It was autumn weather now, and Edina had come on a short visit to Eagles' Nest. She had wished to put off the visit until the following spring, but had yielded to persuasion. One or other of them at Eagles' Nest was perpetually writing to her; and at last Dr. Raynor added his word to theirs. "There is no reason why you should not go, Edina," he said. "Hatman and I get on famously together, you know; and I am better than I was." And so Edina had made the long journey; and—here she was.

Not yet had she been two days at Eagles' Nest; but in that short time she had found much to grieve her. Grieved she was, and full of anxiety. Every one of the family, from her uncle Francis and Mrs. Raynor downwards, had greatly changed. From the simple, unaffected people they had once been, they had transformed themselves into great personages with airs and assumptions. That was not the worst. That might have been left to find its own level in time: they would no doubt have returned to common sense. What pained Edina was the rate at which they lived. Carriages, horses, servants; dinners, dressing, gaiety. Where could it all end? Had the revenues of Eagles' Nest been twice what they were, the major would still have been spending more than his income. It was this that troubled Edina.

And something else troubled her. The *tone* of their mind seemed to be changing: not so much that of Major and Mrs. Raynor, as of the children. Speaking, of course, chiefly of the elder ones. Formerly they were warm-hearted, unassuming, full of sympathy for others. Now all thought seemed to be swallowed up in self; those who wanted help, whether in word or kind, might go where they would for it: selfishness reigned supreme. A latent dread was making itself heard in Edina's heart, that they were being spoiled by sudden prosperity. As many others have been.

The first day she arrived, dinner was served at seven o'clock; a very elaborate one. Soup, fish, entrées, meats, sweets: all quite à la mode. Edina was vexed: she thought this had been done for her: but she was much more vexed when she found it was their daily style of living. To her, with the frugal notions implanted in her by her father's early straits, with her naturally simple tastes, and her conscientious judging of what was right and wrong, this profusion seemed sinful waste. And—they were all so grand! The faded cottons and washed-out muslins, had of course been discarded, but they had given place to costly gossamer fabrics and to silks that rustled in their richness. They were now just as much over-dressed as formerly they were the opposite. Alice had already put off black for her aunt Atkinson, and was in very slight mourning indeed: in lilac or white hues, with black or grey ribbons. With it all, they were acquiring a hard, indifferent tone, as though the world's changes and sorrows could never again concern them.

"All this looks new," mused Edina, referring to the appurtenances of the room. "I don't fancy Aunt Ann had anything so modern: she liked old-fashioned furniture. With all these expenses, Uncle Francis will soon be in greater embarrassment than he ever was at Spring Lawn. And it is bad for Charley. Very bad. It will give him all sorts of extravagant ideas and habits."

As if to escape her thoughts, she rose and stood at the window, looking forth on the landscape. It was very beautiful. There were hills near and far off, a wide extent of wood and snatches of gleaming water, green meadows, and a field or two of yellow corn that had ripened late. The leaves on the trees were already beginning to put on their autumn tints. On the lawn were many beds of bright flowers. Under a tree sat the major, sipping a champagne-cup, of which he was fond. Beyond, three young people were playing at croquet: Charles, Alice, and William Stane; the latter a son of Sir Philip Stane, who lived near them. Through one of the bare fields, where the corn had been already reaped and gathered, walked Mademoiselle Delrue, the French governess, and little Kate. Alfred was at school. Robert was generally with his nurse. Mademoiselle, a finished pianist, superintended Alice's music and read French with her; also took Robert for French: otherwise her duties all lay with Kate. It was, of course, well to have a resident French governess and to pay her sixty guineas a-year if they could afford it: but, altogether, one might have supposed Major Raynor had dropped into an income of five or six thousand a-year, instead of only two thousand.

A shout and a laugh from the croquet lawn caused Edina to look towards the players. The game was at an end. At the same moment Alice saw Edina. She threw down her mallet, and ran upstairs.

"Why don't you come out, Edina? It is a lovely afternoon."

"I came up for my work, dear, and stayed thinking," replied Edina, drawing Alice to her side and keeping her arm round her.

"What were you thinking about?"

"Of many things. Chiefly about you and Charley. You both seem so changed."

"Do we?"

"And not for the better."

Alice laughed. She was nearly eighteen now, and very pretty. Her head was lifted with a conscious air: she played with one of the lilac bows on her white dress.

"I know what you mean, Edina: you heard mamma telling me this morning that I was growing vain."

"No, I did not hear her." But Edina said no more just then.

"Is Mr. Stane often here?" she asked, presently.

"Oh—yes—pretty often," replied Alice with a vivid blush. "He and Charles are good friends. And—and he lives near us, you know."

The blush and the hesitation seemed to hint at a story Edina had not yet glanced at. She had but been wondering whether this young Stane was a desirable companion for Charles: one likely to encourage him in idleness and extravagance, or to turn his ideas towards better things.

"Mr. Stane is older than Charley, Alice."

"Several years older. He is a barrister, and lives at his chambers in the Temple. Just now he is down here a great deal on account of his father's illness."

"Are they rich people?"

"No, I think not. Not very rich. Of course Sir Philip has plenty of money, and he has retired from practice. He used to be a lawyer in the City of London, and was knighted for something or other."

"Is William Stane the only son?"

"He is the second son. The eldest has the law business in the City; and there are two others. One is in the army."

"I like his look," mused Edina, gazing down at the young man, who was now talking to Major Raynor. "And—I think I like his manners. His countenance has pride in it, though."

Pride it certainly had: but it was a pleasant countenance for all that. William Stane was about middle height, with a somewhat rugged, honest, intelligent face, and an earnest manner. His eyes and hair were dark.

"Won't you come down, Edina?"

Edina turned at the appeal, and took up some work that lay on the table. "I was getting short of pocket-handkerchiefs," she said, in reference to it, "so I bought half-a-dozen new ones before I left home, and am now hemming them."

Alice shrugged her pretty shoulders. "Let one of the maids hem them for you, Edina. The idea of your troubling yourself with plain work!"

"The idea of my *not* troubling myself!" returned Edina. "Was life made only for play, Alice, think you? At Spring Lawn hemming handkerchiefs was looked upon as a pastime, compared with the heavier work there was to do."

"Oh, but those days have all passed," said Alice, somewhat resentfully, not at all pleased at having them recalled.

"Yes; and you have all changed with them. By the way, Alice, I was thinking what a beautiful room this is. Is not the furniture new?"

"All of it," replied Alice. "It was quite dingy when we came here; and papa and mamma thought that, as it was to be the state-room for visitors, they would have it done up properly."

Edina sighed. "It is very nice; very; too good for me. I am not used to such a room."

She sat down near Major Raynor under the weeping elm, and went on with her work. Charles, Alice, and young Stane began another game of the everlasting croquet. The major looked on and sipped his champagne-cup, the very image of intense satisfaction. Though he must have known that he was living at a most unjustifiable rate, and that it must again bring upon him the old enemy, debt, he looked as free from thought and care as any one can look in this world. Ay, and felt so, too. Not long yet had he been at this delightful place, Eagles' Nest; the time might be counted by weeks; but he had already flourished upon it. He had been stout enough before, but he was stouter now. The lost bonds or vouchers for the supposed accumulated savings left by Mrs. Atkinson, were depended upon by the major as a certain resource for any little extra expenses not justified by his present means. The bonds had not turned up yet, but he never doubted their coming to light some fine day. Hope, that most precious of our gifts, deceitful though it sometimes proves, was always buoyantly active in Major Raynor.

It was on this very subject of the lost bonds that Edina began to speak. The conversation was led up to. She had scarcely sat down, when a servant came from the house and approached his master, saying that "Tubbs" had come again, and particularly wished his little account settled, if quite convenient to the major, as he had a payment to make up.

"But it's not convenient," was the major's reply. "Tell Tubbs to come again next week."

"Is it any matter of a few shillings or so?" asked Edina, looking up, really thinking it might be so, and that the major did not care to trouble himself to go indoors for the money. "I have my purse in my pocket, Uncle Francis, and—"

"Bless you, my dear, it's a matter of fifteen or twenty pounds," interrupted the major, complacently watching his servant, who was carrying away the message. "For new harness and saddles and things. Tubbs is a saddler in the village, and we thought we would give him a turn. Your aunt Ann employed the tradespeople of the neighbourhood, and we think it right to do the same."

"Perhaps he wants his money, Uncle Francis?"

"No doubt of it, my dear. I'll pay him when I can. But as to ready-money, I seem to be shorter of it than ever. All the spare cash that came to me at your aunt Ann's death has run away in a wonderful manner. Sometimes I set myself to consider what it can have gone in; but I might as well try to count the leaves on that walnut-tree."

"I am very sorry," said Edina. "And you are living at so much expense!"

"Oh, it will be all right when the bonds turn up," cried the major, cheerfully. "Street says, you know, there must be at least fifteen or twenty thousand pounds somewhere."

"But he is not sure that there are any bonds to turn up, Uncle Francis. He does not *know* that the money exists still. Aunt Ann may have speculated and lost it."

"Now, my dear, is that likely?" cried the major. "Ann was never a speculating woman. And, if she had lost the money in any way, she would have been sure to say so. Street tells me she gave him all sorts of injunctions during the last year for the proper keeping-up of this estate, involving no end of cost; she wouldn't have done that if there hadn't been a substantial accumulation to draw upon."

"And do you keep it up well, uncle?"

"Why, how can I, Edina? I've no means to do it with."

"But are the revenues of the estate not sufficient to keep it up?"

"Well, they would be; but then you see I have so many expenses upon me."

Edina did quite two inches of her hemming before speaking again. The course they had embarked upon at Eagles' Nest seemed to be a wrong one altogether: but she felt that it was not her place to take her uncle to task.

"I'm sure I hope the money will be found, Uncle Francis."

"So do I, my dear, and soon too. It shall be better for you when it is. Why Ann should have left my brother Hugh and you unmentioned in her will, I cannot tell; but it was very unjust of her, and I will make it up to you, Edina, in a small way. Frank is to have three thousand pounds when the money turns up, and you shall have the same."

Edina smiled. She thought the promise very safe and very hopeless: though she knew the good-hearted speaker meant what he said.

"Thank you all the same, Uncle Francis, but I do not want any of the money; and I am sure you will have ways and means for every shilling of it, however much it may prove to be. How long does Frank mean to remain abroad?"

"Well, I conclude he is waiting for the money to turn up," said the major.

"Is it wise of him to stay so long, do you think?"

"I'm sure I don't know. When he receives the money he will return to London and settle down."

And so they chatted on. Mrs. Raynor, who had been lying down with a headache, came out and joined them. The afternoon wore on, and croquet came to an end. Mr. Stane approached to say good-bye.

"Won't you stay dinner?" asked the major.

"I should like to very much indeed, but I must go home," replied the young man: and once more, as Edina watched the sincere face and heard the earnest tone, she decided that she liked him. "My father particularly desired me to be at home to dinner: he was feeling less well again."

"Then you must stay with us next time," spoke the hospitable major.

MRS. HENRY WOOD

And Mr. Stane shook hands all round, leaving Alice to the last, and being somewhat longer over it with her than he need have been.

His departure was the signal for a general break-up. Major and Mrs. Raynor went indoors, Charles strolled across the lawn with William Stane. Edina retained her place and went on with her work. Charles soon came back again, and sat down by her.

"What a pity you don't play croquet, Edina! The last game was a good one."

"If I had all my time on my hands as you have, Charley, and nothing to do with it, I might perhaps take up croquet. I can't tell."

"I know what that tone means, Edina. You want to find fault with me for idleness."

"I could find fault with you for a good many things, Charles. The idleness is not the worst of it."

"What is the worst?" asked Charles, amused.

"You have so changed in these few weeks that I ask myself whether you can be the same single-minded, simple-hearted young people who lived at Spring Lawn. I speak of you and Alice, Charley."

"Circumstances have changed," returned Charles. "Alice"—for the girl at that moment came up to them—"Edina's saying we have so changed since leaving Bath that she wonders whether we are ourselves or not. How have we changed, pray, Edina?"

"Your minds and manners are changing," coolly spoke Edina, beginning to turn down the hem on the other side of the handkerchief. "Do you know what sort of people you put me in mind of now?"

"No. What?"

"Of nouveaux riches."

"For shame, Edina!"

"You do. And I think the world must judge you as I judge. You are haughty, purse-proud, indifferent."

"Go on," said Charley. "I like to hear the worst."

Edina did go on. "*You* are the worst, Charles. You seem to think the world was made for you alone. When that poor man came yesterday, a cottager, asking for some favour or assistance, or complaining of some hardship—I did not quite catch the words—you just flung him off as though he were not of the same species of created being as yourself. Have you a bad heart, Charles?"

Charles laughed. "I think I have a very good heart—as hearts go. The man is troublesome. His name's Beck. He has been here three times, and wants I don't know what done to his wretched cottage; says Mrs. Atkinson promised it. My father can't afford to listen to these complaints, Edina: and if he did it for one, he must do it for all. The fact is, Aunt Ann did so much for the wretches that she spoilt them."

"But you might have spoken kindly to the man. Civilly, at any rate."

"Oh, bother!" cried Charley: who was much of a boy still in manner. "Only think of all those years of poverty, Edina: we ought to enjoy ourselves now. Why, we had to look at a shilling before we spent it. And did not often get one to spend."

"But, Charley, you think *only* of enjoyment. Nothing is thought of at Eagles' Nest but the pleasure and gratification of the present hour, day by day, as the days come round."

"Well, I shall have enough work to do by-and-by, Edina. I go to Oxford after the long vacation."

"And you go without any preparation for it," said Edina.

"Preparation! Why, I am well up in classics," cried Charley, staring at Edina.

"I was not thinking of classics. You have had no experience, Charles; you are like a child in the ways of the world."

"I tell you, Edina, I am a very fair scholar. What else do you want at Oxford? You don't want experience there."

"Well for you, Charley, if it shall prove so," was Edina's answer, as she folded her work to go indoors; for the evening was drawing on, and the air felt chilly. Changed they all were, more than she could express. They saw with one set of eyes, she with another.

"What a tiresome thing Edina is getting!" exclaimed Alice to her brother, as Edina disappeared.

"A regular croaker."

"A confirmed old maid."

The only one who could not be said to have much changed, was Mrs. Raynor. She was gentle, meek, simple-mannered as ever: but even she was drawn into the vortex of visiting and gaiety, of show and expense, of parade and ceremony that had set in. She seemed to have no leisure to give to anything else. This day was the only quiet day Eagles' Nest had during Edina's visit. Mrs. Raynor, with her yielding will, could not help herself altogether. But Edina was grieved to see that she neglected the religious training of her young children. Even the hearing of their evening prayers was given over to the governess.

"Mademoiselle Delrue is a Protestant," said Mrs. Raynor; when, on

MRS. HENRY WOOD

this same evening, Edina ventured to speak a word upon the subject, as Kate and Robert said good-night and left the drawing-room.

"I know she is," said Edina. "But none but a mother should, in these vital matters, train her children. You always used to do it, Mary."

"If you only knew how fully my time and thoughts are occupied!" returned Mrs. Raynor, in a tone of great deprecation. "We live in a whirl here: and it is rather too much for me. And, to tell you the truth, Edina, I sometimes wonder whether the old life, with all its straitened means, was not the happier; whether we have in all respects improved matters, in coming to Eagles' Nest."

II

Apprehensions

The fine old house, Eagles' Nest, lay buried in snow. It was Christmas-tide, and Christmas weather. All the Raynor family had assembled within its walls: with the exception of Dr. Raynor and his daughter Edina. Charles had come home from keeping his first term at Oxford; Alfred from school; Frank Raynor and his wife had returned from their sojourn abroad.

All these past months, during which we have lost sight of them, Frank and Daisy had been on the Continent. Almost immediately after their departure from Trennach, Frank, through his medical friend, Crisp, was introduced to a lady who was going to Switzerland with her only son; a sickly lad of fifteen, in whom the doctors at home had hardly been able to keep life. This lady, Mrs. Berkeley, proposed to Frank to travel with them as medical attendant on her son, and she had not the least objection to Frank's wife being of the party. So preliminaries were settled, and they started. Frank considered it a most opportune chance to have fallen to him while waiting for the missing money to turn up.

But the engagement did not last long. Hardly had they settled in Switzerland when the lad died, and Mrs. Berkeley returned to England. Frank stayed on where he was. The place and the sojourn were alike pleasant; and, as he remarked to his wife, who knew but he might pick up a practice there, amongst the many English residents of the town, or those who flocked to it as birds of passage? Daisy was just as delighted to remain as he: they had funds in hand, and could afford to throw care to the winds. Even had care declared itself: which it did not. The young are sanguine, rarely gifted with much forethought. Frank and his wife especially lacked it. A few odds and ends of practice did drop into Frank, just a small case or so, at long intervals: and they remained stationary for some time in perfect complacency. But when Christmas approached, and Frank found that his five hundred pounds would not hold out for ever, and that the idea of a practice in the Swiss town was a mere castle in the air, he took his wife home again. By invitation, they went at once to Eagles' Nest.

Christmas-Day passed merrily, and some of the days immediately succeeding to it. On New-Year's Day they were invited to an entertainment at Sir Philip Stane's; Major and Mrs. Raynor, Charles and Alice; a later invitation having come in for Frank and his wife. William Stane was a frequent visitor at Eagles' Nest whenever he was sojourning at his father's; and, though he had not yet spoken, few could doubt that the chief object to draw him there was Alice Raynor.

Yes. Sunshine and merry-making, profusion and reckless expenditure reigned within the doors of Eagles' Nest; but little except poverty, distress and dissatisfaction existed beyond its gates. Mrs. Atkinson had ever been liberal in her care of the estate; the land had been enriched and thoroughly well kept; the small tenants and labourers were cared for. One thing she had not done so thoroughly as she might: and that was, improving the dwellings of the labourers. Repairs she had made from time to time; but the places were really beyond repair. Each tenement wanted one of two things: to be thoroughly renewed and to have an additional sleeping-room added; or else to be entirely rebuilt. During the last year of Mrs. Atkinson's life, she seemed to awaken suddenly to the necessity of doing something. Perhaps with the approach of death—which will often open our eyes to many things they remained closed to before—she saw the supineness she had been guilty of. Street the lawyer was hastily summoned to Eagles' Nest: he ordered to procure plans and estimates for new dwellings. A long row of cottages, some thirty in number, was hastily begun. Whilst the builders were commencing their work, Mrs. Atkinson died. With nearly her last breath she charged Mr. Street to see that the new houses were completed, and that the old ones were also repaired and made healthy.

Mr. Street could only hand over the charge to the inheritor of the estate, Major Raynor. The reader may remember that the major spoke of it to Edina. The lawyer could not do more than that, or carry out Mrs. Atkinson's wishes in any other way. And the major did nothing. His will might have been good enough to carry out the changes, but he had not the means. So much money was required for his own wants and those of his family, that he had none to spare for other people. The ready-money he came into had chiefly gone in paying back-debts: until these debts stared him in the face in black and white, he had not thought that he owed a tithe of them. It is a very common experience. So the new dwellings were summarily stopped, and remained as they were—so many skeletons: and the tumbledown cottages, wanting space, drainage, whitewash, and everything else that could render them decent and healthy, grew worse day by day, and became an eyesore to spectators and the talk of the neighbourhood.

Not only did *they* suffer from the major's want of money and foresight; many other necessities were crying out in like manner: these are only given as a specimen. Above all, he was doing no good to the land, spending nothing to enrich it, and sparing necessary and ordinary labour. Perhaps had Major Raynor understood the cultivation and requirements of land, he might have made an effort to improve his own: as it was, it deteriorated day by day.

This state of things had caused a certain antagonism to set in between Eagles' Nest and its dependents. The labourers and their families grumbled; the major, conscious of the state of affairs, and feeling some slight shame in consequence, but knowing at the same time that he was powerless to remedy it, shunned them. When complainers came to the house he would very rarely see them. A warm-hearted man, he could not bear to hear them. Mrs. Raynor and the elder children, understanding matters very imperfectly, naturally espoused the major's cause, and looked upon the small tenants as a barbarous, insubordinate set of wretches, next door to insurgents. When the poor wives or children fell ill, no succour was sent to them from Eagles' Nest. With this estrangement reigning, Mrs. Raynor did not attempt to help: not from coldness of heart, but that she considered they did not deserve help, and, moreover, thought it would be flung back on her if she offered it.

There was where the shoe pinched the poor. The insufficient dwellings they were used to; though indeed with every winter and every summer they grew worse than ever; but they were not accustomed to utter, contemptuous neglect, as they looked upon it, in times of need. Mrs. Atkinson had always been a generous mistress: when sickness or sorrow or distress in times of little work set in, her hand and purse were ever open. Coals in severe weather, Christmas cheer, warm garments for the scantily clad, broth for the sick; she had furnished all: and it was the entire withdrawal of this aid that was so much felt now. The winter was unusually severe: it frequently is so after a very hot summer; labour was scarce, food was dear: and a great deal of illness prevailed. So that you perceive all things were not so flourishing in and about Eagle's Nest as they might have been, and Major Raynor's bed was not entirely one of rose-leaves.

But, unpleasant things that are out of sight, are, it is said, for the most part out of mind—Mr. Blase Pellet told us so much a chapter or two ago—and the discomfort out-of-doors did not disturb the geniality within. At Eagles' Nest, the days floated on in a round of enjoyment; they seemed to be one continuous course of pleasure that would never end. Daisy Raynor had never been so happy in all her life: Eagles' Nest, she said, was perfection.

The music and wax-lights, the flowers and evergreens rendered the rooms at Sir Philip Stane's a scene of enchantment. At least it seemed so to Alice Raynor as she entered upon it. William Stane stood near the door, and caught her hand as she and Charles were following their father and mother.

"The first dance is mine, remember, Alice," he whispered. And her pretty cheeks flushed and a half-conscious smile parted her lips, as she passed on to Lady Stane.

Lady Stane, a stout and kindly woman in emerald green, received her kindly. She suspected that this young lady might some day become her daughter-in-law, and she looked at her more critically than she had ever looked before. Alice could bear the inspection to-night. Her new white dress was beautiful; her face was charming, her manner modest and graceful. "The most lady-like girl in the room," mentally decided Lady Stane, "and no doubt will have a fair fortune. William might do worse."

William Stane thought he might do very much worse. Without doubt he was truly attached to Alice. Not perhaps in the wild and ardent manner that some lovers own to: all natures are not capable of that: but he did love her, her only, and he hoped that when he married it was she who would be his wife. He was not ready to marry at present. He was progressing in his profession, but with the proverbial slowness that is said to attend the advancement of barristers: and he did not wish to speak just yet. Meanwhile he was quite content to make love tacitly; and he felt sure that his intentions were understood.

His elder brother was not present this evening, and it fell to William to take his place, and dispense his favours pretty equally amongst the guests. But every moment that he could snatch for Alice, was given to her; in every dance that he could possibly spare her, she was his partner.

"Have you enjoyed the evening, Alice?" he asked in a whisper, as he was taking her to the carriage at three o'clock in the morning.

"I never enjoyed an evening half so much," was the shyly-breathed answer. And Mr. William Stane took possession of her hand as she spoke, and kept it to the last.

If this light-hearted carelessness never came to an end! If freedom from trouble could only last for ever! Pleasure first, says some wise old saw, pain afterwards. With the dawn came the pain to Eagles' Nest.

Amongst the letters delivered to Major Raynor—who, for a wonder, had risen betimes that morning, and was turning places over in his study in search of the lost bonds—was one from Oxford. It enclosed a very heavy bill for wine supplied to his son Charles: heavy, considering Mr. Charles's years and the duration of his one sojourn at the University. The major stared at it, with his spectacles, and without his spectacles; he looked at the heading, he gazed at the foot; and finally when he had mastered it he went into a passion, and ordered Charles before him. So peremptory was the summons, that Charles appeared in haste, half dressed. His outburst, when he found out what the matter was, quite equalled his father's.

"I'm sure I thought you must be on fire down here, sir," said he. "What confounded sneaks they are, to apply to you! I can't understand their doing it."

"Sneaks be shot!" cried the wrathful major. "Do you owe all this, or don't you? That's the question."

"Why, the letter was addressed to *me!*" exclaimed Charles, who had been examining the envelope. "I must say, sir, you might allow me to open my own letters."

But the major was guiltless of any want of faith. The mistake was the butler's. He had inadvertently placed the letter amongst his master's letters, and the major opened it without glancing at the address.

"What does it signify, do you suppose, whether I opened it or you?" demanded the major. "Not that I did it intentionally. I should have to know of it: *you* can't pay this."

"They can wait," said Charles.

"Wait! Do you mean to confess that you have had all this wine?" retorted the major, irascible for once. "Why, you must be growing into—into what I don't care to name!"

"You can't suppose that I drank it, sir. The other undergrads give wine parties, and I have to do the same. They drink the wine; I don't."

"That is, you drink it amongst you," roared the major; "and a nice disreputable lot you must all be. I understood that young men went to college to study; not to drink, and run up bills. What else do you owe? Is this all?"

Charles hesitated in answering. An untruth he would not tell. The major saw what the hesitation meant, and it alarmed him. When we become frightened our wrath cools down. The major dropped into a chair, and lost his fierceness and his voice together.

"Charley," said he in very subdued tones, "I have not the money to pay with. You know I haven't. If it's much, it will ruin me."

"But it is not much, father," returned Charles, his own anger disarmed and contrition taking its place. "There may be one or two more trifling bills; nothing to speak of."

"What on earth made you run them up?"

"I'm sure I don't know; and I am very sorry for it," said Charles. "These things accumulate in the most extraordinary manner. When you fancy that you owe only a few shillings at some place or another, it turns out to be pounds. You have no idea what it is, father!"

"Have I not!" returned the major, significantly. "It is because I have rather too much idea of the insidious way in which debt creeps upon one, that I should like to see you keep out of its toils. Charley, my boy, I have been staving off liabilities all my life, and haven't worried myself in doing it; but it is beginning to tell upon me now. My constitution's changing. I suppose I must be growing fidgety."

"Well, don't let this worry you, father. It's not so very much."

"Much or little, it must be paid. I don't want my son to get into bad odour at college; or have 'debtor' attached to his name. You are young for that, Mr. Charles."

Charles remained silent. The major was evidently in blissful ignorance of the latitude of opinion current amongst Oxonians.

"Go back and dress yourself, Charles; and get your breakfast over; and then, just sit down and make out a list of what it is you owe, and I'll see what can be done."

Now in the course of this same morning it chanced that Frank Raynor took occasion to speak to his uncle about money matters, as connected with his own prospects, which he had not previously entered upon during his present stay. The major was pacing his study in a gloomy mood when Frank entered.

"You look tired, Uncle Francis. Just as though you had been dancing all night."

"I leave that to you younger men," returned the major, drawing his easy-chair to the fire. "As to being tired, Frank, I am so; though I have not danced."

"Tired of what, uncle?"

"Of everything, I think. Sit down, lad."

"I want to speak to you, Uncle Francis, concerning myself and my plans," said Frank, taking a seat near the fire. "It is time I settled down to something."

"Is it?" was the answer. The major's thoughts were elsewhere.

"Why, yes; don't you think it is, sir? The question is, what is it to be? With regard to the bonds for that missing money, uncle? They have not turned up, I conclude?"

"They have not turned up, my boy, or the money either. If they had, you'd have been the first to hear of it. I have been searching for them this very morning."

"What is your true opinion about the money, Uncle Francis?" resumed Frank, after a pause. "Will it ever be found?"

"Yes, Frank, I think it will. I feel assured that the money is lying somewhere—and that it will come to the surface sooner or later. I should be sorry to think otherwise; for, goodness knows, I need it badly enough."

A piece of blazing wood fell off the grate. Frank caught the tongs, and put it up again.

"And I wish it could be found for your sake, also, Frank. You want your share of it, you know."

"Why, you see, Uncle Francis, without money I don't know what to be at. If I were single, I'd engage myself out as assistant to-morrow; but for my wife's sake I wish to take a better position than that."

"Naturally you do, Frank, And so you ought."

"It would be easy enough if I had the money in hand; or if I could with any certainty say when I should have it."

"It's sure to come," said the major. "Quite sure."

"Well, I hope so. The difficulty is—when?"

"You must wait a bit longer, my boy. It may turn up any day. To-night, even: to-morrow morning. Never a day passes but I go ferreting into some corner or other of the old house, thinking I may put my hand upon the papers. They are lying in it somewhere, I know, overlooked."

"But I don't see my way clear to wait. Not to wait long. We must have a roof over our heads, and means to keep it up—"

"Why, you have a roof over your heads," interrupted the major. "Can't you stay here?"

"I should not like to stay too long," avowed Frank in his candour. "It would be abusing your hospitality."

MRS. HENRY WOOD

"Abusing a fiddlestick!" cried the major, staring at Frank. "What's come to you? Is the house not large enough?—and plenty to eat in it? I'm sure you may stay here for ever; and the longer you stay the more welcome you'll be. We like to have you."

"Thank you greatly, Uncle Francis."

"Daisy does not want to go away; she's as happy as the day's long," continued the major. "Just make yourselves comfortable here, Frank, my boy, until the money turns up and I can hand you over some of it."

"Thank you again, uncle," said Frank, accepting the hospitality in the free-hearted spirit that it was offered. "For a little while at any rate we will stay with you; but I hope before long to be doing something and to get into a home of my own. I can run up to town once or twice a week and be looking out."

"Of course you can."

"Had you been a rich man, Uncle Francis, I would have asked you to lend me a thousand pounds, or so, to set me up until the nest-egg is found; but I know you have not got it to lend."

"Got it to lend!" echoed the major in dismayed astonishment. "Why, Frank, my boy, I want to borrow such a sum myself. I wish to my heart I knew where to pick it up. Here's Charles must have money now: has come home from Oxford with a pack of debts at his back!"

"Charles has!" exclaimed Frank in surprise.

"And would like to make me believe that all the rest of the young fellows there run up the same bills! every man Jack of 'em! No, no, Master Charley: you don't get me to take *that* in. Young men can be steady at college as well as at home if they choose to be. Charley's just one that's led any way. He is young, you see, Frank: and he is thrown there, I expect, amongst a few rich blades to whom money is no object, and must needs do as they do. The result is, he has made I don't know what liabilities, and I must pay them. Oh, it's all worry and bother together!"

Not intentionally, but by chance, Frank, on quitting his uncle, came upon Charles. Looking into a room in search of his wife, there sat Charley at a table, pen, ink and paper before him, setting down his debts, as far as he could judge of and recollect them. Frank went in and closed the door.

Charles let off a little of his superfluous discomfort in abuse of the people who had presumed to trouble him with the wine bill. Frank sat down, and drew the paper towards him.

"I had no idea it could be as much as that, Frank," was the rueful avowal. "And I wish with all my heart their wine parties and their fast living had been at the bottom of the sea!"

"*Is* it as much, Charley?"

"To tell the truth, I am afraid it's more," said Charles, with candour. "I've only made a guess at the other amounts, and I know I have not put down too much. That tailor is an awful man for sticking it on: as all the rest of the crew are, for the matter of that. I was trying to recollect how many times I've had horses and traps and things; and I can't."

"Does Uncle Francis know it comes to all this?"

"No. And I don't care to let him know. Things seem to worry him so much now. I do wish that lost money could be found!"

"Just what your father and I have been wishing," cried Frank. "Look here, Charley. I have a little left out of my five hundred pounds. You shall have half of it: just between ourselves, you know: and then the sum my uncle must find will not look so formidable to him. Nay, no thanks, lad: would you not all do as much for me—and more? And we are going to stay on here for a time—and that will save expenses."

It was simply impossible for Frank Raynor to see a difficulty of this kind, or indeed of any kind, and not help to relieve it if he had help in his power. That he would himself very speedily require the money he was now giving away, was only too probable: but he was content to forget that in Charley's need.

The one individual person in all the house that Charles would have kept from the knowledge of his folly—and in his repentance he looked upon it as folly most extreme—was his mother. He loved her dearly; and he had the grace to be ashamed, for her sake, of what he had done, and to hope that she would never know it. A most fallacious hope, as he was soon to find, for Major Raynor had taken the news up to her with open mouth.

She was sitting on the low sofa in her dressing-room that evening at dusk, when Charles went in. The firelight played on her face, showing its look of utter weariness, and the traces of tears.

"What's the matter, mother?" he asked, sitting down beside her and taking her hand. "Are you ill?"

"Not ill, Charley," she answered. "Only tired and—and out of sorts."

"What has tired you? Last night, I suppose. But you have been resting all day."

"Not last night particularly. So much fast living does not suit me."

"Fast living!" exclaimed Charles in wondering accents. "Is it the gravies?—or the plum-puddings?"

Mrs. Raynor could not forbear a smile. "I was not thinking of the table, Charles; the gravies and the puddings; but of our fast, artificial existence. We seem to have no rest at all. It is always excitement; nothing but excitement. We went out last night; we go out to dinner to-morrow night; people come here the next night. Every day that we are at home there is something; if it's not luncheon and afternoon-tea, it's dinner; and if it's not dinner, it's supper. I have to think of it all; the entertainments and the dress, and everything; and to go out when you go; and—and I feel it is getting rather too much for me."

"Then lie up, mother, for a few days," advised Charles, affectionately. "Keep by your own fire, and turn things over to Alice and the servants. You will soon be all right again."

Mrs. Raynor did not answer. She held Charles's hand in her own, and was looking steadfastly at the flickering blaze. A silence ensued. Charles lost himself in a train of thought.

"What about this trouble of yours, Charley?"

It was a very unpleasant awakening for him. Of all things, this is what he had wanted to keep from her. His ingenuous face—and it was an ingenuous face in spite of the wine bills—flushed deeply with annoyance.

"It's what you need not have heard about, mother. I came away from Oxford without paying a few pounds I owe there; that's all. There need be no fuss about it."

"I hear of wine bills, and horses, and things of that kind. Oh, my dear, *need* you have entered into that fast sort of life?"

"Others enter into it," said Charley.

"It is not so much the cost that troubles me," added Mrs. Raynor, in loving tones; "that can be met somehow. It is—" She stopped as if wanting words.

"It is what, mother?"

"Charley, my dear, what I think of is this—that you may be falling into the world's evil ways. It is so easy to do it; you young lads are so inexperienced and confiding; you think all is fair that looks fair; that no poison lurks in what has a specious surface. And oh, my boy, you know that there is a world after this world; and if you were to fall too deeply into the ways of *this*, to get to love it, to be unable to do without it, you might never gain the other. Some young lads that have fallen away from God have not cared to find Him again; never have found Him.

"There has been no harm," said Charley. "And I assure you I don't often miss chapel."

"Charley, dear, there's a verse in Ecclesiastes that I often think of," she resumed in low sweet tones. "All mothers think of it, I fancy, when their sons begin to go out in the world."

"In Ecclesiastes?" repeated Charley.

"The verse that Edina illuminated for us once, when she was staying at Spring Lawn. It was her doing it, I think, that helped to impress it so much on my memory."

"I remember it, mother mine." And the words ran through Charley's thoughts as he spoke.

"Rejoice, O young man, in thy youth and let thy heart cheer thee in the days of thy youth, and walk in the ways of thine heart, and in the sight of thine eyes: but know thou, that for all these things God will bring thee into judgment."

III

A Tiger

The late spring flowers were blooming; the air was soft and balmy. Easter was rather late; in fact, April was passing; and when Easter comes at that period, it generally brings sunshine with it.

Eagles' Nest, amidst other favoured spots, seemed to be as bright as the day was long. Once more Major Raynor had all his children about him; also Frank and Daisy. For anything that could be seen on the surface, merry hearts reigned; none of them seemed to have a care in the world.

Frank decidedly had not. Sanguine and light-hearted, he was content as ever to let the future take care of itself. Yielding to persuasion, he still stayed on at Eagles' Nest. His wife looked forward to being laid up in the course of a month or two: and where, asked the major, could she be better attended to than at Eagles' Nest? Daisy, of course, wished to remain; she should feel safe, she said, in the care of Mrs. Raynor: and who would wish to run away from so pleasant a home? Twenty times at least had Frank gone up to town to see if he could pick up any news, or hear of anything to suit him. Delusive dreams often presented themselves to his mental vision, of some doctor, rich in years and philanthropy, who might be willing to take him in for nothing, to share his first-rate practice. As yet the benevolent old gentleman had not been discovered, but Frank quite believed he existed somewhere.

Another thing had not been discovered: the missing money. But Major Raynor, sanguine as ever was his nephew, did not lose faith in its existence. It would come to light some time he felt certain; and of this he never ceased to assure Frank. Embarrassments decidedly increased upon the major, chiefly arising from the want of ready cash; for the greater portion of *that* was sure to be forestalled before it came in. Still, a man who enjoys from two to three thousand a-year cannot be so very badly off: money comes to the fore somehow: and on the whole Major Raynor led an easy, indolent, and self-satisfied life. Had they decreased their home expenses, it would have been all the better: and they might have done that very materially, and yet not touched on home comforts. But neither Major nor Mrs. Raynor knew how to set about retrenchment: and so the senseless profusion went on.

"What is there to see, Charley?"

The questioner was Frank. In crossing the grounds, some little distance from home, he came upon Charles Raynor. Charles was craning his neck over a stile, by which the high hedge was divided that bordered the large, enclosed, three-cornered tract of land known as the common. On one side of the common were those miserable dwellings, the neglected cottages: in a line with them ran the row of skeletons, summarily stopped in process of erection. On the other side stood some pretty detached cottages, inhabited by a somewhat better class of people; whilst this high hedge—now budding into summer bloom, and flanked with a sloping bank, rich in moss and weeds and wild flowers—bordered the third side. In one corner, between the hedge and the better houses, flourished a small grove of trees. It all belonged to Major Raynor.

"Nothing particular," said Charley, in answer to the question. "I was only looking at a fellow."

Frank sent his eyes over the green space before him. Three or four paths traversed it in different directions. A portion of it was railed off by wooden fencing, and on this some cattle grazed; but on most of it grass was growing, intended for the mower in a month or two's time. Frank could not see a soul; and said so. Some children, indeed, were playing before the huts; but Charles had evidently not alluded to them: his gaze had been directed to the opposite side, near the grove.

"He has disappeared amongst those trees," said Charles.

"Who was it?" pursued Frank: for there was something in his young cousin's tone and manner suggestive of uneasiness; and it awoke his own curiosity.

Charles turned and put his back against the stile. He had plucked a small twig from the hedge, and was twirling it about between his lips.

"Frank, I am in a mess. Keep a look-out yonder, and if you see a stranger, tell me."

"Over-run the constable at Oxford this term, as before?" questioned Frank, leaping to the truth by instinct.

Charles nodded. "And I assure you, Frank," he added, attempting to excuse himself, "that I no more intended to get into debt this last term than I intended to hang myself. When I went down after Christmas, I had formed the best resolutions in the world. I told the mother she might trust me. No one could have wished to keep straighter than I wished: and somehow—"

"You didn't," put in Frank at the pause.

"I have managed to fall into a fast set, and that's the truth," confessed Charles. "And I think the very deuce is in the money. It runs away without your knowing it."

"Well, the tradespeople must wait," said Frank, cheerfully; for he was just as genial over this trouble as he would have been over pleasure. "They have to wait pretty stiffly for others.

"The worst of it is, I have accepted a bill or two," cried Charley, ruefully. "And—I had a writ served upon me the last day of term."

"Whew!" whistled Frank. "A writ?"

"One. And I expect another. Those horrid bills—there are two of them—were drawn at only a month's date. Of course the time's out; and the fellow wouldn't renew; and I expect there'll be the dickens to pay. The amount is not much; each fifty pounds; but I have not the ghost of a shilling to meet it with."

"What do you owe besides?"

"As if I knew! There's the tailor, and the bootmaker, and the livery stables, and the wine— Oh, I can't recollect."

Had Frank possessed the money, in pocket or prospective, he would have handed out help to Charles there and then. But he did not possess it. He was at a nonplus.

"When once a writ's served, they can take you, can't they?" asked Charles, stooping to pluck a pink blossom from the bank, the twig being bitten away to nothing.

"I think so," replied Frank, who had himself contrived to steer clear of these unpleasant shoals, and knew no more of their power than Charles did. "By the way, though, I don't know. Have they got judgment?"

"Judgment? What's that? Sure to have got it if it's anything bad. And I think I am going to be arrested," continued Charles, dropping his voice, and turning to face the common again. "It's rather a blue look-out. I should not so *much* mind it for myself, I think: better men than I have had to go through the same: but it's the fuss there'll be at home."

"The idea of calling yourself a man, Charley! You are only a boy yet."

"By the way, talking of that, Jones of Corpus told me a writ could not be legally served upon me as I was not of age. Jones said he was sure of it. What do you think, Frank?"

"I don't know. To tell you the truth, Charley, I am not at home in these things. But I should suppose that the very fact of the writ having been served upon you is a proof that it can be done, and that Jones of Corpus is wrong. William Stane could tell you: he must have all points of law at his fingers' ends."

"But I don't care to ask William Stane. It may be they take it for granted that I am of age. Any way, I was served with the writ at Oxford: and, unless I am mistaken," added Charles, gloomily, "a fellow has followed me here, and is dodging my heels to arrest me."

"What are your grounds for thinking so, Charley? Have you seen any suspicious person about?"

"Yes, I have. Before you came up just now, I—"

The words were broken off suddenly. Charles leaped from the corner of the stile to hide behind the hedge. Some individual was emerging from the grove of trees; and he, it was evident, had caused the movement.

"If he turns his steps this way, tell me, Frank, and I'll make a dash homewards through the oak-coppice," came the hurried whisper.

"All right. No. He is making off across the common."

"That may be only a ruse to throw me off my guard," cried Charley, from the hedge. "Watch. He will come over here full pelt in a minute. He looks just like a tiger, with that great mass of brown beard. He is a tiger."

Frank, leaning his arms on the stile, scanned the movements of the "Tiger." The Tiger was at some distance, and he could not see him clearly. A thin tiger of middle height, and apparently approaching middle age, dressed in a suit of grey, with a slouching hat on his brows and a fine brown beard. But the Tiger, whosoever he might be, appeared to entertain no hostile intentions for the present moment, and was strolling leisurely in the direction of the huts. Presently Frank spoke.

"He is well away now, Charley: too far to distinguish you, even should he turn round. There's no danger."

Charley came out from the hedge, and took up his former position at the extreme corner of the stile, where he was partly hidden. Every vestige of colour had forsaken his face. He was very young still: not much more than a boy, as Frank had said: and unfamiliar with these things.

"I saw him yesterday for the first time," said he to Frank. "I chanced to be standing here, as we are now, and he was walking towards me across the common. Whilst wondering, in a lazy kind of way, who he

MRS. HENRY WOOD

was and what he wanted here, a rush of fear came over me. It occurred to me that he might be a sheriff's officer. Why the idea should flash on me in that sudden manner—and the fear—I cannot tell; but it did so. I made the best of my way indoors, and did not stir out again. This morning I said to myself what a simpleton I had been—that I had no grounds for fearing the man, except that he was a stranger, and that my own mind was full of bother; and I came out, all bravery. The first person I saw, upon crossing this stile, was he; just in the same spot, near the trees, in which I saw him yesterday; and the rush of fear came over me again. It's of no good your laughing, Frank: I can't help it: I never was a coward before."

"I was not laughing. Did he see you?"

"Not to-day, I think. Yesterday he did, looked at me keenly; and here he is again in the same spot! I am sure he is looking for me. If I were up in funds, I'd be off somewhere and stay away."

"What about home—and Oxford?"

"There's the worst of it."

"And you could not stay away for ever."

"For ever, no. But, you see, that money may turn up any day, and put all things straight."

"Well, you may be mistaken in the man, Charley: and I hope you are."

William Stane was at home for these Easter holidays, and still the shadow of Alice Raynor. It chanced that this same afternoon he and Alice encountered the Tiger—as, from that day, Charles and Frank both called him in private. Strolling side by side under the brilliant afternoon sun, in that silence which is most eloquent of love, with the birds singing above them, and the very murmur of the trees speaking a sweet language to their hearts, they came upon this stranger in grey, sitting on the stump of a tree. The trees, mostly beeches, were thick about there; the path branched off sharply at a right angle, and they did not see him until they were close up: in fact, William Stene had to make a hasty stop or two to pass without touching him. Perhaps it was his unexpected appearance in that spot, or that it was not usual to see strangers there, or else his peculiar look, with the slouching hat and the bushy beard; but certain it was that he especially attracted their attention; somewhat of their curiosity.

"What a strange-looking man!" exclaimed Alice, when they had gone on some distance. "Did you not think so, William?"

"Queerish. Does he live here? I wonder if he is aware that he is trespassing?"

"Papa lets any one come on the grounds who likes to," replied Alice. "He is a stranger. I never saw him before."

"Oh, it must be one of the Easter excursionists. Escaped from smoky London to enjoy a day or two of pure air in the Kentish Wolds."

"As you have done," said she.

"As I have done. I only wish, Alice, I could enjoy it oftener."

Words and the tone alike bore a precious meaning to her ear. His eyes met hers, and lingered there.

"I am getting on excellently," he continued. "By the end of this year, I have no doubt I shall be justified in—in quitting my chambers and taking a house. Perhaps before that."

"Look at that hawthorn!" exclaimed Alice, darting to a hedge they were now passing, for she knew too well what the words implied. "Has it not come out early! It is in full bloom."

"Shall I gather some for you?"

"No. It would be a pity. It looks so well there, and every one who passes can enjoy it. Do you know, I never see the flowering hawthorn but I think of that good old Scotch song, 'Ye banks and braes.' I don't know why."

"Let us sit down here," said he, as they came to a rustic seat under the trees. "And now, Alice, if you would sing that good old song, the charm would be perfect."

She laughed. "What charm?"

"The charm of—everything. The day and hour, the white and pink may budding in the hedges, the wild flowers we crush with our feet, the blue sky and the green trees, the sunshine and the shade, the singing birds and the whispering leaves, and—yourself."

Not another word from either of them just yet. William Stane had allowed his hand to fall on hers. Her head was slightly turned from him, her cheeks were glowing, her heart was beating: it was again another interval of that most sweet and eloquent silence.

"Won't you begin, Alice? The birds 'warbling through the flowering thorn' are waiting to hear you. So am I."

And as if she had no power to resist his will, she began at once, without a dissenting murmur, and sang the song to the end. Excepting the birds above them, there were no listeners: no rover was likely to be near that solitary spot. Her voice was sweet, but not loud; every syllable was spoken distinctly. To sit there for ever, side by side, and not be disturbed, would be a very Eden.

> *"And my fake lover stole my rose,*
> *But ah! he left the thorn wi' me."*

Scarcely had the echoing melody died away, when the unexpected sound of footsteps was heard approaching, and there advanced into view a woman well known to Alice; one Sarah Croft, the wife of a man employed on the estate. They lived in one of the most miserable dwellings on the common, but were civil and quiet; somewhat independent in manner, but never joining in the semi-rebellion that reigned. She looked miserably poor. Her blue cotton gown, though clean, was in rags, her old shawl would hardly hang together, the black bonnet on her head might have been used for frightening the crows. She dropped a curtsy and was passing onwards, when Alice inquired after her sick children.

"They be no better, Miss Raynor, thank you," she answered, halting in front of the bench. "The little one, she be took sick now, as well as the two boys. I've a fine time o't.

"Why don't you have a doctor to them?" said Alice.

"More nor a week agone I went up to the parish and told them I must have a doctor to my children: but he never come till yesterday."

"What did he say?"

"I'll tell ye what he said, Miss Raynor, if ye like. He said doctors and doctors' stuff was o' no good, so long as the houses remained what they was—pes-ti-fe-rus. I should not have remembered the word, though, but for Jetty's lodger repeating of the very self-same word to me a minute or two agone. I've just passed him, a-sitting down under yonder beeches."

Alice, as well as William Stane, instantly recalled the man in grey they had seen there. "Jetty's lodger!" repeated Alice. "Who is he?"

"Some stranger staying in the place, Miss Raynor. He come into it one morning, a week agone, and took Jetty's rooms which was to let."

"What is he staying here for?"

"To pry into people's business, I think," replied the woman. "He's always about, here, there, and everywhere; one can't stir out many yards but one meets him. Saturday last, he walks right into our place without as much as knocking; and there he turns hisself round and about, looking at the rotten floor and the dripping walls, and sniffing at the bad smell that's always there, just as if he had as much right inside as a king. 'Who is your landlord?' says he, 'and does he know what a den this is?' So I told him that our landlord was Major Raynor at Eagles' Nest, and that he did know, but that nothing was done for us. He have gone, I hear, into some o' the other houses as well."

The woman's tone was quite civil, but there could be no doubt that, in her independence, she was talking at Alice as the daughter of Major Raynor.

"As I passed him now he asked me whether my sick children was better—just as you have, Miss Raynor. I told him they was worse. 'And worse they will be, and never better, and all the rest of you too,' says he, 'as long as you inhabit them pes-ti-fe-rus dens!'"

Alice drew up her head in cold disdain, vouchsafing no further word, and feeling very angry at the implied reproach. The woman dropped a slight curtsy again, and went on her way.

"How insolent they all are!" exclaimed Alice to Mr. Stane. "That Sarah Croft would have been abusive in another moment."

"Their cottages are bad," returned the young man, after a pause. "Could nothing be done, I wonder, to make them a little better?"

"It is papa's business, not mine," remarked Alice, in slight resentment. "And the idea of that stranger presuming to interfere! wonder what he means by it?"

"I do not suppose he intends it as interference: he is looking about him by way of filling up his time: it must hang rather monotonously on his hands down here, I presume, away from his books and ledgers," remarked Mr. Stane. "It is the way of the world, Alice; people must be busy-bodies and look into what does not concern them, for curiosity's sake. Nay, just a few moments longer," he said, for she had risen to depart. "To-morrow I shall have no such pleasant and peaceful seat to linger in; I shall not have you. How delightful it all is!"

And so, the disturbing element forgotten, they sat on in the balmy air, under the blue of the sky, the green foliage about them springing into life and beauty, type of another Life that must succeed our own winter, and listening to the little birds overhead warbling their joyous songs. Can none of us, grey now with care and work and years, remember just such an hour spent in our own sweet spring-time?—when all things around spoke to our hearts in one unmixed love-strain of harmony, and the future looked like a charmed scroll that could only bring intense happiness in the unrolling thereof?

"Take my arm, Alice," he half whispered, when they at length rose to return.

She did take it, her face and heart glowing. Took it timidly and with much self-consciousness, never having been in the habit of taking it, or he of offering it. Her hand trembled as it lay gently upon his arm; each might have heard the other's heart beating. And so in the bliss of this, their first love-dream, they sauntered home through the grounds, choosing pleasant glades and mossy by-ways; and arrived to find Eagles' Nest in a commotion.

Mrs. Frank Raynor had been taken seriously and unexpectedly ill. Doctors were sent for; servants ran about. And William Stane said farewell, and went home from an afternoon that would ever remain as a green spot on his memory. It was his last day of holiday.

WITH THE MORNING, DAISY LAY in great danger. The illness, not anticipated for a month or two, had come on suddenly. In one sense of the word the event was over, but not the danger; and the baby, not destined to see the light, was gone.

It was perhaps unfortunate that on this same morning Frank should receive an urgent summons to Trennach. Edina wrote. Her father was very ill; ill, it was feared, unto death; and he most earnestly begged Frank to travel to him with all speed, for he had urgent need of seeing him. Edina said that, unless her father should rally, three or four days were the utmost limits of life accorded to him by the doctors: she therefore begged of Frank to lose no time in obeying the summons; and she added that her father desired her to say the journey should be no cost to him.

"What a distressing thing!" cried Frank, in blank dismay, showing the letter to the major. "I cannot go. It is impossible that I can go whilst Daisy lies in this state."

"Good gracious!" said the major, rubbing his head, as he always did in any emergency. "Well, I suppose you can't, my boy. Poor Hugh!"

"How can I! Suppose I were to go, and—and she died?"

"Yes, to be sure. You must wait until she is in less danger. I hope with all my heart Hugh will rally. And Daisy too."

Frank sat down and wrote a few words to his uncle, telling him why he could not start that day, but that he would do so the moment his wife's state allowed it. He wrote more fully, but to the same effect, to Edina. Perhaps on the morrow, he added. The morrow might bring better things.

But on the morrow Daisy was even worse. A high fever had set in. Frank wrote again to Trennach, but he could not leave Eagles' Nest. Some days went on; days of peril: Daisy was hovering between life and death. And on the first day that a very faint indication of improvement was perceptible and the medical men said she might now live, that there was a bare chance of it, but no certainty; that same day the final news came from Trennach, and it was too late for Frank to take the journey. Dr. Raynor was dead.

The tidings came by letter from Edina: written to Frank. It was only a short note, giving a few particulars. Within this note, however, was a thicker letter, sealed and marked "Private." Frank chanced to be alone at the moment, and opened it with some curiosity. On a single sheet of enveloping paper, enclosing a letter from Dr. Raynor, were the following lines from Edina.

My poor father was so anxious to see you, dear Frank, at the last, that it disturbed his peace. Of course you could not come, under the circumstances; he saw that; but he said over and over again that your not coming was most unfortunate, and to you might be disastrous. At the hours of the day and night when a train was due, nothing could exceed the eagerness with which he looked for you, his restlessness when it grew too late to admit of hope that you had come. The day before he died, when he knew the end was approaching and he should not live to see you, he caused himself to be propped up in bed, and had pen-and-ink brought that he might write to you. He watched me seal up the letter when it was finished, and charged me to send it to you when all was over, but to be sure to enclose it privately, and to tell you to open and read it when you were alone.

E. R.

Sending Edina's short note announcing the death of her father to Major Raynor by a servant, Frank carried these lines and the doctor's letter to his chamber: thereby obeying injunctions, but nevertheless wondering at them very much. What could his uncle have to say to him necessitating secrecy? Breaking the seal, he ran his eyes over the almost illegible lines that the dying hand had traced.

My Dear Nephew Frank,

"I wanted to see you; I ought not to have put it off so long. But this closing scene has come upon me somewhat suddenly: and now I cannot write all I ought to, and should wish: and I must, of necessity, write abruptly.

"*Are you conscious of being in any danger?* Have you committed any act that could bring you under the arm of the law? If so, take care of yourself. A terrible rumour was whispered in my ears by Andrew Float, connecting you with the hitherto unexplained fate of Bell the miner. I charged Float to be silent—and I think he will be, for he is a kind and good man, and only spoke to me that I might put you on your guard—and I questioned Blase Pellet, from whom Float had heard it. Pellet was sullen, obstinate, would not say much; but he did say that he could hang you, and *would* do it if you offended him or put yourself in his way. I could not get anything more from him, and it was not a subject that I cared to inquire into minutely, or could pursue openly.

"My boy, you best know what grounds there may be for this half-breathed accusation; whether any or none. I have scarcely had a minute's peace since it reached me, now three weeks ago: in fact, it has, I believe, brought on the crisis with me somewhat before it would otherwise have come. At≈one moment I say to myself, It is a malicious invention, an infamous lie; I know my boy Frank too well to believe this, or anything else against him: the next moment I shudder at the tale and at the possibility of what may have been enacted. Perhaps through passion—or accident—or—I grow confused: I know not what I would say.

"Oh, my boy, my nephew, my dear brother Henry's only child! my heart is aching with dismay and doubt. I do believe you are innocent of all intention to do harm; but—My sight is growing dim. *Take care of yourself.* Hide yourself if need be (and you best know whether there be need, or not) from Blase Pellet. It is he who would be your enemy. I see it; and Andrew Float sees it; though we know not why or wherefore. In any obscure nook of this wide world, shelter yourself from him. Don't let him know where you are. If he does indeed hold power in his hand, it may be your only chance of safety:

he said it was so. I can write no more. God bless and help you! Farewell.

Your loving and anxious
U<small>NCLE</small> H<small>UGH</small>

Frank Raynor may have drawn many a deep breath in his life, but never so deep a one as he drew now. Mechanically he folded the letter and placed it in an inner pocket.

"Are you there, sir?"

The question came from outside the door, in the voice of one of the servants. Frank unbolted it.

"Lunch is on the table, sir."

"Is it?" returned Frank, half bewildered. "I don't want any to-day, James. Just say so. I am going out for a stroll."

The letters from Cornwall were never delivered at Eagles' Nest until the midday post. Frank took his hat, and went out; bending his steps whithersoever they chose to take him, so that he might be alone. Strolling on mechanically, in deep thought, he plunged into a dark coppice, and asked himself what he was to do. The letter had disturbed him in no ordinary degree. It had taken all his spirit, all his elasticity out of him: and that was saying a great deal for Frank Raynor.

"I wish I could hang Blase Pellet!" he broke forth in his torment and perplexity. "He deserves it richly. To disturb my poor uncle with his malicious tongue! Villain!"

But Frank was unconsciously unjust. It was not Blase Pellet who had disturbed Dr. Raynor. At least, he had not done it intentionally. To do Blase justice, he was vexed that the doctor should have heard it, for he held him in great respect and would not willingly have grieved him. In an evil moment, when Blase had taken rather more than was quite necessary—an almost unprecedented occurrence with him—he had dropped the dangerous words to Andrew Float.

"Yes, I must hide from him, as my uncle says," resumed Frank, referring to the advice in the letter. "There's no help for it. He could be a dangerous enemy. For my own sake; for—every one's sake, I must keep myself in some shelter where he cannot find me."

Emerging on to the open ground, Frank lifted his eyes, and saw, standing near him, the man in grey, whom they had christened the Tiger. He was leaning against the tree with bent head and folded arms, apparently in deep thought. All in a moment, just as a personal fear of him had rushed over Charles, so did it now rush over Frank. His brain grew dizzy.

For the idea somehow struck him that the man was not wanting Charles at all. But that he might be an emissary of Blase Pellet's, come hither to look after himself and his movements.

IV

At Jetty's

John Jetty was the local carpenter. A master in a small way. His workshop was in the village, Grassmere, near to Eagles' Nest; his dwelling-house was on the common already described. In this house he lived with his sister, Esther Jetty; a staid woman, more than ten years older than himself: he being a smart, talkative, active, and very intelligent man of two or three-and-thirty. The house, which they rented of Major Raynor, was larger than they required, and Esther Jetty was in the habit of letting a sitting and bedroom in it when she could find a desirable lodger to occupy them.

On the Thursday in Passion Week, when she was in the midst of her house-cleaning for Easter, and in the act of polishing the outside of the spare sitting-room window, in which hung a card with "Lodgings" inscribed on it, she noticed a man in grey clothes sauntering up from the direction of the railway-station, an overcoat on his arm, and a good-sized black bag in his hand.

"Some traveller from London," decided Esther Jetty, turning to gaze at him; for a stranger in the quiet place was quite an event. "Come down to spend Easter."

The thought had scarcely crossed her mind, when, somewhat to her surprise, the stranger turned out of the path, walked directly towards her, and took off his hat while he spoke.

"Have you lodgings to let?" he asked. "I see a card in your window."

"Yes, sir; I have two rooms," said she, respectfully, for the courtesy of the lifted hat had favourably impressed her, and the tones of his voice were courteous also, not at all like those of an individual in humble station. "What a fine beard!" she thought to herself. "How smooth and silky it is!"

"I want to stay in this place a few days," continued he, "and am looking for lodgings. Perhaps yours would suit me."

Esther Jetty hastened to show the rooms. They were small, but clean, comfortable, and prettily furnished: and the rent was ten shillings per week.

"It is not too much, sir, at this season of the year, when summer's coming on," she hastened to say, lest the amount should be objected to.

"I always try to make my lodgers comfortable, and cook for them and wait on them well. The last I had—a sick young woman and her little girl—stayed here all the winter and spring: they only left three weeks ago."

The stranger's answer was to put down a sovereign. "That's the first week's rent in advance," said he. "With the change you can get me some mutton chops for my dinner. I shall not give you much trouble." And he took possession of the rooms at once.

As the days had gone on, only a few as yet, Esther Jetty found that his promise of not giving much trouble was kept. She had never had a lodger who gave less. He lived very simply. His dinner generally consisted of two mutton chops; his other food chiefly of eggs and bread-and-butter. It was glorious weather; and he passed nearly all his time out-of-doors.

Not a nook or corner of the immediate neighbourhood escaped his keen eye, his, as it seemed, insatiable curiosity. He penetrated into the small dwelling-houses, good and bad, asking questions of the inmates, making friends with them all. He would stand by the half-hour side by side with the out-door labourers, saying the land wanted this and that done to it, and demanding why it was not done. But, there could be no doubt that he was even more curious in regard to the Raynor family, and especially to its eldest son, than he was as to the land and its labourers: and the latter soon noticed that if by chance Charles Raynor came into sight, the stranger would stroll off, apparently without aim, towards him; and when Charles turned away, as he invariably did, the man followed in his wake at a distance. In short, it would seem that his chief business was to look surreptitiously after some of the inmates of Eagles' Nest; and that his visits to the land and the cottages, and his disparaging remarks thereupon, were probably only taken up to pass the time away. These opinions, however, grew upon people as time went on, rather than at the beginning of his stay.

Easter week passed. On the following Sunday the stranger went to church; and, after the service began, took up a place whence he had full view of the large square pew belonging to Eagles' Nest. On Easter Sunday he had sat at the back of the church, out of sight. Charles, Alice, and Frank were in the pew to-day, with the governess and little Kate: Mrs. Raynor was at home with Frank's wife, then lying dangerously ill; the major had not come. This was two days before they received news of Dr. Raynor's death. Charles was rendered miserably uncomfortable during the service by the presence of the Tiger opposite to him—as might be read by any one in the secret of his fears, and was read by Frank. Never did Charles raise his eyes but he saw those of the Tiger fixed on him. In fact, the Tiger studied the faces in Major Raynor's pew more attentively than he studied his book.

"He is taking toll of me that he may know me again: I don't suppose he knew me before, or his work would have been done and over," thought Charles. "What a precious idiot I was to come to church! Thank Heaven, he can't touch me on a Sunday." And when the service was ended, the Tiger coolly stood in the churchyard and watched the family pass him, looking keenly at Charles.

He had in like manner watched them into church. From a shady nook in the same churchyard, he had stood, himself unseen, looking at the congregation as they filed in. When the bell had ceased, and the last person seemed to have entered, then the Tiger followed, and put himself in the best place for seeing the Raynors. It was, however, the first and last time Charles was annoyed in a similar manner. On subsequent Sundays, the Tiger, if he went to church at all, was lost amidst the general congregation.

On this same Sunday evening, John Jetty found himself invited to take a pipe with his lodger. They sat in the arbour in the back-garden, amidst the herbs, the spring cabbages, and the early flowers. Jetty never wanted any inducement to talk. He was not of a wary nature by any means, and did not observe how skilfully and easily the thread of his discourse was this evening turned on the Raynors and their affairs. No man in the place could have supplied more correct information to a stranger than he. He was often at work in the house, was particularly intimate with Lamb the butler, who had lived with Mrs. Atkinson; as had two or three of the other head servants; and they had the family politics at their fingers' ends. Mrs. Raynor had brought one servant from Spring Lawn; the nurse; the woman knew all about her branch of the family, Frank included, and had no objection to relate news for the new people's benefit, who in their turn repeated it to Jetty. Consequently Jetty was as much at home in the family archives as the Raynors were themselves.

"Is the estate entailed on the major's son?" questioned the Tiger, in a pause of the conversation.

"I don't think it's strictly entailed on him, sir, but of course he'll have it," was Jetty's answer. "Indeed, it is no secret that the major has made a will and left it to him. Mrs. Atkinson bequeathed it entirely to the major: she didn't entail it."

"Who was Mrs. Atkinson?" asked the Tiger.

"Why, the possessor of the estate before him," cried Jetty, in accents full of surprise. To him, familiar for many years with Eagles' Nest and its people, it sounded strange to hear any one asking who Mrs. Atkinson was. "She was an old lady, sir, sister to the major, and it all belonged to her. He only came into it last year when she died."

"Had she no sons?"

"No, sir; not any. I never heard that she did have any. Her husband was a banker in London; he bought this place a good many years ago. After his death Mrs. Atkinson entirely lived in it."

"Then—it is sure to come to the major's eldest son?"

"As sure as sure can be," affirmed Jetty, replenishing his pipe at his lodger's invitation. "The major would not be likely to will it away to anybody else."

"I saw two young men in the pew to-day: one quite young, scarcely out of his teens, I should say; the other some years older. Which of them was the son?"

"Oh, the youngest. The other is a nephew; Mr. Frank Raynor. He is very good-looking, he is: such a pleasant face, with nice blue eyes and bright hair. Not but what Mr. Charles is good-looking, too, in a different way."

"Mr. Charles looks to me like an insolent young puppy," freely commented the Tiger. "And has a haughty air with it: as though he were king of the country and all the rest of us were his subjects." The probability was that Charles had honoured the staring Tiger with all the haughty and insolent looks he could call up throughout the service.

"Well, he is a bit haughty sometimes," acknowledged the carpenter. "Folks have found him so. He is just home from Oxford, sir, and I fancy has been spending pretty freely there: Lamb just gave me a hint. But if you want pleasant words and cordial manners, you must go to the nephew, Mr. Frank.

"What is *he* doing here?" dryly asked the stranger, after a pause.

"He is a doctor, sir."

"A doctor? Is he in practice here?"

"Oh no. He is waiting to set up in London, and staying down here till he does it."

"What is he waiting for?"

"Well, sir, for money, I guess. The Raynors are open-natured people and don't scruple to talk of things before their servants, so that there's not much but what's known. When the late Mrs. Atkinson died, a good deal of stir arose about some money of hers that could not be found: thousands and thousands of pounds, it was said. It could neither be found, nor the papers relating to it."

"Is it not found yet?" asked the Tiger, stroking his silky beard.

"Not yet. The major is anxiously waiting for it: not a day passes, Lamb says, but he is sure to remark that it may turn up the next. Mr. Frank Raynor is to have some of this money to set him up in practice."

"Did Mrs. Atkinson not leave any money to him? He must have been a relation of hers?"

"Oh yes, she left him money. I forget what it was now—a good sum, though."

"Why does he not set up with that?" questioned the Tiger, wonderingly.

"He has spent it, sir. He and his young wife went abroad, and lived away, I suppose. Any way, the money's gone, Lamb says. But Mr. Frank's as nice a fellow as ever lived."

"Did he—" began the stranger, and then broke off, as if in doubt whether or not to put the question: but in a moment went on firmly. "Did he ever live at Trennach, in Cornwall?"

"Trennach?" repeated Jetty, considering. "Yes, sir, I think that's where he did live. Yes, I'm sure that is the name. He was in practice there with another uncle, one Dr. Raynor, and might have stopped there and come into the practice after him. A rare good opening for him, it's said: but he preferred to go elsewhere."

"Preferred to travel and see the world," spoke the stranger, cynically. "Are Major Raynor's revenues good ones?"

"Well, sir, I know in Mrs. Atkinson's time this estate was said to bring in a clear two thousand a-year. And Major Raynor had of course an income before he came into it: but that, I hear, is only an annuity, and goes from him at his death."

"Then, if his revenues amount to that—from two to three thousand a-year—how is it that he does not do the repairs necessary on the estate, and keep up the land, and help to ameliorate the condition of the wretched serfs about him?" demanded the stranger.

Jetty shook his head. "I don't think it is the will that's wanting," replied he. "The major seems to be thoroughly good-hearted and Lamb

MRS. HENRY WOOD

says he is one of the easiest masters he could ever wish to serve. No, it is not the will, sir, that is wanting."

"What is it, then? The money?"

Jetty nodded in the affirmative. "They live at such a rate, you see, sir; and it is said the major had a lot of back-debts to pay when he came here. Altogether, he has nothing to spare."

"Then he ought to have," asserted the Tiger, tapping thoughtfully at his pipe, that lay on the table. "Does he never visit his tenements and see into things for himself?"

"No, sir, not he. 'Twould be too much exertion for him. He can't walk about much; never comes beyond his own garden gates; never."

The Tiger paused. "This young Frank Raynor's wife, who is lying ill: had she no money?"

"No, sir. Her family have plenty, I expect, for they live at some grand place down in Cornwall. But she has none. It was a runaway match that she and Mr. Frank made, so she couldn't expect any."

The Tiger nodded two or three times, as if in self-commune. "I see," said he: "these Raynors are an improvident set altogether. Thoughtless, cruel, selfish, upstart and purse-proud. From what little I have noticed during the few days I have been here, that is the impression they make upon me: and what you say confirms it."

He took his pipe up from the table as he spoke, knocked the ashes out of it, and put it into its case. An intimation, John Jetty thought, that their social hour was at an end: and he went away, respectfully wishing his lodger good-evening.

EASTER WAS OVER; AND THE time for going back to Oxford for the coming term was past. Charles Raynor had not gone up to keep it. He had to confess to the major that he did not care to go back without a good sum of money, apart from his allowance; he might have said, dared not go. It was not convenient to find the sum: so the major decided that Charles must miss that one term, and keep the next.

The weeks went on. Charles had in a degree got over his dread of the Tiger—who still remained on in his lodgings—for it was now very evident that if that mysterious man's mission at Grassmere were to take him into custody for debt, it might have been accomplished ere this. Nevertheless, so strongly do first impressions retain their hold upon us, his dislike of the man continued in all its force.

But, as Charles's alarm subsided, Frank's increased. The more evident it became that Charles was not the Tiger's object, the more surely did it seem to Frank that he himself was. It was a fear he could not speak of, but his secret uneasiness was great. Neither he nor Charles could fail to see that the man's daily business appeared to be that of watching the movements of the Raynor family, especially those of the two young men. Not watching offensively, but in a quiet, easy, unobtrusive manner. Frank fully believed that the man was a secret emissary of Blase Pellet's sent there to see that he did not escape his toils.

Major Raynor had never seen this man: and Frank and Charles, each for his own private and individual reasons, had refrained from speaking about him. Of late the major had chiefly confined himself to the gardens immediately attached to his house. There were two reasons for this: the one, that he had now grown so very stout as to render walking a trouble to him, and when he did go out it was in a carriage; the other, that he never went beyond his inner fence but he was sure to meet one or other of those wretched malcontents; who thought nothing of accosting him and asking him to do this, and to do that. So matters remained pretty stationary: the major indolently nursing himself in his easy-chair on the lawn; the young men enjoying their private discomforts; and the Tiger peering into every conceivable spot open to him, and making himself better acquainted with the general shortcomings of the Raynors, in regard to the estate and the people on it, than they were themselves.

It was Saturday evening. Alice sat at the piano in the drawing-room, singing songs in the twilight to the intense gratification of William Stane, who stood over her. The young barrister frequently ran down home the last day of the week, to remain over the Sunday with his family. As a matter of course, he spent a great part of the time at Eagles' Nest. The major sat back in the room, dozing; Charles was listlessly turning over a pile of music. Eagles' Nest had given an afternoon party that day; a fashionable kettledrum; but the guests had departed.

"I can scarcely see," said Alice, as her lover placed a new song before her. She was in the dress she had worn in the afternoon: a black gauze trimmed with white ribbons, with silver bracelets and other silver ornaments, and looked charmingly lovely. They were in mourning for Dr. Raynor.

"I'll ring for lights," said Charles. "I can't see, either."

The talking had aroused the major. "We don't want lights yet," said he. "It is pleasanter as it is."

"Sing the songs you know by heart," whispered William Stane. "After all, they are the best and sweetest."

Presently Lamb came in of his own accord, with the wax-lights. The major, waking up again, made no objection now, but forbade the shutters to be closed.

"It's a pity to shut out that moonlight," said he. Not that the moonlight could have interested him much, for in another minute he was asleep again. He had grown strangely drowsy of late. So the room was lighted up, and the moonlight streamed in at the window.

Frank entered. He had been sitting upstairs with his wife, who was still very ill. In fact, this had been an unusually prolonged and critical sickness. Taking up his position at the window, Frank listened silently to the song then in progress. Charles came up to him.

"How is she to-night, Frank?"

"No better. If— Look there!" he suddenly exclaimed, his voice sunk to a whisper.

Some one had walked deliberately by, outside the window, gazing at what there might be to see within the room. Was it the Tiger? Frank's heart beat nineteen to the dozen.

"Did you see him, Charley?"

"Who was it?" whispered Charley.

"I'm not quite sure; he passed so quickly. The Tiger, I conclude. Yes, I feel sure of it. I know the cut of his hat."

"What consummate impudence, to be trespassing here!"

They both left the room, made their way to a side-door, and looked out. No one was in sight; and yet, whosoever it was that had passed must have come that way.

"He has turned back," said Charley: and as he spoke he advanced cautiously amidst the shrubs that skirted that end of the house, and looked round at the front.

No. Not a soul was to be seen or heard. Had he scampered straight across the lawn and made off? It seemed like it.

"I wonder what it's coming to!" cried Charley. "Could we have him warned off the estate, I wonder?"

"Hardly," spoke Frank, in a dreamy tone.

"I *cannot* think what he does here," exclaimed Charles. "If he had any evil intentions, he—he would have acted upon them before now."

"You mean as to yourself, Charley. Rely upon it, you are out of the matter altogether."

"Who's in it, then?"

"Myself, perhaps."

The answer was given quietly and easily: but there was something in its tone that kept Charles from regarding it as a jest.

"*You* are not in debt, are you, Frank?" he cried hastily.

"Not that I know of."

"I declare for the moment I thought you must be in earnest," said Charles, relieved. "It is uncommonly strange what the fellow can want here!"

Frank said no more. They paced about for some time, without their hats, in the bright moonlight, talking of other matters. In crossing the path to the house; they met Jetty the carpenter coming away from it, a frail in his hand, out of which a saw was standing upright. The man had been doing some repairs indoors.

"Jetty," said Charles, accosting him, and speaking upon impulse, "who is the man that lodges with you? The fellow with the great brown beard, who goes about in a suit of grey."

"I don't know who he is in particular, sir," replied Jetty. "He is a very quiet lodger, and pays regular."

"What is he down here for?"

"Well, I think for his health," said Jetty. "He told us he had not been well for some time before he came to Grassmere."

"What is his name?"

"That I don't know, sir—"

"Not know his name?" interrupted Charles, impatiently.

"Well, sir, I was going to say that I don't know it from himself. He is uncommonly close as to his own affairs: though he likes well enough to hear about other people's. As to his name, he did not mention it when he first came in, and my sister said she did not like to ask him. But—"

"I never knew such a thing as not knowing a lodger's name," went on Charles, getting excited over it, whilst Frank stood by in perfect silence. "Does the man not get any letters?"

"Yes, sir. But they don't come to the house; they are left at the post-office in Grassmere, and he fetches them himself. The other morning, when Esther went into his parlour, he was reading one of these letters, and the cover lay on the table, address upwards. She was not quick enough to read the name on it, for he took it up, but she saw it was a short name and began with a G."

"Grim, no doubt," said Charles.

"'Mr. G—, Post Office, Grassmere.' That was it, sir."

"I must say I should like to know who he is and what he is doing here," continued Charles. "Good-night, Jetty."

Jetty touched his cap and went away with rapid strides. Drawing near to his home, he overtook the Tiger, sauntering along with slow steps.

"You are late to-night, Jetty."

"Yes, sir," replied the carpenter, suiting his pace to that of the speaker. "I had to put some new shelves into one of the kitchen cupboards at Eagles' Nest, and it has taken me longer than I thought for."

"All going on well there?" continued the Tiger.

"First rate," said Jetty. "They had a great party this afternoon; one of those new-fashioned kettledrums. Such an entertainment it was! such fine dresses!"

"I thought the son, Charles Raynor, was keeping his terms at Oxford," resumed the Tiger, after giving himself time to digest the information touching the kettledrum. "Why is he not keeping this term?"

"Well, sir," said Jetty, beginning to answer in his usual favourite mode, and lowering his voice, though they were quite alone on the common: "I believe Mr. Charles can't show his face at Oxford until he is better up in funds; so he is omitting this term."

"Debts—eh?" cried the Tiger, but without any appearance of surprise. "And the major has not the funds to spare for them?"

"Well, sir, that's to be inferred."

"Meanwhile the lad fills up his days and hours at home with dancing, and smoking, and kettledrums, and other good-for-nothing amusements. A nice way of spending one's life!"

"Young men will be young men, sir—though they are but lads," spoke Jetty, deprecatingly.

"Yes; young men will be young men: some of them, at any rate," came the mocking retort. "But in all my days I never saw a young man who appeared more likely to go straight down to ruin than Charles Raynor."

V

SIR PHILIP'S MISSION

Major Raynor sat in his favourite seat on the lawn at Eagles' Nest, at drowsy peace with himself and with the world. Of late the major had always been drowsy: morning, noon, and night, no matter what company he was in, he might be seen nodding. Frank, as a medical man, did not like the signs. He spoke to his uncle of the necessity of rousing himself, of taking more exercise, of indulging somewhat less in good luncheons and dinners. The major made an effort to obey: for two days he actually walked about the lawn for twenty minutes, refused two rich entrées, took at each meal one glass less of wine. But the efforts ended there, and on the third day the major gave up reformation as a bad job.

"It's of no use, Frank, my boy. You young folk can be upon the run all day if you choose, and live upon bread-and-cheese and beer; but we old ones require ease; we can't be put about."

So the major sat at ease this day as usual, lazily thinking, and dropping into a doze. A letter had been received that morning from Edina, in answer to an invitation from Major and Mrs. Raynor to come and make her home with them now that she was alone in the world. Edina declined it for the present. She was staying at Trennach parsonage with Mr. and Mrs. Pine: her plans were not decided upon; but the clergyman and his wife would not yet spare her. She had many affairs to settle at Trennach. Mr. Hatman had taken to the practice, as had been arranged, and to the house; but Edina could not leave the place at present. She hoped to pay Eagles' Nest a visit in the course of the summer.

Thinking of this, and subsiding into dozing, sat the major. The hum of the insects sounded in his ears, the scent of the rich flowering hawthorn was heavy in the air. Though not yet summer by the calendar, for May was still reigning, the season was unusually premature, and the weather was, to all intents and purposes, that of summer. Bees were sipping at the honey-blossoms, butterflies fluttered from flower to flower. All nature seemed conducive to repose, and—the major was soon fast asleep, and choking as though he were being strangled.

"You are wanted, if you please, sir."

The words aroused him. Opening his eyes, and sitting upright in his chair, he saw his butler by his side.

"What do you say, Lamb? Wanted? Who is it?"

"Sir Philip Stane, sir. He is in the drawing-room."

The major took a draught of his champagne-cup, standing on the table by his side. Which cup, it must be confessed, was much more innocent than its name would imply. A quart or two of it would not have hurt any one: and the major was always thirsty. Crossing the lawn, he went into the drawing-room. Sir Philip Stane, a little man with a white shirt-frill, a cold face, and a remarkably composed manner, rose at his entrance. Major Raynor shook hands with him in his hearty way, and they sat down together.

For some few minutes the conversation turned on general topics; but soon the knight gave the major to understand that he had come to speak upon a particular subject: the attachment of his son to Miss Raynor.

"It has for some time been observable that they are thinking of one another," remarked he.

"Well, yes, I suppose it has," said the major. "We have noticed it here."

"William is getting on fairly well; he calculates that he will make at least seven-hundred pounds this year. Quite enough, he thinks, to begin housekeeping upon, with help. With help, major."

"I should have thought it unbounded riches in my marrying days," observed the major.

"William considers that he would be justified in setting up a home, provided he can be met," continued Sir Philip in his deliberate, sententious way, presenting a direct contrast to the major's heartiness. "Young people do not of course expect to begin as they may hope to end: riches must come by degrees."

"Quite right," said the major.

"And therefore, with a view to the consideration of the matter—to finally deciding whether my son may be justified, or not, in settling this year—I have come to ask you, Major Raynor, what portion you intend to bestow upon your daughter."

"Not any," replied the plain-speaking major. "I have none to bestow."

Sir Philip looked at him blankly. He did not appear to understand.

"My will is good, Sir Philip. I would give a portion to Alice heartily if I possessed it. Thousands, I'm sure, the young people should be welcome to, if they needed it."

"Do you mean to say that you—that you will not bestow any portion whatever upon your daughter when she marries?" asked Sir Philip, in a tone of cold astonishment.

"I'm sorry that I can't do it," said the major. "I wish I could. If that lost money of mine would only turn up—"

"Then, I am afraid, I—cannot say what I had come to say," returned Sir Philip, with the air of a man who deliberates aloud, and quite ignoring the major's interrupted sentence. "I could not advise my son to settle upon the few hundreds a-year that make up his present income."

"Why, it's abundance," cried the candid major. "You have just said yourself that young people cannot expect to begin as they will end. Your son's is a rising income: if he makes seven-hundred this year, he may expect to make ten next, and double the seven the year after. It is ample to begin upon, Sir Philip."

"No," dissented Sir Philip. "Neither he nor I would consider it so. Something should be put by for a rainy day. This communication has completely taken me by surprise, Major Raynor. We took it for granted that your daughter would at least add her quota to the income: had it been only three or four hundred a-year. Without money of her own, there could be no settlement on her, you see, my son's not being real property."

The major was growing a little heated. He did not at all like the turn the conversation was taking, or Sir Philip's dictatorial tone.

"Well, you hear, Sir Philip, that Alice has nothing. Those who wish to take her, must take her as she is—portionless—or not at all."

Sir Philip Stane rose. "I am sorry, then, major, that I cannot ask what I was about to ask for—herself. Your daughter—"

"You are not wanted to ask it, sir," hotly interrupted the major.

"The fact of your daughter's being portionless debars it," quietly went on the knight. "I am very sorry indeed to have troubled you, and subjected myself to pain. William must consider his pretensions at an end."

"They are at an end," fired the major. "If it is money he has been thinking of all this time, he ought to be ashamed of himself for a calculating, mercenary young rascal. Were he to come to me on his knees, after this, begging for my daughter, he should not have her. That's my answer, Sir Philip Stane, and you can take it away with you."

The major's tug at the bell-rope sent a peal echoing through the house. But Sir Philip Stane's hand was already on the door-handle, letting himself out with a short "good-morning."

Away went the major, hunting for Alice. He found her with her mother. Hotly and explosively he gave an account of the interview; of what he called the mercenary conduct of Sir Philip and William Stane. Poor Alice turned hot and cold: red and white by turns. She took the indignity—as she was pleased to think it—quite as resentfully as the major.

"I forbid you to have anything to do with him after this, Alice. I forbid you to see him again."

"You need not forbid me, papa," was the answer. "I should not think of it."

Major Raynor was one who could not keep in anything, good or bad, especially any grievance. He went about the house, looking for Charles and Frank, that he might impart the news, and so let off a little of his superfluous anger. But he could not find either of them.

Matters were going on much as usual. Daisy was progressing so far towards recovery that she could sit at the open window of her chamber and revel in the balmy air, while feasting her eyes upon the charming landscape. Charles was in a little extra trouble; for he had been written to twice upon the subject of the fifty-pound bill that was overdue. And Frank, outwardly gay as the flowers of May, was inwardly on thorns and nettles.

That that mysterious personage, the Tiger, was wasting his days and hours at Grassmere on Frank Raynor's account, Frank felt persuaded of. To him it seemed an indisputable fact. The man did not molest him: did not appear to take particular notice of him; he had not yet accosted him: but Frank knew that all the while he was craftily watching his movements, to see that he did not escape. It needed not a conjuror to tell him that the Tiger was the spy of Blase Pellet.

The espionage was growing intolerable to Frank. And on this very day, just about the time that Sir Philip Stane was at Eagles' Nest, he flung prudence to the winds, and questioned the enemy. The Tiger had wandered as near to the house as he could, without being guilty of a positive trespass: and Frank, chancing to turn out of what was called Beech Walk, came face to face with him. It was the first time they had thus closely met. For half-a-minute they gazed at each other. The Tiger stood his ground, and quietly took from his pocket a small note-case of brown morocco leather, with the initials "C.R." stamped upon it in gilt.

"Does this belong to you?" questioned the Tiger.

"Not to me," replied Frank. "But I believe it belongs to my cousin, Mr. Raynor.

"I picked it up a few minutes ago as I was strolling along. Perhaps you will be so good us to give it to its owner."

Frank took the case from the Tiger, and thanked him. Even to this man, suspecting him as he did for a despicable spy, he could only be courteous. And, indeed, but for this suspicion, Frank would rather have liked the man's face, now he saw it closely; the thought passed through his mind that, for a Tiger, he was a civilized one. There was a tone of pleasant freedom in the voice; the dark grey eyes, gazing steadily into Frank's, were earnest and good.

"You come from Trennach," said Frank suddenly, speaking upon impulse.

"From Trennach?" repeated the stranger, vaguely, and evincing no surprise.

"Or from some one there," continued Frank. "Employed by him to—to look after his villainous interests here."

"I am my own employer, young man."

"What is your name, pray?"

"If I thought it concerned you to know it, I might, perhaps, inform you," was the answer, civilly delivered.

"But suppose it does concern me?"

"It is my opinion that it does not."

"At any rate your business here does."

"Does it?"

"Will you deny that you have business here? Business of a private nature?"

"I cannot deny that, for it is true."

"And that your business consists in peeping, and watching, and spying?"

"You are partly right."

"And," continued Frank, growing warm, "don't you think that to peep and to spy is a despicable proceeding?"

"In some cases it may undoubtedly be so regarded," was the calm, cool answer. "In other cases it is perfectly justifiable. When some good end, for instance, has to be obtained: or, let us say, a problem worked out."

"The devil can quote Scripture, we are told, to serve his own purposes," muttered Frank to himself as he turned away, afraid of pursuing the subject, half afraid of what revelation the man might make, and of his fearless grey eyes and their steadfast gaze.

They strode apart one from another at right angles. The stranger with careless, easy steps, with profound composure: Frank less easy than usual.

"I wonder," soliloquized he, "whether Pellet has let him into that unhappy night's secret, or whether he has only given him general instructions to look after me, and has kept him in the dark? Any way, I wish Blase Pellet was—"

The wish, whatever it might have been, was left unspoken. For the Tiger had changed his course. Had turned to follow Frank at a fleet pace, and now came up with him.

"Will you tell me, sir, what induced you to assume that I had come here from Trennach? And for what purpose I am 'spying'?—and upon whom?"

"There's no need to tell you," rejoined Frank. "You know too well already."

"And if I tell you that I do not know?"

"I hope you don't. It's all the same," returned Frank, indifferently, believing he was being played with.

"Perhaps you have run up debts at Trennach, and are mistaking me for a sheriff's officer?" proceeded the Tiger, once more gazing steadfastly at Frank as he spoke. "Your cousin, the major's son, has been taking me for one."

"How on earth did he get to know that?" thought Frank. And it seemed to be so confirmatory of the Tiger's accomplishments in the prying line, that Frank felt as much exasperated as his sweet-tempered nature was capable of feeling.

"Your road lies that way, and mine this," spoke Frank, with a wave of the hand. "Good-morning."

The Tiger stood still, looking after his receding footsteps. A very peculiar expression sat on his face, not altogether complimentary to Frank.

"A curious lot, these Raynors," concluded he to himself, as he turned to pursue his own way.

It was perhaps rather remarkable that Charles Raynor should also, on this same day, be brought into contact with the Tiger for the first time. Charley's troubles were culminating to a point: at least, in so far that he was about to be pressed for one of his debts, though he knew it not. It would come upon Charley something like a shock. Since fear, on the score of the Tiger, had subsided, he had enjoyed a complete immunity from *personal* annoyance; and this had lulled his apprehensions to rest; so that he went about here, there, and everywhere, feeling free as air.

He had been out in the dog-cart all the morning. Upon going indoors on his return, by the entrance that was nearest to the stables, in passing the butler's pantry he saw Lamb standing in it. The man made a sudden movement as though he would speak to him, and it arrested Charley.

"Do you want me, Lamb?" he asked, halting on his way.

Lamb dropped his voice to a mysterious whisper, and Charley instinctively moved inside, and shut the door. Lamb knew nearly as much about his young master's embarrassments as he himself knew.

"A party has been here this morning who wanted to see you, Mr. Charles. When I said you were out—gone up to London, I thought—he seemed as if he hardly believed me. I began to think I shouldn't get rid of him."

"Who was it?" asked Charles.

"It was a respectable-looking man, sir. Highly respectable, one might be tempted to call him, if his errand had not been to bother people for money. Being near the neighbourhood, he had turned aside to Grassmere to see you, he said, and his business with you was particular. Of course I knew what it all meant, Mr. Charles, and I declared you were gone out for the day and couldn't be seen though he waited till night."

"I wonder which of them it was?" mused Charley. "Did he give his name?"

"Yes, sir; Huddles. He—"

"Oh, Huddles, is it?" interrupted Charley, his mouth falling. "I'm glad I didn't see him. Is he gone for good, do you think, Lamb?"

"I should say so, sir. I fully impressed upon him that his waiting would be no earthly use. I even said, Mr. Charles, that there was no answering for your return when you went to London, and that you might be there a week, for all I could say. I told him he had better write to you, sir. 'Very well,' he said in answer, and went off with a quick step: no doubt to catch the next train."

"That's all right then," said Charley, completely reassured. "Any visitors been here, Lamb?"

"Sir Philip Stane called, sir. And some ladies are in the drawing-room now. Would you like some refreshment, Mr. Charles?"

"No, I'll wait till dinnertime."

But it still wanted some two or three hours to dinnertime. Presently Charles went strolling out on foot, digesting the unpleasant item of news that his father had just hastened to impart to him—the sneaking behaviour, as he called it, of William Stane. Charles felt greatly vexed and annoyed at it for Alice's sake. He was sure there was a mutual attachment, and had believed that they understood each other.

Lost in reflections on this subject, and never giving a thought to the matter imparted to him by Lamb, his eyes never raised, his footsteps wandering on almost as they would, Charley found himself passing along the common, on the side of the better houses. Words of salutation greeted him.

"Good-afternoon, sir. A hot day again, is it not?"

They came from Miss Jetty, the carpenter's sister. She was sitting at work at her open window. Charles lifted his eyes to nod to her; and that enabled him to see some one who was approaching at a short distance. *Huddles*. Charley recognized him; and on the spur of the moment darted into the carpenter's to hide.

"I hope and trust he did not see me!"

But Mr. Huddles had seen him. Mr. Huddles came up with a long stride, and was inside the house almost as soon as Charley was. Charley could not pretend to be blind then. He stood just within Esther Jetty's sitting-room; and the applicant stood in the passage facing him.

"I called at Eagles' Nest to-day, Mr. Charles Raynor, and could not see you. You know of course what it was I wanted?"

Charles was taken aback. What with the unpleasantness of the surprise, the consciousness of the helpless state of his finances, and the proximity of Miss Esther Jetty's eyes and ears, raised in curiosity, he was turning frightfully cross. A few sharp, haughty words greeted Huddles, apparently causing him astonishment. This application concerned one of the two "bills" given by Charley; the one on which no proceedings had as yet been taken.

"Can you meet that bill, Mr. Charles Raynor?"

"No, I can't," replied Charles. "I wrote you word that I would meet it as soon as I could; that bill and the other also; and so I will. You must wait."

"For how long, Mr. Raynor? It is inconvenient to wait."

Charles flew into a passion. But for Esther Jetty's presence, he would have managed much better; that of course behoved him to carry matters with a high hand, and he showered abuse on Mr. Huddles in haughty language, forgetful of diplomacy. Mr. Huddles, not at all the sort of man to be dealt with in this manner, repaid him in his own coin. Had Charles met him civilly, he would have been civil also; ay, and forbearing. The bills—he held them both—had only come into his hands in the course of business. He was really respectable, both as a man and a tradesman, not accustomed to be spoken to in such a fashion, and most certainly in this instance did not deserve it. His temper rose. A short, sharp storm ensued, and Mr. Huddles went out of the house in anger, leaving a promise behind him.

"I have been holding the two bills over for you, Mr. Charles Raynor, and staying proceedings out of consideration to you and at your request. And this is the gratitude I get in return! The affair is none of mine, as you know; and what I have done has been simply out of good-nature, for I was sorry to see so young a man in danger of exposure, perhaps of a debtor's prison. I will not delay proceedings another day. The bills shall pass out of my hands, and you must do the best you can for yourself."

Whilst Charles stood knitting his brow and looking very foolish, staring at the front-door, which still vibrated with the bang Mr. Huddles gave it, and not half liking to turn and face Esther Jetty, the parlour-door on the other side of the passage, which had been ajar all the time, opened, and the Tiger appeared at it. He must have been an ear-witness to the whole. It did not tend to decrease Charley's annoyance: and, in truth, the sudden appearance of this man upon the scene, in conjunction with the visit of Huddles, revived Charley's suspicions of him. The Tiger's face wore quite a benevolent aspect.

"Can I be of any use to you?" he asked. "I will be if I can. Step in here, Charles Raynor, and let us talk it over."

Charley lost his head. The words only added fuel to fire. Coming from this sneak of a sheriff's officer, or whatever other disreputable thing he might be, they sounded in his ears in the light of an insult—a bit of casuistry designed to entrap him. And he treated them accordingly.

"*You* be of use to me!" he contemptuously retorted, with all the scorn he could call up. "Mind your own business, man, if you can. Don't presume to interfere with mine."

And out of the house strode Charley, banging the door in his turn, and sending a good-afternoon to Esther Jetty through the open window. The Tiger shrugged his shoulders with a disdainful gesture: as much as to say that the young man was not worth a thought and that he washed his hands of him and his concerns. Taking up his slouching hat, he put it well over his forehead, stood for a few minutes at the outer door, and then passed through the little gate.

"Wouldn't you like your tea, sir?" called Esther Jetty from the window. "I was just about to get it."

"Presently," replied the Tiger.

Meanwhile Charles Raynor was striding towards home, full of bitter repentance. All the folly of his recent conduct was presenting itself before him.

"I wish I had met the fellow differently!" he soliloquized, alluding to Huddles. "There can be no more putting-off now. A day or two and they will be down upon me. I think I was a fool! What a to-do there'll be at home! How on earth will the money be found?—and what will be the upshot of it all?"

Indeed, it seemed that, with one thing and another, Eagles' Nest was not altogether comfortable. Most of its inmates had some secret trouble upon them. And yet not twelve months ago they had entered upon it, all glee and joy, believing their days would henceforth be delightful as a second Paradise!

The next afternoon but one, Saturday, brought William Stane. Alice chanced to be in the shrubbery, and met him. His countenance proved that he felt vexed, doubtful, ill at ease. Instead of the tender glance and smile that had been wont to greet Alice, he had a grave eye and knitted brow. The look angered her, even more than had the reported words of Sir Philip on the Thursday before.

What precisely passed between them perhaps neither could afterwards clearly recall. He said something about how sorry he was that their happy intercourse should have been marred; Alice interrupted him with a sharp and haughty retort. William Stane retorted in his turn; and things were spoken between them, in the moment's ill-feeling, that could neither be unsaid nor qualified. Prejudiced by his father's account of the unsatisfactory interview with the major, he had come, naturally inclined to espouse his father's side; Alice on her part upheld their own cause. Very short indeed was the scene, but it was decisive.

"I am sorry to have been so mistaken in you, Miss Raynor," he said, turning to depart. "No great harm has, however, been done."

"None," returned Alice. "Fare you well."

He raised his hat without speaking, and the echoes of his retreating footsteps died away in the shrubbery.

Thus they parted. The fault being at least as much Alice's as his. Whether he had come to straighten matters, to repudiate the fiat Sir Philip had pronounced, Alice knew not, but she did not allow him the opportunity. If the possession of Eagles' Nest had taught nothing else to Major Raynor's children, it had certainly taught them to be arrogant. The world seemed made for them, and for them alone.

Alice went upstairs humming a gay song, and passed into Daisy's room. She halted at the glass, glancing at her pretty face, at the brightness of the blue eyes, at the unusual flush on her cheeks. Frank's wife turned round.

"You are gay this afternoon, Alice."

"Gay as a fairy," replied Alice. "It is lovely out-of-doors. The sun's shining and the birds are singing."

A few days went on. Charley was in a state of mental collapse. For, not one single minute of those days came and went but he was on the look-out for some dreadful shock, emanating from the enemy, Huddles. Each night, as darkness fell, he felt not at all thankful that the blow had kept off, concluding that the morrow would bring it. It seemed to him at times that its falling would bring relief, by ending his almost unbearable suspense.

Alice continued gay; gay as a lark. Was it assumed, this gaiety, or was it real? Perhaps she herself did not know.

"You could not have cared very much for William Stane, Alice, or he for you," one day remarked her mother, to whom the affair had given pain, interrupting Alice in the carolling of a song, sung to an impromptu dance.

"Cared for him, mamma!" she returned, in her spirit of bravado. "I am well rid of him."

Mrs. Raynor sighed. Alice had so changed: not, she feared, for the better. So had Charles. Good fortune had ruined them all.

VI

Startling News

The first of June. A day destined to be an eventful one at Eagles' Nest. At five o'clock in the morning the house was aroused from its peaceful slumbers by a commotion. Mrs. Raynor's bell was ringing violently; Mrs. Raynor's voice was calling for help in loud and anxious tones. Major Raynor had been taken ill.

Frank was first at the bedside. His uncle lay unconscious, or partly so, exhibiting alarming symptoms. An attack of some kind seemed imminent; Frank thought it would prove apoplexy. Other advice was sent for.

Long before the usual hour for breakfast, breakfast had been taken, and the family hardly knew what to do with themselves. Dr. Selfe, a clever man, residing near, had seen Major Raynor—who now seemed to be somewhat better. The doctor quite agreed with Frank that the symptoms were indicative of apoplexy; but he thought that it might be warded off, at least for the present, by the aid of powerful remedies. These remedies had been applied, and the patient was decidedly improving. He spoke little, but was quite conscious. On these occasions, when one out of the home circle is lying upstairs in sudden and dangerous illness, the house becomes utterly unsettled. Ordinary habits are changed; no one knows what to be at.

"I shall ring for some more coffee," said Charles, rising as he spoke. "There's nothing else to do."

Lamb came in and received the order. The breakfast-things were still on the table. This was one of the pleasantest rooms in the house: small and cosy, with glass-doors opening to the garden. It faced the west, so was free from the morning sun: but, beyond the shade cast by the house, that sun shone brightly on the smooth green grass and clustering flowers.

Whilst waiting for the coffee, which had to be made, Charles leaned against the window, half in, half out-of-doors, whistling softly and keeping a good look-out around, lest any Philistine should be approaching unawares. This illness of his father's terribly complicated matters. In the midst of Charley's worst apprehensions there had lain, down deep in his heart, the vista of a possible refuge. He had whispered to himself, "When things come to a crisis, my father will no doubt find a way to help me;" and the hope had been as a healing balm to his spirit. But his father, lying in this state, could not be applied to: his repose of mind must not be disturbed: and if Charley fell into some tiger's clutches now, what on earth was he to do?

Whistling softly and unconsciously, Charley indulged in these highly agreeable reflections. His mother had not come downstairs at all. Alice had gone up to Daisy: Kate and Mademoiselle were reading French under the distant walnut-tree. Only Frank was there.

"I do think I can smell haymaking!" cried Charley, suddenly.

"Yes," assented Frank. "Some of the fields are down."

"Is it not early for it?"

"We have had an early season."

No more was said. There flashed into Charley's mind a remembrance of the day he had first seen Eagles' Nest: when he had stood at one of the windows, though not this one, gazing out at the charming scenery, the lovely flowers; inhaling their perfume and that of the new-mown hay. Association of ideas is powerful, and probably that scent of the hay had brought the day to his memory now. Barely a twelvemonth had passed since then: and yet—how hopes and anticipations had changed! He had believed then that peace, ease, prosperity must inevitably attend them as the possessors of Eagles' Nest: he remembered picturing to himself the calamity it would have been had the beautiful place passed into others' hands. But he had lived to learn that care and worry could penetrate even there.

"There's the postman!" cried Charley. And glad, probably, of the interruption, he went out, and crossed the lawn to meet the man.

"Only one letter this morning," he exclaimed, coming back, his eyes fixed on it. "I say, Frank, what is to be done? It is from old Street, and he has put 'immediate' on it."

"You had better open the letter yourself, I should say, Charles: my uncle cannot," said Frank, decisively.

"I wonder what he has to write about: it is not often we hear from him. Nothing particular, I dare say: the good old father has not, I am sure, a secret in the world. Or—do you think," added Charley, his face lighting with eager hope, "that the money can have turned up? What a glorious thought! Yes, I will open it."

He broke the seal of the letter. At that moment Lamb came in with fresh coffee. Frank, standing near the mantelpiece, watched the man put it down, and set two or three things in order on the table before going out again. As the door closed, Frank's glance chanced to stray to Charley's face.

What was the matter with it? The eager flush of hope had been succeeded by a look of dismay: nay, almost of horror. The letter seemed very short. Charley was reading it twice over, growing paler the while.

"Can it be a hoax?" he cried, in a voice scarcely raised above a whisper, as he held the letter out. "It cannot be true."

Frank took the letter reluctantly. There was no help for it. But a spasm seized his own face, and a very terrible spasm seized his heart. When we are nourishing some great dread, any new and unexplained event seems to bear upon it. His fears had flown back to that dreadful night at Trennach. Had this letter come to betray him?

But the letter proved in no way connected with that. The news it brought was of a nature perfectly open and tangible. Frank's own fears gave place to consternation and dismay as he read the lawyer's words: dismay for his uncle's sake.

My Dear Sir,
    "I have just heard a very painful rumour, and I think it my duty to communicate it to you. It is said that the will, under which you succeeded to Mrs. Atkinson's estate, proves to have been worthless; a fresh will having been discovered. By this later will, it is Mr. George Atkinson who inherits Eagles' Nest. My information is, I fear, authentic; but I do not yet know full particulars.
    "This is but a brief note to convey such tidings, but the evening post is on the point of closing, and I do not wish to lose it. I would have run down, instead of writing, but am not equal to it, having for the past week or two been confined to the house.
    "Believe me, dear sir,

Sincerely yours,
John Street
Major Raynor

They stood looking at one another, Charles and Frank, with questioning eyes and dismayed faces. Could it be true? No, surely not.

Street the lawyer, in spite of the boasted authenticity of his information, must have been misinformed.

So thought, so spoke Charles. "You see," cried he, "he speaks of it at first as only a rumour."

But Frank, in spite of his sanguine nature, regarded the information differently. He began looking at portions of the letter again, and did not answer.

"Can't you say something, Frank?"

"Charley, I fear it is true. Street would never have written this dismal news to your father whilst there was any doubt about it."

"But it has no right to be true; it ought not to be true," disputed Charley, in his terrible perplexity. "Who is George Atkinson that he should inherit Eagles' Nest? The fellow lives at the other end of the world. In Australia, or somewhere. Frank, it's not *likely* to be true. It would be frightful injustice; a cruel shame. It has been ours for twelve months: who will wrest it from us now?"

And truly, having enjoyed Eagles' Nest for all that time, regarding it as theirs, living at it in perfect security, it did appear most improbable that it should now pass away from them; almost an impossibility.

"Charley, we must keep this letter to ourselves until we know more. I am almost glad my uncle is ill; it would have shocked him so—"

"And how long will it be before we know more?" broke in Charles, who was in a humour for finding fault with every one, especially the lawyer. "Street ought to have come down, no matter at what inconvenience. A pretty state of suspense, this, to be placed in!"

"Drink your coffee, Charley."

"Coffee? Oh, I don't want it now."

The unfortunate news left Charles no inclination for coffee. Of all the calamities, actual or threatened, that had been making his life uneasy, this was the worst. The worst? The rest now seemed as passing shadows in comparison. Frank, with all his sunny nature, could impart no comfort to him. The only possible ray to be discerned, lay in the hope that the tidings would turn out to be untrue. A hope which grew fainter with every moment's thought.

To remain in this suspense was nothing less than torture. It was hastily decided between them that Frank should go up to town, see Mr. Street, and learn more. He had no scruple in doing this: Major Raynor was decidedly better; in no immediate danger, as Frank believed; and Dr. Selfe was at hand in case of need.

Frank lost no time; hastening to the station, and looking in on Dr. Selfe on his way, to explain that important business was calling him for a few hours to London. Mr. Street's residence was near Euston Square, and his offices were in the same house. The morning was well advanced when Frank arrived there and was shown into the lawyer's presence. He seemed less genial than of yore, as he sat half turned from a table covered with papers, his right foot on a rest: his hair was certainly more scanty; his light eyes, seen so clearly through his spectacles, were colder. Frank, who, as it chanced, had never seen him, thought what a hard little man he looked.

"Ah, yes; a sad affair," he remarked, as Frank in a few words introduced himself and his business. "Very embarrassing for the major."

"But I hope that it cannot be true, Mr. Street?"

"That what cannot be true?—that a later will is in existence? Oh, that is true enough. And the major has had an attack, you say? Misfortunes never come singly."

"May I ask how the fact—that there is a later will—has come to your knowledge?"

Mr. Street turned over a few of the papers on the table, and took up a letter lying amongst them. "I received this note from my brother, the banker, yesterday afternoon," he said, running his eyes over it. "It tells me that a will, of later date than the one by which Major Raynor holds Eagles' Nest, has been produced, leaving the estate to Mr. George Atkinson. George Atkinson is now on his homeward voyage from Australia, to take possession of the property."

"What a mercy if the ship should go down with him!" thought Frank, in his dismay, as the faint remnant of hope died out. "Then—I presume you consider that this unpleasant report may be relied on, Mr. Street?"

"Certainly it may. My brother is one of the most cautious men living; he would not have written so decisively"—touching the note with his finger—"had any doubt existed. Most likely he has heard from George Atkinson himself: he would of course write before sailing. Atkinson is virtually his chief partner, you know, head of the bank. I had thought my brother would perhaps call here last night, but he did not. Something or other has come to my ankle, and I can't get out."

"Then—this note from Mr. Edwin Street is all the information you as yet possess?"

"Yes, all. But I know it is to be relied on. I thought it better to write at once and acquaint the major: he will have little time, as it is, to prepare for the change, and see what can be done."

Frank rose. "I will go down and question Mr. Edwin Street," he said. "I suppose I am at liberty to do so?"

"Oh, quite at liberty," was the reply. "He no doubt wrote to me with a view to preparing your family, Mr. Raynor. You will find him at the bank."

The banker received Frank coldly; he seemed just the same hard, ungenial, self-contained sort of man that his brother was. Harder, in fact. This was indeed his general manner: but somehow, Frank caught up an idea that he had a dislike to the name of Raynor.

"I beg to refer you to Callard and Priestleigh, Mr. Atkinson's solicitors," spoke the banker to Frank, as soon as the latter entered on his business. "They will be able to afford you every necessary information."

"But won't you tell me how it has all come about?" cried Frank, his genial manner presenting a contrast to that of the banker. "If Mrs. Atkinson made a later will, where has the will been all this while? Why should it turn up at a twelvemonth's end, and not at the time of her death?"

"The will, as I am informed, has been lying in the hands of Callard and Priestleigh."

"Then why did Callard and Priestleigh not produce it at the proper time?" reiterated Frank.

"Callard and Priestleigh may themselves be able to inform you," was the short, stiff answer.

Apparently no satisfaction could be extracted from Mr. Edwin Street. Frank wished him good-morning, and betook himself to Callard and Priestleigh, who lived near the Temple. "From pillar to post, from post to pillar," thought he. "I ought to arrive at something presently."

Mr. Callard was a white-haired old gentleman; a little reserved in manner also; but nevertheless sufficiently cordial with Frank, and not objecting to give him information. He took him for the son of Major Raynor; and though Frank twice set him right upon the point, the old man went back to his own impression, and persisted in thinking Frank to be the—late—heir to Eagles' Nest. It was a mistake of no consequence.

The reader may remember that when Mrs. Atkinson expressed her intention of making a fresh will in Mr. George Atkinson's favour and leaving Major Raynor's name out of it, she had summoned Street the lawyer to Eagles' Nest to draw it up. Street, as he subsequently informed the major, had represented the injustice of this to Mrs. Atkinson, and prevailed upon her—as he supposed—to renounce her intention, and to let the old will stand. The lawyer went back to London in this belief; and nothing whatever transpired, then or subsequently, to shake it. However, after his departure from Eagles' Nest, it appeared that Mrs. Atkinson had sent for a local solicitor, and caused him to draw up a fresh will, in which she made George Atkinson her heir, and cut off the major. This will she had kept by her until just before her death, when she sent it, sealed up, to Callard and Priestleigh, requesting them to put it amongst Mr. George Atkinson's papers, and hold it at his disposal. There could be no doubt, Mr. Callard thought, that she also, either at the time the new will was made, or close upon her death, wrote to George Atkinson and informed him of what she had done: namely, made her will in his favour, and placed it with his solicitors.

"But, sir," exclaimed Frank to Mr. Callard when he had listened to this explanation, "how was it that you did not bring the will forward at Mrs. Atkinson's death? Why did you suffer the other will to be proved and acted upon, when you knew you held this one?"

"But we did not know it," replied the old man: "you have misunderstood me, my young friend. When Mrs. Atkinson sent the document to us she did not inform us of its nature. I assure you we never suspected that it was a will. It was sealed up in a parchment envelope, and bore no outward indication of its contents."

"Then—how do you know it now?"

"Because we have received written instructions from Mr. George Atkinson to open the parchment, and prove the will. It is by these instructions we gather the fact that Mrs. Atkinson must have written to inform him such a will existed."

"He has taken his time in coming to verify it!"

"It appears—as we hear from Edwin Street—that he was travelling for months in some remote parts of Australia, and did not receive his letters. However, he is on his way home now."

"Is the will opened? Have you seen it?" asked Frank.

"Both seen it and read it," replied the old man, smoothing back his white hair, and looking at Frank with concern. "It will be proved in a day or two. I sympathize with you and your father."

"Who are the executors?"

"George Atkinson and Street the banker. The latter is acting."

"And Mr. Atkinson is really on his way from Australia."

"Yes: by ship. We expect him to land in the course of two or three weeks. His written instructions were received by this last mail, and were conveyed to us through Edwin Street, to whom they were sent. Mr. Atkinson desires that all necessary preliminaries may be executed without delay, as he intends to take possession of Eagles' Nest on his arrival."

"He cannot know that my uncle is in it!"

"I dare say he does. He knew that Major Raynor succeeded to it, for we wrote him to that effect at the time. And he is in regular correspondence with his partner, Edwin Street."

"Then the worst is true!" cried Frank, as he fully realized what this meant for the poor major and his family. "I *wonder* that George Atkinson should accept the estate!—should wrest it from them! from the little I have heard of him, I drew the conclusion that he was a kind and a just man."

Mr. Solicitor Callard opened his eyes very widely. The words surprised him "Kind! Just!" cried he. "Well, he is so: we know him well: but, my good sir, a will is a will. You can't ignore a will as you might a verbal message."

"It will be a terrible shock to my uncle and his family. Utter ruin."

The old gentleman shook his head in pity.

"Ay, it's sad, no doubt; very sad. We lawyers often have to inflict grievous blows; and we cannot help ourselves."

"One last question," said Frank, as he prepared to leave. "In the old will, Major Raynor was left residuary legatee,—and therefore came in for all the accumulated money—though in point of fact the bulk of it has not yet been found. Who comes in for it now?"

"George Atkinson. My good young friend, George Atkinson comes in for *everything*. The one will may be called a counterpart of the other; in regard to the small legacies, and all else; excepting that George Atkinson's name is substituted for Major Raynor's."

"Is nothing left to the major in this later one?"

"Nothing."

Frank Raynor went back to Eagles' Nest, carrying his deplorable news with him. Careless and sanguine-natured though he was, he could not close his eyes to the dark future. It was not only the loss of the estate. That would have been bad enough, in all conscience; but there was also the money the major had spent. The ready-money that had been lying at Eagles' Nest and at her banker's at the time of Mrs. Atkinson's death; and also this past year's revenues from the estate. The major had spent it all: and for this he was now accountable to George Atkinson; he could be legally called upon to refund it. A fear crossed Frank that he would be so called upon: a hard man, as he was now judging George Atkinson to be—perhaps without just cause—would most likely exact his full rights, no matter what misery and ruin they might involve to others. In Frank Raynor's chivalrous good-nature, he was thinking that George Atkinson, already a wealthy man, might have refused Eagles' Nest, and left the major in peaceable possession of it. Perhaps very few men would agree with him: as the old lawyer said, a will was a will. This was certain: that, no matter how large a sum the law might claim from Major Raynor, he had not a shilling to meet it with. Would they confiscate his annuity until it was paid—that five hundred a-year; which was all he and his children would now have to fall back upon? "I wish with all my heart I had a home to offer them, and a good practice to keep it up!" concluded Frank.

Poor Major Raynor! He was never to be subjected to this trouble; or to any other trouble in this world. It was past six when Frank got back to Eagles' Nest, and he found his uncle dying. The attack that was dreaded had seized him about an hour before: just twelve hours after the first threatening in the morning; and there was now little, if any, hope.

"Oh, my dear," gasped Mrs. Raynor, in her pitiable distress, letting her head fall on Frank's shoulder, as her tears rained down, "it is so sudden! If he could only recover consciousness, and speak to us!"

"Aunt," he said, his own eyes misty, "don't you think we had better send for Edina? She would be a comfort to you."

"Edina!" was the sobbing answer. "My dear, she was telegraphed for this morning. Lamb went to the station just after you left. I knew she would come off at once: she is on her way now. I could never bear up under this trouble without Edina."

"But she does not know of the other trouble," thought Frank, looking on Mrs. Raynor, with pitying eyes. "It must be broken to her by Edina."

VII

Frank Raynor Followed

The whole house was steeped in grief—for Major Raynor had died at dawn. As most houses are, when a near and beloved relative is removed: and the anguish is more keenly felt if the blow, as in this case, falls suddenly. Edina was a treasure now; she had travelled by night and was early at Eagles' Nest. Mourning with them sincerely, she at the time strove to cheer them. She whispered of a happier meeting hereafter, where shall be no more parting; she would not let them sorrow without hope. Even Mrs. Raynor felt comforted: and the little children dried their tears, saying that papa was with the angels in heaven, and they should go to him when God saw that they were good enough.

But, of that other misfortune none of the household as yet were cognizant. Frank took an opportunity of revealing it to Edina. It almost overwhelmed even her.

"Not theirs!" she cried, in a dread whisper. "Eagles' Nest George Atkinson's!"

"And the worst of it is," returned Frank, running through a summary of the details he had heard, "that he means to exact his rights at once, and take immediate possession of the place as soon as he lands. Did you not know this George Atkinson once, Edina?"

"Yes—a little," she answered, a faint blush rising to her cheek at the remembrance.

"Was he hard and selfish then?"

"I—cannot quite tell, Frank. He did not appear to me to be so."

"Perhaps not. He was young then: and men grow harder as they grow older. But now, Edina, what is to be done? They will have to turn out of this house, and where will they find another?"

The problem seemed a hard one. Edina sat it an attitude almost of despair as she tried to solve it: her hands folded quietly on her black dress; her usually calm, good face perplexed; her steady eyes anxious. The unexpected blow had fallen on her sharply; and in these first moments it was a hard task to battle with it. So far as she or any one else could see, the Raynors would not have a penny to fall back upon: no income of any sort whatever. The major's annuity has died with him.

"They are all so helpless!" she murmured.

"Of course they are," assented Frank. "Not that that makes it any worse or better."

"It makes it all the worse," said Edina. "Were they experienced and capable, they might do something or other to earn a living."

A whole world of surprise shone in Frank Raynor's candid blue eyes. "Earn a living!" he exclaimed. "Who would earn it?"

"All who are old enough," said Edina. "Mrs. Raynor and Alice to begin with."

"Surely you cannot think of such a thing for them, Edina!"

"But how else will they exist, Frank? Who will keep them? Charley will never be able to do it."

A blank pause. Frank, brought thus practically face to face with the position, was unable to reply.

"I wish to goodness I could keep them!" he exclaimed, at length. "I wish I had a practice and a house over my head! They should all come to it."

"It has surprised me very much indeed, Frank—to leave the other subject for a moment—that you have not sought to establish yourself all this time."

"I was waiting for some money to do it with, Edina. Poor Uncle Francis was constantly expecting those missing funds to turn up. It seems they would have belonged to George Atkinson if they had come to light: but we could not have known that."

"Your uncle Hugh blamed you for it, Frank. 'Better to take a situation as an assistant, than to fritter away his days at Eagles' Nest,' he used often to say."

Frank made no reply. The mention of his uncle Hugh brought vividly to his mind that last ominous letter he had received from him. With his usual incaution, he spoke on the moment's impulse.

"Is Blase Pellet at Trennach still?"

Not quite immediately did Edina answer. Raising his eyes, he met hers fixed on him. And he saw something in their depths that he did not like: an anxious, questioning, half-terrified expression.

"Edina knows about it," thought he. And he turned as cold as the winter frost.

"Yes, Blase Pellet is there as usual," she replied, averting her eyes. "And Mrs. Bell has left Trennach for good and has gone to live at Falmouth."

Why, the very answer; that last gratuitous sentence; would itself have been enough to betray her cognizance of the matter. Else why should she have connected the Bells with Blase Pellet? Frank quitted the topic abruptly.

Not until after the funeral—which took place, as was deemed expedient, on the fourth day from the death—were the tidings of their penniless state conveyed to Mrs. Raynor and the others. How Charles had contrived to keep counsel he never knew. He was looked upon as the successor to Eagles' Nest. Servants and others continually came to him for directions: Is this to be done, sir; is the other to be done: treating him as the master.

Mrs. Raynor received the news with amazement, astonishment contending with incredulity. Alice burst into tears; Alfred went into a passion. They talked foolishly at first, saying they would go to law: the newly-found will should be disputed; the property flung into Chancery. The only two capable of bringing reason to bear upon the matter were Frank and Edina: and they might have been nearly as bad as the rest, had the tidings only just come upon them. They pointed out how worse than futile any opposition would be. Not a shadow of doubt could exist that the second will was perfectly correct and legal, and that the whole property belonged to George Atkinson.

On the second day after Frank's return from London, while the poor major lay dead in the house, Charles received an official letter from Street the lawyer. It gave in detail the particulars already known, and stated that Mr. George Atkinson was then on his voyage to Europe, with sundry other hints and statements. This letter Frank read aloud now.

"You see," he said, "even our own lawyer gives in. He says not a word about opposition. No, there's no help for it; Eagles' Nest must go from you. But I think old Aunt Atkinson ought to have been ashamed of herself."

"She must have been dreadfully wicked," sobbed Alice.

One thing they did not tell Mrs. Raynor—that she could be made responsible for the money received and spent during the past twelvemonth. The claim was not yet made; would not be made until Mr. George Atkinson's arrival; time enough to tell her then.

What their plans were to be, or where they could go, or how live, was the subject of many an anxious thought, as the days passed on.

Edina suggested this and that; but poor Mrs. Raynor and Alice shrunk from all. As yet they could not realize what the turning-out of Eagles' Nest would be, and instinctively shunned the anticipation.

But upon none did the blow fall so bitterly as upon Charles. He was suddenly flung from his position on the height of a pinnacle to its base. A few days ago he was an independent gentleman, an undergraduate of Oxford, the heir to Eagles' Nest; now all these desirable accessories had melted like icicles in the sunbeams. He must work for a living, if he were to live; he must take his name off the college books, failing the means to return to college; he must, for his mind's best peace, forget that there was such a place as Eagles' Nest.

Work for a living! How was he to do anything of the kind, he asked himself. And even if he were willing, and the work presented itself (some charming, rose-coloured vision of a sinecure post would now and again arise indistinctly before his imagination) how would he be free to fulfil it, with those wretched debts at his heels?

One little matter did surprise Charles—he heard nothing of Huddles. He had fully expected that within a day or two of that worthy man's departure certain sharks of the law, or—as he seemed to prefer to call them—tigers, would attack him. But nothing of the sort occurred. The days went on, and Charles was still not interfered with.

About a fortnight after the death of Major Raynor, a letter arrived from Mr. Street. And, by the way, speaking of the major's death, what a grievous farce his will sounded when it was read. Eagles' Nest was bequeathed to Charles, with liberty to Mrs. Raynor to reside in it for the next ten years; after that, if Charles should deem it expedient that she should leave with the younger children, he was charged to provide her with a home. The major recommended that a portion of the missing money, when found, should be put out at interest, and allowed to accumulate for her benefit. Quite a large sum was willed away in small bequests. This to one child, that to another; some to Edina, some to Frank, and so on. The horses and carriages, the linen, plate, ornaments and trinkets, with sundry other personalities that had come to him with Eagles' Nest, were left to Mrs. Raynor. All this, when read, sounded like a painful farce, a practical joke. These things were all George Atkinson's; and, of the legacies, the poor major possessed not a shilling to bequeath.

Mr. George Atkinson safely arrived in England and in London. Lawyer Street wrote to Eagles' Nest to state the fact, and that he had held a business interview with him in the presence of Mr. Callard. Mr. Atkinson, he hinted, was not inclined to deal harshly with the Raynor family, but leniently. He gave them one month in which to vacate Eagles' Nest, when he should himself enter into possession of it; and with regard to the money spent in the past twelvemonth, which did in reality belong to him, and to the mesne profits, he made no claim. Let them leave his house quietly, and he should say nothing about arrears. It had been spent by Major Raynor under the misapprehension that it was his own, and he would not exact it of the major's children.

The conditions were, perhaps, as favourable as could be expected from a man of the world. Mr. Solicitor Callard pronounced them to be wonderfully so, cruelly hard though they sounded to the Raynors. *They* thought, taking all circumstances into consideration—his own wealth, which must be accumulating yearly, his want of relationship to the former mistress of Eagles' Nest, and consequent absence of just claim to inherit it—that Mr. Atkinson should have quietly resigned it to them, and left them in undisturbed possession of it. Frank, once hearing Charley say this, shook his head. *He* should have done this himself, he said, were he George Atkinson; but he feared the world, as a whole, would not: we did not live in Utopia.

And now came in Edina's practical good sense. After allowing them a day to grieve, she begged them to listen to her ideas for the future. She had been thinking a great deal, but could only hit upon one plan that seemed at all feasible. It was, that Mrs. Raynor and Alice should establish a school. Alice, a well-educated girl, a good musician and otherwise accomplished, would be of valuable aid in teaching.

Three weeks ago, they would—Alice, at any rate—have turned from the proposition with indignation. But those three weeks had been working their natural effect; and neither Mrs. Raynor nor Alice spoke a dissenting syllable. They had begun to realize the bitter fact that they must work to live. The world lay before and around them: a cold, cruel, and indifferent world, as it now seemed to them; and they had no shelter in it. To keep a ladies' school would be less objectionable than some things, and was certainly preferable to starving. Better than setting up a shop, for instance, or taking to a boarding-house. It was Edina who alluded to these unpleasant alternatives, and Alice did not thank her for it. Poor Alice had still many lessons to learn. It is true that Alice might go out as a governess, but that would not keep Mrs. Raynor and the younger ones.

MRS. HENRY WOOD

"I see only one objection to this school idea of yours, Edina," spoke poor Mrs. Raynor, who was the first to break the silence which had ensued; while Alice sat with downcast eyes and an aching heart. "And that is, that I do not know how it is to be accomplished. We have no money and no furniture. It would be easy enough to take a house in some good situation, as you suggest; but how is it to be furnished?"

Edina did not immediately answer. Perhaps the problem was rather too much for herself. She sat in thought; her steadfast eyes gazing with a far-away look over the beautiful landscape they were so soon to lose.

"Mr. Atkinson intimates that we are at liberty to remove any furniture, or other articles, we may have bought for Eagles' Nest; that he only wishes it left as it was left by Mrs. Atkinson," continued Mrs. Raynor: who, in these last few days of trouble, seemed to have quite returned to the meek-spirited, humble-minded woman she used to be, with not a wish of her own, and thoroughly incapable. "But, Edina, the furniture would be too large, too grand for the sort of house we must have now, and therefore I am afraid useless. Besides, we shall have to sell these things with the carriages, and all that, to pay outstanding debts here that must be settled: the servants' wages, our new mourning, and other things."

"True," replied Edina, somewhat absently.

"Perhaps we could hire some articles: chairs and tables, and forms for the girls to sit on, and beds?" suggested Mrs. Raynor. "Sometimes furniture is let with a house. Edina, are you listening?"

"Yes, I am listening; partly at least; but I was deep in thought just then over ways and means," replied Edina, rousing herself to her usual mental activity. "A furnished house would never do; it would be too costly; and so, I fear, would be the hiring of furniture. Now and then, I believe, when a house is to be let, the furniture in it can be bought very cheaply."

"But if we have no money to buy it with, Edina?"

"Of course: there's the drawback. I think the neighbourhood of London would be the best locality for a new school: the most likely one to bring scholars. Should not you, Mary?"

"Yes," assented Mrs. Raynor, with a sigh. "But you know all about these things so much better than I do, Edina."

The plans, and the means of carrying them out, seemed, as yet, very indistinct; but at length Edina proposed to go to London and look about her, and see if she could find any suitable place. Mrs. Raynor, always thankful that others should act for her, eagerly acquiesced. Though, indeed, to find a house—or, rather, to find one full of furniture—appeared as a very castle-in-the-air. Chairs and tables do not drop from the skies: and Edina was setting her face resolutely against running into debt.

"Now you understand," Edina said, the morning of her departure, calling Charles and Mrs. Raynor to her, "that I shall depend upon you to arrange matters here. If I am to find a house for you in London, I may have too much to do to return, and you must manage without me. Set about what has to be done at once, Charles: get the superfluous furniture out of the house, for sale; and have your boxes packed, ready to come up. You must be out of Eagles' Nest as soon as possible; on account of the heavy expenses still going on while you are in it. Mr. George Atkinson allowed you a month: I should leave it in less than half that time. Besides, Mary: you should be on the spot to begin school before the Midsummer holidays are over; it will give you a better chance of pupils."

They agreed to all: Charles rather gloomily, Mrs. Raynor in simple confidence: anything suggested by Edina was sure to be for the best. It was impossible for Charles to rise up yet from the blow. With him, the aspect of things, instead of growing brighter, grew darker. Each morning, as it dawned, was only more gloomy than the last. A terrible wrong had been dealt to him—whether by Fate, or by that unjust defunct woman, his aunt Ann, or by George Atkinson, he could not quite decide, perhaps by all three combined—and he felt at variance with the whole world. Edina had talked to him of plans for himself, but Charles did not hear her with any patience. To contrast the present with the past drove him half-mad. That he must do something, he knew quite well, and he intended to do it: but he did not know what that something was to be; he could not see an opening anywhere. Moreover, he also knew that he must make some arrangement with the people at Oxford to whom he owed money.

Another thing had yet to be done—taking his name off the college books. Charles went down to do this; and to confer with his creditors. Very young men are often most sensitive on the score of debt: Charles Raynor was so: and it seemed to him a formidable and distressing task to meet these men, avow his poverty, and beg of them to be lenient and wait.

"I declare I'd rather meet his Satanic majesty, and hold a battle with *him!*" cried Charley, as he started forth to the encounter.

But he found the creditors considerate. They had heard of his reverse of fortune. The news of the fresh will put forward, and the consequent transfer of Eagles' Nest from the Raynors to George Atkinson the banker, had been made much of in the newspapers. One and all met Charles pleasantly; some actuated by genuine pity for the young man, others by the remembrance that you cannot get blood out of a stone. Half the sting was taken from Charley's task. He told them truly that he had no present means whatever, therefore could not offer to pay: but he assured them—and his voice was earnest, and they saw he meant it—that he would pay them whenever it should be in his power to do so, though that might not be for years to come. So he and they parted cordially. After all, no individual debt was very much, though in the aggregate the sum looked formidable.

Mr. Huddles was left until last. Charles dreaded him most. That debt was the largest. The two bills were for fifty pounds each, making a hundred; and mischief alone knew what the added expenses would be. Not only did Charles dread him because he would have to eat humble-pie, which he hated and detested, and beg the man to hold the bills on, but he believed that Mr. Huddles could arrest him without ceremony. Nevertheless he had no choice but to enter on the interview for he must know his own position before he could plan out or venture on any career of life. He went forth to it at dusk; some dim idea pervading him that tigers and kidnappers might not exercise their functions after sunset.

Mr. Huddles sat alone in his parlour when Charles was shown in: a well-lighted and well-furnished room. Instead of the scowl and the frown Charles had anticipated, he rose with a smile and a pleasant look, and offered Charles a chair.

"We were both a little out of temper the other day, Mr. Raynor," said he; "and both, I dare say, felt sorry for it afterwards. What can I do for you?"

To hear this, completely took Charles aback. Down he sat, with some indistinct words of reply. And then, summoning up what courage he could, he entered upon the subject of the bills.

"No one can regret more than I that I cannot pay them," he said. "I have come here to-night to beg of you to be so kind as hold them over. The expenses, I suppose—"

"I don't understand you, sir," interrupted Mr. Huddles. "What bills are you talking of?"

"The two bills for fifty pounds each—I have no others. Although I know how unjust it must seem to ask you to do this, Mr. Huddles, as you are only a third party and had nothing whatever to do with the transaction, I have no resource but to throw myself upon your good feeling. I am quite unable to take the bills up; you have probably heard of our reverse of fortune; but I will give you my word of honour to do so as soon as—

"The bills are paid," cried Mr. Huddles, not allowing him to go on.

"Paid?" echoed Charley.

"Paid; both of them. Why—did you not know it?"

"No, that I did not. Who has paid them?"

"Some legal firm in London."

"What firm?"

"The name was—let me see—Symmonds, I think. Yes, that was it: Symmonds and Son, solicitors."

Charley could only stare. He began to think Mr. Huddles was playing off a joke upon him; perhaps to turn round on him afterwards.

"I don't know any people of the name of Symmonds, or they me," said he. "How *came* they to pay?"

"I think Major Raynor—I was sorry to see his death in the *Times* so soon afterwards—gave them the necessary orders."

Charles shook his head; it was not at all likely, as he knew. He lost himself in a maze of thought.

"The evening I saw you, I was running into the station to catch a train, having lingered rather too long at the inn over some late refreshment," explained Mr. Huddles, perceiving that Charles was altogether puzzled, "when a gentleman accosted me, asking if my errand in the place had not been connected with Major Raynor's son. I replied that it had. This gentleman then said that if I would furnish the particulars of the debt to Messrs. Symmonds and Son, solicitors, of London, they would no doubt see that I was paid; and he handed me their address. I sent the particulars up the next day, and in the course of a post or two received the money."

"It must have been Frank," thought Charles, the idea flashing into his mind. "What was this gentleman like, Mr. Huddles?"

"Upon my word, sir, I can hardly tell you," was the reply. "The train dashed in just as he began to speak to me; several passengers were waiting for it, and there was a good bit of confusion. It was dusk also. Nearly dark, in fact."

"A good-looking, pleasant-speaking fellow?"

"Yes, I think so. He had a pleasant voice."

"No one but Frank," decided Charles. "It's just like him to do these good-natured things. I wonder how he found the money? And why in the world did he not tell me he had done it?"

So this trouble was at an end; and Charles might for the present be pronounced free from worry on the score of debt. If the Fates had been hard to him latterly, it seemed that they yet hold some little kindness in store for him.

But this visit to the University city was productive of the most intense chagrin in other ways to Charles Raynor; of the keenest humiliation. "Only a short while ago, I was one of *them*, with the world all before me to hold my head up in!" he kept telling himself, as he watched the undergraduates passing in the street, holding aloof from them, for he had not the courage to show his face. If by unavoidable chance he encountered one or two, he drew away as quickly as he could, after exchanging a few uncomfortable sentences. Whilst they, knowing his changed circumstances, his blighted prospects, made no effort to detain him; and if their manner displayed a certain restraint, springing from innate pity, or delicacy of feeling, Charles put it down to a very different cause, and felt all the deeper mortification.

As he left Oxford by an early morning train on his way home, his thoughts were busy with what had passed. For one thing, he found that his days of torment at Eagles' Nest, when he went about in fear of writs and arrest, had been without foundation. With the exception of Mr. Huddles—and that was much later—not a single creditor, as all assured him, had followed him there: neither had any of them written to him, excepting the one whose letter had by misadventure fallen into the hands of Major Raynor. Who then was the Tiger, Charles asked himself. Could it be that, after all, the man had positively held no mission that concerned him? It might be so: and that Charles had dreaded and hated him for nothing. The Tiger had left Grassmere now, as Charles happened to know. Jetty had said so the other day when he was at Eagles' Nest. To return sometime Jetty believed, for the gentleman had said as much to his sister Esther when leaving: he liked the lodgings and liked the place, and should no doubt visit them again.

And so, Charles Raynor returned home, relieved on the whole, in spite of his ever-present trouble, and with a lively feeling of gratitude to Frank Raynor in his heart.

He could not yet personally thank Frank; for Frank and his wife had quitted Eagles' Nest soon after the funeral of Major Raynor. With the fortunes of its hitherto supposed owners come to an end, Frank could not any longer remain, a weight on their hospitable hands. It was at length necessary that he should bestir himself in earnest, and see in what manner he could make a living for himself and Daisy. One great impediment to his doing this comfortably was, that he had no money. Excepting a few spare pounds in his pocket for present exigencies, he had positively none. The sum he had privately furnished Charles with at Christmas-time would have been useful to him now; but Frank never gave a regret to it. Daisy was not very strong yet, and could not be put about. She was going to stay with her sister, Captain Townley's wife, for two or three weeks, who had just come over from India with her children, and had taken a furnished house in London. Daisy wrote to her from Eagles' Nest proffering the visit: she saw what a convenience it would be to Frank to be "rid" of her, as she laughingly said, whilst he looked about for some place that they could settle in. Mrs. Townley's answer had been speedy and cordial. "Yes, you can come here, Daisy; I shall be delighted to see you. But what a silly child you must have been to make the undesirable runaway marriage they tell me of! I thought all the St. Clares had better sense than that."

But the Tiger is not done with yet. On the day that Frank and his wife said farewell to Eagles' Nest, and took train for London, Frank jumped out of the carriage at an intermediate station to get a newspaper. On his way into it again, he had his eyes on the newspaper, and chanced to go up to the wrong compartment, the one behind his own. Opening the door, Frank saw to his surprise that there was no room for him, and at the same moment found his face in pretty close contact with another face; one adorned with a silky brown beard and the steadfast grey eyes Frank had learned to know.

"This compartment is full, sir."

How far Frank recoiled at the words, at the sight, he never knew. *It was the Tiger.* With a sinking of the heart, a rush of dismay, he made his way to his own carriage; and let the newspaper, that he had been eager for, drop between his knees.

"He is following me to town," cried Frank, mentally, in his firm conviction. "He means to track me. How shall I escape him? How am I to escape Blase Pellet?"

MRS. HENRY WOOD

VIII

The New Home

A cold, drizzling rain was falling. We have wintry weather sometimes in July, as was the case now. The lovely summer seemed to have come to an abrupt end, and to have flown for good. At least, it appeared so to those who were turning out of their late happy and prosperous home, to enter on another of which they knew little. Knew nothing, in fact, except that it would have to be one of poverty and labour. For this was the day that Mrs. Raynor and her children were quitting Eagles' Nest.

All superfluous effects had been disposed off, even to their personal trinkets. Charles's watch, that he set store by because it had been his father's, and had only just come into his possession, had to go. Without the sale of these things they could not have paid all their debts and kept sufficient for pressing requirements. A fly took Mrs. Raynor, Alice, and the two younger children to the station, Charles and Alfred having walked on; and a cart conveyed the luggage. The rain beat against the windows of the fly, the wind swept by in gusts, shaking the branches of the trees. Everything looked dreary and wretched, even Eagles' Nest itself. Oh, what a change it was, inwardly and outwardly, from that day, bright with hope and sunshine, when they had entered it only twelve short months before!

Charles was at the fly door when it drew up. "What tickets am I to take?" he asked of his mother: and a blank pause ensued. They were accustomed to first-class; but that would not do now.

"Either second, or—*third*, Charley," spoke poor Mrs. Raynor.

"There is no third-class to this train," replied Charley, glad perhaps to have to say it, as he turned away to the ticket-office.

And so they travelled up to London, Mrs. Raynor leaning back in the carriage with closed eyes, grateful for the rest. It had been a long scuffle to get away: and every one of them had mentally reproached Edina for not coming to their help.

"It is just as though she had deserted us," said Mrs. Raynor. "I suppose she will be at the new house to receive us, as she says; but I think she might have come all the same: she knows how incapable I am."

The "new house" was situated in the southern district of London, some three miles, or so, from the heart of the bustle. It was about five o'clock when they approached it in two cabs, through the dirt and drizzle. The spirits of all were depressed. With the very utmost difficulty Mrs. Raynor kept down her tears.

"I expect to find an empty barn," she said, looking out on the dreary road. "Perhaps there will not be as much as a mattress to sleep on."

The cabs stopped before the door of a convenient, roomy, but old-fashioned-looking house, standing a little back from the road, with a garden behind it. A rosy servant-girl opened the door. She was not as fashionable-looking as the maids they had left, but she was neat and active, and very willing—a remarkably desirable quality in a maid-of-all-work. Edina came forward; a bright smile of welcome on her face as she took all the hands into hers that she could hold, and led the way to the sitting-room. It was quite furnished, and the tea-things stood on the table.

Instead of the empty barn Mrs. Raynor had expected, she found a house plainly but well furnished throughout. The schoolroom, the airy bedrooms, the sitting-rooms, the kitchen, all had their appropriate appointments. Useful furniture, and quite new. Mrs. Raynor halted in the kitchen, which was not underground, and gazed about her. The fire threw its warmth on the red bricks, a kettle was singing away, plates and dishes stood on the dresser shelves, every necessary article seemed at hand.

"I cannot understand it, Edina. You must have obtained the things on credit, after all. Oh, that the school may succeed!—so that we may soon be enabled to pay for them."

"No credit has been asked or given, Mary," was Edina's answer. "The furniture has been bought and paid for, and it is yours."

"Bought by whom?"

"By me. You will not be too proud to accept it from your poor friend, Edina!"

Mrs. Raynor sat down on the nearest wooden chair, and burst into tears.

"You thought, I am sure, that I might have come back to help you away from Eagles' Nest, Mary, but I could not: I had too much to do here," explained Edina. "I find there is an opening in this neighbourhood for a school, and I also found this house, that is so suitable for one, to be let. I took it, and with Frank's help, furnished it, plainly as you see: and then I went about amongst the neighbours, and put an advertisement or two in the papers, asking for pupils. Two boarders, sisters, will enter to-morrow; two more on Monday, and five day-pupils. This is not so bad a beginning, and I dare say others will drop in. I feel sure you will succeed; that you and Alice may get a very good school together in time: and I hope Heaven will bless and prosper you."

Mrs. Raynor was looking up in her rather helpless manner. "I—I don't understand, Edina. Did you buy the furniture, or did Frank?"

"Not Frank, poor fellow: he has need of help himself. Be at rest, Mary: I bought it, and I have made it over to you by a deed of gift. The house is taken in your name, and I am responsible for the first half-year's rent."

"Oh, Edina! But I thought you had no money—except the small income Dr. Raynor secured to you."

"Please don't disparage my income," said Edina, gaily. "It is fifty pounds a-year: quite enough for me. As to the money, I had a hundred pounds or two by me that my dear father left me over and above the income. In laying it out for you and yours in your hour of need, Mary, I think it well spent."

"And we used to call Edina mean and stingy!" thought Mrs. Raynor in her repentant heart. "At least, Charles and Alice did."

With the next week, all the expected pupils had entered; four boarders and five day-pupils. Another day-pupil, not expected, made six. It was a very good opening, affording hope of ultimate success.

"What do you think of it, Charley?" asked Mrs. Raynor, on the third evening, as they sat together after the little boarders and Kate and Robert were in bed, Edina being out.

"Oh, I think it's first-rate," answered Charley, half seriously, half mockingly. "You and Alice will be making a fortune by-and-by."

The remark did not please Alice. *She*, at least, was not reconciled to the new home and its duties.

"*You* may think it first-rate," she retorted. "It is widely different from Eagles' Nest. We were gentlepeople there; we are poor governesses here."

Charley made no response. The very name of Eagles' Nest would give him an unpleasant turn.

"And it is nothing but work all day," went on Alice. "Lessons this hour, music that, writing the next. Oh, it is wearisome!"

"Don't grumble, my dears," interposed Mrs. Raynor. "It might have been so much worse. After the strange turn our affairs took, we might now be without a roof over our heads or a morsel of bread to eat. So far as I can see, we should have been, but for Edina."

The tears were raining down Mrs. Raynor's cheeks. Alice started up and threw her arms round her in repentance. "Forgive me, dear mamma, forgive me! I was wrong to speak so repiningly."

"You were wrong, dear Alice. In dwelling so much upon the advantages we have lost, you overlook the mercies remaining to us. And they are mercies. We are together under one roof; we have the prospect of making a fair living."

"Yes," acquiesced Charley, throwing regrets behind him. "It is a very nice home indeed, compared with what might have been."

"And I think we may yet be very happy in it," said Mrs. Raynor.

Alice strove to think so too, and put on a cheerful face. But the old days were ever present with her; and she never recalled the past hopes connected with William Stane, but her heart turned sick and faint in its despair.

"It will be your turn next, Charles," observed Edina, taking the opportunity of speaking to him the following morning, when they were alone.

"My turn?" repeated Charles, vaguely: conscious that he knew what she meant, but not choosing to acknowledge it.

"To do something for yourself," added Edina. "You cannot intend to live upon your mother."

"Of course I do not, Edina. How stupid you are."

"And the question is, what is that something to be?" she continued, passing over his compliment to herself.

"I should like to go into the army, Edina."

Edina shook her head. Her longer experience of life, her habits of forethought, enabled her to see obstacles that younger people did not see.

"Even if you had the money to purchase a commission, Charley—"

"But I did not think of purchasing. I should like to get one given to me."

"Is there a chance of it?"

Charles did not reply. He was standing before the window, gazing abstractedly at a young butcher boy, dashing about in a light cart for his morning orders. There was not very much chance of it, he feared, but there might be a little.

"Let us suppose that you had the commission, Charley, that it arrived here for you this very day direct from the Horse Guards—or whatever place may issue them," pursued Edina. "Would it benefit you?"

"Benefit me!"

"I mean, could you take it up? How would you find your necessary outfit? Regimentals cost a great deal: and there must be many other preliminary expenses. This is not all—"

"I could get things on credit," interrupted Charles, "and pay as I went on."

"But this would not be the only impediment, Charley. I have heard that it takes every officer more than his pay to live. I have often thought that were I an officer it should not take me more; but it may be that I am mistaken there. You would not have anything besides your pay, Charley."

"Oh, I expect I should get along."

"Taken at the best, you would have nothing to spare. I had thought you might choose some calling which would enable you to help them here at home."

"Of course. It is what I should wish to do."

"Alfred must be educated; and little Robert as he comes on. Your mother may not be able to do this. And I do not see that you will have it in your power to aid her if you enter the army."

Charles began scoring the window-pane with a pencil that he held, not knowing what to answer. In truth, his own intentions and views as to the future were so vague and purposeless, that to dwell on it gave him nightmare.

"What should you propose, Edina?"

"A situation," replied Edina, promptly, "in some good city house."

But for the obligations they were just now under to Edina, Mr. Charles Raynor would have abused her well for the suggestion. It suited neither himself nor his pride. A situation in some city house! That meant a clerk, he supposed. To write at desks and go on errands!

"I wish you wouldn't talk so, Edina," he peevishly said, wishing he might box her ears. "Did you ever hear of a Raynor becoming a tradesman?"

"Did you ever hear of a Raynor with no means of living?" retorted Edina. "No profession, and no money? Circumstances alter cases, Charley."

"Circumstances can't make a common man a gentleman; and they can't make a gentleman take up the rôle of a common man."

"Can't they! I think they often do. However, Charley, I will say no more just now, for I perceive you are not in the humour for it. Consider the matter with yourself. *Don't* depend upon the commission, for indeed I do not see that you have a chance of one. Put it out of your thoughts, if you can, and look to other ways and means. I shall be leaving you in a day or two, you know; by that time you will perhaps have decided on something."

Edina went into the schoolroom, and Charles stood where he was. Alfred came in with his Latin books. Mrs. Raynor was going to send Alfred to a day-school close by; but it did not open for another week or two, and meanwhile Charles made a show of keeping him to his Latin.

"What am I to do this morning, Charley?"

"Copy that last exercise over again, lad. It was so badly written yesterday that I could not read it."

Alfred's pen went scratching over the copy-book. Charles remained at the window, deep in thought. He had no more wish to be living on his mother than any other good son has; but he did not see where he could go, or what he could do. The doubt had lain on his mind during these recent days more than was agreeable to its peace. His whole heart was set upon a commission; but in truth he did not feel much more sanguine of obtaining one than Edina seemed to feel.

He wished he was something—wished it there as he stood. *Anything*, rather than remain in this helpless position. Wished he was a doctor, like Frank; or a banker, like that wretch, George Atkinson; or a barrister, like that other wretch, Stane. Had he been brought up to one of these callings he should at least have a profession before him. As it was, he felt incapable: he was fit for nothing, knew nothing. If he could get a commission given to him, he should be on his legs at once; and *that* required no special training.

But for Charles Raynor's inexperience, he might have found that a candidate for a commission in the army does require a special training now. In his father's young days the case was otherwise. The major had been very fond of talking of those days; Charles had thence gathered his impressions, and they remained with him.

Yes, he said to himself, making a final score on the window-pane, he must get the commission; and the sooner the better. Not to lose time, he thought it might be well to see about it at once. An old acquaintance of his father's, one Colonel Cockburn, had (as Charles was wont to put it to himself) some interest in high quarters: his brother, Sir James Cockburn, being one of the Lords of the Admiralty. Of course, reasoned

Charles, Sir James must be quite able to give away posts indiscriminately in both army and navy; and it was not likely he would refuse one to his brother, if the latter asked for it. So if he, Charles, could only get Colonel Cockburn to interest himself, the affair was done.

"Are you going out?" questioned Alfred, as Charles began to brush his coat and hat.

"Yes, I am going to see Colonel Cockburn," was the reply. "No good putting it off any longer. When you have finished copying that exercise, youngster, you can do another. And mind you stick at it: don't go worrying the mother."

Away went Charles, on the top of a passing omnibus. Colonel Cockburn's club was the Army and Navy. Charles possessed no other address of his; and to that building he found his way, and boldly entered.

"Colonel Cockburn, sir?" was the answer to his inquiry. "I don't think he is in town."

"Not in town!" cried Charles, his ardour suddenly damped. "Why do you think that?"

"He has not been here for a day or two, sir: so we conclude he is either absent or ill. The colonel is sometimes laid up with gout for a week together."

"Can you tell me where he lives? I'll go and see him."

"In St. James's Street," replied the man, giving at the same time the number of the house.

To St. James's Street proceeded Charles, found the house in which the colonel occupied rooms, and saw the landlady. Colonel Cockburn was at Bath: had gone to stay with a brother who was lying there ill.

"What a dreadful bother!" thought Charles. "Cockburn must have a whole regiment of brothers!" And he stood in indecision.

"Will the colonel be back soon?" inquired he.

"I don't know at all," was the landlady's answer. "Should he be detained in Bath, he may not come back before October. The colonel always leaves London the end of July. Sometimes he leaves earlier than that."

"What on earth am I to do?" cried Charles, half aloud, his vivid hopes evaporating considerably. "My business with him was urgent."

"Could you write to him?" suggested the landlady.

"I suppose I must—if you have his address. But I ought to see him."

She took an envelope from the mantelpiece, on which was written an address in the Crescent, Bath. Charles copied it down, and went out. He stood a moment, considering what he should do. The day was so fine and the town so full of life, that to go off to that pokey old southern suburb seemed a sin and a shame. So he decided to make a day of it, and began with the Royal Academy.

Time slips away in the most wonderful manner when sight-seeing, and the day was over before Charles thought it half through. When he reached home, it was past nine. The children were in bed; his mother also had gone to bed with headache; Edina and Alice were sewing by lamplight. Alice was at some fancy work; Edina was mending a torn pinafore: one of a batch that required repairing.

While taking his supper, Charles told them of his ill-luck in regard to Colonel Cockburn. And when the tray went away, he got paper and ink and began to write to him.

"He is sure to have heard of our misfortunes—don't you think so, Edina? I suppose I need only just allude to them."

"Of course he has heard of them," broke in Alice, resentfully. "All the world must have heard of them."

Charley went on writing. The first letter did not please him; and when it was nearly completed he tore it up and began another.

"It is always difficult to know what to say in this kind of application: and I don't think I am much of a letter-writer," observed he, candidly.

Alice grew tired, nodded over her embroidery, and at length said good-night and went upstairs. Edina sent the servant to bed, and stitched on at another pinafore.

"I think that will do," said Charley: and he read the letter aloud.

"It will do very well," acquiesced Edina. "But, Charley, I foresee all sorts of difficulties. To begin with, I am not at all sure that you are eligible for a commission: I fancy you ought to go first of all to Sandhurst or Woolwich."

"Not a bit of it," replied Charley, full of confidence. "What other difficulties do you foresee, Edina?"

"I wish you would give up the idea."

"I dare say! What would you have me do, if I did give it up?"

"Pocket your pride, and find a situation."

Charles tossed his head. Pride was almost as much in the ascendant with him as it ever had been. He thought how old and silly Edina was growing. But he remembered what she had done for them, and would not quarrel with her.

"Time enough to talk of that, Edina, when I have had Colonel Cockburn's answer."

Edina said no more for a few moments. She rose; shook out Robert's completed pinafore, and folded it. "I had a scheme in my head, Charley; but you don't seem inclined to hear anything I may say upon the subject."

"Yes, I will," replied Charley, opening his ears at the rather attractive word "scheme." "I will hear that."

"I cannot help thinking that if George Atkinson were applied to, he would give you a post in his bank. He ought to do it. After turning you out of Eagles' Nest—"

"I wouldn't apply to him; I wouldn't take it," interrupted Charles, fiercely, his anger aroused by the name. "If he offered me the best post in it to-morrow, I would fling it back in his face. Good-night, Edina: I'm off. I don't care to stay to hear of suggested obligations from *him*."

On the day of Edina's departure for Trennach, the morning post brought Colonel Cockburn's answer to Charles. It was very short. Edina, her bonnet on, stood to read it over his shoulder. The colonel intimated that he did not quite comprehend Charles's application; but would see him on his return to London.

"So there's nothing for it but to wait—and I hope he won't be long," remarked Charles, as he folded the briefly-worded letter. "You must see there's nothing else, Edina."

IX

Mr. Max Brown

In a populous and somewhat obscure part of Lambeth, not a hundred miles away from the great hospital, Bedlam, there ran a narrow street. Amongst the shops, on the left of this street in going from London, stood a house that could not strictly be called a shop now; though it had been one recently, and the two counters within it still remained. It had formerly been a small chemist's shop. About a year ago, a young medical man named Brown had taken it, done away with the drugs and chemicals, so far as retailing them to the public went, and there set himself up as a doctor. He dispensed his own medicines, so the counters were useful still, and his jars of powders and liquids occupied the pigeon-holes above, where the chemist's jars had once stood. The lower half of the windows had been stained white; on one of them was written in black letters, "Mr. Max Brown, surgeon;" on the other, "Mr. Max Brown, general medical practitioner."

It was now about a year since Mr. Max Brown had thus established himself; and he had done very fairly. If his practice did not afford a promise that he would speedily become a millionaire, it at least was sufficient to keep him. And to keep him well. Mr. Brown had himself been born and reared in as crowded a part of London as this, somewhere towards Clerkenwell, therefore the locality did not offend his tastes. He anticipated remaining in it for good, and had not the slightest doubt that his practice would steadily increase, and afford him a carriage and a better house in time. The tradespeople around, though far below those of Bond Street in the social scale, were tradespeople of sufficient substance, and could afford to pay Mr. Brown. He was a little dark man, of affable nature and manners, clever in his profession, liked by his patients, and winning his way more surely amongst them day by day.

In the midst of this humble prosperity a check occurred. Not to the prosperity, but to Mr. Brown's plans and projects. Several years before, his elder brother had gone to the West Indies, and his widowed mother and his sister had subsequently followed him out. The sister had married there. The brother, Kenneth Brown, was for some years successful manager of a planter's estate; he now managed one of his own. Altogether they were extremely prosperous; and the only one of the family left in England, Max, received pleasant letters from them by each fortnightly mail, and was quite at ease with regard to them. It therefore took him completely by surprise in the midst of this ease, to find himself suddenly summoned to Jamaica.

One day in this same hot summer, early in the month of June—for we must go back two or three weeks in our story—Mr. Brown, having completed his morning round of calls on patients, stood behind his counter making up the physic required by them, and waiting for his queer old maid-servant, Eve, to come and tell him his one-o'clock dinner was ready. The door stood open to the hot street, and to the foot-passengers traversing the pavement; and Sam, the young boy, was waiting at the opposite counter with his covered basket until the physic should be ready.

"That's all to-day, Sam," said his master, pleasantly, as he folded the white paper round the last bottle, and motioned to the lad to bring the basket forward. "And, look here"—showing one of the packets—"this is for a fresh place, Number 26, you see, in The Walk. It's a grocer's shop."

"All right, sir. I shall find it."

"Maximilian Brown, Esq.," interrupted a voice at this juncture. It was that of the postman. He came in at the open door, and read out the address of the letter—his usual custom—as he put it down.

"Oh, the mail's in, I see," observed the doctor to him.

"Yes, sir."

Postman and boy went out together. Mr. Brown, leisurely turning down his coat-cuffs, which were never allowed to come in contact with the physic, took up the West Indian letter, and broke the seal. By that seal, as well as by the writing, he knew it was from his mother. Mrs. Brown always sealed her letters.

The letter contained only a few shaky lines. It told her son Max that she was ill; ill, as she feared, unto death. And it enjoined him to come out to Jamaica, that she might see him before she died. A note from his brother was enclosed, which contained these words—

"Do come out, dear Max, if you can in any way manage it. Mother's heart is set upon it. There is no immediate danger, but she is breaking fast. Come by next mail if you can, the middle of June; but at any rate don't delay it longer than the beginning of July. I enclose you an order on our London bankers, that the want of funds may be no impediment to you.

Your affectionate brother,
KENNETH

It took a great deal to disturb the equable temperament of Max Brown. This did disturb him. He stood staring at the different missives: now at his mother's, now at his brother's, now at the good round sum named in the order. A thunderbolt could not more effectually have taken him back. Eve, a clean old body in a flowery chintz gown, with a mob-cap and bow of green ribbon surmounting her grey hair, came in twice to say the loin of lamb waited: but she received no reply in return.

"I *can't* go," Max was repeating to himself. "I don't see how I *can* go. What would become of my practice?"

But his mother was his mother: and Max Brown, a dutiful son, began to feel that he should not like her to die before he had seen her once again. She was not sixty yet. The whole of the rest of the day and part of the night he was revolving matters in his mind; and in the morning he sent an advertisement to the *Times* and to a medical journal.

For more than a week the advertisement brought no result. Answers there were to it, and subsequent interviews with those who wrote them; but none that availed Max Brown. Either the applicants did not suit him, or his offer did not suit them. He then inserted the advertisement a second time.

And it chanced to fall under the notice of Frank Raynor. Or, strictly speaking, under the notice of Frank's friend Crisp. This was close upon the return of Frank from Eagles' Nest. Daisy was with her sister in Westbourne Terrace, and Frank had been taken in by Mr. Crisp, a young surgeon who held an appointment in one of the London hospitals. He occupied private rooms, and could accommodate Frank with a sofa-bedstead. Mr. Crisp saw the advertisement on the morning of its second appearance in the *Times*, and pointed it out to Frank.

"A qualified medical practitioner wanted, to take entire charge for a few months of a general practice in London during the absence of the principal."

"It may be worth looking after, old fellow," said Crisp.

Frank seized upon the suggestion eagerly. Most anxious was he to be relieved from his present state of inactivity. An interview took place between him and Max Brown; and before it terminated Frank had accepted the post.

To him it looked all couleur-de-rose. During the very few days he had now been in London, that enemy, the Tiger, had troubled his mind more than was pleasant. That the man had come up in the same train, and absolutely in the compartment immediately behind his own, for the purpose of keeping him in view, and of tracking out his place of abode in town, appeared only too evident to him. When Frank had deposited his wife at her sister's door, the turnings and twistings he caused the cab to take in carrying him to Crisp's, would have been sufficient to baffle a detective. Frank hoped it had baffled the Tiger: but he had scarcely liked to show himself abroad since. Therefore the obscurity of the locality in which Mr. Brown's practice lay, whilst it had frightened away one or two dandies who had inquired about it, was a strong recommendation in the eyes of Frank.

The terms proposed by Mr. Brown were these: That Frank Raynor should enter the house as he went out of it, take his place in all respects, carry on the practice for him until he himself returned, and live upon the proceeds. If the returns amounted to more than a certain sum, the surplus was to be reserved for Mr. Brown.

Frank agreed to all: the terms were first-rate; just what he should have chosen, he said. And surely to him they looked so. He was suddenly lifted out of his state of penniless dependence, had a house over his head, and occupation. The very fact of possessing a home to bring Daisy to, would have lent enchantment to the view in his sanguine nature.

"And by good luck I shall dodge the Tiger," he assured himself. "He will never think of looking for me *here*. Were he to find me out, Mr. Blase Pellet would be down upon me for hush-money—for that I expect will be his move the moment he thinks I have any money in my pocket. Yes, better to be in this obscure place at present, than flourishing before the West-end world as a royal physician."

So when preliminaries were arranged he wrote to Mrs. Raynor, saying what a jolly thing he had dropped into.

But Mr. Max Brown reconsidered one item in the arrangement. Instead of Frank's coming in when he left, he had him there a week beforehand that he might introduce him to the patients. Frank was to take to the old servant, Eve, and to the boy, Sam: in short, nothing was to be altered, nothing changed excepting the master. Frank was to walk in and Mr. Brown to walk out; all else was to go on as before. Mr. Brown made no sort of objection to Frank's wife sharing the home: on the contrary, he made one or two extra arrangements for her comfort. When he sailed, the beginning of July, Frank was fully installed, and Daisy might come as soon as she pleased. But her sister wished to keep her a little longer.

On one of the hot mornings in that same month of July, a well-dressed young fellow in deep mourning might be seen picking his way through the narrow streets of Lambeth, rendered ankle-deep in mud by the prodigal benevolence of the water-cart. It was Charles Raynor. Having nothing to do with his time, he had come forth to find out Frank.

"It *can't* be here!" cried Charley to himself, sniffing about fastidiously. "Frank would never take a practice in a low place like this! I say—here, youngster," he cried, arresting the steps of a tattered girl, who was running out of a shop, "do you chance to know where Mark Street is?"

"First turning you comes to," promptly responded the damsel, with assured confidence.

Charles found the turning and the street, and went down it, looking on all sides for the house he wanted. As he did not remember, or else did not know, the name of Frank's predecessor, the words "Mr. Max Brown" on some window-panes on the opposite side of the way afforded him no guide; and he might have gone on into endless wilds but for catching sight within the house of a shapely head and some bright hair, which he knew belonged to Frank. He crossed the street at a bound, and entered.

"Frank!"

Standing in the identical spot in which Max Brown was standing when we first saw him, was Frank, his head bent forward over an account-book, in which he was writing. He looked up hastily.

"Charley!"

Their hands met, and some mutual inquiries ensued. They had not seen each other since quitting Eagles' Nest.

"We thought you must be dead and buried, Frank. You might have come to see us."

"Just what I have been thinking—that you might have come to see me," returned Frank. "*I* can't get away. Since Brown left, and for a week before it, I have not had a moment to myself: morning, noon and night, I am tied to my post here. Your time is your own, Charley."

"I have been about at the West-end, finding out Colonel Cockburn, and doing one thing or another," said Charley, by way of excusing his laziness. "Edina left us only yesterday."

"For Trennach?"

"Yes, for Trennach. We fancy she means to take up her abode for good in the old place. She does not feel at home anywhere else, she says, as she does there. It was good of her, though, was it not, Frank, to set us up in the new home?"

"Very good—even for Edina. And I believe few people in this world are so practically good as she is. I did a little towards helping her choose the furniture; not much, because I arranged with Brown. How is the school progressing?"

"All right. It is a dreadful come-down: but it has to be put up with. Alice cries every night."

"And about yourself? Have you formed any plans?"

"I am waiting till Cockburn returns to town. I expect he will get me a commission."

"A commission!" exclaimed Frank, dubiously; certain doubts and difficulties crossing his mind, as they had crossed Edina's.

"It will be the best thing for me if I can only obtain it. There is no other opening."

Frank remained silent. His doubts were very strong indeed; but he never liked to inflict thorns where he could not scatter flowers, and he would not damp Charley's evident ardour. Time might do that quickly enough.

Charley was looking about him. He had been looking about him ever since he entered, somewhat after the fastidious manner that he had looked at the streets, but more furtively. Appearances were surprising him. The small shop (it seemed no better) with the door standing open to the narrow street; the counters on either side; the glass jars above; the scales lying to hand, and sundry packets of pills and powders beside them: to him, it all savoured of a small retail chemist's business. Charley thought he must be in a sort of dream. He could not understand how or why Frank had condescended to so inferior a position as this.

"Do you *like* this place, Frank?"

"Uncommonly," answered Frank: and his honest blue eyes, glancing brightly into Charley's, confirmed the words. "It is a relief to be in harness again; and to have a home to bring Daisy to."

"Will Daisy like it?" questioned Charles. And the hesitation in his tone, which he could not suppress, plainly betrayed his opinion—that she would not like it.

Frank's countenance fell. It was the one bitter drop in the otherwise sufficiently palatable cup.

"I *wish* I could have done better for her. It is only for a time, you know, Charley."

"I see," said Charley, feeling relieved. "You are only here whilst looking out for something better."

"That's it, in one sense. I stay here until Brown comes back. By that time I hope to—to pick myself up again."

The slight pause was caused by a consciousness that he did not feel assured upon the point. That Mr. Blase Pellet and his emissary, the Tiger, and all their unfriendly machinations combined, would by that time be in some way satisfactorily disposed of, leaving himself a free agent again, Frank devoutly hoped and most sanguinely expected. It was only when his mind dipped into details, and he began to consider how and by what means these enemies were likely to be subdued, that he felt anxious and doubtful.

"Something good may turn up for you, Frank, before the fellow—Brown, if that's his name—comes home. I suppose you'll take it if it does."

"Not I. My bargain with Brown is to remain here until he returns. And here I shall remain."

"Oh, well—of course a bargain's a bargain. How long does he expect to be away?"

"He did not know. He might stay four or six months with his people, he thought, if things went on well here."

"I say, why do you keep that street-door open?"

"I don't know," answered Frank. "From habit, I suppose. Brown used to keep it open, and I have done the same. I like it so. It gives a little liveliness to the place."

"People may take the place for a shop, and come in."

"Some have done so," laughed Frank. "It was a chemist's shop before Brown took to it. I tell them it is only a surgery now."

"When do you expect Daisy?" asked Charles, after a pause.

"This evening."

"This evening!"

"I shall snatch a moment at dusk to fetch her," added Frank. "Mrs. Townley is going into Cornwall on a visit to The Mount, and Daisy comes home."

"Have the people at The Mount forgiven Daisy yet?"

"No. They will not do that, I expect, until I am established as a first-rate practitioner, with servants and carriages about me. Mrs. St. Clare likes show."

"She wouldn't like this, I'm afraid," spoke Charles, candidly, looking up at the low ceiling and across at the walls.

Frank was saved a reply. Sam, the boy, who had been out on an errand, entered, and began delivering a message to his master.

"Would you like some dinner, Charley?" asked Frank. "Come along, I don't know what there is to-day."

Passing through a side-door behind him, Frank stepped into an adjoining sitting-room. It was narrow, but comfortable. The window looked to the street. The fireplace was at the opposite end, side by side with the door that led to the house beyond. A mahogany sofa covered with horsehair stood against the wall on one side; a low bookcase and a work-table on the other. The chairs matched the sofa; on the centre table the dinner-cloth was laid.

"Not a bad room, this," said Charley, thinking it an improvement on the shop.

"There's a better sitting-room upstairs," observed Frank.

"Well furnished, too. Brown liked to have decent things about him; and his people, he said, helped him liberally when he set up here. That work-table he bought the other day for Daisy's benefit."

"He must be rather a good sort of a fellow."

"He's a very good one. What have you for dinner, Eve? Put a knife and fork for this gentleman."

"Roast beef, sir," replied the old woman, who was carrying in the dishes, and nodded graciously to Charles, as much as to say he was welcome. "I thought the new mistress might like to find a cut of cold meat in the house."

"Quite right," said Frank. "Sit down, Charley."

Charley sat down, and did ample justice to the dinner, especially the Yorkshire pudding, a dish of which he was particularly fond, and had not lost his relish for amidst the dainties of the table at Eagles' Nest. He began to think Frank's quarters were not so bad on the whole, compared with no quarters at all, and no dinner to eat.

"Have you chanced to see that man, Charley, since you came to London?" inquired Frank, putting the question with a certain reluctance, for he hated to allude to the subject.

"What man?" returned Charley.

"The Tiger."

"No, I have not seen him. I learnt at Oxford that I had been mistaken in thinking he was looking after me—"

"He was not looking after you," interrupted Frank.

"My creditors there all assured me— Oh, Frank, how could I forget?" broke off Charley. "What an ungrateful fellow I am! Though, indeed, not really ungrateful, but it had temporarily slipped my memory. How good it was of you to settle those two bills for me! I would not write to thank you: I preferred to wait until we met. How did you raise the money?"

Frank, who had finished his dinner, had nothing to do but to stare at Charles. And he did stare, "I don't know what you are talking about, Charley. What bills have I settled for you?"

"The two wretched bills I had accepted and went about in fear of. You know. Was it not you who paid them?"

"Are they paid?"

"Yes. All paid and done with. It must have been you, Frank. There's no one else that it could have been."

"My good lad, I assure you I know nothing whatever about it. Where should I get a hundred pounds from? What could induce you to think it was I?"

Charles told the tale—all he knew of it. They wasted some minutes in conjectures, and then came to the conclusion that it must have been Major Raynor himself who had paid. He had become acquainted in some way with Charles's trouble and had quietly relieved it. A lame conclusion, as both felt: for setting aside the fact that the poor major was short of money himself, to pay bills for his son secretly was eminently uncharacteristic of him: he would have been far more likely to proclaim it to the whole house, and reproach Charley in its hearing. But they were fain to rest in the belief, from sheer want of any other benefactor to fix upon. Not a soul was there in the wide world, as far as Charley knew, to come forth in this manner, excepting his father.

"I think it must have been so," concluded Charles. "Perhaps the dear old man got to know, through Lamb, of Huddles's visit that day."

"And what of Eagles' Nest?" asked Frank, as he passed back into the surgery with Charles, and sent the boy into the kitchen to his dinner. "Has George Atkinson taken possession yet?"

"We have heard nothing of Eagles' Nest, Frank; we don't care to hear anything. Possession? Of course he has. You may depend upon it he would make an indecent rush into it the very day after we came out of it, the wretch! If he did not the same night."

Frank could not help a smile at the outburst of indignation. "Atkinson ought to do something for you, Charley," he said. "After turning you out of one home, the least he could do would be to find you another. I dare say he might put you into some post or other."

"And do you suppose I'd take it!" fired Charles, his eyes blazing. "What queer ideas you must have, Frank! You are as bad as Edina. As if—"

"Oh, please, Dr. Brown, would you come to mother," interrupted a small child, darting in at the open door. "She have fell through the back parlour window a-cleaning of it, and her arm be broke, she says."

"Who is your mother, little one?"

"At the corner shop, please, sir. Number eleven."

"Tell her I will come directly."

Charles was taking up his hat, to leave. "Why does she call you Dr. Brown?" he questioned, as the child ran off, and Frank was making ready to follow her and summoning Sam to the surgery.

"Half the people here call me so. It comes more readily to them than the new name. Good-bye, Charley. My love to all at home. Come again soon."

He sped away in the wake of the child. Charley turned the other way on his road homewards, carrying with him a very disparaging opinion of Lambeth.

In the small back sitting-room, underneath its two lighted gas-burners, stood Mrs. Frank Raynor, her heart beating faster than usual, her breath laboured. She felt partly frightened, partly confused by what she saw—by the aspect of the place she was brought to, as her new home. Frank had in a degree prepared her for it as they came along in the cab which brought them, Daisy's boxes piled upon it: but either he had done it insufficiently, or she had failed to realize his description of what he called the "humble den," for it came upon her with a shock. Both as Margaret St. Clare and as Margaret Raynor her personal experiences of dwelling-places had been pleasant and sunny.

The clock was striking ten when the cab had drawn up in Mark Street. She looked out to see why it stopped. She saw a narrow street, an inferior locality, small shops on either side. The one before which they had halted appeared to be a shop too: the door stood open, a gas-burner was alight within.

"Why are we stopping here, Frank?"

Frank, hastening to jump out, did not hear the question. He turned to help her.

"This is not the place?" she cried in doubt.

"Yes, this is it, Daisy."

He took her in, piloted her between the counters into the lighted side-room, and turned back to see to the luggage; leaving her utterly aghast, bewildered, and standing as still as a statue.

The door at the end of the room opened, and a curious old figure, attired in a chintz gown of antique shape, with a huge bow of green ribbon on her muslin cap, appeared at it. Eve curtsied to her new mistress: the new mistress stared at the servant.

"You are welcome, ma'am. We are glad to see you. And, please, would you like the supper-tray brought in?"

"Is—is this Mr. Raynor's?" questioned Daisy, in tones that seemed to say she dreaded the answer.

"Sure enough it is, ma'am, for the present. He is here during the master's absence."

Daisy said no more. She only stood still in her grievous astonishment, striving to comprehend it all, and to hush her dismayed heart. The luggage was being brought in, and Eve went to help with it. Frank found his wife seated on the horsehair sofa, when he came in; and caught the blank look on her pale face.

"You are tired, Daisy. You would like to take your things off. Come upstairs, and I will show you your bedroom."

Lighting a candle, he led the way, Daisy following mechanically up the steep, confined staircase, to which she herself seemed to present a contrast, with her fashionable attire of costly black gauze, relieved by frillings of soft white net.

"The room's not very large, Daisy," he said, entering one on the first floor, the window looking out on some back leads. "There's a larger one in front on the upper landing, but I thought you would prefer this, and it is better furnished. It was Brown's room. He said I had better take to it, for if I went up higher I might not hear the night-bell."

"Yes," replied Daisy, faintly, undoing the strings of her bonnet. "Was it a—a shop we came through?"

"That was the surgery. It used to be a shop, and Brown never took the trouble to alter its arrangement."

"Have you always to come through it on entering the house?"

"Yes. There is no other entrance. The houses in these crowded places are confined in space, you see, Daisy. I will help Sam to bring up the boxes," added Frank, disappearing.

When finally left to herself, Margaret sat down and burst into a passionate flood of tears. It seemed to her that, in coming to dwell here, she must lose caste for ever. Frank called to her presently, to know whether she was not coming down.

Drying her eyes as she best could, she took up the candle to descend. On the opposite side of the small landing, a door stood open to a sitting-room, and she looked in. A fair-sized room this, for it was over both the surgery and the parlour, and a very nice room too, its carpet of a rich dark hue, with chairs and window-hangings to match, and furniture that was good and handsome. She put the candle on a console, crossed to one of the windows, and gazed down at the street.

Late though it was, people were surging to and fro; not at all the sort of people Daisy had been accustomed to. Over the way was a small fish-shop: a ragged man and boy, standing before it, were eating mussels. To pass one's days in such a street as this must be frightfully depressing, and Mrs. Raynor burst into tears again.

"Why, my darling, what is the matter?"

Frank, coming up in search of her, found her sobbing wildly, her head buried on the arm of one of the chairs. She lifted it, and let it rest upon his shoulder.

"You are disappointed, Daisy. I see it."

"It—it is such a wretched street, Frank; and—and such a house!"

Frank flushed painfully. He felt the complaint to his heart's core.

"It is only for a time, Daisy. Until I can get into something better. If that may ever be!" he added to himself, as Blase Pellet's image rose before his mind.

Daisy sobbed more quietly. He was holding her to him.

"I know, my poor girl, how inferior it is; altogether different from anything you have been accustomed to; but this home is better than none at all. We can at least be together and be happy here."

"Yes, we can," replied Daisy, rallying her spirits and her sweet nature, as she lifted her face to look into his. "I married you for worse, as well as for better, Frank, my best love. We *will* be happy in it."

"As happy as a king and queen in a fairy-tale," rejoined Frank, a whole world of hope in his tones.

And that was Daisy's instalment in her London home.

X

A Night Alarm

Misfortunes seldom come singly. Many of us, unhappily, have had good cause only too often to learn the truth of the saying; but few, it is to be hoped, have experienced it in an equal degree with the Raynors. For another calamity was in store for them: one that, taking the difference between their present and past circumstances into consideration, was at least as distressing as the ejection from Eagles' Nest.

But it did not happen quite immediately. The weeks were calmly passing, and Mrs. Raynor felt in spirits; for two more day-scholars had entered at the half-quarter, and another boarder was promised at Michaelmas. So that matters might be said to be progressing satisfactorily though monotonously. Monotony, however, does not suit young people, especially if they have been suddenly plunged into it. It did not suit Charles and Alice Raynor. Ever contrasting, as they were, the present enforced quiet and obscurity with the past life at Eagles' Nest, its show, society, and luxuries, no wonder that they felt well-nigh weary unto death. At first it was almost unbearable. But they could not help themselves: it had to be endured. Charles was worse off than Alice; she had her school duties to occupy her during the day; he had nothing. Colonel Cockburn had not yet returned to London, and Charles told himself and his mother that he must wait for him. As the weeks went on, some relief suggested itself from this dreariness—perhaps was the result of it.

The alleviation was found in private theatricals. They had made the acquaintance of some neighbours named Earle; had become intimate with them. The circumstances of the two families were much alike, and perhaps this at first drew them together. Captain Earle—a post-captain in the Royal Navy—had left only a slender income to his wife at his death: just enough to enable her to live quietly, and bring up her children inexpensively. They were gentlepeople; and that went a long way with the Raynors. The young Earles—four of them—were all in their teens: the eldest son had a post in Somerset House, the younger one went to a day-school in the neighbourhood, the two daughters had finished their education, and were at home. It chanced that these young people had a passion just now for private theatricals, and the Raynors caught the infection. After witnessing a performance at Mrs. Earle's of a popular comedy, Charles and Alice Raynor got up from it wild to perform one at their own home.

And probably the very eagerness with which they pursued the fancy, arose out of the recent monotony of their lives. Mrs. Raynor looked grave: she did not know whether the parents of her pupils would approve of private theatricals. But her children overruled her objection, and she could only yield to them. She always did so.

They fixed upon Goldsmith's comedy, "She Stoops to Conquer." A thoroughly good play in itself. Charles procured some sixpenny copies of it, and drew his pen through any part that he considered unsuited to present taste, which shortened the play very much. He chose the part of Charles Marlowe; Alice that of Miss Hardcastle; Mrs. Earle, who liked the amusement as much as her children did, would be Mrs. Hardcastle; her eldest daughter Constance Neville: and the young Somerset-House clerk Tony Lumpkin. The other characters were taken by some acquaintances of the Earles.

And now, fairly launched upon this new project, the monotony of the house disappeared: for the time they even forgot to lament after Eagles' Nest. Dresses, gauzes, tinsel, green-baize curtains, and all the rest of it, were to be lent by the Earles; so that no cost was involved in the entertainment. The schoolroom was to be the theatre, and the pupils were to have seats amongst the audience.

Charles entered into it with wonderful energy. He never now had a minute for lying on three chairs, or for stretching his hands above his head to help a mournful yawn. A letter that arrived from Edina, requiring him to transact a little matter of business, was wholly neglected; it would have involved his going to the City, and he said he had no time for it.

Edina had intended to insure the new furniture in the same Cornish office that her father had insured his in for so many years. Perhaps she had more faith in it than in the London offices. However, after some negotiations with the Cornish company upon her return to Trennach, they declined the offer, as the furniture it related to was so far away, and recommended a safe and good insurance company in the City of London. She wrote to Mrs. Raynor, desiring that Charles should at once go to the City to do what was necessary and secure the policy. Charles put it off upon the plea that he was too busy; it could wait.

"Charley, I think you ought to do it, if only to comply with Edina's wish," urged Mrs. Raynor.

"And so I will, mother, as soon as I get a little time."

"It would only take you half-a-day, my dear."

"But I can't spare the half-day. Do you think the house is going to be burnt down?"

"Nonsense, Charley!"

"Then where's the need of hurry?" he persisted. "I have looked after every one else's part so much and the arrangements altogether, that I scarcely know a word yet of my own. I stuck yesterday at the very first sentence Charles Marlowe has to say."

Mrs. Raynor, never able to contend against a stronger will than her own, gave in as usual, saying no more. And Charles was left unmolested.

But in the midst of this arduous labour, for other people as well as for himself, Charles received news from Colonel Cockburn. The colonel wrote to say he was in London for a couple of days, and Charles might call in St. James's Street the following morning.

This mandate Charles would not put off, in spite of the exigencies of the theatricals; and of the first rehearsal, two evenings hence. The grand performance was to take place during the few days' holiday Mrs. Raynor gave at Michaelmas; and Michaelmas would be upon them in a little more than a week.

Charles went to St. James's Street. And there his hopes, in regard to the future, received a very decided check. Colonel Cockburn—who turned out to be a feeble and deaf old gentleman—informed Charles that he could not help him to obtain a commission, and moreover, explained many things to him, and assured him that he had no chance of obtaining one. No one, the colonel said, could get one now, unless he had been specially prepared for it. He would advise Charles, he added, to embrace a civil profession; say the law. It was very easy to go to the Bar, he believed; involving only, so far as he knew, the eating of a certain number of dinners. All this sounded very cruel to Charles Raynor. Otherwise the colonel was kind. He kept him for the day, and took him to dine at his club.

It was late when Charles reached home; thoroughly tired. Disappointment alone inflicts weariness. Mrs. Raynor felt terribly disheartened at the news.

"There have been so many weeks lost, you see, Charley!"

"Yes," returned Charles, gloomily. "I'm sure I don't know what to be at now. Cockburn suggested the Bar. He says one may qualify for almost nothing."

"We will talk about it to-morrow Charley," said Mrs. Raynor. "It is past bedtime, and I am tired. You were not thinking of sitting up later, were you, my dear?" she added, as Charles took up "She Stoops to Conquer" from a side table.

"Oh, well—I suppose not, if you say it is so late," he replied.

"The dresses have come, ready for the rehearsal, Charley," whispered Alice, as they were going upstairs. "I have put them in your room. Charlotte Earle and I have been trying on ours. I mean to wear one of Edina's brown holland aprons while I am supposed to be a barmaid."

"I'll be shot if I know half my part," grumbled Charley. "It *was* a bother, having to go out to-day!"

"You can learn it before Michaelmas."

"Of course I can. But one likes to be perfect at rehearsal. Good-night."

Charles turned into his room, and shut the door. It was a good-sized apartment, one that Mrs. Raynor destined for boarders, when the school should have increased. The first thing he saw, piled up between the bed and the wall, partly on a low chest of drawers, partly on the floor, was a confused heap of gay clothes and other articles: the theatrical paraphernalia that had been brought round from Mrs. Earle's. Upon the top of all, lay a yellow gauze dress edged with tinsel. Charles, all his interest in the coming rehearsal reviving at the sight, touched it gingerly here and there, and wondered whether it might be the state robe for one of the younger ladies, or for Tony Lumpkin's mother.

"I wish to goodness I was more perfect in my part!" cried he, pulling corners out of the other things to see what they consisted of. "Suppose I give half-an-hour to it, before I get into bed?"

The little book was still in his hand. He lodged the candle on the edge of the drawers amidst the finery, and sat down near, pausing in the act of taking off his coat. Alfred lay on the far side of the bed fast asleep. A night or two ago, for this was by no means the first time he had sat down in his chamber to con the sayings of young Marlowe, Charles took his coat off, dropped asleep, and woke up cold when the night was half over. So he concluded that he would keep his coat on now.

Precisely the same event took place: Charles fell asleep. Tired with his day's journey, he had not studied the book five minutes when it fell from his hands. He was soon in a sound slumber. How long he remained in it he never knew, but he was awakened by a shout and a cry. Fire!

A shout and a cry, and a great glare of light. Fire? Yes, it was fire. Whether Charles had thrown out his arm in his sleep and turned the candle over, or whether a spark had shot out from it, he knew not, never would know; but the pile of inflammable gauzes and other stuffs lying there had caught light. The flames had penetrated to the bed, and finally awakened Alfred. It was Alfred who shouted the alarm. Perhaps Charles owed his life to the fact that he had kept his coat on: its sleeve was scorched.

These scenes have been often described before: it is of no use to detail another here. A household aroused in the depth of the night; terrified women and children crying and running: flames mounting, smoke suffocating. They all escaped with life, taking refuge at the dwelling of a neighbour; but the house and its contents were burnt to the ground.

My Dear Edina,

"I never began a letter like this in all my life: it will have nothing in it but ill news and misery. Whether I am doing wrong in writing to you, I hardly know. My mother would not write. She feels a delicacy in disclosing our calamities to you, after your generous kindness in providing us with a home; and she must be ashamed to tell you about me. The home is lost, Edina, and I am the cause of it.

"I am too wretched to go into details: and, if I did, you might not have patience to read them; so I will tell the story in as few words as I can. We—I, Alice, and the Earles: you may remember them as living in the low, square house, near the church—were going to act a play, 'She Stoops to Conquer.' I sat up last Wednesday night to study my part, dropped asleep, and somehow the candle set light to some stage dresses that were lying ready in my chamber. When I woke up, the room was in flames. None of us are hurt; but the house is burnt down; and everything that was in it.

"This is not all. I hate to make the next confession to you more than I hated this one. The insurance on the furniture

MRS. HENRY WOOD

had not been effected. I had put it off and off; though my mother urged me more than once to go and do it.

"You have spoken sometimes, Edina, of the necessity of acting rightly, so that we may enjoy a peaceful conscience. If you only knew what mine is now, and the torment of remorse I endure, even you might feel a passing shade of pity for me. There are moments when the weight seems more than I can bear.

"We have taken a small, cheap lodging near; number five, in the next street; and what the future is to be I cannot tell. It of course falls to my lot now to keep them, as it is through me they have lost their home, and *I shall try and do it*. Life will be no play-day with me now.

"I thought it my duty to tell you this, Edina. Whilst holding back from the task, I have yet said to myself that you would reproach me if I did not. And you will not mistake the motive, since you are aware that I know you parted with every shilling you had, to provide us with the last home.

"Write a few words of consolation to my mother; no one can do it as you can; and *don't spare me to her*.

Your unhappy cousin,
CHARLES

Frank Raynor once made the remark in our hearing that somehow every one turned to Edina in trouble. Charley had instinctively turned to her. Not because it might lie in his duty to let her know what had come to pass, to confess his own share in it, his imprudent folly; but for the sake of his mother. Though Edina had no more money to give away, and could not help them to another home, he knew that if any one could breathe a word of comfort to her, it was Edina.

One thing lay more heavily upon his conscience than all the rest; and if he had not mentioned this to Edina, it was not that he wished to spare himself, for he was in the mood to confess everything that could tell against him, almost with exaggeration, but that in the hurry of writing he had unintentionally omitted it. On one of the previous nights that he had been studying his part, Mrs. Raynor caught sight of the light under his door. Opening it, she found him sitting on the bed in his shirt-sleeves, reading. There and then she spoke of the danger, and begged him never to sit up at night again. The fact was this: Charles

Raynor had nothing on earth to do with his time; an idle young fellow, as he was, needed not the night for work; but his habits had grown so desultory that he could settle to no occupation in the daytime.

The answer from Edina did not come. Charles said nothing about having written to her; but he did fully hope and expect Edina would write to his mother. Morning after morning he posted himself outside the door to watch for the postman; and morning after morning the man passed and gave him nothing.

"Edina is too angry to write," concluded Charles, at last. "This has been too much even for her." And he betook himself to his walk to London.

No repentance could be more thoroughly sincere than was Charles Raynor's. The last dire calamity had taken all his pride and elevated notions out of him. The family were helpless, hopeless; and he had rendered them so. No clothes, no food, no prospects, no home, no money. A few articles of wearing apparel had been thrown out of the burning house, chiefly belonging to Alice, but not many. All the money Mrs. Raynor had in the world—four banknotes of five pounds each—had been consumed. There had chanced to be a little gold in Charles's pockets, given him to pay the insurance, some taxes, and other necessary matters; and that was all they had to go on with. Night after night Charles lay awake, lamenting his folly, and making huge resolves to remedy the evil results of it.

They must have food to eat; though it were but bread-and-cheese; they must have a roof over them, let it be ever so confined. And there was only himself to provide this. Any thought of setting up a school again could not present itself to their minds after the late ignominious failure: they had no means of doing it, and the little pupils had gone from them for ever. No; all lay on Charles. He studied the columns of the *Times*, and walked up and down London until he was footsore; footsore and heart-sick; trying to get one of the desirable places advertised as vacant. In vain.

He had been doing this now for four or five days. On this, the sixth day, when he reached home after his weary walk, the landlady of the house stood at the open door, bargaining for one of the pots of musk that a man was carrying about for sale. Charles wished her good-evening as he passed on to the parlour; and there he met with a surprise, for in it sat Edina. She had evidently just arrived. Her travelling-cloak was thrown on the back of a chair, her black mantle was only unfastened, her bonnet was still on. Katie and Robert sat at her feet; the tea-things were on the table, Alice was cutting bread-and-butter, and Mrs. Raynor was sobbing. Charles held out his hand with hesitation, feeling that it was not worthy for Edina to touch, and a red flush dyed his face.

After tea the conversation turned on their present position, on plans and projects. Ah what poor ones they were! Mrs. Raynor acknowledged freely that she had only a few shillings left.

"Have you been paid for the pupils?" asked Edina.

"No," said Mrs. Raynor. "I have not yet sent in the accounts. The children were not with me quite a quarter, you know, and perhaps some of the parents may make that an excuse, combined with the termination, for not paying me at all. Even if I get the money, there are debts to be paid out of it: the tradespeople, the stationer, the maidservant's wages. Not much will be left of it."

"Then, Mary, let us settle to-night what is to be done."

"What can be settled?" returned Mrs. Raynor, hopelessly. "I see nothing at all before us. Except starvation."

"Don't talk of starvation while Heaven spares us the use of our minds to plan, and our hands to work," said Edina, pleasantly; and the bright tone cheered Mrs. Raynor. "For one thing, I have come up to live with you."

"Edina!"

"I cannot provide you with another home: you know why," continued Edina: "but I can share with you all I have left—my income. It is so small a one that perhaps you will hardly thank me for it, saddled with myself; but at least it is something to fall back upon, and we can all share together."

Mrs. Raynor burst into tears again. Never strong in resources, the repeated calamities she had been subjected to of late had tended to render her next-door to helpless both in body and spirit. Charles turned to Edina, brushing his eyelashes.

"I cannot presume to thank you, Edina: you would not care to receive thanks from me. *I* am hoping to support them."

"In what manner, Charles?" asked Edina; and her tone was as kind as usual. "I hear you have lost hopes of the commission."

"By getting into some situation and earning a weekly salary at it," spoke Charles, bravely. "The worst is, situations seem to be so unattainable."

"How do you know they are unattainable?"

"I have done nothing the last few days but look for one. Besides the places advertised, I can't tell you how many banks and other establishments I have made bold to go into, asking if they want a clerk. A hundred a-year would be something."

"It would be a great deal," replied Edina, significantly. "Salaries to that amount are certainly hard to find. I question if you would get half of it at first."

A blank look overspread Charley's face. Edina's judgment had always been sound.

"But why do you question it, Edina?"

"Because you are inexperienced: totally unused to business; to work of any kind."

"Yes, that's what some of the people say when they question me."

"There is one person who might help you to such a situation, if he would," observed Edina, slowly. "But I shall offend you if I speak of him, Charles: as I did once before."

"You mean George Atkinson!"

"I do. If he chose to put you into his bank, he might give you any salary he pleased; and he might be willing to do it, whether you earned it or not. I think he would, if I asked him."

There was a pause. Edina's thoughts were carrying her back to the old days when George Atkinson had been all the world to her. It would cost her something to apply to him; but for the sake of this helpless family, she must bring her mind to doing it.

"What do you say, Charles?"

"I say yes, Edina. I have nothing but humble-pie to eat just now: it will be only another slice of it. Banking work seems to consist of everlastingly adding up columns of figures: I should grow expert at it no doubt in time."

"Then I will go to-morrow and see whether he is in town," decided Edina. "If not, I must travel down to Eagles' Nest."

"You might write instead," suggested Mrs. Raynor.

"No, Mary, I will not write. A personal interview gives so much more chance of success in an application of this nature."

"*I* could not apply to him personally," sighed Mrs. Raynor.

But Edina never shrank from a duty; and the next morning saw her at the banking-house of Atkinson and Street, the very house where she had spent those few happy days of her early life when she had learned to love. Mr. Street and his wife lived in it now. She went to the private door and asked for him. He had known her in those days; and a smile actually crossed his calm cold face as he shook hands with her: and to her he proved more communicative than he generally showed himself to the world.

"Is Mr. Atkinson in town?" she inquired, when a few courtesies had passed.

"No. He—"

"I feared not," quickly spoke Edina, for she had quite anticipated the answer. "I thought he would be at Eagles' Nest."

"But he is not at Eagles' Nest," interposed the banker. "He is on the high seas, on his way to New Zealand."

"On his way to New Zealand!" echoed Edina, hardly thinking, in her surprise, that she heard correctly.

"He went away again immediately. I do not suppose he was in London a fortnight altogether."

"Then he could not have made much stay at Eagles' Nest?"

"He did not make any stay at it," replied Edwin Street. "I don't think he went down to Eagles' Nest at all. If he did go, he came back the same day, for he never slept one night away from this house throughout his sojourn."

"But what could be his reason?" reiterated Edina, wonderingly. "Why has he gone away so soon again?"

"He put it upon the score of his health, Miss Raynor. England does not agree with him. At least, he fancies it does not."

"And who is living at Eagles' Nest?"

"A Mr. Fairfax. He is a land-agent and steward, a thoroughly efficient man, and he has been appointed steward to the estate. His orders are to take care of it, and to renovate it by all possible means that money and labour can do. Mr. Atkinson was informed on good authority that it had been neglected by Major Raynor."

"That's true," thought Edina.

"The first thing Mr. Atkinson did on his arrival, was to inquire whether the estate had been well cared for and kept up since Mrs. Atkinson's death. I was not able to say that it had been: I was obliged to tell him that the contrary was the fact. He then questioned my brother, and other people who were acquainted with the truth. It vexed him: and, as I tell you, he is now doing all he can to remedy the late neglect."

"I am very much surprised that Mr. Atkinson did not himself go down to see into it!" said Edina.

"Long residence in foreign lands often conduces to indolent habits," remarked the banker.

Edina sighed. Was her mission to be a fruitless one? Taking a moment's counsel with herself, she resolved to disclose its purport to Edwin Street. And she did so: asking him to give Charles Raynor a stool in his counting-house, and a salary with it.

But Mr. Street declined. His very manner seemed to freeze at the request. A young man, brought up as Mr. Charles Raynor had been, could not possibly be of any use in a bank, he observed.

"Suppose Mr. Atkinson were here, and had complied with my request to put him in?—what then?" said Edina.

"In that case he would have come in," was the candid answer. "But Mr. Atkinson is not here; in his absence I exercise my own discretion; and I am bound to tell you that I cannot make room for the young man. Don't seek to put Charles Raynor into a bank: he is not fitted for the post in any way, and might do harm in it instead of good. Take an experienced man's advice for once, Miss Raynor."

"It has spared me the pain of an interview with *him*," thought Edina, as she said good-morning to Mr. Street. "But what a strange thing that he should go away again without seeing Eagles' Nest!"

MRS. HENRY WOOD

PART THE THIRD

I

LAUREL COTTAGE

It was a roomy cottage in a small by-road of the environs of Kennington, bordering on South Lambeth. Frost and snow lay on the ground outside, and bitter blasts in the air: within, sitting round the scanty fire in a bare-looking but not very small parlour, were Mrs. Raynor, Edina, and the younger children, the two former busily employed making brown chenile nets for the hair.

When Edina was out one day searching for some abode for them, this dwelling fell under her eye. It was called Laurel Cottage, as the white letters on a slate-coloured wooden gate testified: probably because a dwarf laurel tree flourished between the palings and the window. In the window was a card, setting forth that "lodgings" were to be let: and Edina entered. Could the Raynors have gone into the country, she would have taken a whole cottage to themselves; but then there would have been a difficulty about furniture. It was necessary they should remain in London, as Charles still expected to find employment there, and they must not be too far from the business parts of it, for he would have to walk to and fro night and morning. Laurel Cottage possessed a landlady, one Mrs. Fox, and a young boy, her son. The rooms to let were four in number; parlour, kitchen, and two bedrooms. She asked ten shillings a-week: but that the house was shabby and badly furnished, she might have asked more. Edina freely said she could afford to give only eight shillings a-week; and at length the bargain was struck. Edina's income was just a pound a-week, fifty-two pounds a-year; eight shillings out of it for rent was a formidable sum. It left only twelve shillings for all necessities: and poor, anxious Edina, who had all the care and responsibility on her own shoulders, and felt that she had it, did not see the future very clearly before her; but at present there was nothing to be done but to bow to circumstances. So here they were in Laurel Cottage, with a dreary look-out of waste-ground for a view, and a few stunted trees overshadowing the gate.

Alice had gone into a school as teacher. It was situated near Richmond, in Surrey, and was chiefly for the reception of children whose parents were in India. She would have to stay there during the holidays: but that was so much the better, as there was no place for her at home. Alfred ran on errands, and made a show of saying his lessons to his mother between whiles. Mrs. Raynor taught Kate and little Robert; Edina did the work, for they were not waited upon; Charles spent his time tramping about after a situation. To eke out their narrow income, Edina had tried to get some sewing, or other work, to do; she had found out a City house that dealt largely in ladies' hairnets, and the house agreed to supply her with some to make. All their spare time she and Mrs. Raynor devoted to these nets, Charles carrying the parcels backwards and forwards. But for those nets, they must certainly to a great extent have starved. With the nets, they were not much better off.

In some mysterious way, Edina had managed to provide them all with a change of clothing, to replace some of that which had been lost in the fire. They never knew how she did it. Only Edina herself knew that. A few articles of plate that had been her father's; a few ornaments of her own: these were turned into money.

The light of the wintry afternoon was fading; the icicles outside were growing less visible to the eye. Little Robert, sitting on the floor, said at last that he could not see his picture-book. Mrs. Raynor, looking young still in her widow's cap, let fall the net on her lap for a minute's rest, and looked at the fire through her tears. Over and over again did these tears rise unbidden now. Edina, neat and nice-looking as ever, in her soft black dress, her brown hair smoothly braided on either side her attractive face—attractive in its intelligence and goodness—caught sight of the tears from the low chair where she sat opposite.

"Take courage, Mary," she gently said. "Things will take a turn some time."

Mrs. Raynor caught up her work and suppressed a rising sob. Katie, in a grumbling tone, said she was sure it must be tea-time. Edina rose, brought in a tray from the small kitchen, which was on the same floor as the room they sat in, and began to put out the cups and saucers.

"What a long time Alfred is!" cried the little girl.

Alfred came in almost as he spoke, a can of milk in his hand. By sending to a dairy half-a-mile off, Edina had discovered that she could get pure milk cheaper than any left by the milkman: so Alfred went for it morning and night.

"It is so jolly hard!" exclaimed he, with a glowing face, alluding to the ice in the roads. "The slides are beautiful."

"Don't get sliding when you are carrying the milk," advised Edina. "Take off your cap and comforter, Alfred."

She was cutting slices of bread for him to toast. Unused to hard fare, the children could not eat dry bread with any relish: so, when there was neither butter nor dripping, neither treacle nor honey in the house, Edina had the bread toasted. Alfred knelt down before the fire—the only fire they had—and began to toast. The kettle was singing on the hob. Edina turned the milk into a jug.

They were sitting down to the tea-table when Charles came in. A glance at his weary and dispirited face told Edina that he had met with no more luck to-day than usual. Putting down a brown-paper parcel that he carried, containing a fresh supply of material to be made into nets, he took his place at the table. How hungry he was, no one but himself knew. And how scanty the food was that he could be supplied with!

But for his later experience, Charles could not have believed that it was so difficult for a young man to obtain a situation in London. Edina, less hopeful than he, would not have believed it. Charles Raynor had not been brought up to work of any sort, had never done any; and this seemed to be one of the stumbling-blocks in his way. Perhaps he looked too much of a gentleman; perhaps his refined manners and tones told against him in the eyes of men of business, betraying that he might prove unfit for work: at any rate, he had not found any one to take him. Another impediment was that no sooner did a situation fall vacant, than a large number of applicants made a rush to fill it. Only one of them could be engaged: and it never happened to be Charles. Charles looked through the *Times* advertisements every morning, through the friendliness of a neighbouring newsvendor. He would read of a clerk being wanted in some place or other in the great mart of London, and away he would go, to present himself. But he invariably found other applicants before him, and as invariably he never seemed to have the slightest chance.

The disappointment was beginning to tell upon him. There were times when he felt almost maddened. His conscience had been awake these last many bitter weeks, and the prolonged strain often seemed more than he could bear. Had it been only himself! All, then, as it seemed to Charles Raynor, all would have been easy. He could enlist for a soldier; he could join the labourers' emigration society and go out for a term of years to Australia or Canada; he could turn porter at a railway-station. These wild thoughts (though perhaps they could not be called so very wild in his present circumstances) continually passed through his mind: but he had to put them aside as visionary.

Visionary, because his object was, not to support himself alone, but the family. At least to help to support them. Charles Raynor was sensitive to a degree; and every mouthful he was obliged to eat seemed as though it would choke him, because it lessened the portion of those at home. A man cannot quite starve: but it often seemed to Charles that he really and truly would prefer to starve, and to bear the martyrdom of the process, rather than be a burden upon his mother and Edina. Sometimes he came home by way of Frank's and took tea there—and Frank, suspecting the truth of matters, took care to add some substantial dish to the table. But Charles, in delicacy of feeling, would not do this often: the house, in point of fact, was Mr. Max Brown's, not Frank's.

How utterly subdued in spirit his mother had become, Charles did not like to see and note. She kept about, but there could be no mistaking that she was both ill and suffering. Oh, if he could only lift her out of this poverty to a home of ease and plenty! he would say to himself, a whole world of self-reproach at work within him. If this last year or two could be blotted out of time and memory, and they had their modest home again near Bath!

No; it might not be. The events that time brings forth must endure in the memory for ever; our actions in it must remain in the Book of the Recording Angel as facts of the past. The home at Bath had gone; Eagles' Nest had gone; the transient weeks of the school-life had gone: and here they were, hopeless and without prospect, eating hard fare at Laurel Cottage.

They had left off asking him now in an evening how he succeeded during the day, and what his luck had been. His answer was ever the same; he had had no luck; had done nothing: and it was given with pain so evident, that they refrained in very compassion. On this evening Charles himself spoke of it; spoke to Edina. The children were in bed. Mrs. Raynor had gone, as usual, to hear them say their prayers, and had not yet returned.

"I wonder how much longer this is to go on, Edina?"

Edina looked up from her work. "Do you mean your want of success, Charley?"

"Could I mean anything else!" he rejoined, his tone utterly subdued. "I think of nothing but that, morning, noon, and night."

"It is a long lane that has no turning, Charles. And I don't think patience and perseverance often go unrewarded in the long-run. How did you fare to-day?"

"Just as usual. Never had a single chance at all. Look, Edina—my boots are beginning to wear out."

A rather ominous pause. Charley was stretching out his right foot.

"You have another pair, you know, Charley. These must be mended."

"But I am thinking of the time when neither pair will mend any longer. Edina, I wonder whether life is worth living?"

"Charley, we cannot see into the future," spoke Edina, pausing for a moment in her work to look at him, a newly begun net in her hand. "If we could, we might foresee, even now, how good and necessary this discipline is for us. It may be, Charley, that you needed it; that we all needed it, more or less. Take it as a cross that has come direct from God; bear it as well as you are able; do your best in it and trust to Him. Rely upon it that, in His own good time, He will lighten it for you. And He will take care of you until it passes away."

Charles took up the poker; recollected himself, and put it down again. Fires might not be lavishly stirred now, as they had been at Eagles' Nest. Mrs. Raynor had been obliged to make a rule that no one should touch the fire excepting herself and Edina.

"It is not for myself I am thus impatient to get employment," resumed Charles. "But for the rest of them, I would go off to-morrow and enlist. If I could only earn twenty pounds a-year to begin with, it would be a help; better than nothing."

Only two or three months ago he had said, If I can only get a hundred a-year. Such lessons of humility adversity teaches!

"Twenty pounds a-year would pay the rent," observed Edina. "I never thought it could be so hard to get into something. I supposed that when young men wanted employment they had only to seek it. It does seem wrong does it not, Charley, that an able and willing young fellow should not be able to work when he wishes to do so?"

"Enlisting would relieve you of myself: and the thought is often in my mind," observed Charles. "On the other hand—"

"On the other hand, you had better not think of it," she interposed firmly. "We should not like to see you in the ranks, Charley. A common soldier is—"

"Hush, Edina! here comes the mother."

But luck was dawning for Charley. Only a small slice of luck, it is true; and what, not so very long ago, he would have scorned. Estimating things by his present hopeless condition, it looked fair enough.

One bleak morning, a day or two after the above conversation, Charley was slowly pacing Fleet Street, wondering where he could go next, what do. A situation, advertised in that morning's paper, had brought him up, post haste. As usual, it turned out a failure: to be successful, the applicant must put down fifty pounds in cash. So that chance was gone: and there was Charles, uncertain, and miserable.

"Halloa, Raynor! Is it you?"

A young stripling about his own age had run against him. At the first moment Charles did not know him: but recollection flashed on his mind. It was Peter Hartley: a lad who had been a schoolfellow of his in Somersetshire.

"I am going to get my dinner," said Hartley, after a few sentences had passed. "Will you come and take some with me?"

Too thankful for the offer, Charles followed him into the Rainbow. And over the viands they grew confidential. Hartley was in a large printing and publishing establishment close by: his brother Fred was at a solicitor's, almost out of his articles.

"Fred's ill," observed Peter. "He thinks it must be the fogs of this precious London that affect him: and I think so too. Any way, he coughs frightfully, and has had to give up for a day or two. I went to his office this morning to say he was in bed with a plaster on his chest; and a fine way they were in at hearing it: wanting him to go, whether or not. One of their copying-clerks has left; and they can't hear of another all in a hurry."

"I wonder whether I should suit them?" spoke Charles on the spur of the moment, a flush rising to his face and a light to his eyes.

"*You!*" cried Peter Hartley.

And then Charles, encouraged perhaps by the good cheer, told a little of his history to Hartley, and why he must find a situation of some sort that would bring in its returns. Hartley, an open-hearted, country-bred lad, became eager to help him, and offered to introduce him to the solicitor's firm there and then.

"It is near the Temple: almost close by," said he: "Prestleigh and Preen. A good firm: one of the best in London. Let us go at once."

Charles accompanied him to the place. Had he been aware that this same legal firm counted Mr. George Atkinson amongst its clients, he might have declined to try to enter it. It had once been Callard and Prestleigh. But old Mr. Callard had died very soon after Frank held the interview with him that has been recorded: and Charles, under the new designation of Prestleigh and Preen, did not recognize the old firm.

Peter Hartley introduced Charles to the managing-clerk, Mr. Stroud. Mr. Stroud, a tall man, wearing silver-rimmed spectacles, with iron-grey hair and a crabbed manner, put some questions to Charles, and then told him to sit down and wait. Mr. Prestleigh was in his private room; but it would not do to trouble him with these matters: Mr. Preen was out. Peter Hartley, in his good-nature, said all he could in favour of Charles, particularly "that he would be sure to do," and then went away.

Charles sat down, and passed an hour gazing at the fire and listening to the pens scratching away at the desks. People were constantly passing in and out: the green-baize door seemed to be ever on the swing. Some brought messages; some were marshalled into Mr. Prestleigh's room. By-and-by, a youngish man—he might be thirty-five, perhaps—came in, in a warm white overcoat; and, from the attention and seriousness suddenly shown by the clerks generally, Charles rightly guessed him to be Mr. Preen. He passed through the room without speaking, and was followed by the head-clerk.

A few minutes more, and Charles was sent for to Mr. Preen's room. That gentleman—who had a great profusion of light curling hair and a pleasant face and manner—was alone, standing with his back to the fire near his table. He asked Charles very much the same questions that Mr. Stroud had asked, and particularly what his recent occupation had been. Charles told the truth: he had not been brought up to any occupation, but an unfortunate reverse of family circumstances was obliging him to seek one.

"You have not been in a solicitor's office, then! Not been accustomed to copying deeds?" cried Mr. Preen.

Charles confessed he had not. But he took courage to say he had no doubt he could do any copying required of him, and to beg that he might be tried.

"Is your handwriting a neat one?"

"Yes, it is," said Charles, eagerly, for he was speaking the truth. "Neat and good, and very plain."

"You think you could copy quickly and correctly?"

"I am sure I could, sir. I *hope* you will try me," he added, a curious entreaty in his tone, that perhaps he was himself unconscious of; but which was nevertheless apparent to Mr. Preen. "I have been seeking something so long, day after day, week after week, that I have almost lost heart."

Perhaps that last avowal was not the best aid to Charles's success; or would not have been with most men of business. With Mr. Preen, who was very good-natured, it told rather for than against him. The lawyer mused. They wanted a copying-clerk very badly indeed; being two hands short, including Fred Hartley, and extremely busy: but the question was, could this young man accomplish the work? A thought struck him.

"Suppose you were to stay now and copy a few pages this afternoon?" suggested Mr. Preen. "You see, if you cannot do the work, it would be useless your attempting it: but if you can, we will engage you."

"I shall only be too happy to stay, sir."

"Very well," said Mr. Preen, ringing his bell for the managing-clerk. "And you shall then have an answer."

Charles was put to work by Mr. Stroud: who came and looked at him three or four times whilst he was doing the copying. He wrote slowly: the result of his extra care, his intensely earnest wish to succeed: but his writing was good and clear.

"I shall write quickly enough in a day or two, when I am used to it," he said, looking up: and there was hope in his face as well as his tone.

Mr. Preen chanced to be standing by. The writing would do, he decided; and Mr. Stroud was told to engage him. To begin with, his salary was to be fifteen shillings a-week: in a short time—as soon, indeed, as his suiting them was assured—it would be raised to eighteen. He was to enter on the morrow.

"Where do you live?" curtly questioned Mr. Stroud.

"Just beyond Kennington."

"Take care that you are punctual. Nine o'clock is the hour for the copying-clerks. You are expected to be at work by that time, therefore you must get here before the clock strikes."

A very easy condition, as it seemed to Charles Raynor, in his elation. A copying-clerk in a lawyer's office at fifteen or eighteen shillings a-week! Had any one told him a year ago that he would be capable of accepting so degrading a post—as he would then have deemed it—he had surely said the world must first turn itself upside down. *Now* he went home with a joyous step and a light heart, hardly knowing whether he trod on his head or his heels.

MRS. HENRY WOOD

And at Laurel Cottage they held quite a jubilee. Fifteen shillings a-week added to the narrow income of twenty, seemed at the moment to look very like riches. Charles had formed all sorts of mental resolutions as he walked home: to manage his clothes carefully lest they should grow shabby; scarcely to tread on his boots that they might not wear out: and to make his daily dinner of bread-and-cheese, carried in his pocket from home. Ah, these resolves are good, and more than good; and generous, wholesome-hearted young fellows are proud to make them in the time of need. But in their inexperience they cannot foresee the long, wearing, depressing struggle that the years must entail, during which the efforts and the privation must be persevered in. And it is well they cannot.

It wanted a quarter to nine in the morning, when Charles entered the office, warm with the speed at which he had walked. He did all that he was put to do, and did it correctly. If Mr. Stroud did not praise, he did not grumble.

When told at one o'clock that he might go to dinner, Charles made his way to the more sheltered parts in the precincts of the Temple, and surreptitiously ate the bread-and-cheese that he had brought from home in his pocket. That was eaten long and long before the time had expired when he would be expected to go in again: but he did not like to appear earlier, lest some discerning clerk should decide he had not been to dinner at all. It was frightfully dull and dreary here, the bitterly cold wind whistling down the passages and round the corners; so he turned into the open streets: they, at least, were lively with busy traversers: and walked about the Strand.

"I must go and see Peter Hartley, to tell him of my success and thank him; for it is to him I owe it," thought Charles, as he left the office in the evening. "Let me see! The address was somewhere near Mecklenburgh Square."

Taking out a small note-case, in which the address was entered, he halted at a street corner whilst he turned its leaves: some one came round the corner hastily, and Charles found himself in contact with William Stane. The gas in the streets and shops made it as light as day: no chance had they to pretend not to see each other. A bow, coldly exchanged, and each passed on his way.

"I won't notice him at all, if we meet again," said Charles to himself. And it might have been that Mr. Stane was saying the same thing. "Now for Doughty Street. I wonder which is the way to it?" deliberated he.

"Does Mr. Hartley live here?" inquired Charles of the young maid-servant, when he had found the house.

"In the parlour," replied the girl, pointing to a room on her left.

Without further ceremony, she went away, leaving him to introduce himself. A voice, that he supposed was Peter's, bade him "come in," in answer to his knock.

But he could not see Peter. A young fellow was stretched on the sofa in front of the fire. Charles rightly judged him to be the brother, Frederick Hartley. Young men are not, as a rule, very observant of one another, but Charles was struck with the appearance of the one before him. He was extremely good-looking; with fair hair, all in disorder, that shone like threads of gold in the firelight, glistening blue eyes, and a hectic flush on his thin cheeks.

"I beg your pardon," said Charley, as the invalid—for such he evidently was—half rose and gazed at him. "I came to see Peter."

"Oh yes; sit down," was the answer, given in cordial but very weak tones. "I expect him in every minute."

"You are Fred," observed Charles. "I dare say he told you about meeting me on Tuesday: Charles Raynor."

"Yes, he did. Do sit down. You don't mind my lying here?"

"Is it a cold you have taken?" asked Charles, bringing a chair to the corner of the hearth.

"I suppose so. A fresh cold. You might have heard me breathing yesterday over the way. The doctor kept me in bed. He wanted to keep me there to-day also; but to have to lie in that back-room is so wretchedly dull. Poke up the fire, will you, please, and make a blaze."

With every word he spoke, his breath seemed laboured. His voice was hollow. Now he had a fit of coughing; and the cough sounded as hollow as the voice had done.

Peter came in, welcomed Charles boisterously, and rang for tea. That, you may be sure, was acceptable to poor Charles. Fred, saying he was glad Charles had obtained the place at Prestleigh's, plunged into a few revelations touching the office politics, as well as his frequent cough and his imperfect breathing allowed, with a view of putting him au courant of affairs in general in his new position.

"I shall make things pleasant for you, after I get back," said he. "We articled fellows hold ourselves somewhat aloof from the working clerks; but I shall let them know who you are, and that it is only a temporary move on your part."

Fred Hartley, warm-hearted as his brother, said this when Charles was bidding him good-evening. That last look, taken when the invalid's face was raised, and the lamp shone full upon it, impressed Charles more than all. Peter went with him to the door.

"What does the doctor say about your brother?" asked Charles, as they stood on the pavement, in the cold.

"Says he must take care of himself."

"Don't you think he looks very ill?"

"I don't know," replied Peter, who had been in the habit of seeing his brother daily; and therefore had not been particularly impressed by his looks. "Does he?"

"Well, it strikes me so. I should say he is ill. Why don't you send for his mother to come up?"

"So I would, if we had a mother to send for," returned Peter. "Our mother died two years ago; and—and my father has married again. We have no longer any place in the old Somersetshire homestead, Raynor. Fred and I stand alone in the world."

"And without means?" cried Charles, quickly; who had lately begun to refer every evil the world contained to the want of money.

"Oh, he allows us something. Just enough to keep us going until we have started on our own account. I get a hundred a-year from the place I'm at. Fred gains nothing yet. He is not out of his articles."

"Well, I'll come and see him again soon," cried Charley, vaulting off. "Good-night, Peter."

Was Fred indeed seriously ill? Was it going to be one of those cases, of which there are too many in London: of a poor young fellow, just entering on the hopeful threshold of life, dying away from friends, and home, and care? Whether caused by Charles's tone or Charles's words, the shadowy thought, that it might be so, entered for the first time into the mind of Peter.

And Charles never had "things made pleasant for him," at the office, in pursuance of the friendly wish just expressed: the opportunity was never afforded. Exactly twenty days from that evening, he was invited to attend the funeral of Frederick Hartley. And could not do so, for want of suitable clothes to wear.

II

Jealousy

The room was smartened up for the occasion. At least, as much as a room furnished with cane-seated chairs, a threadbare carpet not half covering the boards, and a stained green-baize table-cover, can be smartened. It was Mrs. Raynor's birthday. Frank Raynor and his wife had come down to wish her many happy returns of it and to take tea with her; Alice had been invited; Charles had said he would be home early. But tea was over, and neither Charles nor Alice had put in an appearance; and the little fête, without them, had seemed a failure to their mother.

Mrs. Raynor was altered: worn, spiritless, always ailing, in the past year she had aged much. Disappointment and straitened circumstances told on her health as well as on her mind. It was not for herself she grieved and suffered, but for her children. For Charles especially. His prospects had been blighted; his standing in the world utterly changed. Edina's hands were full, for Mrs. Raynor could help very little now. What Mrs. Raynor chiefly did was to gather the young ones around her, and talk to them, in her gentle voice, of resignation to God's will, of patience, of that better world that they were travelling on to; where there will be neither sickness nor sorrow, neither mortification nor suffering. The children needed such lessons. It seemed very hard to them that they should sometimes have nothing but dry bread for dinner, or baked potatoes without meat. Even with all Edina's economy and with Charles's earnings, meat could not always be afforded. The joint must be carved sparingly, and made to last the best part of the week. They generally had a joint on a Sunday, and that was as much as could be said. Clothes cost so much: and Charles, at least, had to be tolerably well-dressed. But there are many items in a household's expenses besides eating and drinking; and this especially applies to fallen gentlepeople, whose habits have been formed, and who must still in a degree keep up appearances.

If the Raynors had needed discipline, as some who knew them at Eagles' Nest had declared, they were certainly experiencing it in a very marked degree. Twelve months had slipped by since they took up their abode at Laurel Cottage, and there had been no change. The days and the weeks had drifted on, one day, one week after another, in the same routine of thrift, struggle and privation. Charles was at Prestleigh and Preen's, working to that firm's satisfaction, and bringing home a sovereign a-week: Alice was teaching still in the school at Richmond. Alfred went to a day-school now. Edina had sought an interview with its principal, and by dint of some magic of her own, when she told him confidentially of their misfortunes, had persuaded him to admit the lad at an almost nominal charge. It was altogether a weary life for them, no doubt; one requiring constant patience and resignation; but, as Edina would cheerfully tell them, it might have been worse, and they had many things to be thankful for even yet.

October was passing, and the falling leaves strewed the ground. The afternoon was not sunny, but warm and dull; so sultry, in fact, as to suggest the idea of tempest in the air. They had gathered in the square patch of ground at the back of the house, called by courtesy a garden: Frank, his wife, Edina, Mrs. Raynor, and the children. Some of them stood about, looking at the bed of herbs Edina's care had planted; Mrs. Raynor was sitting on the narrow bench under the high window. For this garden had to be descended into by several steps; and as you stood in it the back-parlour window (Mrs. Raynor's bedroom) looked perched quite a long way up.

"Herbs are so useful," remarked Edina, as they praised the bed. "When a stew is nothing in itself, thyme or mint will give it quite a fine flavour. Do you remember, Frank, how poor papa liked thyme in the Irish stews?"

"And very good they used to be," said Frank. "Eve calls them ragoûts. I often tell her they are not half as good as those I had at Trennach. Remember, Daisy, it is thyme Eve's ragoûts want."

Daisy, playing with little Robert, turned round with dancing eyes. She was as pretty as ever, in spite of the distasteful existence in Lambeth. And she had put on for this occasion one of her old grand silks.

"I'll try and remember, Frank," she laughed. "I hope I shall not say rue instead of thyme. What did you plant this great bush of rue for, Edina?"

"That bush is not mine but the landlady's; it was here when we came," replied Edina. "Mrs. Fox hangs some of it at the foot of her bed, and declares that it mysteriously keeps away gnats and moths."

When Mr. Max Brown departed for the West Indies, he had thought the very utmost extent of his term of absence would be less than six months. But considerably more than twice six months had elapsed, and he had not returned. Apparently he liked the life there; apparently was quite satisfied with Frank's management of his practice at home. In writing to Frank, he put the delay down to his mother. She was dying, but very slowly: that is, her complaint was one for which there is no remedy: and she wanted to keep him with her to the end. Thus Max wrote, and it was the only excuse he gave for his prolonged stay. Frank could not help thinking there was some mystery about it; but he was quite content to remain at his post. It was very seldom indeed that he could take an hour or two's recreation, such as this. The practice was exacting, and he had no assistant.

"That's the postman's knock!" cried Kate.

The postman was not a frequent visitor at Laurel Cottage. When he did bring a letter it was always for the Raynors: Mrs. Fox never had one at all, and never seemed to expect one. Kate ran to the door and brought back the letter. It proved to be from Alice: stating why she was not able to come.

"Daisy, my darling, you must put your bonnet on," whispered Frank. "I want to get home before dark: I have been away now longer than I care to be."

"I should send the practice to York for one evening," cried Alfred, who chanced to overhear the words.

"No doubt you would," laughed Frank.

"Well, Frank, I'm sure you seem to put that precious practice before everything else. One would think it was an idol, with a golden body and diamond wings."

"And so I ought to put it before everything else, Master Alfred. A steward must do his duty."

Daisy went in unnoticed. She felt tired, wanted to be at home herself, and began arranging her bonnet before the glass at the window of the crowded back-room. Two beds were in the chamber, besides other furniture. In one of them slept Mrs. Raynor and Kate, in the smaller one, Edina. What a change it all was for them! Suddenly, while Daisy's attention was still given to her bonnet, certain words, spoken by Edina, broke upon her ear. She and Frank had sat down on the bench under the window, and were talking of Trennach. Mrs. Raynor and the children were at the end of the garden, bending their heads together over the untidy path, as if trying to determine what sort of coarse gravel it might be composed of.

"Do you ever hear anything of Mrs. Bell, Frank?"

"I saw her to-day," was Frank's unexpected answer. "Saw her yesterday as well."

"Where did you see her? Is she in London?" quickly repeated Edina.

"They have come to live in London. She and Rosaline."

"What has made them do that?" continued Edina quite sharply, as if she did not altogether approve of the information. Daisy's fingers, tying her bonnet-strings, could not have dropped more suddenly, had they been seized with paralysis.

"I'm sure I don't know. They have come into money, through the death of some relative at Falmouth, and thought, I believe, that they would like to live in London. Poor Mrs. Bell is worse than she used to be: the complaint, feared for her, is making progress—and must do so until the end. I am attending her."

"They live near you, then?"

"Close by."

A short silence ensued. Edina was probably busy with her thoughts. She spoke again.

"Is Rosaline as pretty as ever?"

"Not quite so pretty, perhaps: more beautiful."

"Ah, well—I would not go there too much, Frank; illness, or no illness," cried Edina.

She spoke in a dreamy tone, as if her reflections were back in the past. In her heart she believed he must have cared more or less for Rosaline. Frank laughed slightly in answer: a laugh that was somewhat constrained. His thoughts also had gone back; back to that fatal night at Trennach.

A sudden shout in Alfred's voice from the group in the garden. "Here it is! here it is, mamma!" Mrs. Raynor's thin gold ring had slipped off her slender finger, and they had been searching for it in the twilight.

Daisy seemed to see and hear no more until some of them came running into the bedroom, saying that Frank was waiting for her. She went out, said good-night in a mechanical sort of manner, and they started homewards, arm-in-arm. The old jealousy she had once felt of Rosaline Bell had sprung up again with tenfold force.

A short distance from the cottage, they met Charles. He was walking along at full speed, and greeted them in a storm of anger.

"It was an awful shame! Just because I wanted to get home an hour earlier than usual, it is an hour later. The office is full of work, and some of us had to stay behind and do it."

"Never mind, Charley," said Frank, with his genial smile. "Better luck next time."

"Yes, it's all very well to say next time; that will be next year, I suppose. You hardly ever come to see us, you know, Frank."

"I come when I can. You must come to us instead. Spend next Sunday with us, Charley. I can't stay talking now."

"All right," said Charley, vaulting off. "Good-night to you both." And neither of them had noticed that Daisy had not spoken a word.

Daisy was tormenting herself in a most unnecessary manner. Rosaline Bell in London! Living near to them; *close* to them, he had said. He had seen her to-day, and yesterday as well: no doubt he saw her every day. No doubt he loved this Rosaline!—and had thrown off all affection for herself, his wife. Even Edina could see the state of affairs. What a frightful thing it was!—and how far had it gone?—and what would it end in?

After this, the ordinary fashion of a jealous woman, did Mrs. Frank Raynor reason; believing her fancies to be all true as gospel. Had some angelic messenger essayed to set her right, it would have availed nothing in her present frame of mind. Jealousy is as much a disease as intermittent fever: it may have its lighter intervals, but it must run its course.

"Daisy, I think we shall have a storm!" cried Frank. "How still and hot the air is!—and look at that great black cloud coming up! We must hasten as much as possible."

Daisy silently acquiesced. And the pace they went prevented much attempt at talking. So that he had no opportunity of noticing that she had suddenly become strangely silent.

The storm burst forth when they were within a few doors of their own home. Lightning, thunder, a heavy downpour of rain. As they turned into the surgery, where Sam stood under the gas-light, his arms on the counter, his heels kicking about underneath it, Frank caught up a note that was lying there, addressed to him.

"Who brought this note?" asked Frank as he read it.

"It was a young lady," replied Sam. "When I told her you were not at home, she asked me for a sheet o' paper and pen-and-ink, and wrote that, and said it was to be gave you as soon as you came in. And please, sir, they have been round twice from Tripp's to say the baby's worse."

Frank Raynor went out again at once, in spite of the storm. His wife, who had heard what passed, turned into the parlour, her brain at work.

"I wonder how long this has been going on!—how long she has been coming here?" debated Mrs. Frank, her fingers twitching with agitation, her head hot and throbbing. "*She* wrote that note—barefaced thing! When she found she could not see him, she wrote it, and left it for him: and he has gone out to see her!"

Jealousy in its way is as exciting as wine; acting very much in the same manner on any patient who is under its influence. Mrs. Frank's blood was surging in her veins; her thoughts were taking a wild turn; her trembling fingers could hardly throw off her bonnet. In point of fact, the note concerned a worthy tradesman, who feared he was sickening for some complaint, and "the young lady," his daughter, had written it, in preference to leaving a message, begging for Mr. Raynor's speedy attendance.

"Have you had your supper, Sam?" asked Mrs. Frank, appearing at the intervening door.

"No, ma'am."

"Then go and get it."

Sam passed her on his way to the kitchen. She stepped forward to the counter, opened the day-book, and began searching for Dame Bell's address. The front-door was usually kept closed now, not open as formerly; and Daisy went to it on tiptoe, and slipped the bolt. There was no one to hear her had she stepped ever so heavily; but we are all apt to think that secret transactions require silent movements. Taking up her place behind the counter, she turned the leaves of the book again. The windows were closed in with shutters; she was quite in privacy. But, turn and look as she would, she could not see the address sought for. It is true she was looking in a desperate hurry, for what if Frank were to return suddenly? Or Sam from his supper?

"No, the address is not there!"—shutting the book, and pushing back the pretty hair from her beating temples. "He is too cautious to have entered it. Other patients' names are there, but Dame Bell's is not. The affair is clandestine from beginning to end."

And from that night Mrs. Frank Raynor began a course of action that she would previously have believed herself incapable of. She watched her husband. In her eagerness to discover where these Bells lived—though what service the knowledge could render her she would have been at a loss to declare—she occasionally followed him. Keeping her bonnet downstairs in readiness, she would put it on hastily when he went out, and steal after him. Three or four times a-week she did this. Very contemptible indeed Daisy felt it to be, and her cheeks blazed consciously now and again: but jealousy has driven a woman to do more contemptible things than even this. But for the unsuitability of her present life, as contrasted with her previous tastes and habits and surroundings, and for its utter monotony, causing her to feel weary unto death day after day, Margaret Raynor might never so far have forgotten herself. The pursuit was quite exciting, bringing a sort of relief to her; and she resolutely put away from her all inconvenient qualms of conscience.

So, imagine that you behold them. Frank turning out at the surgery-door, and hastening this way or that way, as if his feet were aided by wings: and when he is a few yards off, Daisy turns out after him. It would generally be a tedious and tormenting chase. He seemed to have so many patients to visit, here, there, and everywhere; on this side the street and on that side, and round the corners, and down courts, that his pursuer was generally baffled, lost him for good, and had to return home in despair.

Meanwhile, as time went on, Frank, unconscious of all this, was destined to receive a shock himself. One evening, when he had been called out to a case of emergency near home, upon quitting the sick man's house, he entered a chemist's for the purpose of directing some article, which it was not in his province to supply, to be sent to the sufferer. Dashing into the shop hurriedly, for his time was not his own, he was beginning to give his order.

"Will you send—"

And there his speech failed him. He stopped as suddenly and completely as though his tongue had been paralyzed. The young man to whom he was addressing himself, with the attentive red-brown eyes in which gleamed a smile of intelligence, and the clean white apron tied round his waist, was Blase Pellet. They looked at one another in the full glare of the gas-light.

Blase was the first to speak. "How do you do, Mr. Raynor?"

"Is it *you?*" cried Frank, recovering himself somewhat. "Are you living here?"

"Since a week past," replied Blase.

"Why have you left Trennach?"

"I came up to better myself," said Blase demurely. "One hears great things of fortunes being made in London."

"And of being lost, Pellet," rejoined Frank.

"I can go back at any time," observed Blase. "Old Float would be only too glad to have me. The young fellow he has now in my place is not *me*, Float writes word. Float will have to attend to business a little more himself now, and I expect it will not suit him."

Vouchsafing no answer to this, Frank left the order he had gone in to give, and passed out of the shop, his mind in a very disagreeable state of ferment.

"He has come up here to spy upon me; he is watching my movements," said Frank to himself. "How did he know I was here—in this part of London?—how did he find it out?" A positive conviction, that it was utterly useless to try to evade Blase Pellet, had taken sudden possession of him; that he had been tracking him all along by the means of spies and emissaries, and had now come to do it in person. He felt that if he were to sail away over the seas and set up his tent in an African desert, or on the shores of some remote fastness of the Indian Empire, or amidst the unexplored wilds of a prairie, he should see Blase Pellet in another tent, side by side with him, the next morning.

For the moment, his several pressing engagements had gone out of his head. His patients, lying in expectation of him, might lie: self was all in all. The uneasiness that had taken hold of him amounted to tribulation.

"I wonder what Dame Bell knows of this?" it suddenly occurred to him to think. And no sooner did it occur than, acting on the moment's impulse, he determined to ask her, and walked towards her lodging at his usual quick rate. She had taken rooms in a quiet street, West Street, where the small houses were chiefly private. It was nearly a week since Frank had seen her, for her complaint was very fluctuating, and latterly she had felt better, not requiring regular attendance.

Opening the front-door without knocking, as was his custom, he went upstairs to the small sitting-room: this room and the bedchamber behind it comprising Mrs. Bell's apartments. She had come into a little money by the death of her sister at Falmouth, John Pellet's wife: and this, combined with her previous small income, enabled her to live quietly. When Mrs. Pellet died, it had been suggested that Rosaline should take to her millinery business, and carry it on: but Rosaline positively declined to do so. Neither Rosaline nor her mother liked Falmouth, and they resolved to go up to London. Chance alone—or at least, that apparently unconscious impulse that is called chance—had caused them to choose this particular part of London for their abode; and neither of them had the slightest idea that it was within a stone's-throw of Frank Raynor. On the third day after settling in it, Rosaline and Frank had met in Mark Street: and he then learnt the news of their recent movements.

Mrs. Bell was at her old employment this evening when Frank entered—knitting. Lifting her eyes to see who had come in, she took the opportunity to snuff the candle near her, and gazed at Frank over her spectacles.

"Hey-day!" she cried. "I thought it was Rosaline." This was the first time Frank had seen her alone. During all his previous visits Rosaline had been present. Rosaline had gone a long way that afternoon, Dame Bell proceeded to explain, as far as Oxford Street, and was not back again yet. The girl seemed to have some crotchet in her head, she added, and would not say what she went for. Frank was glad of her absence, crotchet or no crotchet: he felt an invincible distaste to naming the name of Blase Pellet in her hearing.

Seen Blase Pellet to-night!—what had Blase Pellet come to town for? repeated Dame Bell, in answer to Frank's introduction of the subject. "Well, sir," she added, "he tells us he was grown sick and tired of Trennach, and came up here to be near me and Rose. I'm sure you might have knocked me down with a feather, so surprised was I when he walked into this room last Sunday afternoon. I had dozed off in my chair here, and Rose was reading the Bible to herself, when he came in. For a minute or two I did not believe my eyes, and that's the truth. As to Rose, she turned the colour of chalk, just as if he had frightened her."

"Did he know you were living here?"

"Of course he knew that, Mr. Frank. Blase, I must say, has always been as dutiful to me as if he had been really my nephew, and he often wrote to us at Falmouth. One of his letters was sent after us from Falmouth, and I wrote to tell him where we were in return."

"Did you tell him *I* was here?" questioned Frank.

"Well no, I did not: but it is curious you should ask the question, Mr. Frank," cried the dame. "I was just going to add to my letter that I hoped I should get better now Mr. Raynor was attending me again, but Rosaline stopped me. Mr. Raynor was nothing to Blase, she said: better not name him at all. Upon that, I asked her why she did not write herself, if she thought she could word the letter better than me: but she never will write to him. However, you were not mentioned, sir."

"What is his object in coming to London?" repeated Frank, unable to dismiss the one important point from his mind.

"I shouldn't wonder but it's Rosaline," said Dame Bell, shrewdly. "Blase has wanted to make up to her this many a day; but—"

"What an idiot the man must be!" struck in Frank.

"But she will not have anything to say to him, I was going to add," concluded Dame Bell. "Why should you call him an idiot, Mr. Frank?"

"He must be one, if he thinks he can persuade Rosaline to like him. See how ugly he is!"

"She might do worse, sir. I don't say Blase is handsome: he is not: but he is steady. If men and women were all chosen by their looks, Mr. Frank, a good many would go unmarried. Blase Pellet is putting by money: he will be setting up for himself, some day; and he would make her a good husband."

"Do you tell your daughter that he would?" asked Frank.

"She won't let me tell her, sir. I say to her sometimes that she seems frightened at hearing the young man's very name mentioned: just as though it would bring some evil upon her. I know what I think."

"What?" asked Frank.

"Why, that Rosaline pressed this settling in London upon me, on purpose to put a wider distance between herself and Blase. Falmouth was within reach, and he now and then came over there. I did not suspect her of this till last Sunday, Mr. Frank. When tea was over, and Blase had gone, she just sat with her hands before her, looking more dead than alive. 'After all, it seems we had better have stayed at Falmouth,' said she suddenly, as if speaking to herself: and that gave me the idea that she had come here to be farther away from him."

Frank made no remark.

"Blase has found a place at a druggist's close by," continued Mrs. Bell: whose chatter, once in full flow, was not easily stopped. "I don't suppose he'll like London as well as Trennach, and so I told him. *I* don't. Great noisy bustling place!"

It seemed that there was nothing more to ask or learn, and Frank bethought himself of his patients. Wishing the old dame good-night, he departed. His first visit led him past the druggist's; and his glance,

III

CROPPING UP AGAIN

W hy, Daisy. Out marketing, my dear?"
The salutation to Mrs. Frank Raynor came from her husband. One winter's morning, regardless of the extreme cold and the frost that made the streets partly deserted, she followed her husband when he went out after breakfast. The dwelling-place of Mrs. Bell and her daughter in West Street had become known to her long ago; and Daisy was always longing to see whether her husband's footsteps took him to it.

That most unreasoning jealousy, which had seized upon her mind, increased in force. It was growing almost into a disease. She felt as sure as if she had seen it written in letters of divination, that her husband's love had been, was, and ever would be Rosaline Bell's: that it never had been hers: and over and over again she asked herself the question—why had he married her?

It all appeared so plain to Daisy. Looking back, she could, as she fully believed, trace out the past, in regard to it, bit by bit. First of all, there was the girl's unusual and dangerous beauty; Frank Raynor's attendance at the house on the Bare Plain, under the plea of visiting the mother professionally; and the intimacy that was reported to have existed between himself and Rosaline. A great deal more frequently than was wise or necessary, Daisy recalled the evening when Frank had been dining at The Mount, and the conversation had turned upon the mysterious disappearance of Bell, the miner, and the beauty of his daughter. Frank's signs of agitation—his emotional voice, his flushings from red to white—Daisy had then been entirely unable to comprehend: she had considered them as unaccountable as was the absence of the man of whom they were speaking. Now the reason was very apparent to her: the emotion had arisen from his love of Rosaline. She remembered, as though it had been yesterday, the tales brought home by Tabitha, and repeated to herself—that this beautiful daughter of Bell the miner was Frank Raynor's best and only love, and that the girl worshipped the very ground he trod on. It was too late then to be influenced by the information, for the secret marriage had taken place in the church at

Trennach. Daisy had hardly known whether to believe the story or not; but it had shaken her. Later, as time went on, and she and her husband moved far away from the scene of events, and Rosaline Bell seemed to have faded out of sight; almost, so far as they were concerned, out of existence; Daisy had suffered herself to forget the doubt and jealousy. But only to call it up with tenfold force now.

And so, Mrs. Frank Raynor had amused herself, if the word may be applied to a state of mind so painful as was hers, with the pastime of watching her husband. Not often of course; only now and then. Her steps, as of their own uncontrollable will, would take her to the quiet street in which Dame Bell lived, and she had on one or two rare occasions been rewarded by seeing him pass in or out of the house. Of course she could not watch very often. She dared not do so. She would have been ashamed to do so. As it was, she knew that Sam's eyes had taken to opening with wonder whenever she followed her husband through the surgery, and that the boy's curiosity was much exercised as to the cause. Therefore, as she was unable to make Frank's shadow frequently, and as, with all her expectation, she had been gratified so rarely by seeing what she looked for, she drew the conclusion that fortune did not favour her, and that Frank's times for going to the house were just those when she did not happen to be out herself. An ingenious inference: as all sensible people must allow, but one that jealousy would be certain to invent.

On one of those rare occasions, Frank came out of the house accompanied by Rosaline.

They turned the opposite way to where Daisy was standing, but not before she had caught a glimpse of the beautiful face. Where were they going together? she passionately asked herself. The probability was that their coming out together was only incidental; for in a very few minutes Daisy met the girl coming back alone, carrying a paper of rusks, which she had no doubt been out to buy. All the more necessary was it, thought Daisy, after this little incident, that she should continue to look after her husband.

Daisy was becoming quite an adept at the work, and might have taken service as a lady detective. Of course the chief care to be exercised was to keep herself out of her husband's view. It was not so difficult to do this as it would have been with some husbands; for Frank's time was always so precious, and his movements were in consequence obliged to be so rapid, that he went flying through the streets like a lamplighter, never looking to the right or left. More than once, though, Daisy had been obliged to dart into a doorway; and it was at those times that she especially felt the humiliation of what she was doing.

But, the pitcher that goes too often to the well gets broken at last, we are told. On this bitter January day, when of a surety no one would venture out who could keep in, Daisy came face to face with her husband. She had seen him enter Mrs. Bell's house; fortune for once had so far favoured her. She saw him make for the quiet street upon first leaving home, skim down it with long strides, and go straight in at the door. Her heart beat as though it would burst its bounds; her pulses coursed on with fever-heat. Nothing in the world can be so good for the doctors as jealousy: it must inevitably tend to bring on heart disease. "I wonder how long he will stay?" thought Daisy in her raging anger. "Half-an-hour, perhaps. Of course he does not hurry himself when he goes *there*."

Sauntering onwards with slow steps, some idea in her head of waiting to see how long he did stay, and believing herself perfectly safe for many minutes to come, went Daisy. She longed to cross over the street and so obtain a sight of the upstairs window. But she did not dare; he might chance to look out and see her. She knew all about the position of the Bells' rooms, having, in a careless, off-hand manner, questioned Sam, who took out Mrs. Bell's medicine. In front of the closed door, her face turned towards it, was Daisy, when—she found herself confronted with her husband. He had come quickly forth, without warning, not having remained two minutes.

"Why, Daisy! Out marketing, my dear?"

The question was put laughingly. Daisy never did any marketing: she was not much of a housekeeper as yet, and the Lambeth shops did not tempt her to begin. Eve did all that. Had she been committing a crime, she could not have felt more taken aback in her surprise, or more awkward at finding an excuse.

"I—had a headache," she stammered, "and—came out for a little walk."

"But it is too cold for you, Daisy. The wind is in the north-east. I have never felt it keener."

"It won't hurt me," gasped Daisy, believing his solicitude for her was all put on. She had believed that for some time now. The kinder Frank showed himself, the more she despised him.

"You have been there to see a patient?" questioned Daisy, hardly knowing and certainly not caring what she did say.

"Yes," replied Frank. "But she is better this morning; so I am off to others who want me more than she does."

"Is it that Mrs. Bell from Trennach? I saw a bottle of medicine directed to West Street for her one day. Sam was putting it into his basket."

"It is Mrs. Bell. She is worse than she used to be, for the disorder has made progress. And I fear she will grow worse, day by day now, until the end."

"What a hypocrite he is!" thought Daisy: "I dare say there is as much the matter with her as there is with me. Of course he needs some plea of excuse—to be going there for ever after that wretched girl."

"Do you come here pretty often?" went on Daisy, coughing to conceal the spleen in her tone, which she was unable to suppress.

"I shall have to come here oftener in future, I fear," returned Frank, not directly answering the question; of which delay she took due note. Just for these few minutes, he had slackened his pace to hers, and they were walking side by side. "I am glad she is near me: I don't think any stranger would give her the care that I shall give her."

"You speak as though you were anxious about her!" resentfully cried Daisy.

"I am more than anxious. I would give half I am worth to be able to cure her."

"Well, I'm sure!" exclaimed Daisy. "One would think you and these people must possess some bond of union in common."

"And so we do," he answered.

Perhaps the words were spoken incautiously. Daisy, looking quickly up at him, saw that he seemed lost in thought.

"What is it?" she asked in a low tone: her breathing just then seeming a little difficult.

"What is what?"

"The bond of union between you and these Bells."

The question brought him out of his abstraction. He laughed lightly: laughed, as Daisy thought, and saw, to do away with the impression the words had made: and answered carelessly.

"The bond between me and Dame Bell? It is that I knew her at Trennach, Daisy, and learnt to respect her. She nursed me through a fever once."

"Oh," said Daisy, turning her head away, indignant at what she believed was an evasion. The "bond," if there were any, existed, not between himself and the mother, but between himself and the daughter.

"I dare say you attend them for nothing!"

"Of course I do."

"What would Mr. Max Brown say to that?"

"What he pleased. Max Brown is not a man to object, Daisy."

"You can't tell."

"Yes, I can. If he did, I should pay him the cost of the medicines. And my time, at least, I can give."

Daisy said no more. Swelling with resentment and jealousy, she walked by his side in silence. Frank saw her to the surgery-door, and then turned back rapidly. She went in; passed Sam, who was leisurely dusting the counter, and sat down in the parlour by the fire.

Her state of mind was not one to be envied. Jealousy, you know, makes the food it feeds on. Mrs. Frank Raynor was making very disagreeable food for herself, indeed. She gave the reins to her imagination, and it presented her with all sorts of suggestive horrors. The worst was that she did not, and could not, regard these pictured fancies as possible delusions, emanating from her own brain, and to be cautiously received; but she converted them into undoubted facts. The sounds of Sam's movements in the surgery, his answers to applicants who came in, penetrated to her through the half-open door; but, though they touched her ear in a degree, they did not touch her senses. She was as one who heard not.

Thus she sat on, until midday, indulging these visions to the full extent of her fancy, and utterly miserable. At least, perhaps not quite utterly so: for when people are in the state of angry rage that Daisy was, they cannot feel very acutely. A few minutes after twelve, Sam appeared. He stared to see his mistress sitting just as she had come in, not even her cloak removed, or her bonnet unfastened.

"A letter for you, please, ma'am. The postman have just brought it in."

Daisy took the letter from him without a word. It proved to be from her sister Charlotte, Mrs. Townley. Mrs. Townley wrote to say that she was back again at the house in Westbourne Terrace, and would be glad to see Daisy. She, with her children, had been making a long visit of several months to her mother at The Mount, and she had only now returned. "I did intend to be back for the New Year," she wrote; "but mamma and Lydia would not hear of it. I have many things to tell you, Daisy: so come to me as soon as you get this note. If your husband will join us at dinner—seven o'clock—there will be no difficulty about your getting home again. Say that I shall be happy to see him."

Should she go, or should she not go? Mrs. Frank Raynor was in so excited a mood as not to care very much what she did. And—if she went, and he did not come in the evening, he would no doubt take the opportunity of passing it with Rosaline Bell.

She went upstairs, took her things off, and passed into the drawing-room. The fire was burning brightly. Eve was a treasure of a servant, and attended to it carefully. Frank had given orders that a fire should be always kept up there: it was a better room for his wife than the one downstairs, and more cheerful.

Certainly more cheerful: for the street and its busy traversers could be seen. The opposite fish-shop displayed its wares more plainly to this room than to the small room below. Just now, Monsieur and Madame, the fish proprietors, were enjoying a wordy war, touching some haddock that Madame had sold under cost price. He held an oyster-knife in his hand, and was laying down the law with it. She stood, in her old brown bonnet, her wrists turned back on her capacious hips, and defied his anger. Daisy had the pleasure of assisting at the quarrel, as the French say; for the tones of the disputants were loud, and partly reached her ears.

"What a frightful place this is!" exclaimed Daisy. "What people! Yes, I will go to Charlotte. It is something to get away from them for a few hours, and into civilized life again."

At one o'clock, the hand-bell in the passage below was rung: the signal for dinner. Daisy went down. Frank had only just come in, and was taking off his overcoat.

"I have hardly a minute, Daisy," he said. "I have not seen all my patients yet."

"Been hindering his time with Rosaline," thought Daisy. And she slowly and ungraciously took her place at the table. Frank, regardless of ceremony, had already begun to carve the boiled leg of mutton.

"You have *generally* finished before one o'clock," she coldly remarked, as he handed her plate to her. For Eve, good servant though she was, had no idea of remaining in the room during meals to wait upon them.

"Yes, generally. But a good many people are ill: and I was hindered this morning by attending to an accident. A little boy was run over in the street."

"Is he much hurt?"

"Not very much. I shall get him right again soon."

The dinner proceeded in silence. Frank was eating too rapidly to have leisure for anything else; Daisy's angry spirit would not permit her to talk. As she laid down her knife and fork, Frank pressed her to take some more mutton, but she curtly refused it.

"I have said no once. This is luncheon; not dinner."

Frank Raynor had become accustomed to hearing his wife speak to him in cold, resentful tones: but to-day they sounded especially cold. He had long ago put it down in his own mind to dissatisfaction at their blighted prospects; blighted, at least, in comparison with those they had so sanguinely entertained when wandering together side by side at Trennach and picturing the future to each other. It only made him the more patient, the more tender with her.

"Mrs. Townley has written to ask me to go to her. She is back again in Westbourne Terrace. She bids me say she shall be happy to see you to dinner at seven. But I suppose you will not go."

"Yes, I will go," said Frank, rapidly revolving ways and means, as regarded the exigencies of his patients. "I think I can get away for an hour or two, Daisy. Is it dress?"

"Just as you please," was the frosty answer. "Mrs. Townley says nothing about dress; she would be hardly likely to do so; but she is accustomed to proper ways."

"And how shall you go, my dear?" resumed Frank, passing over the implication with his usual sweetness of temper. "You had better have a cab."

"I intend to have one," said Daisy.

She arrayed herself in some of her smartest things, for the spirit of bravado was upon her: if her husband did not choose to dress, *she* should: and set out in a cab for Westbourne Terrace. Once there, she put away her troubles; outwardly at any rate: and her sister never suspected that anything was amiss.

"I shall give you a surprise, Daisy," said Mrs. Townley in the course of the afternoon. "An old beau of yours is coming to dinner."

"An old beau of mine! Who is that?"

"Sir Paul Trellasis."

"What an idea!" cried Daisy. "*He* a beau of mine! Mamma must have put that into your head, Charlotte. Sir Paul came to The Mount once or twice; as he was a bachelor, mamma at once jumped to the conclusion that he must come for Lydia or for me. He married Miss Beauchamp that same year, you know."

"He and his wife are in London, and I asked them to come and dine with us to-day without ceremony," resumed Mrs. Townley. "Had you married Sir Paul, Daisy, you would not have been buried alive amongst savages in some unknown region of London."

"No, I should not," replied the miserable wife with stern emphasis.

But there was another surprise in store for Daisy. For Mrs. Townley as well. At dusk, a caller was ushered into the drawing-room, and proved to be the Reverend Titus Backup. The curate had never quite severed his relations with Trennach. He had taken three-months' duty there again the past autumn, when the Rector was once more laid aside by illness. He had then made the acquaintance of Mrs. Townley; and being now in London, had called upon her.

Mrs. Frank Raynor flushed red as a rose when he entered. The sight brought back to her memory the old time at Trennach, and its doings, with vivid intensity. She seemed to see herself once more standing with Frank Raynor before him at the altar, when he was making them *One* together, until death should part them. Mr. Backup had lost somewhat of his former nervousness, but he was shy still, and held out his hand to Mrs. Frank Raynor with timidity.

"Ah, I remember—it was you who married Daisy," observed Mrs. Townley. "My mother at first would not forgive you, I believe, Mr. Backup, until she found you did not know it was a stolen match. And for how long are you in town?"

"I am not sure," replied the parson. "I have come up to see about a curacy."

"Well, you must stay and dine with us," returned Mrs. Townley. "Nonsense! You must. I shall not let you say no. Sir Paul and Lady Trellasis are coming—you know them—and Mr. Raynor."

The curate, perhaps lacking courage to press his refusal, stayed. In due time Sir Paul and his wife arrived; and, as the clock was striking seven, Frank: dressed.

All this need not have been noticed, for in truth Mrs. Townley and her visitors have little to do with the story, but for an incident that occurred in the course of the evening. Mrs. Townley was on the music-stool, playing some scientific "morceau" that was crushingly loud, and seemed interminable, with Sir Paul at her elbow turning over for her, and Daisy on the other side. Lady Trellasis, a pretty young woman with black hair, sat talking with Mr. Backup on the sofa near the fire: and Frank stood just behind them, looking at photographs. In a moment, when he was least thinking of trouble, certain words spoken by the curate caught his ear.

"Josiah Bell: that was his name. No; the particulars have never come to light. He was found eventually, as of course you know, and buried in the churchyard at Trennach."

"The affair took great hold on my imagination," observed Lady Trellasis. "I was staying at The Mount with papa and mamma at the time the man was lost. It was a story that seemed to be surrounded with romance. They spoke, I remember, of the daughter, saying she was so beautiful. Papa thought, I recollect, that the poor man must have fallen into some pit or other; and so it proved."

"Yes," said Mr. Backup, "a pit so deep that the miners call it the Bottomless Shaft. The mystery of course consisted in how he got there."

"But why should that be a mystery? Did he not fall into it?"

"The fact is, that some superstition attaches to the place, and not a single miner, it is said, would willingly approach it. Bell especially would not go near it: for in all matters of superstition he was singularly weak-minded."

"Then how did he get in?" quickly asked Lady Trellasis.

"There was a suspicion of foul play. It was thought the man was thrown in."

"How very dreadful! Thrown in by whom?"

"I cannot tell you. A faint rumour arose later—as I was told by Mr. Pine—that some one in a higher walk of life was supposed to have been implicated in the matter: some gentleman. The Rector tried to trace the report to its source, and to ascertain the name of the suspected man. He could get at nothing: but he says that an uncomfortable feeling about it remains still on his mind. I should not be surprised at the affair cropping up again some day."

The "morceau" came to an end with a final crash, and the conversation with it. Frank woke up with a start, to find a servant standing before him with a tray and tea-cups. He took one of the cups, and drank the tea quite scalding, never knowing whether it was hot or cold. Certain of the words, which he could not help overhearing, had startled all feeling out of him.

"Is it not time to go, Daisy?" he asked presently.

"If you think so," she freezingly answered.

"Then will you put on your bonnet, my dear," he said, never noticing the ungraciousness of her reply. After those ominous words, all other words, for the time being, fell on his ear as though he heard them not.

Not a syllable was exchanged between them as they sat together in the cab, speeding homewards. Frank was too unpleasantly absorbed to speak; Daisy was indulging resentment. That last sentence of Mr. Backup's, "I should not be surprised at the affair cropping up again," kept surging in his mind. He asked himself whether it was spoken prophetically; and, he also asked, what, if it did crop up, would be the consequences to himself?

"He is thinking of *her*," concluded Daisy, resenting the unusual silence, although she herself by her manner invoked it. And, in good truth, so he was.

Handing Daisy out of the cab when it stopped, Frank opened the surgery-door for her, and turned to pay the driver. At that self-same moment some man came strolling slowly along the pavement. He was wrapped up in a warm coat, and seemed to be walking for pleasure.

He looked at the cab, looked at the open door of the house, looked at Frank. Not straightforwardly; but by covert sidelong glances.

"Good-night, Mr. Raynor," said he at length, as he was passing.

"Good-night to you," replied Frank.

And Mr. Blase Pellet sauntered on, enjoying the icicles of the winter night. Frank went in, and barred and bolted his door.

"I wish to Heaven it needed nothing but bars and bolts to keep the fellow out!" spoke Frank in his dismay. "How long he will be kept out, I know not. Talk of whether the affair will crop up again!—why, it *is* cropping up. And I have a bitter enemy in Blase Pellet."

IV

Humiliation

Again the weeks and the months went on, bringing round the autumn season of another year. For in real life—and this is very much of a true history—time passes imperceptibly when there are no special events to mark its progress. Seasons succeed each other, leaving little record behind them.

It was a monotonous life at best—that of the Raynors'. It seemed to be spent in a quiet, constant endeavour to exist; a patient, perpetual struggling to make both ends meet: to remain under the humble roof of Laurel Cottage, and not to have to turn from it; to contrive that their garments should be decent, something like gentlepeople's, not ragged and shabby.

But for Edina they would never have done it. Even though they had her fifty pounds a-year, without her presence they would never have got on. She managed and worked, and had ever a cheerful word for them all. When their spirits failed, especially Mrs. Raynor's, and the onward way looked unusually dark and dreary, it was Edina who talked of a bright day-star to arise in the distance, of the silver lining that is sure to be in every cloud. But for Edina they might almost have lost faith in Heaven.

The one most altered of all was Charles. Altered in looks, bearing, manner; above all, in spirit. All his pride had flown; all his self-importance had disappeared as summer mist before the sun: disappeared for ever. Had the discipline he was subjected to been transient, lasting for a few weeks, let us say, or even months, its impressions might have worn away with renewed prosperity, had such set in again, leaving no lasting trace for good. But when this sort of depressing mortification continues for years, the lesson it implants in the mind is generally permanent. Day by day, every day of his life, and every hour in the day, Charles was subjected to the humiliations (as he looked upon them, and to him they were indeed such) that attend the position of a working clerk. He who had been reared in the habits and ideas of a gentleman, had believed himself the undoubted heir to Eagles' Nest, found himself reduced by fate to this subordinate capacity, ordered about by the articled clerks, and regarded as an individual not at all to be ranked with them. He was at their beck and call, and obliged to be so; he had to submit to them as his superiors, not only his superiors in the office, but his superiors socially; above all, he had to submit to their off-hand tones, which always implied, unwittingly, perhaps, to themselves, but all too apparent to Charles, a consciousness of the distinction that existed between them.

How galling it all was to Charles Raynor, the reader may imagine; but it can never be described. At first it was all but unbearable. Over and over again he thought he must run away from it, and escape to a land where these distinctions do not exist. He might dig for gold in California; he might clear a settlement for himself in the back-woods of America: and the life in either place would be as paradise compared with this one at Prestleigh and Preen's. Nothing but the broad fact that the wages he earned were absolutely necessary to his mother's and the family's support, detained him. To give that aid was his imperative duty before God: for had it not been through him and his carelessness that they were reduced to this terrible extremity? So Charles Raynor, helped on by the ever-ready counsel of Edina, *endured* his troubles, put up with his humiliation, and bore onwards with the best resolution he could call up. Who knew, who could ever know, *how much* of this wonderful change was really due to Edina?

And, as the time went on, he grew to feel the troubles somewhat less keenly: habit reconciles us in a degree to the worst of things, no matter what that worst may be. But he had learnt a lesson that would last him his whole life. Never again could he become the arrogant young fellow who thought the world was made for his especial delectation. He had gained experience; he had found his level; he saw what existence was worth, and that those who would be happy in it must first learn and perform their duties in it. His very nature had changed. Self-sufficiency, selfish indifference, had given place to modesty, to a subdued thoughtfulness of habit, to an earnest sense of other's needs as well as his own. Frank Raynor, with all his sunny-heartedness and geniality, could not be more ready with a helping hand, than was Charles. He could give nothing in money, but he could in kind. No other discipline, perhaps, would have had this effect upon Charles Raynor. It had made a man of him, and, if a subdued, a good one. And so, he went on, reconciled in a degree to the changed life after his two years' spell at it, and looking forward to no better prospect in the future. Prospect of every sort seemed so hopeless.

MRS. HENRY WOOD

A little fresh care had come upon them this autumn, in the return of Alice. Changes had taken place in the school at Richmond, and her services were no longer required. Edina borrowed the advertisement sheet of the *Times* every morning, and caused Alice to write to any notice that appeared likely to suit her. As yet—a fortnight had gone on—nothing had come of it.

"No one seems to want a governess," remarked Alice one Monday morning, as they rose from breakfast, and Charles was brushing his hat to depart. "I suppose there are too many of us."

"By one half," assented Edina. "The field is too crowded. Some lady in this neighbourhood recently advertised for a governess for her daughters, directing the answers to be addressed to Jones's library, where we get these papers. Mr. Jones told me that the first day's post brought more than a hundred letters."

"Oh dear!" exclaimed Alice.

"The lady engaged one of the applicants," continued Edina, "and then discovered that she was the daughter of a small shopkeeper at Camberwell. That put her out of conceit of governesses, and she has sent her children to school."

"I should not like to be hard, I'm sure, or to speak against any class of people," interposed Mrs. Raynor, in her meek, deprecating voice; "but I do think that some of the young women who came forward as governesses would do much better as servants. These inferior persons are helping to jostle the gentlewomen out of the governess field—as Edina calls it."

"Will they jostle me out of it?" cried Alice, looking up in alarm. "Oh, Charley, I wish you could hear of something for me!—you go out into the world, you know."

Charles, saying good-bye and kissing his mother, went off with a smile at the words: he was thinking how very unlikely it was that he should hear of anything. Governesses did not come within the radius of Prestleigh and Preen's. Nevertheless, it was singular that Charles did hear of a vacant situation that self-same day, and heard it in the office.

In the course of the afternoon the head-clerk had despatched Charles to Mr. Preen's room with a message. He was about to deliver it when Mr. Preen waved his hand to him to wait: a friend who had been sitting with him had risen to leave.

"When shall we see Mrs. Preen to spend her promised day with us?" asked the gentleman, as he was shaking hands. "My wife has been expecting her all the week."

"I don't know," was the reply. "The little girls' governess has left; and, as they don't much like going back to the nursery to the younger children, Mrs. Preen has them with her."

"The governess left, has she?" was the answering remark. "I fancied you thought great things of her."

"So we did. She suited extremely well. But she was summoned home last week in consequence of her mother's serious illness, and now sends us word that she will not be able to leave home again."

"Well, you will easily find a successor, Preen."

"Two or three ladies have already applied, but Mrs. Preen did not care for them. She will have to advertise, I suppose."

Charles drank in the words. He delivered the message, and took Mr. Stroud the answer, his head full of Alice. If she could only obtain the situation! Mrs. Preen seemed a nice woman, and the two little girls were nice: he had seen them occasionally at the office. Alice would be sure to be happy there.

Sitting down to his desk, he went on with his writing, making one or two mistakes, and drawing down upon him the wrath of Mr. Stroud. But his mind was far away, deliberating whether he might, or could, do anything.

Speak to Mr. Preen? He hardly liked to do it: the copying-clerks kept at a respectful distance. And yet, why should he not speak? It seemed to be his only chance. Then came a thought that made Charley's face burn like fire: would *his* sister be deemed worthy of the post? Well, he could only make the trial.

Just before the time of leaving for the night, Charles went to Mr. Preen's room, knocked at the door, and was told to enter. Mr. Preen was standing in front of his desk, in the act of locking it, and a gentleman sat close before the almost-extinguished fire in the large easy-chair which had been old Mr. Callard's. Charles could see nothing but the back of his head, for the high, well-stuffed chair hid all the rest of him. He had a newspaper in his hand, and was reading it by the light of a solitary gas-burner; the other having been put out. To see this stranger here took Charles aback.

"What is it?" questioned Mr. Preen.

Charles hesitated. "I had thought you were alone, sir."

"All the same. Say what you want."

"I have taken the liberty of coming to speak to you on a private matter, sir; but—" There he stopped.

"What is it?" repeated Mr. Preen.

"When I was in this room to-day, sir, I heard you say that your little girls were in want of a governess."

"Well?"

"What I am about to say may seem nothing but presumption—but my sister is seeking just such a situation. If you—if Mrs. Preen—would only see her!"

"Your sister?" returned the lawyer; with, Charles thought, chilling surprise. It damped him: made him feel sensitively small.

"Oh, pray do not judge of my sister by me, sir!—I mean by the position I occupy here," cried Charles, all his prearranged speeches forgotten, and speaking straight from his wounded feelings, his full heart. "You only know me as a young man working for his daily bread, and very poor. But indeed we are gentlepeople: not only by birth and education, but in mind and habits. I was copying a deed to-day: the lease of a farm on the estate of Eagles' Nest. Do you know it, sir?"

"Know what?" asked Mr. Preen. "That you were copying the deed, or the estate?"

"Eagles' Nest."

"I know it only from being solicitor to its owner. As my predecessor, Mr. Callard, was before me."

"That estate was ours, sir. When Mr. George Atkinson came into possession of it he turned us out. It had come to my father from his sister, Mrs. Atkinson, and we lived in it for a year, never dreaming it possible that it could be wrested from us. But at the year's-end a later will came to light: my aunt had left Eagles' Nest to Mr. George Atkinson, passing my father over."

Charles stopped to gather breath and firmness. The remembrance of his father, and of their subsequent misfortunes and privations, almost unnerved him. Mr. Preen listened in evident surprise.

"But—was your father Major Raynor, of Eagles' Nest?"

"Yes, sir."

"You never mentioned it."

"To what end?" returned Charles; while the stranger took a momentary glance over his shoulder at him, and then bent over his newspaper again, as though the matter and the young clerk were no concern of his. "Now that my position in life has so much altered, I would rather let people think I was born a copying-clerk, than that I was heir to Eagles' Nest."

"It sounds like a romance," cried Mr. Preen.

"For us it has been, and is, only too stern reality. But I do not wish to trouble you with these affairs, sir; and I should not have presumed to allude to them, but for wishing to prove to you that Alice is superior to what you might imagine her to be as my sister. She is a very excellent governess indeed, accomplished, and a thorough lady."

"And you say she is in want of a situation?"

"Yes, sir. She has been for two years teacher in a school at Richmond. If Mrs. Preen would but consent to give her a trial, I know she would prove worthy. I do not say so merely to get her the post," he continued, earnestly, "but because I really believe she could and would faithfully fulfil its duties. I would not otherwise urge it: for we have learnt not to press ourselves forward at the expense of other people's interests, whatever the need."

"Well, Raynor: I cannot say anything myself about this matter; it is Mrs. Preen's business and not mine," spoke the lawyer, upon whom Charles's story and Charles's manner had made an impression. "If your sister likes to call and see Mrs. Preen she can do so."

"Oh, thank you; thank you very much, sir," said Charles. "I am sure you will like Alice."

"Stay; not so fast"—for Charley was leaving the room in eager haste. "Do you know where my house is?"

"To be sure I do, sir—in Bayswater. I have been up there with messages for you."

"So that's young Raynor!" cried the gentleman at the fire, turning as Charles went out, and taking a look at him.

"It is young Raynor, one of our copying-clerks," acquiesced Mr. Preen. "But I never knew he was one of the Raynors who were connected with Eagles' Nest."

"Is he steady?—hardworking?"

"Quite so, I think. He keeps his hours punctually, and does his work well. He has been here nearly two years."

"Is not upstart and lazy?"

Mr. Preen laughed. "He has no opportunity of being either. I fancy he and his family have to live in a very humble, reduced sort of way. If they were the Raynors of Eagles' Nest—and of course they were, or he would not say so—they must have been finding the world pretty hard of late."

"So much the better," remarked the stranger. "By what I have heard, they needed to find it so."

"He has to make no end of shifts, for want of means. At first the clerks made fun of him; but they left it off: he took it so helplessly and patiently. His clothes are often threadbare; he walks to and fro, instead of riding as the others do, though I fancy it is close upon three miles. I don't believe he has a proper dinner one day out of the six."

The stranger nodded complacently: as if the information gave him intense satisfaction.

"I wish I could persuade you to come home and dine with me," resumed Mr. Preen, as he concluded his preparations for departure.

"I am not well enough to do so. I am fit for nothing to-night but bed. Will one of your people call a cab for me? Oh, here's Prestleigh."

As Charles had gone out, dashing along the passage from his interview, he nearly dashed against Mr. Prestleigh, who was coming up, some papers in hand.

"Take care, Raynor! What are you in such a hurry about? Is Mr. George Atkinson gone?"

"Who, sir?" asked Charles, struck with the name.

"Mr. George Atkinson. Is he still with Mr. Preen?"

"Some gentleman is with him, sir. He is sitting over the fire.

"The same, no doubt. He is a great invalid just now."

Charles felt his face flush all over. So, it was the owner of Eagles' Nest before whom he had spoken. What a singular coincidence! The only time that a word had escaped his lips in regard to their fallen fortunes, *he* must be present and hear it! And Charley felt inclined to wish he had lost his tongue first. All the world might have been welcome to hear it, rather than George Atkinson.

The way home was generally long and weary, but this evening Charles found it light enough: he seemed to tread upon air. His thoughts were filled with Alice, and with the hope he was carrying to her. Never for a moment did he doubt she would be successful. He already saw her in imagination installed at Mrs. Preen's.

Edina went to Bayswater with Alice in the morning. A handsome house, well appointed. Mrs. Preen, interested in what she had heard from her husband, received them graciously. She liked them at first sight. Though very plain in dress, she saw that they were gentlewomen.

"It cannot be that I am speaking to Mrs. Raynor?" she cried, puzzled at Edina's youthful look.

Edina set her right: she was *Miss* Raynor. "The result of possessing no cards," thought Edina. "I never had more than fifty printed in my life, and most of those got discoloured with years. Mrs. Raynor is not strong enough to walk as far as this," she said aloud.

"But surely you did not walk?" cried Mrs. Preen.

"Yes, for walking costs nothing," replied Edina with a smile.

"The Raynors, if I have been rightly informed, have experienced a reverse of fortune."

"A reverse that is rarely experienced," avowed Edina. "From wealth and luxury they have been plunged into trouble and poverty. If you, madam, are what, from this short interview, I judge you to be, the avowal will not tell against our application."

"Not in the least," said Mrs. Preen, cordially, for she was a warm-hearted, sensible woman. "We do not expect young ladies who are rich to go out as governesses."

The result was that Alice was engaged, and they were asked to stay luncheon. Alice played, and her playing was approved of; she sang one short song, and that was approved of also. Mrs. Preen was really taken with her. She was to have thirty guineas a-year to begin with, and to enter the day after the morrow.

"I can buy mamma a new black silk, by-and-by, with all that money," said Alice, impulsively, with a flushed, happy face. And though Mrs. Preen laughed at the remark, she liked her all the better for it: it was so naïve and genuine.

"Oh my dear child, I am sure God is helping you!" breathed Mrs. Raynor, when they got back home and told her the news.

On the afternoon appointed, Thursday, Alice went to take up her abode at Mrs. Preen's, accompanied, as before, by Edina. Poverty makes us acquainted with habits before unknown, and necessity, it is said, is a hard taskmaster; nevertheless, it was deemed well that Alice should not walk alone in the streets of London. Edina left her in safety, and saw for a moment her pupils—two nice little girls of eight and ten years old.

Alice was taking off her bonnet in the chamber assigned her when Mrs. Preen entered it.

"We shall have a few friends with us this evening, Miss Raynor," she said. "It may give you a little pleasure to come to the drawing-room and join them."

"Oh, thank you," said Alice, her face beaming at the unexpected, and, with her, very rare treat. "If I can—if my boxes arrive. They were sent off this morning by the carrier."

The boxes arrived. Poor Alice might have looked almost as well had they been delayed, for her one best dress was an old black silk. Prettily made for evening wear, it is true; but its white lace and ribbon trimmings could not conceal the fact that the silk itself was worn and shabby.

The few friends consisted of at least thirty people, most of them in gay evening dress. Mrs. Preen introduced her to a young lady, a Miss Knox, who was chatty and pleasant, and told her many of the names of those present. But after a while Miss Knox went away into the next room, leaving Alice alone.

She felt something like a fish out of water. Other people moved about here and there talking with this acquaintance and laughing with that; but Alice, conscious of being only the governess, did not like to do so. She was standing near one of the open windows, within shade of the curtains that were being swayed about by the draught, turning her gaze sometimes upon the rooms, sometimes to the road below.

Suddenly, her whole conscious being seemed struck as by a blow. Her pulses stopped, her heart felt faint, every vestige of colour forsook her cheeks. Walking slowly across the room, within a yard of her, came William Stane.

Not until he was close up did he see her standing there. A moment's hesitation, during which he seemed to be as surprised as she, and then he held out his hand.

"It is Miss Raynor, I think?"

"Yes," replied Alice, her hand meeting his, and the hot crimson flushing her cheek again. How well he was looking! Better, far better looking than he used to be. And he was of more importance in the world, for he had risen into note as a pleader, young at the Bar though he was, and his name was often on the lips of men. His presence brought back to Alice the old Elysian days at Eagles' Nest, and her heart ached.

"Are Sir Philip and Lady Stane quite well?" she asked, in sheer need of saying something; for the silence was embarrassing.

"My mother is well; my father is very poorly indeed. He is a confirmed invalid now."

His tone was frigid. Alice felt it painfully. She stood there before him in the blaze of light, all too conscious of her shabby dress, her subdued manner, all her other disadvantages. Not far off sat a young lady in rich white silk and lace, diamond bracelets gleaming on her arms. Times had indeed changed!

"Are any of your family here to-night, Miss Raynor? I do not see them."

"No; oh no;—I am only the governess here," replied poor Alice, making the confession in bitter pain. And he might hear it in her voice.

"Oh—the governess," he assented, quite unmoved. "I hope Mrs. Raynor is well."

"Not very well, thank you."

Mr. Stane moved away. She saw him several times after that in different parts of the room; but he did not come near her again.

And that, the first night that Alice spent at her new home, was passed in the same cruel pain, her pillow wet with tears. Pain, not so much for the life of ease she had once enjoyed, the one of labour she had entered upon, not so much in regret for the changed position she held in the world, as for the loss of the love of William Stane.

V

The Missing Desk

B ut there is something yet to relate of the afternoon. It was about five o'clock when Edina reached home. Very much to her astonishment she saw a gentleman seated by Mrs. Raynor. The tea-things were on the table. Bobby sat on the floor. Kate stood, her back to the window, gazing with some awe at the visitor—so unusual an event in the retired household. He was a scanty-haired little gentleman, with cold, light eyes, and a trim, neat dress. Edina knew him at once, and held out her hand. It was Street, the banker.

It was evident that he had come in only a minute before her, for he had not yet entered upon his business. He began upon it now. Edina silently took off her things as she listened, put them on the side-table, and made the tea. There he sat, talking methodically, and appearing to notice nothing, but in reality seeing everything: the shabby room, the scanty attire of the young children, the faded appearance of Mrs. Raynor, as she sat putting fresh cuffs on a jacket of Alfred's. Edina began to pour out the tea, and brought him a cup, handing him the sugar and milk.

"Is it cream?" asked Mr. Street. "I can't take cream."

"It is skim-milk," said Edina. "But it is good: not at all watered. We buy it at a small farmhouse."

He had come to ask Mrs. Raynor whether she remembered a small ebony desk that had been at Eagles' Nest. It had belonged to the late Mrs. Atkinson, he observed: "she kept papers in it: receipts and things of that sort."

"I remember it quite well," replied Mrs. Raynor. "My husband took it into use, and kept papers of his own in it. He used to put all the bills there."

"Do you know what became of the desk, madam?"

"It was left in the house," said Mrs. Raynor.

"Ay: we supposed it would be," nodded the banker. "But, madam, it cannot be found. I was at Eagles' Nest myself all day yesterday, searching for it. Mr. Fairfax says he does not remember to have seen it."

The name struck unfamiliarly on Mrs. Raynor's ear. "Mr. Fairfax? Who is he?"

"The land-steward, who lives in the house. He thinks that had the desk been there when he entered into possession, he should have noticed it."

"Is the desk particularly wanted?" interposed Edina, struck with the fact that so busy a man as Mr. Street should have been down in search of it.

"We should be glad to find it," was the answer, as he turned again to Mrs. Raynor. "Lamb, the butler, who remained in the house for some two or three weeks after you left it, says he does not remember to have seen it there after your departure. So I procured your address from my brother, madam, and have come to ask you about it."

Mrs. Raynor, who had put aside her work soon after Mr. Street entered, sat with her cup and saucer in her hand, looking a little bewildered. He proceeded to explain further.

On the evening of Mr. George Atkinson's arrival in London— which had only taken place on Monday, the day Charles Raynor saw him in Mr. Preen's office—he and the banker were conversing together on various matters, as would naturally be the case after his long absence. Amongst other subjects touched upon was that of the lost money and the vouchers: neither of which had ever been discovered. Whilst they were recalling, in a desultory sort of way, every probable and improbable place in which these vouchers, if they existed, could have been placed, Mr. Atkinson suddenly asked whether the ebony desk had been well examined. Of course it had, and all the other desks, was Mr. Street's answer. "But," said George Atkinson, "that ebony desk had a false bottom to it, in which things might be concealed. I wonder I never thought of that before. It may be that the Raynors never found that out; and I should not be much surprised if Mrs. Atkinson put the bonds in it, and if they are in it to this day."

Of course the suggestion was worth following up. Especially worthy of it did it appear to Street, the banker, who had a keen scent for money, whether his own or other people's. He went down himself to Eagles' Nest to search the desk: but of the desk he could find no traces. The land-agent who had since occupied the house did not remember to have seen anything of the kind. He next inquired for Lamb, the former butler, and heard that he was now living with Sir Philip Stane. To Sir Philip Stane's proceeded Mr. Street, and saw Lamb. Lamb said he knew the desk quite well; but he could not recollect seeing it after the family had left, and he had no idea what became of it. Mr. Street, feeling baffled, had returned to town without learning anything of the desk. He had now come down to question Mrs. Raynor.

"I wish, madam, I could hear that you had brought it away with you," he observed, the explanation over. It had been rather a long one for curt-speaking Mr. Street.

"We should not be likely to bring it away," said poor Mrs. Raynor, in her mild, meek voice. "We were told that we must not remove anything that had been Mrs. Atkinson's."

"True. Those instructions were issued by Mr. George Atkinson, through me, madam."

"And I can assure you, sir, that we did *not* remove anything," she replied, a little flurried. "All that we brought away belonged strictly to ourselves. But I fancy Mr. George Atkinson must be mistaken in supposing the bonds were in that desk. Had they been there my husband could not have failed to see them."

"Did he know of the false bottom?"

"I am not aware that he did. But still—he so often used the desk. It frequently stood in the little room, upon the low cabinet, or secretaire. I have seen him turn it upside down, when searching for some particular bill he had mislaid."

"That does not prove the bonds were not in the secret compartment," remarked the banker.

"Did you know of this secret compartment?" inquired Edina.

"I did not, Miss Raynor. Or you may be sure it would have been searched when we were first looking for the bonds. This desk George Atkinson himself brought from Ceylon the first time he went there, and gave it to Mrs. Atkinson. It was not, I believe, really of ebony, but of black wood peculiar to the country; handsomely carved, as you no doubt remember, if you made acquaintance with the desk at Eagles' Nest. Mr. George Atkinson cannot imagine how he could have forgotten the desk until now; but it had as completely slipped his memory, he says, as though it had never existed."

"I'm sure I wish it could be found!" spoke Mrs. Raynor. "It may be that the bonds are in it. That my husband never discovered the compartment you speak of, I feel assured. If he had, we should all have known it."

"And—just one more question, madam," said the banker, rising to depart. "Do you chance to remember in what room that desk was left when you quitted Eagles' Nest?"

Mrs. Raynor paused in thought; and then shook her head hopelessly. "No, I do not," she answered. "I know the desk must have been left there because we did not bring it away, but I have no especial recollection about it at all. Dear me! What a strange thing if the bonds were lying concealed in it all that time!"

"That they are lying in it I think more than likely—provided there are any to lie anywhere," observed the banker, "for it is most singular that none have come to light. It is also to be regretted that Mr. Atkinson did not think of the desk before this. Good-evening, madam."

"We heard that Mr. Atkinson was in London," remarked Edina, as she accompanied Mr. Street to the front-door.

"For a few days only."

"For a few days only! When does he intend to enter into possession of Eagles' Nest?"

"I cannot tell: he is an invalid just now," was the hurried answer, as if the banker did not care to be questioned. "Good-day, Miss Raynor." And away he went with a quick step.

Edina began to wash up the tea-things, that she might get to some ironing. Her mind was busy, and somewhat troubled. Reminiscences of George Atkinson, thoughts of the missing desk and of the lost bonds that were perhaps in it, kept rapidly chasing each other in her brain—and there seemed to be no comfort in any one of them.

"Had the desk been brought away from Eagles' Nest, I must have seen it," she remarked at length, but in doubtful tones, as if not feeling altogether sure of her assertion.

"But surely, Edina, you don't think we *should* bring it!" cried Mrs. Raynor, looking up from her work, which she had resumed.

"Not intentionally, of course, Mary. The only chance of it would be if Charles, or any one else, inadvertently packed it up."

"I am sure he did not," said Mrs. Raynor. "Had it been brought away by accident we should certainly have seen it, and sent it back to Eagles' Nest."

"I remember that desk quite well," spoke up Kate, looking off the spelling-lesson she was learning. "I remember seeing Frank empty all the papers out of it one morning.

"Frank did?" cried Edina.

"Why, yes: it was Frank who examined the desk," said Mrs. Raynor. "I now recollect as much as that. It was the day after the funeral. You were upstairs, Edina, helping to pack Daisy's things for London. I was crying about the money we owed, not knowing whether it was much or little, and Frank said we had better examine the bills. I told him the bills were most likely all in the little ebony desk—and he went to get them.

"I saw him do it," reiterated Kate. "I was in the little room with Mademoiselle Delrue. He came and unlocked the desk, shook all the papers out of it, and took them away with him."

"And what did he do with the desk?" asked Edina. "Did he leave it there?"

"I don't know. I think he took that away too."

"I wonder whether Frank would remember anything of it?" mused Edina. "Perhaps he put up the desk somewhere for safety, after taking the papers out of it: in some cupboard or closet?"

"Perhaps he did," added Mrs. Raynor. "It is so strange a thing that it cannot be found."

"I may as well walk over to Frank's, and hear what his recollections are upon the subject," said Edina after a pause.

"But you must be so tired, Edina, after that walk to Bayswater."

"Not very. I meant to iron the boy's collars and Charley's wristbands this evening, but I can do that to-morrow."

Mrs. Raynor made no further objection; and Edina set out. The visit of the banker seemed to have saddened rather than cheered her—as so unusual a little change in the monotony of their home life might have been expected to do. They all felt faint and weary with their depressing prospects. Were things to go on for life as they now were? It was a question they often asked themselves. And, for all they could see, the answer was—Yes. Even Edina at times lost heart, and indulged in a good cry in secret.

Matters were not in a much better state at Frank Raynor's. It is true no poverty was there, no privation; but the old happiness that existed between him and his wife had disappeared. Daisy was much changed. The once warm-hearted girl had become cold and silent, and frightfully apathetic. Her husband never received a kindly look from her, or heard a loving tone. She did not complain. She did not reproach him. She did not find fault with any earthly thing. She just went through life in a listless kind of manner, as if all interest had left her for ever. Frank put it down to dissatisfaction at their changed circumstances; to the obscure manner in which they lived. Ever and anon he would try to breathe a word of hope that things would be different sometime: but his wife never responded to it.

Steeped in her miserable jealousy, was Mrs. Frank Raynor. All through this past year had she been silently indulging it. It had become a chronic ailment; it coloured her mind by day and her dreams by night. The most provoking feature of it all was, that she could not obtain any tangible proof of her husband's delinquency, anything very special to make a stir about: and how intensely aggravating that is to a jealous woman, let many confess. That her husband did go to Mrs. Bell's frequently, was indisputable: but then, as a counterbalance to that, there was the fact that he went in his professional capacity. No end of pills and potions were entered in Mrs. Bell's name in the medicine-book, and Daisy was therefore unable to assert that the plea for his visits was a mere pretence. But she believed it was so. Once, chance had given her an opportunity of speaking of these visits. A serious accident happened in the street just opposite their door, through a vicious horse. Daisy watched it from the drawing-room window; saw the injured man brought into the surgery. She ran down in distress. Frank was not at home. The boy flew one way in search of him, Eve ran another: but Frank could not be found, and the poor man had to be carried insensible elsewhere. "I'm very sorry," said Frank, when he returned, speaking rather carelessly; "I was at Mrs. Bell's." "You appear to be pretty often there," retorted Daisy, an angry sound in her usually cold tones. "I go every two or three days," said he. And how much oftener, I wonder! thought Daisy: but she said nothing more.

No, there was no tangible proof of bad behaviour to be brought against him. Not once, during the whole past twelvemonth, had she even seen them abroad together. She did not watch Frank as at first; she had grown ashamed of that, perhaps a little weary; and she had not once been rewarded by the sight of Rosaline. Had that obnoxious individual been a myth, she could not have more completely hidden herself from her neighbours and from Daisy on a week-day. On Sundays Daisy generally saw her at church. The girl would be sitting quietly in her pew wearing a plain black silk gown; still, devout, seeming to notice no one: had she been training for a nun, the world could not have appeared to possess less interest for her. Her black lace veil was never lifted from her face: but it could not hide that face's beauty. As soon as church was over Rosaline seemed to glide away before any one else stirred, and was lost to sight.

In this unsatisfactory manner the seasons had passed, Frank and his wife living in an estranged atmosphere, without any acknowledged cause for the unhappy state of affairs.

On this self-same evening when Edina was on her way to them, the West Indian mail brought a letter to Frank from Mr. Max Brown. That roving individual wrote regularly once a month, all his letters being filled, more or less, with vague promises of return. Vague, because no certain time was ever given. Frank called Eve to light the lamp, and stood by the fire in the little parlour whilst he read his letter. It was a genial autumn, and very few people had taken to fires; but Daisy ever seemed chilly, and liked one lighted at twilight.

"He says he is really coming, Daisy," cried Frank in quick tones as he looked over the letter. "Listen: 'I am now positively thinking of starting for home, and may be with you soon after the beginning of the new year. I know that you have thought my prolonged absence singular, but I will explain all in person. My mother is, I fear, sinking!'"

Mrs. Frank Raynor made no reply of any sort. For days together she would not speak to her husband, unless something he might say absolutely demanded an answer.

"And when Brown comes, we shall have to leave," went on Frank. "You will be glad of it, I am sure."

"I don't care whether we leave or not," was the ungracious retort.

And she really did not seem to care. Life, for her, had lost its sweetness. Nay, she probably would prefer, of the two, to remain where she was. If away, the field would be so free and open for her husband and that obnoxious young woman, Rosaline Bell.

"I shall be at liberty, once Brown is here again to take to his own practice," continued Frank; "and I will try to place you in a more genial atmosphere than this. I know you have felt it keenly, Daisy, and are feeling it still; but I have not been able to help myself."

His tone was considerate and tender; he stooped unexpectedly and kissed her forehead. Daisy made no response: she passively endured the caress, and that was all. The tears sprang to her eyes. Frank did not see them: he carried his letter into the surgery, where very much of his home time was passed.

His thoughts were far away. Would Mr. Blase Pellet tolerate this anticipated removal when it came? Or, would he not rather dodge Frank's footsteps and establish himself where he could still keep him in view? Yes: Frank felt certain that he would. Unconscious though Frank was of his wife's supervision, he felt persuaded in his mind that he was ever subjected to that of Blase Pellet. It was not, in one sense of the word, offensive; for not once in three months did he and Pellet come into contact with each other: but Frank felt always as a man chained—who can go as far as the chain allows him, but no farther. With all his heart he wished that he could better his position for Daisy's sake; had long wished it; but in his sense of danger he had been contented to let things go on as they were, dreading any attempt at change. Over and over again had he felt thankful for the prolonged wanderings of Mr. Max Brown, which afforded him the plea for putting up with his present lot.

Daisy set on with her discontented face. A very pretty face still; prettier, if anything, than of yore; with the clear eyes and their amber light, the delicate bloom on the lovely features, the sunny, luxuriant hair. She often dressed daintily, wishing in her secret heart, in spite of her resentment, to win back her husband's allegiance. This evening she wore a dark blue silk, one of the remnants of better days, with some rich white lace falling at the throat, on which rested a gold locket, attached to a thin chain. Very, very pretty did Edina think her when she arrived, and was brought into the room by Frank.

"You never come to see me now," began Daisy, in fretful tones of complaint. "I might be dead and buried, for all you or any one else would know of it, Edina."

"Ah, no, Margaret, you might not," was Edina's answer. "Not while you have Frank at your side. If you really needed us, he would take care that we should be sent for."

"All the same, every one neglects me," returned Daisy. "I am glad you have thought of me at last."

"I came this evening with a purpose," said Edina: who would not urge in excuse the very little time she had to give to visiting, for Daisy must be quite aware of it. And she forthwith, loosening her bonnet-strings, told Frank of Mr. Street's visit, of its purport, and of their own conjectures at Laurel Cottage after the banker had departed.

"Why, yes, it was I who emptied that ebony desk," said Frank. "A false bottom! I really can't believe it, Edina. Some of us would have found it out."

"We cannot doubt Mr. Street. He knew nothing of it himself, you hear, until Mr. George Atkinson spoke about it."

"But why in the world did not Atkinson speak about it before? When he was last in England these bonds were being hunted for, high and low."

"He says, I tell you, that he forgot all about the desk and its secret compartment. But, Frank, we cannot remedy the omission if we talk

MRS. HENRY WOOD

of it for ever; what I wanted to ascertain from you is, whether you remember where you left the desk."

"No, that I don't. I remember turning the bills and papers out of it wholesale, and carrying them into the room where Mrs. Raynor was sitting. As to the desk, I suppose it remained upon the table."

"You are sure you emptied it of all the papers?"

"Quite sure," replied Frank. "I turned the desk upside down and shook the papers out, and saw that the desk was quite empty."

"Kate says she saw you do it. But she does not recollect what became of the desk."

"Neither do I. No doubt it was left in the room. I dare say it still remained there when you all came away from the house."

"Well, it cannot be found," concluded Edina. "I think the probability is, that the desk was packed up by the servants and brought away in one of the large boxes, and was lost in the fire. If it had remained at Eagles' Nest, it would no doubt be there still?"

"Then I suppose they will never find the lost money as long as oak and ash grow," observed Frank. "It is a very unsatisfactory thing. George Atkinson ought to have remembered and spoken in time."

He was called away into the surgery, and Edina began to retie her bonnet-strings. Daisy had picked up some crochet-work.

"Why don't you take your bonnet off, Edina, and stay?"

"Because I must go home, dear."

"Not before you have had some supper. Not stay for it! Why can't you stay?"

"I do not like going back so late."

"As if any one would hurt you!"

"I do not fear that. But I am not London bred, you know, Margaret, and cannot quite overcome my dislike to London streets at night."

"Oh, very well. No one cares to be with me now."

Edina looked at her. It was not the first indication by several that Mrs. Frank Raynor had given of a spirit of discontent.

"Will you tell me what is troubling you, Margaret? Something is, I know."

"How do you know?"

"Because I perceive it. I detect it every time I see you."

"It's nothing at all," returned Daisy—who would not have spoken of her jealousy for the world. "That is, nothing that any one could help or hinder."

"My dear," said Edina, bending nearer to her, her sweet voice sounding like music, "that some grievance or other is especially trying you, I think I cannot mistake. But oh, remember one thing, and take comfort. In the very brightest and happiest lot, lurks always some sorrow. Every rose, however lovely, must have its thorn. We ought not, in the true interest of our lives, to wish it otherwise. God sends clouds, Margaret, as well as sunshine. He will guard you whilst trouble lasts, if you only bear patiently and put yourself under His care; and He will bring you out of trouble in His own good time. *Trust to Him*, my dear, for He is a sure refuge."

And when Edina had left, Frank escorting her through the more narrow streets, Daisy burst into tears, and sobbed bitterly. Indulging this jealousy might be very gratifying to her temper; but it had lasted long, and at times she felt ill and weak.

"If God cared for me He would punish that Rosaline Bell," was her comment on Edina's words. "Lay her up with a broken leg, or something."

VI

Under the Church Walls

I cannot buy the bonnet unless you will make the alteration at once. Now: so that I may take it home with me in the carriage."

The speaker was Mrs. Townley. Daisy was spending the day with her in Westbourne Terrace, and they had come out shopping. Mrs. Townley had fallen in love with a bonnet she saw in a milliner's window in Oxford Street; she entered the shop and offered to buy the bonnet, subject to some alteration. The proprietor of the business seemed rather unwilling to make it.

"I assure you, madam, it looks better as it is," she urged. "Were we to substitute blue flowers for the grey and carry the side higher, it would take away all its style at once."

Mrs. Townley somewhat hesitated. If there was one thing she went in for, above all else, it was "style." But she liked to have her own way also, and thought a great deal of her own taste.

"Three parts of these milliners object to any suggested alteration only to save themselves trouble," she said aside to Daisy. "Don't you think it would look better as I propose?"

"I hardly know," replied Daisy. "If we could first see the alteration, we might be able to judge."

But, to make the change, unless the bonnet was first bought, Madame François, the milliner, absolutely refused. It would ruin it, she said, for another customer. Of course she would alter it, if madam insisted after purchasing the bonnet; but she must again express her opinion that it would spoil its style.

The discussion was carried on with animation, madame's accent being decidedly English, in spite of her name. Mrs. Townley still urged her own opinion, but less strenuously; for she would not have risked losing the "style" for the world.

"I will call my head milliner," said madame at length. "Her taste is very superior. Mam'selle, go and ask Miss Bell to step here."

Mam'selle—a young person, evidently French—left her place behind the counter and went into another room. Every pulse in Daisy's body seemed to tingle to her fingers' ends when she came back with

Rosaline. Quiet, self-contained, without a smile on her face to betray any gladness of heart there might be within, Rosaline gave her opinion when the case was submitted to her. She took the bonnet in her hand, and kept it there, for a minute, or so, looking at it.

"I think, madame," she said to her mistress, "that if some grey flowers of a lighter shade were substituted for these, it would be prettier. Blue flowers would spoil the bonnet. As to the side, it certainly ought not to be carried higher. It is the right height as it is."

"Then take it, and change the flowers at once, Miss Bell," said madame, upon Mrs. Townley's signifying her assent to the suggestion. "The lady will wait. Miss Bell's taste is always to be depended upon," added madame, as Rosaline went away with the bonnet.

"How extremely good-looking she is!" exclaimed Mrs. Townley: who had never seen Rosaline before, and of course knew nothing about her. "Quite beautiful."

"Yes," assented madame. "When I engaged her I intended her to be in this front-room and wait on customers; for it cannot be denied that beauty attracts. But Miss Bell refused, point-blank: she had come to be in my work-room, she said, not to serve. Had I insisted, she would have left."

"Is she respectable?"

The question came from Daisy. Swelling with all sorts of resentful and bitter feelings, she had allowed her anger to get the better of her discretion; and the next moment felt ashamed of herself. Madame François did not like it at all.

"Res-pect-able!" she echoed with unnecessary deliberation. "I do not understand the question, madam."

Daisy flushed crimson. Mrs. Townley had also turned a surprised look upon her sister.

"Miss Bell is one of the best-conducted young persons I ever knew," pursued madame. "Steady and quiet in manner at all times, as you saw her now. She is very superior indeed; quite a lady in her ways and thoughts. Before she came to me, nearly two years ago, she had a business of her own down in Cornwall. That is, her aunt had; and Miss Bell was with her."

"She looks very superior indeed, to me," said Mrs. Townley, wishing to smooth away her sister's uncalled-for remark: "her tones are good. Have you any dentelle-de-Paris?"

The bonnet soon reappeared: but it was not brought by Rosaline.

Mrs. Townley chose some lace; paid the bill, and left. As Daisy followed her sister into the carriage, her mind in a very unpleasant whirl, she knew that the matter which had puzzled her—never seeing her husband abroad with Rosaline—was now explained. Rosaline was here by day; but, she supposed, went home at night.

It was so. The reader may remember that one evening when Frank went in to see Dame Bell soon after she had come to London, she had told him that Rosaline had gone to Oxford Street on some mysterious errand: mysterious in so far as that Rose had not disclosed what she went for. The fact was, that Rosaline had then gone to this very milliner's by appointment, having procured a letter of introduction to her from a house of business in Falmouth, with the view of tendering her services. For she knew that her mother's income was too small to live on comfortably, and it would be well if she could increase it. Madame François, pleased with her appearance and satisfied with the letter she brought, engaged her at once. Rosaline had been there ever since: going up in a morning and returning home at night. The milliner had wished her to be entirely in the house, but she could not leave her mother.

On this day, as usual, Rosaline sat at her work in the back-room, planning out new bonnets—that would be displayed afterwards in the window as "the latest fashion from Paris:" and directing the young women under her. That she had a wonderful and innate taste for the work was recognized by all, and Madame François had speedily made her superintendent of the room. The girl, as madame thought, always seemed to have some great care upon her: when questioned upon the point, Rosaline would answer that she was uneasy respecting the decaying health of her mother.

More thoughtful than usual, more buried in the inward life, for the appearance of Mrs. Frank Raynor, whom she knew by sight, had brought back old reminiscences of Trennach, Rosaline sat to-day at her employment until the hours of labour had passed. Generally speaking she went home by omnibus, though she sometimes walked. She walked this evening: for it was mild and pleasant, and she felt in great need of fresh air. So that it was tolerably late when she arrived home: very nearly half-past nine.

The first thing to be noticed was, that her mother's chair was empty: the room also. Rosaline passed quickly into the bedchamber, and saw that her mother had undressed and was in bed.

"Why, mother! what's this for? Are you not well?"

"Not very," sighed the dame. "Your supper is ready for you on the table, Rose."

"Never mind my supper, mother," replied Rose, snuffing the candle, and putting two or three things straight in the room generally, after taking off her bonnet. "Tell me what is the matter with you. Do you feel worse?"

"Not much worse—that I know of," was the answer. "But I grew weary, and thought I should be better in bed. For the past week, or more, I can't get your poor father out of my head, Rose: up or in bed, he is always in my mind, and it worries me."

"But you know, mother, this cannot be good for you—as I have said," cried Rosaline: for she had heard the same complaint once or twice lately.

"What troubles me is this, child—how did he come by his death? That's the question I've wanted answered all along; and now it seems never to leave me."

Rosaline drooped her head. No one but herself knew how terribly the subject tried her.

"Blase Pellet called in at dusk for a minute or two to see how I was," resumed Mrs. Bell. "When I told him how poor Bell had been haunting my mind lately, and how the prolonged mystery of his fate seemed to press upon me, he nodded his head like a bobbing image. 'I want to know how he came by his death,' I said to him. 'The want is always upon me.' 'I could tell, if I chose,' said he, speaking up quickly. 'Then why don't you tell? I insist upon your telling,' I answered. Upon that, he drew in, and declared he had meant nothing. But it's not the first time he has thrown out these hints, Rosaline."

"Blase is a dangerous man," spoke Rosaline, her voice trembling with anger. "And he could be a dangerous enemy."

"Well, I don't see why you should say that, Rose. He is neither your enemy nor mine. But I should like to know what reason he has for saying these things."

"Don't listen to him, mother; don't encourage him here," implored Rosaline. "I'm sure it will be better for our peace that he should keep away. And now—will you have some arrowroot to-night, or—"

"I won't have anything," interrupted Dame Bell. "I had a bit of supper before I undressed and a drop of ale with it. I shall get to sleep if I can: and I hope with all my heart that your poor father will not be haunting me in my dreams."

Rosaline carried away the candle, and sat down to her own supper in the next room. But she could not eat. Mr. Blase Pellet's reported words were quite sufficient supper for her, bringing before her all too vividly the horror of that dreadful night. Would this state of thraldom in which she lived ever cease, she asked herself; would she ever again, as long as the world should last for her, know an hour that was not tinged with its fatal remembrances and the fears connected with them.

In the morning her mother said she was better, and rose as usual. This was Saturday. When Rosaline reached home in the afternoon, earlier than on other days, she found her stirring about at some active housework. But on the Sunday morning she remained in bed, confessing that she felt very poorly. Rosaline wanted to call in Mr. Raynor: but her mother told her not to be silly; she was not ill enough for that.

The internal disorder which afflicted Mrs. Bell, and would eventually be her death, was making slow but sure progress. Frank Raynor—and his experience was pretty extensive now—had never known a similar case develop so lingeringly. He thought she might have a year or two's life in her yet. Still, it was impossible to say: a change might occur at any moment.

On this Sunday afternoon, when she and Rosaline were sitting together after dinner, Mr. Blase Pellet walked in. Rosaline only wished she could walk out. She would far rather have done so. But she forced herself to be civil to him.

"Look here," said Blase, taking a newspaper out of his pocket when he had sat some minutes. "This advertisement must concern those Raynors that you know of. I'll read it to you."

"'Lost. Lost. A small carved ebony desk. Was last seen at Eagles' Nest in the month of June more than two years ago. Any one giving information of where it may be found, or bringing it to Mr. Street, solicitor, of Lawyers' Row, shall receive ten guineas reward.'

"Those Raynors, you know, came into the Eagles' Nest property, and then had to turn out of it again," added Blase.

"Ten guineas reward for an ebony desk!" commented Mrs. Bell. "I wonder what was in it?"

Blase did not receive an invitation to stay tea this afternoon, though he probably expected it. However, he was not one to intrude unwished for, and took his departure.

"I had a great mind to ask him what he meant by the remark he made the other evening about your poor father," said Mrs. Bell to Rosaline as he went out.

"Oh, mother, let it be!" exclaimed Rosaline in piteous tones, her pale face turning hectic. "He cannot know anything that would bring peace to you or me."

"Well, I should like my tea now," said Dame Bell. "And I should have asked him to stay, Rose, but for your ungracious looks."

Rosaline busied herself with the tea, which they took almost in silence. While putting the things away afterwards, Rosaline made some remark: which was not answered. Supposing her mother did not hear, she spoke again. Still there came no reply, and Rose looked round. Mrs. Bell was lying back on the sofa, apparently insensible.

"It was the pain, child," she breathed, when Rosaline had revived her; but she had not quite fainted; "the sharp, sudden pain here. I never had it, I think, as badly as that."

Like a ghost she was still, with a pinched look in her face. Rosaline was frightened. Without saying anything to her mother, she wrote a hasty line to Frank, to ask if he would come round, twisted it up three-cornered fashion, and despatched it by the landlady's daughter.

The note arrived just as Frank Raynor and his wife were beginning to think of setting out for evening service. Frank chanced to have gone into a small back-room near the kitchen, where he kept his store of drugs, and Daisy was alone when Sam came in, the note held between his fingers.

"For master, please, ma'am; and it is to be given to him directly."

With an impatient word—for Daisy knew what these hastily-written, unsealed missives meant, and she did not care to go to church at night alone—she untwisted it, and read the contents.

Dear Mr. Raynor,
  "If you could possibly come round this evening, I should be very much obliged to you. My mother has been taken suddenly worse, and I do not like her looks at all.

Very truly yours,
R. B.

"The shameless thing!" broke forth Mrs. Frank Raynor in her rising anger. "She writes to him exactly as if she were his equal!"

Folding the note again, she threw it on the table, and went upstairs to put on her bonnet. It did not take her long. Frank was only returning to the parlour as she went down.

"Oh," said he, opening the note and reading it, "then I can't go with you to-night, Daisy. I am called out."

No answer.

"I will take you to the church-door and leave you there," he added, tossing the note into the fire.

"Of course you could not stay the service with me and attend to your patient afterwards!" cried Daisy, not attempting to suppress the sarcasm in her tone.

"No, I cannot do that. It is Mrs. Bell I am called to."

"Oh! Of all people *she* must not be neglected."

"Right, Daisy. I would neglect the whole list of patients rather than Mrs. Bell."

He spoke impulsively, pained by her look and tone. But had he taken time to think, he would not have avowed so much. The avowal meant nothing—at least, as Daisy interpreted it. But for him, Francis Raynor, Mrs. Bell's husband might have been living now. This lay on his conscience, and rendered him doubly solicitous for the poor widow. To Frank it had always seemed that, in a degree, she had belonged to him since that fatal night.

But Daisy knew nothing of this; and the impression the words made upon her was unfortunate, for she could only see matters from her own distorted point of view. It was for Rosaline's sake he was anxious for the mother, reasoned her mind, and it had now come to the shameful pass that he did not hesitate to declare it—even to her, his wife! Perhaps the woman was not even ill—the girl had resorted to this ruse that they might spend an evening together!

She kept her face turned to the fire lest he should see her agitation: she pressed her hands upon her chest, to still its laboured breathing. Frank was putting on his overcoat, for it was a cool night, and noticed nothing. Thus they started: Daisy refusing to take his arm, on the plea of holding up her dress: refusing to let him carry her Prayer-book; giving no reply to the few remarks he made. The church bells were chiming, the stars were bright in the frosty sky.

Under the silence and gloom of the church walls, away from the lights inside and out, Frank stopped, and laid his hand upon his wife's.

"You are vexed, Daisy, because I cannot go to church; but when my patients really need me I must not and will not neglect them. For a long time now you have seemed to live in a state of constant discontent and resentment against me. What the cause is, I know not. I do not give you any, as far as I am aware. If it is that you are dissatisfied with our present position—and I am not surprised that you should be—I can only say how much for your sake I regret that I cannot alter it. But that is what I am not yet able to do; and to find your vexation constantly turned upon me is hard to bear. Let us, rather, look forward to better days, and cheer on one another with the hope."

He wrung her hand and turned away. His voice had been so loving and tender, and yet so full of pain, that Daisy found her eyes wet with sudden tears. She went into church. What with resentment against her husband, her own strong sense of misery, and this softened mood, life seemed very sad to her that night.

And as the service proceeded, and the soothing tones of the sweet chant chosen for the *Magnificat* fell on her ear and heart, the mood grew more and more softened. Daisy cried in her lonely pew. Hiding her face when she knelt she let the tears rain down. A vision came over her of a possible happy future: of Frank's love restored to her as by some miracle; of Rosaline Bell and these wretched troubles, lost in the memory of the past; of the world being fair for them again, and she and her husband walking hand in hand, down the stream of time. Poor Daisy let her veil fall when she rose, that her swollen eyes should not be seen.

And the sermon soothed her too. The text was one that she especially loved: "Come unto me, all ye that labour and are heavy laden, and I will give you rest." Daisy thought none had ever been so heavily laden before as she was; just as the lightly chastened are apt to think.

"If I can only be a little more pleasant with him, and have patience," said she to herself, "who knows but things may work round again."

But the heart of man is rebellious, as all the world knows; especially rebellious is the heart of woman, when it is filled with jealous fancies. The trouble to which Mrs. Frank Raynor was subjected might bear precious fruit in the future, but it was not effecting much good in the present. No sooner was she out of church, and the parson's impressive voice and the sweet singing had faded on her ear, than all the old rancour came rushing up to the surface again.

"I wonder if he is there still?" she thought. "Most likely. I wish I could find out!"

Instead of turning her steps homeward, she turned them towards West Street, and paced twice before the house that contained Dame

Bell and her daughter. A light shone behind the white window blind, indicating the probability that the room had inmates; but Daisy could not see who they were. She turned towards home, and had almost reached it when Frank came hastily out of the surgery, a bottle of medicine in his hand.

"Is it you, Daisy? I began to think you were late. I meant to come to the church and fetch you, but found I could not."

"Shall I walk with you?" asked Daisy, trying to commence carrying out the good resolutions she had made in church, and perhaps somewhat pacified by his words. "It is a fine night."

For answer he took her hand, and placed it within his arm. Ah, never would there have been a better husband than Frank Raynor, if she had only met him kindly.

"Who is the medicine for?" asked Daisy.

"For Dame Bell. I am walking fast, Daisy, but she ought to have it without delay."

"Have you been with her all this time?"

"Yes. I was coming away when she had a sort of fainting-fit, the second this evening; and it took more than half-an hour to get her round."

"She is really ill, then?"

"Really ill!" echoed Frank in surprise. "Why, Daisy, she is dying. I do not mean dying to-night," he added; "or likely to die immediately; but that which she is suffering from will gradually kill her. My uncle suspected from the first what it would turn out to be."

Daisy said no more, and the house was gained. As Frank rang the bell, she left his arm and went a few steps away; beyond sight of any one who might open the door, but not beyond hearing of any conversation that might take place.

Rosaline appeared. Frank put the bottle into her hand.

"I brought it round myself, Rosaline, that I might be sure it came quickly. Has there been another fainting-fit?"

"No, not another, Mr. Frank," replied Rosaline. "She is in bed now and seems tranquil."

"Well, give her a dose of this without delay."

"Very well, sir. I—I wish you would tell me the truth," she went on in a somewhat agitated voice.

"The truth as to what?"

"Whether she is much worse? Dangerously so."

"No, I assure you she is not: not materially so, if you mean that. Of course—as you know yourself, Rosaline, or I should not speak of it to you—she will grow worse and worse with time."

"I do know it, sir, unfortunately."

"But I think it will be very gradual; neither sudden nor alarming. This evening's weakness seems to me to be quite exceptional. She must have been either exerting or exciting herself: I said so upstairs."

"True. It is excitement. But I did not like to say so before her. For the past few days she has been complaining that my father worries her," continued Rosaline, dropping her voice to a whisper. "She says he seems to be in her mind night and day: asleep, she dreams of him; she dwells on him. And oh, what a dreadful thing it all is!"

"Hush, Rosaline!" whispered Frank in the same cautious tones: and as Daisy's ears could not catch the conversation now, she of course thought the more. "The fancy will subside. At times, you know, she has had it before."

"Blase Pellet excites her. I know he does. Only the other day he said something or other."

"I wish Blase Pellet was transported!" cried Frank quickly. "But it—it cannot be helped, Rosaline. Give your mother half a wine-glass of this mixture at once."

"I am so much obliged to you for all, sir," she gently said, as he shook hands with her. "Oh, and I beg your pardon for asking another question," she added as he was turning away. "I have been thinking that I ought perhaps to leave my situation and stay at home with my mother. I always meant to do so when she grew worse. Do you see any necessity for it?"

"Not yet. Later of course you must do it: and perhaps it might be as well that you should be at home to-morrow, though the people of the house are attentive to her. You may rely upon me to tell you when the necessity arrives."

"Thank you, Mr. Frank. Good-night."

"Good-night, Rose."

Frank held out his arm to his wife. She took it, and they walked home together. But this time she was very chary in answering any remark he made, and did not herself volunteer one. The interview she had just witnessed had only served to augment the sense of treason that filled the heart of Mrs. Frank Raynor.

VII

Meeting Again

Time flew on. Summer had come round again: and it was now close upon three years since Mrs. Raynor and her children had quitted Eagles' Nest. Certainly, affairs could not be said to be progressing with them. The past winter and spring had again brought trouble. The three younger children were attacked with scarlatina, and it had left Kate so long ill that much care had to be taken with her. Mrs. Raynor was laid up at the same time for several weeks with bronchitis; and the whole nursing fell upon Edina.

With so much on her hands, and Mrs. Raynor invalided, Edina could not continue to do the work which helped to keep them. A little of it she continued to take, but it was very little: and she had to sit up at night and steal hours from her rest to accomplish even so much. This did not please the people who supplied her with it; they evidently did not care to continue to supply her at all; and when things came round again, and she and Mrs. Raynor would have been glad to do the same quantity of work as before, the work was not forthcoming. Their employment failed.

Such, in these early days of June, was the state of affairs: the family pinching and starving more than ever, Charles wearing out his days at the office, Alice teaching at Mrs. Preen's. Never had the future looked so dark as it was looking now.

One day when they were at dinner, Alice came in. Perhaps the little pinched faces around the scanty board—and both Kate's and Robert's looked pinched—struck unpleasantly upon Alice, for she was evidently in less good spirits than usual. She had come down by the omnibus, and taken them by surprise.

An idea, like a fear, flashed into the mind of Mrs. Raynor. It was so very unusual for Alice to come down in this unexpected manner. "You have brought bad news, child!" she faintly said. "What is it?"

And, for answer, Alice burst into tears. The knowledge of their home privations was to her as a very nightmare, for she had a warm heart. What with that and other thoughts, her spirits were always more or less subdued.

"I don't know how to tell you," she cried; "but it is what I have come to do. Mamma, I am going to leave Mrs. Preen's."

Mrs. Raynor sank back in her chair. "Oh, child! For what reason?"

Alice explained as she dried her eyes. Mrs. Preen, who had not been in strong health lately, was ordered for a lengthened term to her native place, Devonshire, where she would stay with her mother. She could not take her two elder children with her, neither did she care to leave them at home during her absence. So they were to be placed at school, and Alice had received notice to leave at the end of a month.

"If I were sure of getting another situation at once, I would not mind it so much," she said. "But it is the uncertainty that frightens me. I cannot afford to be out of a situation."

"Misfortunes never come alone," sighed Mrs. Raynor.

"Let us hope for the best," said Edina. "A whole month is a good while, Alice, and we can make inquiries for you at once. Perhaps Mr. Jones at the library can hear of something. I will speak to him: he is very kind and obliging."

"Do you ever come across that Bill Stane now, Alice?" cried Alfred, as he picked up his cap to go off to school. "We saw in the paper that Sir Philip was dead. That is, we saw something about his will."

"He comes now and then to Mrs. Preen's," replied Alice, blushing vividly, for she could not hear William Stane's name without emotion. "What did you see about Sir Philip's will?" she added, as carelessly as she could speak.

"Oh, I don't know—how his money was left, I think Charley reckoned up that Bill Stane would have ten thousand pounds to his share. Charley says he is getting on at the Bar like a house on fire."

"Shall you not be late, Alfred?"

"I am off now. Good-bye; Alice. It will be jolly, you know, if you come home."

"Not jolly for the dinners," put in poor Katie, who had learnt by sad experience what a difference an extra one made.

"Oh, bother the dinners!" cried Alfred, with all a schoolboy's improvidence. "I'll eat bread-and-cheese. Goodbye, Alice."

"Did you chance to hear what Sir Philip died of, Alice?" questioned Mrs. Raynor, when the doors had done banging after Alfred.

"No, mamma."

"But you see William Stane sometimes, don't you?"

"Yes, I see Mr. Stane now and then. Not often. He has not said anything about his father in my hearing. When I first went to Mrs. Preen's he was very cold and distant; but lately he has been much more friendly. But we do not often meet."

"Well, child, I can only say how unfortunate it is that you should lose your situation. It may be so difficult to get another."

Another matter, that had been giving Mrs. Raynor and Edina concern for some little time, was the education of the children. Alfred ought now to go to a better school; Robert ought to be at one. The child was eight years old. Sometimes it had crossed Edina's mind to wish he could be got into Christ's Hospital: she thought it high time, now that Alice was coming home, to think about it practically. If poor little Bob could be admitted there, it would make room for Alice.

Talking it over with Mrs. Raynor and Charles that same evening, it was decided that the first step towards it must be to obtain a list of the governors. It might be that one of that body had known something of Major Raynor in the days gone by, and would help his little son. How was the list to be procured? They knew not, and went to bed pondering the question.

"I will go to the library and ask Mr. Jones," said Edina the next morning. "Perhaps he has one."

Mr. Jones had not a list, but thought he knew where he could borrow one. And he did so, and left it at the door in the after-part of the day. Edina sat down to study it.

"Here is a name almost at the beginning that we know," she said, looking up with a smile.

"Is there!" exclaimed Charles, with animation, and taking an imaginative view of Robert, yellow-stockinged and bareheaded. "Whose name is it, Edina?"

"George Atkinson, Esquire, Eagles' Nest," read out Edina.

"How unfortunate!" exclaimed Mrs. Raynor. "The very man to whom we cannot apply."

"The very man to whom we will apply," corrected Edina. "If you will not do so, Mary, I will."

"Would you ask a favour of *him?*"

"Yes," said Edina emphatically. "Mr. Atkinson has not behaved well to you: let us put it in his power to make some slight reparation."

"Edina, I—I hope I am not uncharitable or unforgiving, but I do not feel that I *can* ask him," breathed poor Mrs. Raynor.

"But I don't want you to ask him, Mary; I will do that," returned Edina. "Perhaps I shall not *like* doing it more than you would; but the thought of poor little Robert will give me courage."

"Those governors have only a presentation once in three years, I fancy," observed Charles. "George Atkinson may have given away his next turn."

"We can only ascertain, Charley. And now—I wonder how we are to find his address? I hope he is in England!"

"He is at Eagles' Nest, Edina."

"At Eagles' Nest!" repeated Edina.

"He took possession of it six months ago, and gave Fairfax, who was in it, a house close by. And I know he is there still, for only a day or two ago I saw Preen address a letter to him."

"Well, I am glad to hear it, for now I shall go to him instead of writing," concluded Edina. "In these cases a personal application is generally of more use than a written one. And, Mary, you will, at any rate, wish me God speed."

"With my whole heart," replied Mrs. Raynor.

Once mere Edina Raynor stood before the gates of Eagles' Nest. As she walked from the station, the great alteration in the place struck her. Not in Eagles' Nest itself: that looked the same as ever: but in its surroundings. The land was well-cared for and flourishing; the cottages had been renovated into decent and healthy tenements; the row of ugly skeletons had been completed; all were filled with contented inhabitants; and the men and women that Edina saw about as she passed, looked respectable and happy. None could look on the estate of Eagles' Nest as it was now, and not see how good and wise was its ruler.

"Is Mr. Atkinson at home?" asked Edina, as a servant whom she did not know answered her ring.

"He is at home, ma'am, but I do not think you can see him," was the answer. "Mr. Atkinson is very unwell, and does not see visitors."

"I think he will perhaps see me," said Edina. And she took a leaf from her pocket-book, and wrote down her name, adding that she wished to see him very much.

The man showed her to a room. He came back immediately, and ushered her into his master's presence. As she entered, George Atkinson rose from a sofa on which he had been lying near the window, and went forward to meet her.

"Edina!"

The old familiar name from the once loved lips—nay, perhaps loved still: who knew?—in the old familiar voice, brought a tremor to her heart and a tear to her eye. Mr. Atkinson handed her to a chair and sat down in another. The window stood open to the delicious summer air, the morning sunshine—for Edina had come early, and it was not yet much past eleven—to the charming landscape that lay stretched around in the distance. But the impulse that had prompted the warm greeting seemed to die away again, and he addressed her more coldly and calmly.

"Your coming here this morning seems to me to be a very singular coincidence. You see that letter on the table, just ready for the post: have the kindness to read the address."

Edina did so. It bore her own name: and was addressed to the "Care of Charles Raynor, Messrs. Prestleigh and Preen's."

"I did not know your address. That it was somewhere in or near London, I did know, but not the exact locality. The letter contains only a request that you would kindly come down to me here."

"I!" exclaimed Edina.

"Yes. I wanted to see you. But I will ring for my housekeeper to show you to a room where you can take your bonnet off.

"I have not come to remain," replied Edina. "Half-an-hour will be more than enough to transact my business with you.

"But half-an-hour will not transact mine with you. Remain the day with me," he pleaded, "and enliven a poor invalid for a short time." And Edina made no further objection.

When she returned to the room, looking cool and fresh in her summer muslin, old though it might be, with her brown hair braided from her pleasant face, and the brown eyes sweet and earnest as of yore, George Atkinson thought how little, how very little she was altered. It is these placid faces that do not change. Neither had he changed very much. He looked ill, and wore a beard now; a silky brown beard; but his face and eyes and voice were the same. And somehow, now that she was in his presence, heard that musical voice, and met the steadfast, kindly look in the grey eyes, she almost forgot her resentment against him for his conduct to the Raynors.

"You are a governor of Christ's Hospital, I believe," she began, entering upon her business at once as she resumed her seat.

"I am."

"I came here to ask for your next presentation to it. Is it promised?"

"Not yet. It falls due next year."

"Then will you promise it to me?" continued Edina. "It is for the youngest child of Mrs. Raynor. Will you give it to him?"

"No."

"No!" she repeated, tone and spirit falling with the disappointment. "But why not?"

"I have a boy in my eye who is badly in want of it: more than Mrs. Raynor's son will be."

"It is almost impossible that any boy can want it more than poor Robert does."

"In that matter our opinions differ, Miss Raynor."

"And it would be making some trifling reparation to the family."

"Reparation for what?"

"For—what you did," answered Edina, hesitating for a moment and then speaking up bravely. "For turning them out of Eagles' Nest."

"What would you have done in my place?" questioned Mr. Atkinson good-humouredly. "Have left them in quiet possession of Eagles' Nest?"

"I—don't—know—whether I should, or not," hesitated Edina, for the question puzzled her. "Of course Eagles' Nest was legally yours, and I cannot say you were wrong to take it. But I think you might in some way have softened the blow. *I* could not have turned a family from their home and not inquired how they were to live in the future."

"I am aware you could not: for, unless I am mistaken, it was you who provided them with another. The Raynors wanted a lesson read to them, and it was well they should have it. What did I find when I came home; what did I hear? Was there a single good act done by any one of them whilst they were at Eagles' Nest? How did they use the property they came into: well?—or disgracefully? Yes, I repeat it, disgracefully. Things were going to rack and ruin. The poor tenants were ground down to the dust, the uttermost farthing of rent was exacted from them, whilst they were uncared for; body and soul alike abandoned, to get through life as they could, or to perish. And all for what?—to add to the pride, the folly and the prodigality of the Raynors. Could you approve of all this, Edina, or find excuse for it?"

She shook her head in the negative. He seemed to have called her Edina again unconsciously.

"It was self with them all; nothing but self, from Major Raynor downwards," he continued. "Show, extravagance, and vanity! Not a sound moral, or prudent, or worthy aim was inculcated on the children, not a penny given away in charity. Charles Raynor, the supposed heir, was an apt pupil in all this. He even had writs out against him, though he was under age."

Edina could not gainsay a word. It was all too true. "You had this reported to you on your return, I presume, Mr. Atkinson?"

"I had. But I did not take the report uncorroborated. I came down here, and saw for myself I was here for many weeks, watching."

Edina felt surprised. "How could that have been? The Raynors did not see you?"

"I came down unknown. No one knew me in the place, and I stayed on in my lodgings at Jetty the carpenter's and looked about me. The natives took me for an inquisitive man who was fond of poking himself into matters that did not concern him; a second Paul Pry. Mr. Charles Raynor, I heard, christened me the Tiger," added the speaker, with a smile.

Edina held her breath. What a singular revelation it was!

"I was in Australia when I heard that Mrs. Atkinson had left Eagles' Nest to me," he resumed. "The news reached me in a letter from herself, written only a day or two before her death; written chiefly to tell me where her will would be found—in the hands of my solicitors, Callard and Prestleigh. She also stated that a duplicate copy of the will was kept in this, her own house. But that, I think, must have been a mistake."

"Had one been here, it would have been found at the time of her death," remarked Edina.

"Just so. When this letter of hers arrived at Sydney," continued Mr. Atkinson, "I was travelling in the more remote and unfrequented parts of the country, and I did not receive it for some six months afterwards, on my return to Sydney. Rather an accumulation of letters awaited me at Sydney, as you may suppose; and I found, by those from my partner, Street, and his brother the lawyer, that the former will was alone known to exist, and that Major Raynor had entered into possession of Eagles' Nest. Now what did I at once resolve to do? Why, to leave him in possession of it; never to speak of this later will, but destroy it when I got back to England, and say nothing about it. The major had a right to Eagles' Nest; I had not any right at all to it: and the resolve did not cost me a moment's thought—"

"It is just as I should have expected you to act," put in Edina, her cheeks flushing.

"Don't give me more credit than I deserve, Miss Raynor. I cannot tell what I might have done had I been a poor man. Kept the estate, perhaps. But I was a rich one, and I did not want it. I sailed for England; and, on landing, went direct to London, to Street the banker's, arriving there at night. He chanced to be at home alone; his wife and children were at Brighton, and we had a few hours' quiet chat. The first thing I heard of, was the miserable state of affairs down here. Eagles' Nest was going to ruin, Street said, and the major and his son were probably going to ruin with it. 'I will go down incog. and see for myself,' I said to Street, 'and you need not tell any one of my return at present.' I did go down, as I have told you: went down the next day; and Street kept counsel as to my having returned to Europe, and when he wrote to me at Grassmere, addressed his letters to 'Mr. George.' There I stayed, looking about at my leisure."

"How was it my uncle Francis did not recognize you?"

"He never saw me. At first I kept out of his way lest he should do so; but I soon learnt that there was little chance of our meeting, as he never went beyond his own gates. Had he met me, I don't think he would have known me, my beard altered me so much; and I always pulled my broad-brimmed hat well on. No, I felt quite easy, and remained on until my purpose was answered."

He paused, as if recalling the scenes of that past time. Edina made no remark. Presently he resumed.

"What I saw here shocked me. I could not detect one redeeming point in the conduct of Major Raynor and his family, though I assure you I should have been glad to do so. To leave the estate in their hands would be little less than a sin, as I looked upon it, and a cruel wrong upon the poor people who lived on it. So I deliberated on my measures, and finally took them. Edwin Street announced my speedy return, and conveyed a letter from me (apparently written in Australia) to Callard and Prestleigh, informing them that they held the will, and ordering them to produce it, that it might be proved and acted upon. I was more than justified in what I did, as I thought then," emphatically concluded Mr. Atkinson, "and as I think now."

"Well—yes, I cannot say you were not," acquiesced Edina. "But it seemed to us so bitterly hard—never to inquire what became of the Raynors; never to offer them any help."

"Stay," said he. "I did inquire. I heard that Miss Edina Raynor had come forward from Trennach with her help, and had established

Mrs. Raynor in a school in which she was likely to do well. I heard that Charles Raynor was about to be taken by the hand by an old friend of his father's, one Colonel Cockburn, who meant to put him forward in the world. In short, I left England again in the belief that the Raynors were, in a smaller way, as prosperous as they had been at Eagles' Nest."

"What misapprehensions exist!" exclaimed Edina. "That home was soon lost again through a fire, and Colonel Cockburn only saw Charles to tell him he could not help him. Their life for the last three years has been one long course of humiliation, poverty and privation."

"Ay! and you have voluntarily shared it with them," he answered, looking straight into her eyes. "Well, they needed the lesson. But I would have been a friend to Charles Raynor had he allowed me, and not shown himself so haughtily upstart; and to his cousin the doctor also. When Charles was in a mess at Eagles' Nest, in danger of being arrested for debt, I asked him to confide his trouble to me and let me help him. Not a bit of it. He flung my words back in my face with as much scorn as if I had been a dog. So I let him go his own way: though I privately settled the debt for him. Had he known who I was, and that I had power to eject him and his family from their heritage, I could have understood his behaviour: but that was impossible, and I think I never met with so bad an example of conduct shown to a stranger. Yes: Charles Raynor needed a lesson read to him, and he has had it."

"Indeed he has. They all have. Charles Raynor is as true and good a young man now as he was once thoughtless and self-sufficient. There will be no fear of his lapsing in this life."

"I saw him a year ago in Preen's office," remarked Mr. Atkinson, "and liked his tones. Preen gives me an excellent account of him and his sister."

"They deserve it," said Edina. "But oh, you do not know what a struggle it is for us all," she added, her voice almost broken by emotion, "or what a boon it would be to get Robert into the Bluecoat School. If you did, I think you would grant it me."

"No, I should not," persisted he, smiling. "The presentation falls due next year; and by that time little Raynor will not want it. He may be back here again at Eagles' Nest."

Edina gazed at him. "What do you mean?" she gasped.

"I have not had particularly strong health—as you know; but a couple of months ago I was so ill as to fear the worst. It caused me to wish to revise my will, and to consider certain of its provisions. I think I shall leave Eagles' Nest to you."

"I won't have it," cried Edina, bursting into tears. "I will not. How can you be so unjust, Mr. Atkinson? What right have I to Eagles' Nest?"

"Right! You have shared your home with the Raynors when it was a humble one—for the home is virtually yours, I am told: you can do the like, you know, when you become rich."

"I will not have Eagles' Nest," she cried. "It is of no use to think of such a thing, for I will not. I have told you the Raynors are worthy of it themselves."

He almost laughed at her alarm; at the frightened earnestness with which she spoke.

"Well, well, the bequest is not made," he said in a changed tone; and an idea flashed over Edina that he had only been joking with her. "Very thankful I am to say that health and strength appear to be returning to me; the doctors think I have taken a turn, and shall soon be quite well again; better than I have been for years. So, as my death seems improbable, I have thought of making over Eagles' Nest to Charles Raynor by deed of gift. That request for your presence here," glancing at the letter on the table, "was to ask you whether he was so changed in heart and conduct that it might safely be done."

"Oh yes, indeed he is," responded Edina, drying her happy tears. "I told you so before I knew of this, and I told you only the truth."

"I fully believe you. But I must have an interview with him. Let him come down here on Saturday and remain with me until Monday morning. If I find that he may be fully trusted for the future, in a short time he and his mother will be back at Eagles' Nest. London will be hereafter my chief home. They shall come and see me there when they please: and I shall doubtless be welcome to come here occasionally."

"And you do not intend to go wandering again?"

"Never again. I have had enough of it. It may be, that I should have enjoyed better health had I been contented to take more rest. I have purchased the lease of a house in London, to which I shall remove on quitting Eagles' Nest. I am also looking out for some snug little property in this neighbourhood—which I have learned to like— and, when I can find it, shall purchase that."

"How was it," asked Edina, "that you did not take possession of Eagles' Nest when the Raynors left it? We were told you would do so."

George Atkinson smiled. "I had seen enough of Eagles' Nest

while staying at Jetty's. And perhaps I did not care to be recognized immediately by the community for that same prying individual."

"Have the lost bonds been found?"

"No. I feel more than ever convinced that they are in the ebony desk. Unless, indeed, your aunt left no money behind her; in which case there would of course be no bonds anywhere. I begin to think that whoever has the desk must have found and used the bonds."

"You have not heard of the desk?"

"No. The advertisements Street inserted in the newspapers brought forth no more result than the previous inquiries."

"Perhaps if a larger reward had been offered?" said Edina. "We thought the sum small."

"Ten guineas was the sum offered first; twenty afterwards. I suggested increasing it to fifty, or a hundred: but the cautious lawyers said no. Such a reward offered for a desk, would have betrayed that it contained something of value—if the possessor of the desk had not already found that out for himself. It was certainly singular that I should not have thought to ask whether the secret compartment of that desk had been searched when I first knew the bonds were being looked for; but I did not. It altogether escaped my memory."

A servant came in to lay the cloth for dinner: since his illness Mr. Atkinson had taken that meal at one o'clock. The tears rose to Edina's eyes as she sat down to the abundant table, and a choking sensation to her throat. George Atkinson noticed her emotion.

"What is it, Edina?"

"I was only wishing I could transport some of this to London," she answered, glancing at him through her wet eyelashes with a smile.

They sat at the open window again after dinner, talking of the past and the future, and Edina stayed to make tea for him—which came in early. As she put her hand into his, on saying farewell, he left a small case of money in it.

"Shall you be too proud to accept it for them?"

"I have not any pride," answered Edina with a grateful smile. "If I ever had any, the experience of the past three years has taken it out of me."

"I never intended to keep Eagles' Nest," he whispered. "I think you might have divined that, Edina. You knew me well once."

"And suppose Charles Raynor had continued to be unworthy?"

"Then Eagles' Nest would have passed away from him for ever. Its inheritor would have been Edina."

THE EVENING WAS GETTING ON at Mrs. Raynor's. Charles, who had been detained late at the office was sitting down to his frugal supper, which had been kept warm over the fire, and little Robert was in bed. They had been saying how late Edina was. Mrs. Raynor had a very bad headache.

"Let me place that cushion more comfortably for you mamma," said Charles.

"It will do very well as it is, my dear," she answered. "Get your supper: you must want it."

"Oh, not very much," said Charles, making a pretence of eating slowly, to conceal his hunger. "Alfred, do be quiet!—don't you know mamma is ill? Kate, sit down."

"There's Edina!" cried Alfred, clattering out to meet her in the passage.

She came in, looking pleased and gay, with sundry parcels in her hand. Kate and Alfred jumped round her.

"How have you sped, Edina?" asked Mrs. Raynor. "Has George Atkinson given Robert the presentation?"

"No; he will not give it him."

"I feared so. He must be altogether a hard-hearted man. May Heaven have mercy upon us!"

"It will, it will," said Edina. "I have always told you so."

She was undoing the papers. The young eyes regarding them were opened to their utmost width. Had a fairy been out with Edina? Buns, chocolate, a jar of marmalade, a beautiful pat of butter, and—what could be in that other parcel?

"Open it, Charley," said Edina.

He had left his supper to look on with the others, and did as he was told. Out tumbled a whole cargo of mutton chops. Ah, that was the best sight of all, dear as cakes and sweets are to the young! Mrs. Raynor could see nothing clearly for her glistening tears.

"I thought you could all eat a mutton chop for supper, Mary. I know you had scarcely any dinner."

"Are we *all* to have one?" demanded Alfred, believing Aladdin's lamp must really have been at work.

"Yes, all. Charley and mamma can have two if they like. Don't go on with your miserable supper, Charles."

"Robert," cried Kate, flying to the door, "Edina's come home, and she has brought up so many things, and a mutton chop apiece."

　　　　　　　　　　　　　　　　　　MRS. HENRY WOOD

Why, there he was, the audacious little Bob, peeping in in his white nightgown!

"A *whole* mutton chop!" cried he, amazed at the magnitude of the question.

"Yes, a whole one, dear," said Edina turning to him. "And not only for to-night. Every day you shall have a whole mutton chop, or something as good."

"And puddings too!" stammered Kate, the idea of the fairy becoming a certainty.

"And puddings too," said Edina. "Ah, children, I bring you such news! Did I not always tell you that God would remember us in His own good time? Mary, are you listening? Very soon you will all be back again at Eagles' Nest."

Charles's heart beat wildly. He looked at Edina to see if she were joking, his eyes fearfully earnest.

"I am telling you the truth, dear ones: Eagles' Nest is to be yours again, and our struggles and privations are over. George Atkinson never meant to keep it from you. You are to go down to him on Saturday, Charley, and stay over Sunday."

"I'll never abuse him again," said Charley, smiling to hide a deeper emotion. "But—my best coat is so shabby, you know, Edina. I am ashamed of it at church."

"Perhaps you may get another between now and then," nodded Edina.

"What's *this?*" cried Kate, touching the last of the parcels.

"A bottle of wine for mamma. She will soon look so fit and rosy that we shan't know her, for we shall have nothing to do but nurse her up."

"My goodness!" cried Kate. "Wine! Mamma, here's some wine for you!"

But there was no answer. Poor Mrs. Raynor lay back in her chair unable to speak, the silent tears stealing down her worn cheeks.

Charles bent over and kissed her. Little Bob, in his nightgown, crouched down by her side at the fire; whilst Edina, throwing off her shawl and bonnet, began to prepare for supper.

VIII

Hard Lines

Lying in her darkened chamber, sick almost unto death, was Mrs. Frank Raynor. A baby, a few days old, slept in a cot by the wall. No other child had been born to her, until now, since that season of peril at Eagles' Nest: and just as her life had all but paid the forfeit then, so it had again now. She was in danger still; she, herself, thought dying.

An attentive nurse moved noiselessly about the room. Edina stood near the bed, fanning the poor pale face resting on it. The window was wide open, behind the blind: for the invalid's constant cry throughout the morning had been, "Give me air!"

A light, quick step on the stairs, and Frank entered. He took the fan from Edina's tired hand, and she seized the opportunity to go down to the kitchen, to help Eve with the jelly ordered by Dr. Tymms; a skilful practitioner, who had been in constant attendance. Daisy opened her eyes to look at her husband, and the nurse quitted the room, leaving them together.

"You will soon be about again, my darling," said Frank, in his low, earnest, hopeful tones, that were worth more than gold in a sick chamber. "Tymms assures me you are better this morning."

"I don't want to get about," faintly responded Daisy.

"Not want to get about!" cried Frank, uncertain whether it would be best to treat the remark as a passing fancy arising from weakness, or to inquire farther into it—for everything said by his wife now bore this depressing tenor.

"And you ought to know that I cannot wish it," she resumed.

"But I do not know it, Daisy, my love. I do not know why you should speak so."

"I shall be glad to die."

Frank bent a little lower, putting down the fan. "Daisy, I honestly believe that you will recover; that the turning-point has come and gone. Tymms thinks so. Why, yesterday you could not have talked as you are talking now."

"I know I am dying. And it is so much the better for me."

He put his hand under the pillow, raising it slightly to bring her face nearer his, and spoke very tenderly and persuasively. He knew that she was *not* dying; that she was, in fact, improving.

"My darling, you are getting better; and will get better. But, were it as you think, Daisy, all the more reason would exist for telling me what you mean, and why you have so long been in this depressed state of mind. Let me know the cause, Daisy."

For a few minutes she did not reply. Frank thought that she was deliberating whether or not she should answer—and he was not mistaken. She closed her eyes again, and he took up the fan.

"I have thought, while lying here, that I should like to tell you before I die," spoke Daisy at last. "But you don't need to be told."

"I do. I do, indeed."

"It is because you no longer love me. Perhaps you never loved me at all. You care for some one else; not for me."

In very astonishment, Frank dropped the fan on the counterpane. "And who is—'some one else'?"

"Oh, you know."

"Daisy, this is a serious charge, and you must answer me. I do not know."

She turned her face towards him, without speaking. Frank waited; he was ransacking his brains.

"*Surely* you cannot mean Edina!"

A petulant, reproachful movement betrayed her anger. Edina! Who was an angel on earth, and so good to them all!—and older, besides. The tears began to drop slowly from her closed lashes, for she thought he must be trifling with her.

"You will be sorry for it when I am gone, Frank. *Edina!*"

"Who is it, Daisy?"

A flush stole into her white cheeks, and the name was whispered so faintly that Frank scarcely caught it.

"Rosaline Bell!" he repeated, gazing at her in doubt and surprise, for the thought crossed him that her senses might be wandering. "But, Daisy, suppose we speak of this to-morrow instead of now," he added as a measure of precaution. "You—"

"We will speak of it now, or never," she interrupted, as vehemently as any one can speak whose strength is at the lowest ebb. And the sudden anger Frank's words caused her—for she deemed he was acting altogether a deceitful part and dared not speak—nerved her to tell out her grievances more fully than she might otherwise have had courage to do. Frank listened to the accusation with apparent equanimity; to the long line of disloyal conduct he had been indulging in since the early days at Trennach down to the present hour. His simple attempt at refutation made no impression whatever: the belief was too long and firmly rooted in her mind to be quickly dispelled.

"I could have borne any trial better than this," concluded she, with laboured breathing: "all our misfortunes would have been as nothing to me in comparison. Don't say any more, please. Perhaps she will feel some remorse when she hears I am dead."

"We will let it drop now then, Daisy," assented Frank. "But I have had no more thought of Rosaline than of the man in the moon."

"Will you go away now, please, and send the nurse in?"

"What on earth is to be done?" thought Frank, doing as he was ordered. "With this wretched fancy hanging over her, she may never get well; never. Mental worry in these critical cases sometimes means death."

"How is she now?" asked Edina, meeting him on the stairs.

"Just the same."

"She seems so unhappy in mind, Frank," whispered Edina. "Do you know anything about it?"

"She is low and weak at present, you see," answered Frank, evasively. And he passed on.

Frank Raynor lapsed into a review of the past. Of the admiration he had undoubtedly given to Rosaline Bell at Trennach; of the solicitude he had evinced for her (or, rather, for her mother) since their stay in London. Of his constant visits to them: visits paid every three or four days at first; later, daily or twice a day—for poor Mrs. Bell was now near her end. Yes, he did see, looking at the years carefully and dispassionately, that Daisy (her suspicions having been, as she had now confessed, first aroused by the waiting-maid Tabitha) might have fancied she saw sufficient grounds for jealousy. She could not know that his friendship and solicitude for the Bells proceeded from a widely different cause. That clue would never, as he believed, be furnished to her so long as she should live.

"What a blessing it would be if some people were born dumb!" concluded Frank, thinking of Tabitha Float.

The slight symptoms of improvement continued; and at sunset Frank Raynor knew that his wife's condition would bear the carrying out of an idea he had formed. It was yet daylight outside, though the drawn curtains made the room dark, when Daisy was conscious of a sad, beautiful face bending over her, and an entreating voice whose gentle tones told of sadness.

"Don't shrink from me, Mrs. Frank Raynor," whispered Rosaline—for she it was. "I have come to strive to put straight what I hear has been so long crooked."

And the few words she spoke, spoke earnestly and solemnly, brought peace to the unhappy wife's heart. Daisy was too ill to feel much self-reproach then, but it was with some shame she learnt how mistaken she had been.

"Oh, believe me!" concluded Rosaline, "I have never had a wrong thought of Mr. Frank Raynor; nor he one of me. Had we been brother and sister, our intercourse with each other could not have been more open and simple."

"He—he liked you at Trennach, and you liked him," murmured poor Daisy, almost convinced, but repentant and tearful. "People talked about it."

"He liked me as an acquaintance, nothing more," sighed Rosaline, passing over all mention of her own early feelings. "He was fond of talking and laughing with me, and I would talk and laugh back again. I was light-hearted then. But never, I solemnly declare it, did a word of love pass between us. And, in the midst of it, there fell upon me and my mother the terrible grief of my father's unhappy death. I have never laughed since then."

"I have been thinking these past two years that he went to West Street only to see you," sobbed Daisy.

Rosaline shook her head. "He has come entirely for my mother. Without fee, for he will not take it, he has been unremittingly kind and attentive, and has soothed her pains on the way to death. God bless him for it! A few days, and I shall never see him again in this world. But I shall not forget what he has done for us; and God will not forget it either."

"*You* are not going to die, are you?" cried poor puzzled Daisy.

"I am going out to New Zealand," replied Rosaline. "As soon as I have laid my dear mother in her last home—and Death's shadow is even now upon her—I bid farewell to England for ever. We have relations who are settled near Wellington, and they are waiting to receive me. Were Mr. Raynor a free man and had never possessed any other ties on earth, there could be no question, now or ever, of love between him and me."

Daisy's delicate hand went out to clasp the not less delicate one that rested near her on the bed, and her cheeks took quite a red tinge for her own folly and mistakes in the past. A wonderful liking, fancy, admiration, esteem—she hardly knew what to call it—was springing up in her heart for this sad and beautiful young woman, whom she had so miserably misjudged.

"Forgive me my foolish thoughts," she whispered, quite a painful entreaty in her eyes. "I wish I had known you before: I would have made a friend of you."

"Thank you, thank you!" warmly responded Rosaline. "That is all I came to say; but it is Heaven's truth. I, the unconscious cause of the trouble, am more sorry for it than you can be. Farewell, Mrs. Raynor: for now I must go back to my mother. I shall ever pray for your happiness and your husband's."

"Won't you kiss me?" asked Daisy with a sob. And Rosaline bent over her and kissed her.

"Are you convinced now, Daisy?" questioned Frank, coming into the room when he had seen Rosaline out of the house. "Are you happier?"

All the answer she made was to lie on his arm and cry silently, abjectly murmuring something that he could not hear.

"I thought it best to ask Rosaline to come, as you would not believe me. When I told her of the mischief that was supposed to have been afloat, she was more eager to come than I to send her."

"Forgive me, Frank! Please don't be harsh with me! I am so ashamed of myself; so sorry!"

"It is over now; don't think about it any more," kissing her very fervently.

"I will never be so stupid again," she sobbed. "And—Frank—I think I shall—perhaps—get well now."

ROSALINE HAD SAID THAT DEATH's shadow lay upon her mother even while she was talking with Mrs. Raynor. In just twenty-four hours after that, Death himself came. When the day's sunlight was fading, to give place to the tranquil stars and to the cooler air of night, Mrs. Bell passed peacefully away to her heavenly home. She had been a great sufferer: she and her sufferings were alike at rest now.

It was some two hours later. The attendant women had gone downstairs, and Rosaline was sitting alone, her eyes dry but her heart overwhelmed with its anguish, when Blase Pellet came to make a call of inquiry. He had shown true anxiety for the poor sick woman, and had often brought her little costly dainties; such as choice fruit. And once—it was a positive fact—once when Rosaline was absent, Blase had sat down and read to her from the New Testament.

"Will you see her, Blase?" asked Rosaline, as he stood quiet and silent with the news. "She looks so peaceful."

Blase assented; and they went together into the death-chamber. Very peaceful. Yes: none could look more so.

"Poor old lady!" spoke Blase. "I'm sure I feel very sorry: almost as though it was my own mother. Was she sensible to the last?"

"Quite to the very last; and collected," replied Rosaline, suppressing a sob in her throat. "Mr. Frank Raynor called in the afternoon; and I know he saw that nothing more could be done for her, though he did not say so. She was very still after he left, lying with her eyes closed. When she opened them and saw me, she put up her hand for me to take it. 'I have been thinking about your father and that past trouble, dear,' she said. 'I am going to him: and what has never been cleared here will be made clear there.' They were nearly the last words she spoke."

"It's almost a pity but it had been cleared up for her here," said Blase. "It might have set her uncertainty at rest, don't you see. Sometimes I had three parts of a mind to tell her. She'd have thought a little less of Mr. Frank Raynor if I had told."

Rosaline, standing on one side the bed, cast a steady look on the young man, standing on the other. "Blase," she said, "I think the time has come for me to ask you what you mean. As you well know, it is not your first hint, by many, in regard to what you saw that fatal night at Trennach. I have wanted to set you right; but I was obliged to avoid the subject whilst my mother lived; for had the truth reached her she might have died of it."

"Died of it! Set me right!" repeated Blase, gazing back at Rosaline.

"By the words which you have allowed to escape you from time to time, I gather that you have believed my unfortunate father owed his death to Mr. Frank Raynor."

"So he did," said Blase.

"So he did *not*, Blase. It was I who killed my father."

The assertion seemed to confound him. But for the emotion that Rosaline was struggling with, her impressive tones, and the dead woman lying there, across whom they spoke, Blase might have deemed she was essaying to deceive him, and accorded her no belief.

"Are you doubting my words, Blase?" she asked. "Listen. In going home from Granny Sandon's that night, I took the street way, and saw you standing outside the shop, preparing to shut it up. You nodded to me across the street, and I thought you meant to follow me as soon as you were at liberty. When I was out of your sight, I quickened my pace, and should have been at home before you could have caught me up, but for meeting Clerk Trim's wife. She kept me talking for I cannot tell how long, relating some sad tale about an accident that had happened to her sister at Pendon. I did not like to leave her in the middle of it; but I got away as soon as I could, though I dare say a quarter-of-an-hour had been lost. As I reached the middle of the Plain, I turned and saw some one following me at a distance, and I made no doubt it was you. At that same moment, Mr. Frank Raynor met me, and began telling me of a fight that had taken place between Molly Janes and her husband, and of the woman's injuries, which he had then been attending to. It did not occupy above a minute, but during that time, whilst I was standing, you were advancing. I feared you would catch me up; and I wished Mr. Frank a hurried good-night, and ran across to hide behind the mounds whilst you passed by. He did not understand the motive of my sudden movement, and followed me to ask what was the matter. I told him: I had seen you coming, and I did not want you to join me. When I thought you must have gone by, I stole out to look; and, as I could not see you, thought what good speed you had made, to be already out of sight. It never occurred to me to suppose you had come to the mounds, instead of passing on."

"But I had come to them," interrupted Blase eagerly. "My eyes are keener than most people's, and I knew you both; and I saw you dart across, and Raynor after you. So I followed."

"Well—in very heedlessness, I ran up to the mouth of the shaft, and pretended to be listening for Dan Sandon's ghost. Mr. Raynor seized hold of me; for I was too near the edge, and the least false step might have been fatal. Not a moment had we stood there; not a moment; when a shout, followed by a blow on Mr. Raynor's shoulder, startled us. It was my poor father. He was raising his stick for another blow, when I, in my terror, pushed between him and Mr. Raynor to part them. With all my strength—and a terrified woman possesses strength—I flung them apart, not knowing the mouth of the pit was so near. *I flung my father into it, Blase.*"

"Good mercy!" exclaimed Blase.

"Mr. Frank Raynor leaped forward to save him, and nearly lost his own life in consequence; it was an even touch whether he followed my father, or whether he could balance himself backwards. I grasped his coat, and I believe—he believes—that that alone saved him."

"I saw the scuffle," gasped Blase. "I could have taken my oath that it was Raynor who pushed your father in."

"I am telling the truth in the presence of my dead mother and before Heaven," spoke Rosaline, lifting her hands in solemnity. "Do you doubt it, Blase Pellet?"

"No—no; I can't, I don't," confessed Blase. "Moonlight's deceptive. And the wind was rushing along like mad between my eyes and the shaft."

"I only meant to part them," wailed Rosaline. "And but that my poor father was unsteady in his gait that night, he need not have fallen. It is true I pushed him close to the brink, and there he tottered, in his unsteadiness, for the space of a second, and fell backwards: his lameness made him awkward at the best of times. A stronger man, sure of his feet, need not and would not have fallen in. But oh, Blase, that's no excuse for me! It does not lessen my guilt or my misery one iota. It was I who killed him: I, I!"

"Has Mr. Raynor known this all along?" asked Blase, whose faculties for the moment were somewhat confused.

Rosaline looked at him in surprise. "*Known it?* Why, he was an actor in it. Ah, Blase, you have been holding Mr. Raynor guilty in your suspicious heart; he knows you have; and he has been keeping the secret out of compassion for me, bearing your ill thoughts in patient silence. All these four years he has been dreading that you would bring the accusation against him publicly. It has been in your heart; I know it has; to accuse him of my father's murder."

"No, not really," said Blase, knitting his brows. "I should never have done it. I only wanted him to think I should."

"And, see you not what it would have involved? I honestly believe that Frank Raynor would never have cleared himself at my expense, whatever charge you might have brought, but he feared that I should speak and clear him. As I should have done. And that confession would have gone well-nigh to kill my poor mother. For my sake Mr. Raynor has borne all this; borne with you; and done what lay in his power to ward off exposure."

"He always favoured you," spoke Blase in crestfallen tones.

"Not for the sake of *that* has he done it," quickly returned Rosaline. "He takes his share of blame for that night's work; and *will* take it, although blame does not attach to him. Had he gone straight home as I bade him, and not followed me to the mounds, it would not have happened, he says; so he reproaches himself. And, so far, that is true. It was a dreadful thing for both of us, Blase."

"I wish it had been him instead of you," retorted Blase.

"It might have been better, far better, had I spoken at the time—or allowed Mr. Raynor to speak. To have told the whole truth—that I had done it, though not intentionally; and that my poor father was lying where he was—dead. But I did not; I was too frightened, too bewildered, too full of horror: in short, I believe I was out of my senses. And, as I did not confess at the time, I could not do so afterwards. Mr. Raynor would have given the alarm at the moment, but for me: later, when I in my remorse and distress would have confessed, he said it must not be. And I see that he was right."

Blase could only nod acquiescence to this: but his nod was a sullen one.

"You know that our old clergyman at Trennach, Mr. Pine, was in London last Easter and came here to see my mother," resumed Rosaline. "I privately asked him to let me have half-an-hour alone with him, and he said I might call on him at his lodgings. I went; and I told him what I have now told you, Blase; and at my request he got a lawyer there, who drew up this statement of mine in due form, and I swore to its truth and signed it in their presence. A copy of this, sealed and attested, has been handed to Mr. Raynor; Mr. Pine keeps another copy. I do not suppose they will ever have to be used; but there the deeds are, in case of need. It was right that some guarantee of the truth should be given to secure Mr. Raynor, as I was intending to go to the other end of the world."

"It sounds altogether like a tale," cried Blase.

"A very hideous one."

"And as to your going to the end of the world, Rosaline, you know that you need not do it. I am well off, now my father's dead, and—"

She held up her hand warningly. "Blase, *you* know that this is a forbidden subject. I shall never, never marry in this world: and, of all men in it, the two whom I would least marry are you and Mr. Raynor. He takes a share of that night's blame; you may take at least an equal share: for, had you not persisted in following me from Trennach, when you knew it would be distasteful to me, I should have had no need to seek refuge in the mounds, and the calamity could not have occurred. Never speak to me of marriage again, Blase."

"It's very hard lines," grumbled Blase.

"And are not my lines hard?—and have not Mr. Frank Raynor's been hard?" she asked with emotion. "But, oh, Blase," she softly added, "let us remember, to our consolation, that these 'hard lines' are only sent to us in mercy. Without them, and the discipline they bring, we might never seek to gain heaven."

IX

Tears

Alice Raynor was sitting in a small parlour at Mrs. Preen's, dedicated to herself and the children's studies, busily employed in correcting exercises. The afternoon sun shone upon the room, and she had drawn the table into the shade. Her head and hands were given to their work, but her deeper thoughts were far away: for there existed not a minute in the day that the anxiety caused by her uncertain prospects was not more or less present to her mind. She knew nothing of the new hopes relative to Eagles' Nest. In truth, those hopes, both to Mrs. Raynor and Edina, seemed almost too wonderful to be real; and as yet they refrained from giving them to Alice.

The corrections did not take very long, and then Alice laid down the pen and sat thinking. She felt hot and weary, and wished it was nearer tea-time. The old days at Eagles' Nest came into her thoughts. They very often did so: and the contrast they presented to these later ones always made her sad.

A slight tap at the door, and a gentleman entered: William Stane. Alice blushed through her hot cheeks when she saw who it was, and brushed the tears from her eyes. But not before he had seen them.

"I beg your pardon, Miss Raynor. Mrs. Preen is out, I hear."

"Yes, she is out with the two little girls."

"I am sorry. I have brought up some admission tickets for the Botanical flower-show: they were only given me this morning. Do you think Mrs. Preen will be back soon?"

"Not in time to use the tickets. They have gone to an afternoon-tea at Richmond."

"What a pity! It is the rose show. I—suppose you could not go with me?" added Mr. Stane in some hesitation.

"Oh dear, no," replied Alice, glancing at him in astonishment. "Thank you very much."

"Mrs. Preen would not like it, you think?"

"I am sure she would not. You forget that I am only the governess."

Down sat Mr. Stane on the other side the table, and began fingering absently one of the exercise-books, looking occasionally at Alice while he did so.

"What were you crying about?" he suddenly asked.

Alice was taken aback. "I—I don't think I was quite crying."

"You were very near it. What was the matter?"

"I am very sorry to have to leave," she truthfully answered. "Mrs. Preen is about to stay for a time in Devonshire, as perhaps you know, and the little girls are to go to school. So I am no longer wanted here."

"I should consider that a subject for laughter instead of tears. You will be spared work."

"Ah, you don't know," cried Alice, her tone one of pain. "If I do not work here, I must elsewhere. And the next place I get may be harder than this."

"And you were crying at the anticipation?"

"No. I was crying at the thought of perhaps not being able speedily to find another situation. I—suppose," she timidly added, "you do not happen to know of any situation vacant, Mr. Stane?"

"Why, yes, I believe I do. And I think you will be just the right person to fill it."

Her blue eyes brightened, her whole face lighted up with eagerness.

"Oh, if you can only obtain it for me! I shall be so thankful, for mamma's sake."

"But it is not as a governess."

"Not as a governess! What then?"

"As a housekeeper."

"Oh dear!" cried Alice in dismay. "I don't know very much about housekeeping. People would not think me old enough."

"And as a wife."

She did not understand him. He was rising from his seat to approach her, a smile on his face. Alice sat looking at him with parted lips.

"As *my* wife, Alice," he said, bending low. "Oh, my dear, surely our foolish estrangement may end! I have been wishing it for some time past. I am tired of chambers, and want to set up a home for myself. I want a wife in it. Alice, if you will be that wife, well: otherwise I shall probably remain as I am for ever."

Ah, there could be no longer any doubt: he was in earnest. His tender tones, his beseeching eyes, the warm clasp of his hands, told her all the happy truth—his love was her own still. She burst into tears of emotion, and William Stane kissed them away.

"You don't despise me because I have been a governess?" she sobbed.

"My darling, I only love you the better for it. And shall prize you more."

He sat down by her side and quietly told her all. That for a considerable period after their parting, he had steeled his heart against her, and done his best to drive her from it. He thought he had succeeded. He believed he should have succeeded but for meeting her again at Mrs. Preen's. That showed him that she was just as dear to him as ever. Still he strove against his love; but he continued his visits to the Preens, who were old friends of his and each time, that he chanced to see Alice, served to convince him more and more that he could not part with her. He was about to tell his father that he had made up his mind to marry Miss Raynor, when Sir Philip died, and then he did not speak to Alice quite immediately. All this he explained to her.

"And but for your coming into this house, Alice, and my opportunities of seeing you in it, we should in all human probability have remained estranged throughout life. So, you see that I would not have had you not become a governess for the world."

She smiled through her tears. "It was not in that light I spoke."

"I am aware of it. But you are more fitted to make a good wife now, after your experiences and your trials, than you would have been in the old prosperous days at Eagles' Nest. I shall be especially glad for one thing—that when you are mine I shall have a right to ease your mother's straits and difficulties. She has deemed me very hard-hearted, I dare say: but I have often and often thought of her, and wished I had a plea for calling on and helping her."

His intention showed a good heart. But William Stane and Alice were both ignorant of one great fact—that Mrs. Raynor no longer needed help. She would shortly be back again at Eagles' Nest, all her struggles with poverty over.

The hot sun still streamed into the little room, but Alice wondered what had become of its oppression, what of her own weariness. The day and all things with it, without and within, had changed to Elysium.

FRANK RAYNOR ATTENDED THE FUNERAL of old Mrs. Bell. He chose to do so: and Rosaline felt the respect warmly, and thanked him for it. He would have been just as well pleased not to have Mr. Blase Pellet for his companion mourner: but it had to be. On his return home from the cemetery, Frank's way led him through West Street, and he called in just to see Rosaline, who had been too disturbed in health, too depressed in spirits, to attend herself. Not one minute had he been there when Mr. Blase Pellet also came in. On the third day from that, Rosaline was to sail for New Zealand.

"And I say that it is a very cruel thing of her to sail at all," struck in Blase, when Frank chanced to make some remark about the voyage. "As my wife, she would—"

"Blase, you know the bargain," quietly interrupted Rosaline, turning her sad eyes upon him. "Not a word of that kind must ever be spoken by you to me again. I will not hear it, or bear it."

"I'm not going to speak of it; it's of no use speaking," grumbled Blase. "But a fellow who feels his life is blighted can't be wholly silent. And you might have been so happy at Trennach! You liked the place once."

"Are you going back to Trennach?" asked Frank in some surprise.

"Yes," said Blase. "I only came to London to be near her; and I shan't care to stay in it, once she is gone. Float, the druggist, has been wanting me for some time. I am to be his partner; and the whole concern will be mine after he has done with it."

"I wish you success, Blase;" said Frank heartily. "You can make a better thing of the business than old Float makes, if you will."

"I mean to," answered Blase.

"I will take this opportunity of saying just a word to you, Blase," again spoke up Rosaline, smoothing down the crape of her gown with one hand, in what looked like nervousness. "I have informed Mr. Raynor of the conversation I had with you the night my mother died, and that you are aware of the confession he and Mr. Pine alike hold."

Frank turned quickly to Blase. "You perceive now that you have been lying under a mistake from the first, with regard to me."

"I do," said Blase. "I am never ashamed to confess myself in the wrong, once I am convinced of it. But I should never have brought it against you, Mr. Frank Raynor; never; and that, I fancy, is what you have been fearing. In future, the less said about that past night the better. Better for all of us to try and forget it."

Frank nodded an emphatic acquiescence, and took up his hat to depart. Yes, indeed, better forget it. He should have to allude to it once again, for he meant to tell the full truth to Edina; and then he would put it from his mind.

He went home, wondering whether any urgent calls had been made upon him during this morning's absence; and was standing behind the counter, questioning Sam, when a sunburnt little gentleman walked in. Frank gazed at him in amazement: for it was Mr. Max Brown.

"How are you, Raynor?" cried the traveller, grasping Frank's hand cordially.

"My goodness!" exclaimed Frank. "Have you dropped from the moon?"

"I dropped last from the Southampton train. Got into port last night."

"All well?"

"*Very* well. And my good old mother is not dead yet."

There was no mistaking the stress upon the first word: no mistaking the perfectly contented air that distinguished Mr. Max Brown's whole demeanour. Whatever cause might have detained him so long from his home and country, it did not appear to be an unpleasant one.

"There was a young lady in the case," he acknowledged, entering on his explanation with a smile on his bronzed face. "Lota Elmaine; old Elmaine the planter's only daughter. The old man would not let us be married: Lota was too young, he said; the marriage should not take place until she was in Europe. Will you believe it, Raynor, old Elmaine has kept me on like that all the blessed time I have been away, perpetually saying he was coming over here, and never coming! Never a month passed but he gave out he should sail the next."

"And so you stayed also!"

"I stayed also. I would not leave Lota to be snapped up by some covetous rascal in my absence. Truth to tell, I could not part with her on my own score."

"And where is Miss Lota Elmaine?"

"No longer in existence. She is Mrs. Max Brown."

"Then you have brought her over with you!"

"Poor Elmaine died a few months ago; and Lota had a touch of the native fever, which left her thin and prostrate: so I persuaded her to marry me off-hand that I might bring her here for a change. She is better already. The voyage has done her no end of good."

"Where is she?"

"At a private hotel in Westminster. We have taken up our quarters there for the time being."

"Until you can come here," assumed Frank. "I suppose you want me to clear out as soon as possible. My wife is ill—"

"I want you to stay for good, if you will," interrupted Mr. Brown. "The business is excellent, you know, better than when I left it. If you will take to it I shall make it quite easy for you."

　　　　　　　　　　　　　　　　　　MRS. HENRY WOOD

"What are you going to do yourself?" questioned Frank.

"Nothing at present," said Mr. Max Brown. "Lota's relatives on the mother's side live in Wales, and she wants to go amongst them for a time. Perhaps I shall set up in practice there. Lota's fortune is more than enough for us, but I should be miserable with nothing to do. Will you take to this concern, Raynor?"

"I think not," replied Frank, shaking his head. "My wife does not like the neighbourhood."

"Neither would my wife like it. Well, there's no hurry; it is a good offer, and you can consider it. And, look here, Raynor: if you would like a day or two's holiday now, take it: you have been hard at work long enough. I will come down and attend for you. I should like to see my old patients again: though some of them were queer kind of people."

"Thank you," said Frank mechanically.

Thought after thought was passing through his mind. No, he would not stay here. He had no further motive for seeking obscurity, thank Heaven, and Daisy should be removed to a more congenial atmosphere. But—what could he do for means? He must be only an assistant yet, he supposed; but better luck might come in course of time.

And better luck, though Frank knew it not, was on his way to him even then.

What with one thing and another, that day seemed destined to be somewhat of an eventful day to Frank Raynor. In the evening a letter was delivered to him from Mr. George Atkinson, requesting him to go down to Eagles' Nest on the morrow, as he wished particularly to see him.

"What can he want with me?—unless he is about to appoint me Surgeon-in-Ordinary to his high and mighty self!" quoth Frank, lightly. "But I should like to go. I should like to see the old place again. *Can* I go? Daisy is better. Max Brown has offered me a day or two's rest. Yes, I can. And drop Max a note now to say his patients will be waiting for him to-morrow morning."

X

Mademoiselle's Letter

"A parcel for you, sir."

"A parcel for me!" repeated Mr. Atkinson to his servant, some slight surprise in his tone. For he was not in the habit of receiving parcels, and wondered what was being sent to him.

The parcel was done up rather clumsily in brown paper, and appeared, by the label on it, to have come by fast train from Hereford. Mr. George Atkinson looked at the address with curiosity. It did not bear his name, but was simply directed to "The Resident of Eagles' Nest."

"Undo it, Thomas," said he.

Thomas took off the string and unfolded the brown paper. This disclosed a second envelope of white paper: and a sealed note, similarly superscribed, lying on it. Mr. Atkinson took the note in his hand: but Thomas was quick, and in a minute the long-lost ebony desk stood revealed to view, its key attached to it.

"Oh," said Mr. Atkinson. "What does the letter say?"

The letter proved to be from Mademoiselle Delrue, the former governess at Eagles' Nest. In a long and rather complicated explanation, written partly in French, partly in English, the following facts came to light.

When about to leave Eagles' Nest; things and servants being at that time at sixes-and-sevens there; the kitchen-maid, one Jane—or, as mademoiselle wrote it, Jeanne—a good-natured girl, had offered to assist her to pack up. She had shown Jeanne her books piled ready in the small study, and Jeanne had packed them together in several parcels: for mademoiselle's stock of books was extensive. After leaving Mrs. Raynor's, Mademoiselle Delrue had gone into a family who spent a large portion of their time in travelling on the Continent and elsewhere: much luggage could not be allowed to mademoiselle, consequently her parcels of books had remained unpacked from that time to this. She had now settled down with the family in Herefordshire, had her parcels forwarded to her, and unpacked them. To her consternation, her grief, her horror—mademoiselle dashed all three of the words—in one of these parcels she discovered not books, but the black desk, one that she well remembered as belonging to Major Raynor: that stupid Jeanne must have taken it to be hers, and committed the error of putting it up. Mademoiselle finished by asking whether she could be forgiven: if one slight element of consolation could peep out upon her, she observed, it was to find that the desk was empty. She had lost not an instant in sending it back to Eagles' Nest, and she begged the resident gentleman there (whose name, she had the pain of confessing, had quite escaped her memory) to be so kind as to forward it, together with this note of contrition and explanation, to Mrs. Raynor—whose present residence she was not acquainted with. And she had the honour to salute him with respectful cordiality.

"Don't go away, Thomas," said his master. "I want you to stay while I search the private compartment of this desk: I fancy those missing papers may be in it. Let me see? Yes, this is the way—and here's the spring."

With one touch, the false bottom was lifted out. Beneath, quietly lay the lost bonds; also a copy of Mrs. Atkinson's last will—the one made in favour of George Atkinson, and a few words written by her to himself.

"You see them, Thomas? See that I have found them here?"

"Indeed I do, sir."

"That's all, then. People are fond of saying that truth is stranger than fiction," said Mr. Atkinson to himself with a smile, as the man withdrew. He examined the bonds; ascertained, to his astonishment, that the money they related to had been invested in his name, and in one single profitable undertaking. And it appeared that Mrs. Atkinson had given directions that the yearly interest, arising, should remain and be added to the principal, until such time as he, George Atkinson, should come forward to claim the whole.

"Little wonder we could not find the money," thought he. "And now—what is to be done with it?" And taking only a few minutes for consideration, he addressed the letter spoken of in the foregoing chapter, to Frank Raynor. Which brought the latter down in person.

"I never heard of so romantic a thing!" cried Frank with his sweet smile and gay manner, that so won upon everybody; and was now winning upon George Atkinson, as he listened to the narrative on his arrival at Eagles' Nest. "I am sure I congratulate you very heartily. The hunts that poor Uncle Francis used to have over those very bonds! And to think that they were lying all the time close under his hand!"

"I expect that very little of the money would have been left for me had he found them," significantly remarked Mr. Atkinson.

Frank laughed. "To speak the truth, I don't think it would. Is it very much?"

"A little over twenty-one thousand pounds. That is what I make it at a rough calculation—of course including the interest to this date."

"What a heap of money!" exclaimed Frank. "You can set up a coach-and-six," added he, joking lightly.

"Ay. By the way, Mr. Francis Raynor, how came *you* to treat me so cavalierly when I was playing 'Tiger' here?—the name you and Charles were pleased to bestow—"

"Oh, Charley gave you that name," interrupted Frank, his blue eyes dancing with merriment. "He took you for a sheriff's officer about to capture him. I'm sure I never was so astonished in all my life as when Charley told me the other day that the Tiger had turned out to be, not a Tiger, but Mr. George Atkinson.

"I can understand his shunning me, under the misapprehension. But why, I ask, did you do it? You were not in fear, I presume, of a sheriff's officer?"

Frank's face grew grave at once. "No, I was not in fear of that," he said, dropping his voice, "but I had fears on another score. I had reason to fear that I was being watched—looked after—tracked; and I thought you were doing it. I am thankful to say," he added, his countenance brightening again, "that I was under a misapprehension altogether: but I only learnt that very lately. It has been a great trouble to me for years, keeping me down in the world—and yet I had done nothing myself to deserve it. I—I cannot explain further, and would be glad to drop the subject," he continued, raising his eyes ingenuously to George Atkinson's. "And I heartily beg your pardon for all the discourtesy I was guilty of. It is against my nature to show any—even to a Tiger."

"As I should fancy. It gave me a wrong impression of you. Made me think all you Raynors were alike—worthless. It's true, Frank. I was ready to be a good friend to you then, had you allowed me. And now tell me of your plans."

Frank, open-natured, full of candour, told freely all he knew about himself. That he did not intend to remain at Mr. Max Brown's, for Daisy disliked the neighbourhood, and he should look out for a more desirable situation at the West End as assistant-surgeon.

"Why not set up in practice for yourself at the West End?" asked George Atkinson.

"Because I have nothing to set up upon," answered Frank. "That has been a bar all along. We must live, you see, whilst the practice is coming in."

"You could do it on seven thousand pounds."

"Seven thousand pounds!" echoed Frank. "Why, yes on half of it; on a quarter. But I have no money at all, you understand."

"Yes, you have, Frank. You have just that sum. At least you will have it in the course of a few days!"

Frank's Frank's pleasant lips were parting with a smile. He thought it was meant as a joke.

"Look here. This money that has come to light, of your aunt Atkinson's—you cannot, I hope, imagine for a moment that I should keep it. By law it is mine, for she willed it to me; but I shall divide it into three portions, and give them to those who are her rightful heirs: her brothers' families. One portion to Mrs. Raynor; one to that angel of goodness, Edina—"

"And she is an angel," interrupted Frank hotly, carried away by the praise. "How we should all have got on without Edina, I don't know. But, Mr. Atkinson, you must not do this that you are talking of: at least as far as I am concerned. It would be too chivalrously generous."

"Why not to you?"

"I could not think of taking it. I have no claim upon you. Who am I, that you should benefit me?"

"I benefit you as your father's son. Were he living, this money would be his: it will now be yours. There, say no more, Frank; you cannot talk me out of doing bare justice. You will own seven thousand pounds next week, and you can lay your plans accordingly."

"I shall not know how to thank you," cried Frank, with a queer feeling in his throat. "Eagles' Nest first, and twenty-one thousand pounds next! You must have been taking a lesson from Edina. And what will Max Brown say when he hears that I shall leave him for certain? He does not believe it yet."

"Max Brown can go promenading."

XI

SUNSHINE

It was a warm September day. The blue sky was without a cloud; the sunbeams glinted through the foliage, beginning to change with the coming autumn, and fell on the smooth velvet lawn at Eagles' Nest. On that same green lawn stood a group of people in gala attire, for this had been a gala day with them. William Stane and Alice Raynor were married that morning. They had now just driven from the gates, around which the white satin shoes lay, and the rice in showers.

It had been Mr. George Atkinson's intention to resign Eagles' Nest at the end of June, almost immediately after he first spoke of doing so. But his intention, like a great many more intentions formed in this uncertain world of ours, was frustrated. The Raynors could not come down so soon to take possession of it. Charles had given notice at once to leave Prestleigh and Preen's; but he was requested, as a favour, not to do so until the second week in August, for the office had a hard task to get through its work before the long vacation. And as Charles had learnt to study other people's interests more than his own, he cheerfully said he would remain. It was a proud moment for him, standing amongst the fellow-clerks who had looked down upon him, when one of those very clerks copied out the deed of gift by which Eagles' Nest was transferred to him by George Atkinson, constituting him from henceforth its rightful owner. Charles, who knew a little of law by this time, proposed to himself to commence reading for the Bar: he had acquired the habit of work and knew its value, and did not wish to be an idle man. But George Atkinson, their true friend and counsellor, spoke against it. The master of Eagles' Nest need be no idle man, he said; rather, if he did his duty faithfully, too busy a one. Better for Charles to learn how to till his land and manage his property, than to plead in a law court; better to constitute himself the active manager of his estate. Charles saw the advice was sound, and meant to follow it.

Neither was Alice ready to leave London as soon as she had expected, for Mrs. Preen's intended departure from home was delayed for some weeks, and she also requested Alice to remain. Alice was nothing loth.

She saw William Stane frequently, and Mrs. Preen took a warm interest in the arrangement of her wedding clothes.

But the chief impediment to their departure from Laurel Cottage, the poor home which had sheltered them so long, lay with Mrs. Raynor. Whether the reaction, at finding their miserable troubles at an end and fortune smiling again, told too strongly upon her weakened frame; or whether that headache, which you may remember she complained of the night Edina reached home with the joyful news from Eagles' Nest, was in truth the advance symptom of an illness already attacking her, certain it was that from that night Mrs. Raynor drooped. The headache did not leave her; other symptoms crept on. At the end of a few days: days that Edina had spent at Frank's in attendance on his sick wife: a doctor was called in. He pronounced it to be low fever. Edina left Daisy, who was then out of danger, to return home, where she was now most wanted. For some weeks Mrs. Raynor did not leave her bed. Altogether there had been many hindrances.

It was getting towards the end of August before the day came when they went down to take possession of Eagles' Nest. Mrs. Raynor was better then; almost well; but much reduced, and still needing care.

"This place will bring back your health and spirits in no time, mother," cried Charles, bending towards her, as they drove up to the gates of Eagles' Nest. She was leaning back in the carriage, side by side with Edina, and tears were trickling down her pale cheeks. He took her hand. "You don't speak, mother."

"Charley, I was thanking God. And wondering what we can do to show our thanks to Him in the future. I know that my life will be one long, heartfelt hymn of gratitude."

Charley leaned from the carriage window. Talking to the lodge-keeper was Jetty the carpenter. Standing with them and watching the carriage was a man whom Charles remembered as one Beck; remembered, to his shame, what his own treatment had been of the poor fellow in the days gone by. Good Heavens! that he should have been so insolent, purse-proud, haughty a young upstart! his cheeks reddened now with the recollection. Ungenerous words and deeds generally come flashing back upon us as reminders when we least want them.

Could that be Charles Raynor!—their future master? Jetty and Beck scarcely believed that in the pale, self-contained, gentle-faced man, who looked so much older than his years, they saw the arrogant youth of other days: scarcely believed that the sweet smile, the passing word of greeting, the steadfast look shining from the considerate eyes, could be indeed meant for them. Ah yes, they might cast out fear; it was Charles Raynor. And they saw that the good news whispered to them all by Mr. Atkinson was indeed true: their new master would be as good and faithful a friend to them as he himself had been during these past three years.

"God ever helping me to be so!" aspirated Charles to his own heart. A whole lifetime of experience, spent in prosperity, could not have worked the change wrought in him by this comparatively short period of stern adversity.

George Atkinson stood at the door to receive them. He had not left Eagles' Nest. For a week or so they were to be his guests in it: or he theirs. Some hearty joking and laughter was raised in this the first moment of meeting, as to which it would be, led to by a remark of Mrs. Raynor's: that she hoped he would not find the children—coming on with Alice in another carriage—troublesome guests.

"Nay, the house is yours, you know, not mine: you cannot be my guests," laughed George Atkinson. "How do you say, Miss Raynor?"

"I say we are your guests," answered Edina. "And very glad to be so."

"At least I did not think *you* would side against me," said George Atkinson, with pretended resentment. "For this day, let it be so, then. To-morrow I subside into my proper place, and Mrs. Raynor begins her reign."

"I have been wondering how we can ever be sufficiently grateful to God," she whispered with emotion, taking his hand in hers. "I know not how we can ever thank *you*."

"Nay, my dear lady, I have done only what was right and just; right and just in His sight, and according to His laws," was George Atkinson's solemn answer. "We must all strive for that, you know, if we would ensure peace at the last. Here comes the other fly with the young ones!—and that curly-headed urchin, gazing at us with his great blue eyes, must be my disappointed little candidate for the Bluecoat School."

The week passed soon; and the wedding morning dawned. And now that was past, and the bridal carriage had driven off; and the white slippers and the rice were thrown, and they had all collected on the lawn in the afternoon sun. The only guests were Frank Raynor and his wife, who had arrived the night before. Street the lawyer and a brother of William Stane's had come for the morning; but had already left again by an afternoon train.

Frank Raynor, aided by the seven thousand pounds made over to him, had taken to the house and practice of a deceased medical man in Mayfair, and was securely established there and doing already fairly well. Mr. Max Brown, who, with his wife, had been spending a week with them, had disposed of the Lambeth practice to another purchaser. Daisy was happy again, and just as pretty and blooming as in the old days at Trennach. Frank, without entering into actual particulars (he did that only to Edina), had disclosed to her enough of that past night's fatal work to account for his interest in, and care of, Mrs. Bell and poor Rosaline. A dozen times at least in the day, Daisy, with much contrition and many repentant tears, would whisper prayers to her husband to be forgiven; saying at the same time she could never forgive herself. Frank would kiss the tears away and tell her to let bygones be bygones; they were beginning life afresh. Rosaline had sailed for her new home and country—was probably by this time nearing its shores. Most earnestly was it to be hoped she would regain happiness there.

Who so proud as Daisy, flitting about the lawn with her three-months' old baby in her arms, resplendent in its white robes! The little thing was named Francis George, and George Atkinson was its godfather. So many interests had claimed their attention that day, that not a minute had yet been found for questions and answers; and it was only now, at the first quiet moment, that Mr. Atkinson was beginning to inquire how Frank was prospering.

"First-rate," said sanguine Frank, his kindly face glowing. "I wish with all my heart every beginner was getting on as well as I."

"And my mother has recovered her amiability," put in Daisy, irreverently, handing the baby over to its nurse, who stood by. "I had quite a long letter from her yesterday morning, Mr. Atkinson, in which she graciously forgives me, and says I shall have my share of the money that my uncle Tom left her last year. That will be at least some thousands of pounds."

"It never rains but it pours, you know," smiled Frank. "Money drops in, now that we don't particularly want it."

"And so," added Daisy, "we mean to set up our brougham. Frank needs one very badly."

"Frank needs it for use and you for show," cried George Atkinson, laughing.

"Yes that is just it," acknowledged Daisy. "I expect I shall not have much of it, though, as his practice increases. When do you take possession of your town house, Mr. Atkinson? You will not be very far from us."

"I go up to it from Eagles' Nest to-morrow," was the reply. "Perhaps not to remain long in it at present. I am not yet able to form my plans."

"Not able to form your plans!" echoed Daisy, in her saucy, engaging way; her bright eyes gazing questioningly into his. "Why, I should have thought you might have laid your plans on the first of January for all the year, having no one to consult but yourself."

"But if I am uncertain—capricious?" returned he, in half-jesting tones.

"Ah, that's a different thing. I should not have thought you that at all. But—pray tell me, Mr. Atkinson! What do the people down here say, now they have found out that it was you, yourself, who lived amongst them three years ago?"

"They say nothing to me. I dare say they conjecture that I had my reasons for it. Or perhaps they think I was only amusing myself," continued George Atkinson, glancing at Edina.

Edina smiled at him in return. All's well that ends well: and that incognito business had turned out very well in the end. To her only had George Atkinson spoken out fully of the motives that swayed him, the impressions he received.

Edina stood near them in all her finery. She had never been so grand in her life: and perhaps had never looked so well. A lilac-silk dress, and a lovely pink rose in her bosom, nestling amidst white lace. Edina was rich now—as *she* looked upon riches. Seven thousand pounds, and all her own! She had held out strenuously against receiving it, pointing out to George Atkinson that it would be wrong and unfair to give it to her, as her aunt Ann had never meant to leave her any money at all. But Edina's arguments and objections proved of no avail. Mr. Atkinson quietly closed his ears, and transferred the money to her, in spite of her protests. The first use Edina made of her cheque-book was to send a hundred pounds to Mr. Pine, that he might distribute it amongst the poor of Trennach.

Like George Atkinson, as he had just avowed, Edina had not formed her plans. She could not decide where her chief residence should be. Mrs. Raynor and Charles naturally pressed her to remain at Eagles' Nest: but she hesitated. A wish to have a home of her own, some little place of her own setting up, was making itself heard in her heart: and she could visit Eagles' Nest from time to time. Should the little homestead be near to them?—or at Trennach? It was this that she could not yet decide. But she must do so very shortly, for she wished to give them her decision on the morrow.

Turning away from the busy talkers, from the excited children; Kate in white, and little Bob, not in a long skirted blue coat and yellow stockings, but in black velvet and knickerbockers; Edina wandered away, her mind full, and sat down on a bench shaded by clustering trees, out of sight and sound of all. The small opening in the trees before her disclosed a glimpse of the far-off scenery—the Kentish hills, with their varying foliage, lying under the calm, pale blue sky.

"I like Trennach," she argued with herself. "I love it, for it was my girlhood's home; and I love those who are in it. I could almost say with Ruth, 'The people there shall be my people, and their God my God.' On the other hand are the claims of Eagles' Nest, and of Frank and Daisy. I love them all. Mary Raynor says she cannot get on unless I am near her; and perhaps the young ones need me too. If I only knew!"

"Knew what?" cried a voice at her elbow—for she had spoken the last sentence aloud.

The interruption came from George Atkinson. He had been about looking for her, and at last had found her. Edina blushed at having allowed her words to be heard: as he sat down beside her.

"I was only wishing I knew whether it would be better for me to settle near London or at Trennach," she answered with a smile. "It was very silly of me to speak aloud."

"Charles Raynor has just informed us that you intend to remain for good at Eagles' Nest."

"Oh no, I do not. I have never said I would; and to-morrow I shall tell them why. I should like to have a little place of my own; ever so little, but my very own. Either at Trennach, or in this neighbourhood: or perhaps—in London."

"Both in this neighbourhood and in London," he interrupted. "And, sometimes sojourning elsewhere: at the seaside or at Trennach. That is what I should recommend."

"You have made me a millionaire in my own estimation, but not quite so rich as that," laughed Edina.

"The houses are ready for you, and waiting."

Some peculiarity in his tone made her heart stand still. He turned and took her hands in his, speaking softly.

"Edina! Don't you know—have you not guessed—that I want you in my houses, my home? Surely you will come to me!—you will not say me nay! I know that it is late, very late, for me to say this to you: but I will try and make you happy as my wife."

Her pulses went rushing on tumultuously. As the words fell on her ear and heart, the truth was suddenly opened to her—she loved him still.

"I am no longer young, George," she whispered, the tears slowly coursing down her cheeks.

"Too young for me, Edina. The world may say so."

"And I—I don't know that others can spare me."

"Yes, they can. Had I been wise I should have secured you in the days so long gone by, Edina. I have never ceased to care for you. Oh, my best friend, my first and only love, say you will come and make the sunshine of my home! Say you will."

"I will," she whispered.

And Mr. George Atkinson drew her to him and sheltered her face on his breast. After all the sadness and vicissitudes of her life, what a haven of rest it felt to Edina!

"There shall be no delay; we cannot afford it. As soon as possible, Edina, I shall take you away. And that seven thousand pounds that you tried hard to fight me over—you can now transfer it to the others, if you like."

"As you will," she breathed. "All as you will from henceforth, George. I have found my home: and my master."

"God bless you, my dear one! May He be ever with us, as now, and keep us both to the end, in this world and in the next."

The birds sang in the branches; the distant hills were fair and smiling; the pale blue sky had never a cloud: all nature spoke of peace. And within their own hearts reigned that holy peace and rest which comes alone from Heaven; the peace that passeth all understanding.

THE END

MRS. HENRY WOOD

A Note About the Author

Ellen Price (1814–1887) was an English novelist and translator, better known by her penname, Mrs. Henry Wood. Wood lived with her husband, Henry Wood, and four children in Southern France for twenty years, until moving back to England when Henry's business failed. In England, Wood supported her family with her writing, becoming an international bestseller. Wood was praised for her masterful storytelling of middle-class lives, and often advocated for faith and strong morals in her work. Wood's most celebrated work was *East Lynne*, a sensation novel popular for its elaborate plot. In 1867, Wood became the owner and editor of Argosy Magazine, which she continued to publish until her death in 1887. By the end of her career, Wood published over thirty novels, many of which were immensely popular in England, the United States, and in Australia.

A Note from the Publisher

Spanning many genres, from non-fiction essays to literature classics to children's books and lyric poetry, Mint Edition books showcase the master works of our time in a modern new package. The text is freshly typeset, is clean and easy to read, and features a new note about the author in each volume. Many books also include exclusive new introductory material. Every book boasts a striking new cover, which makes it as appropriate for collecting as it is for gift giving. Mint Edition books are only printed when a reader orders them, so natural resources are not wasted. We're proud that our books are never manufactured in excess and exist only in the exact quantity they need to be read and enjoyed. To learn more and view our library, go to minteditionbooks.com

bookfinity & ▰ MINT EDITIONS

Enjoy more of your favorite classics with Bookfinity,
a new search and discovery experience for readers.
With Bookfinity, you can discover more vintage
literature for your collection, find your Reader Type,
track books you've read or want to read,
and add reviews to your favorite books.
Visit www.bookfinity.com, and click on
Take the Quiz to get started.

Don't forget to follow us
@bookfinityofficial and @mint_editions